DESTINED
FOR THE
FAE KING

MEGAN VAN DYKE

Copyright © 2024 by Megan Van Dyke

All rights reserved.

No portion of this book may be reproduced in any form without written permission from the publisher or author, except as permitted by U.S. copyright law and in the case of brief quotations embodied in critical articles or reviews.

This is a work of fiction. Names, characters, places, and incidents either are the product of the author's imagination or are used fictitiously. Any resemblance to actual persons, living or dead, events, or locales is entirely coincidental.

This book and all related artwork are original human creations, and may not be used in any way to train any AI.

Published by Megan Van Dyke

Author's Website: www.authormeganvandyke.com

Credits:

Editing: Jeni Chappelle of Jeni Chappelle Editorial

Cover and Interior Design: Megan Van Dyke

All images licensed appropriately.

Author's Note

Destined for the Fae King is a new adult fantasy romance which contains some content that readers may find distressing, including: adult language, drinking, consensual sex, violence, death/murder, mourning and loss, war, gender role expectations, abuse (not of the FMC or MMC), and the death of a parent (remembered/off-page).

Chapter 1

Today I become a queen of Faery.

Okay, not today, exactly. But I finally get to leap onto that path and sprint down it.

People have many dreams for their future: wealth, love, success, happiness. Most run toward something, or many somethings, even if they don't exactly know what those things are. But there are also some that run away—from failure, heartbreak, mistakes. My mother has it set in her head that I'm doing the latter. Running away. Leaving her and my younger brothers to fend for themselves. She doesn't grasp, or doesn't want to grasp, that I'm doing this for them.

Okay, not fully for them. I'm doing it for me too.

For most of my life, days have chased each other one after the next, mostly indistinguishable from one another. It's a routine that blurs around me like a blanket, providing a sense of stability that's grown too comfortable to step away from. Only twice before has something happened that ripped that blanket away, shredding it into little pieces and forcing me to craft a new life from the remnants.

Now it's happening again.

Only this time, I'm glad it's been shredded. I helped claw it apart and reveled in its destruction. Because finally I have the chance to do the one thing I've dreamed of since I was a small child: run away to Faery.

Uncle Matias drives the black SUV down the winding forest roads, noonday light shining down bright and hot overhead. The miles speed by, each one twisting the knot of anxiety building in me a little bit tighter. He takes a curve a little too sharply, and I slide on the pristine leather seat.

"*Mierda*," my cousin Selena grumbles as she shoves back a lock of her black hair that fell from behind her ear. "Get us there in one piece, why don't you?"

He grunts something unintelligible in return. Aunt Dalia, completely in her own little world, checks her makeup in a compact mirror for about the fourth time before snapping it closed. If one didn't know better, we'd look like a happy little family on a road trip. And I suppose we are on a trip, but not to somewhere most people can visit.

Today, we're due to arrive in Faery for The Choosing, the competition to select the King of Fire's human bride, and I'm to be one of the candidates. Human spirits give power to the fae and enliven their magic. The closer the relationship, the bigger boost of power. It's for that reason fae royals most always choose human consorts. That the King of Fire hasn't taken one to date is a wonder in itself, but apparently he's decided it's time to change that.

"Seriously," Selena continues. "Mira can't become queen if we all die on the way there." She glances over at me from across the back seat. "Right?"

I flash her a tight smile. *Queen.* That's right. Hearing it said out loud still makes my stomach do a weird flip-flop. I actually have a chance to become a queen of Faery. And more than that, my family expects me to do everything I can to make sure the crown lands on my head.

If Uncle Matias had his way, it would be Selena instead—his prized and only child—but she outright refused. Threatened to run away and never come back. And she'd do it too. It's not that she dislikes Faery. Actually, she's one of the most knowledgeable people I've met on the topic, not that the list is very long. However, she loves technology. *Loves* it. Her laptop is basically an extension of herself. Over the last few years, Selena has made herself infinitely useful to the gifted community—those of us that can see fae—using her technological skills. No one can fault her impressive hacking skills which she leverages for the benefit of the community, hiding income in the form of gifts from the fae, falsifying records for those who go to Faery never to return, that sort of thing. In this day and age, it's a skill we can't live without, and even my uncle realizes what a fool he'd be to push her too far and lose that.

And of course, there's the fact that Uncle Matias, the head of our family, just happens to have another eligible woman to compete for the king's hand. Me. Much as it begrudges him to admit that I might have some use or that the reputation of our family will be on my shoulders. The daughter of his beloved late brother and that woman he once called— Actually, I try not to think about the things he's called my mother. It'll just piss me off more and kick this trip off on a bad note. I might be gifted, but my mother isn't, and his brother marrying an outsider is a travesty Uncle Matias has never gotten over. A mar on the Rivera family line, he once called it.

I get to *fix* that now by winning this competition, making our family legendary among the gifted, and securing us all financially for generations to come.

No pressure or anything.

My uncle and I may have our differences, loads of them, but I'm glad Selena is here. Her rebellious streak made sure she turned out nothing like her parents, in most ways, and we've been close as sisters all our lives. There's no one else I'd rather have at my side today. Besides, she was here the first time my life changed too.

It's impossible to forget that day, the way the whole earth seemed to tip on its axis and show me dazzling new possibilities while withholding them at the same time, like a treat I would have to wait years for.

I'd been sitting with Selena in the formal living room of her house. The location should have been the first giveaway. That room is literally never used by family. With its ornate and uncomfortable chairs, original art with spotlights and gilded frames, and bookshelves filled with leather-bound titles no one has cracked the spine on, it's not really meant for living. In fact, I'm still convinced its sole purpose is to make unwanted visitors as uncomfortable as possible so that they leave quickly. It was that room that my dad led us to in our fancy dresses and kitten heels. My aunt settled us on the stiff paisley cushions of the loveseat, giving us a too-bright smile before she retreated to stand beside my uncle and my dad.

"What is it, Daddy?" I'd asked as I looked between him and Selena. We look about the same now since we're only a year apart. Not then. Then, she seemed so much smaller. Some protective instinct rose up in me urging me to take her hand in mine, so I did.

Dad adjusted his tie, a tell I didn't know then. He and my uncle had been at one of their meetings that day, another thing I didn't really understand at that time.

My dad looked over at Uncle Matias, maybe for reassurance or maybe in hope that he'd take on the task. Who really knew? But my uncle took up the task all the same, crouching down before us to say, "Our family is gifted. Special. And we're going to take a little trip to see if either of you are as well."

"We might not be special?" I asked my dad, deeply offended.

"Of course you are, *mi luz*," Dad replied before looking sharply at his brother. "But you might be extra special, and it's time to find out."

That day was the first time we went to the coven house, the same place we're headed now. Most children present at the testing that day saw nothing, but not us. We *were* gifted. Special. As my father and uncle hoped. The door to Faery opened, and we both saw through, gasping and squealing in delight as a fae lingering in the threshold in all their brilliant glory—features a little too perfect, a little taller and longer, a stunning outfit, and a glow of power about them.

To have two children in the same family pass the testing on the same day was a rare thing, especially nowadays when the gift has worn thin in so many of the old bloodlines.

We couldn't go to Faery yet. Not until we matured.

But I never forgot that moment, the wonder and majesty, the promise of something more.

We felt special then. *I* felt it. And ever since then, I yearned to come back and finally step into that world I'd merely glimpsed.

The car ride passes far too quickly, special thanks to my uncle's lead foot, and suddenly we're pulling down the drive toward an old manor house whose elaborate iron gate sits open wide. Several other cars are already parked in a grassy section of the yard. A couple lingers on the white-railed front porch, probably waiting to greet coven members as they arrive.

To say we're witches, as coven implies, wouldn't quite be accurate. Not anymore. No true magic runs in our veins except the ability to see fae, and even that is sparsely doled out amongst the bloodline. A few of the oldest members can do little things—minor charms and such—but even that seems to have vanished with my generation. In fact, no one in my direct bloodline has had any real magic for generations, not since one of my ancestors cursed a fae King of the Forest for sleeping with someone else. The act was frowned upon and still taught as something not to do, not that we can, but I can't help but think the bastard deserved it.

My cousin packs her laptop away. We park. Everyone is unbuckling and getting out, but I'm frozen in the seat. I've been excited for weeks, ever since I knew I'd have this opportunity, but now that it's here, it feels all too real and overwhelming. It doesn't help that Mom's been a tearful mess for days and that I practically had to peel her off me when I left yesterday. She fully believes that I'm destined for the crown and will never come back once I step foot in Faery. A tragedy in her mind. I spent the night at Uncle Matias and Aunt Dalia's house before our short trip today—I needed that break from Mom, that space, to get my head on straight. Or at least I thought I did, but now I'm more of a mess than ever.

My uncle opens the door for me, but it's Selena's cheerful smile that finally pulls me from the seat and out of the car. I've barely stepped onto the grass when she wraps me in a tight hug.

"Have I mentioned how glad I am that you're here?" I ask.

"Only about fifty times."

By the time she releases me, her parents are already walking toward the house, their overstuffed suitcase and my smaller one in tow. Ironic, considering I'm the one staying. All they really need is an overnight bag, if they choose to stay. We're all already dressed for the opening ball of The Choosing, the competition to select the king's bride, though it might do me good to make sure the car ride didn't damage the waves I'd added to my hair. At least my crimson dress seems unwrinkled.

Selena loops her arm through mine and just about drags me toward the manor. The door to Faery, to the Court of Fire, that our coven uses sits in a clearing behind the house, which has existed since the early days of the country—refurbished and added onto over the years of course. Even so, it's still way newer than the door itself, which has stood open longer than any of our records can say.

To an outsider, it looks like a historical home, meticulously maintained and used only for special events. Which is true actually, though coven families take turns having a caretaker in residence, a job my uncle scoffed at when I once asked about it.

It seemed like a better opportunity than waiting tables. Plus, it put me one step outside Faery. Who would notice if I just wandered in from time to time? That was three years ago. I didn't realize then that he already had a plan for me, that he intended to offer me up as a potential bride for the King of Fire as a sort of payment for taking care of my mom, brothers, and me since my father died unexpectedly when I was just thirteen.

I should hate it, being his pawn, his sacrificial lamb, but the truth is, I would have run headlong into Faery years earlier if he'd have let me, and if Mom hadn't been so opposed to me leaving. She's convinced I'll never come back, says she knows without a doubt that I'll be stuck there if I step foot through the door, and her tears guilted me into staying far longer than I ever planned. By eighteen, I was mature enough to enter Faery without risk. I'd always planned on that. And yet, five years later and I've still never stepped foot in that world.

Probably why I got stuck in the same routine for so long. Wait tables. Cheer on my non-gifted little brothers. Help Mom around the house. And basically, just wait for my life to begin, like Rapunzel in her tower. Why bother with college when we can't afford it and I wouldn't be around to use the degree anyway? Why try to find a steady boyfriend when that would just be one more thing holding me back from my dreams?

"I know you've been excited about Faery," Selena says as we walk. "But I was still so worried you were gonna bail." She's dressed in black today, her usual color of choice an odd one for the occasion, but has toned down her signature dark eyeliner and even skipped the black nail polish for once. She almost looks like a proper bridesmaid. Rather fitting, given the circumstances. "Did you know that my mom hinted at trying to force me to enter that damned contest if you didn't show. Me. I'd be the *worst* possible bride candidate for anyone." She hurries on before I can even respond. "But married *and* stuck in Faery? No thank you."

A world without the technology she loves? No, that certainly wouldn't work for her. To say nothing of the fact that she loathes the idea of an arranged marriage. Or marriage in general really.

"Way to be encouraging." I nudge her side.

She winces. "I meant to say, bad for me, good for you. Come on." She bumps her shoulder into mine. "I love you, but you know we're not the same." She pats my arm. "You're going to do great. I know it."

We enter the manor through the front door and walk right down the main hall and out into the backyard. It might as well have been a garden gate for how little time we spent within in, though it'd be a lie to say the impressive spread of food and drinks set just off the main hall didn't snare my attention and make my mouth water.

As we exited the back door out onto the stone pathway through the manicured yard, I bit my lip and cast a longing glance back over my shoulder. There's no time for that though. Uncle Matias is determined for us to be early, though from the number of cars out front, others had the same idea and have beaten us to it. Already, he's impatiently waving Selena and me toward the circle of trees lingering just ahead.

A breeze tugged at the styled dark brown waves of my hair, bringing with it the crispness of autumn. Only a few golden leaves spot the trees, but that will change soon enough. Too bad I'll miss it this year, but maybe next year—

A pang of homesickness makes me skip a step. If I win, there won't be a next year, at least not here on Earth, not for me. A fae king won't want his little human bride leaving Faery.

"Mira?" Selena stares at me, her brows pinched, but I have no words, no way to describe the sudden terror that's stuck my feet to the ground and won't let me take another step.

I want this, don't I?

I feel like the kid at the theme park who has been waiting all day to ride the biggest and baddest rollercoaster but has finally made it to the front of the line and is now too scared to get on.

If I run now, I might never get to Faery, and I've waited so long. I suck in a deep breath and do everything I can to force the feeling deep down and far away.

"It's okay," I say. "I've got this."

The circle of trees ahead is odd. Anyone, gifted or not, wouldn't be able to look at it and say it's natural. But with the way the gardens are designed behind the manor, with their careful designs and lush vegetation, someone might just think the tree circle was part of the carefully curated space. A clever disguise, like much of our lives.

To anyone else, we're normal families. Albeit most are well-off from years of fae gifts we've leveraged over generations into a financial legacy of wise investments. It's the reason Uncle Matias and Aunt Dalia are rich and the reason my mother has been able to not work these past years since Dad died. She never did before he passed, and after... Well, she was a mess for a while. And then there was my uncle generously taking care of us—generous in that we had a roof over our head and food on the table, if not a life near as nice as theirs.

I might not agree with him often, but I know better than to bite the hand that feeds. After all, my waitressing tips only go so far. And I know him getting me into this contest isn't only out of the goodness of his heart, but it's still his reputation and connections that have carried me here. After today, I'll be on my own though. In this contest, it'll be each woman for herself to try to win the hand of the king and secure a place in history. After all, fae live longer than us, so this chance probably won't come again in any of our lifetimes, at least not with the Court of Fire, which our coven pledged its support to ages ago.

A few older coven members linger around the circle of trees, probably there to make sure everything goes smoothly. If any of the other women have arrived, they must already be in Faery.

My aunt and uncle wait at the base of the largest tree. Its branches reach toward the one next to it and form an archway just the right size for us to pass under. As we near the threshold of trees, the tightness in my chest releases and flows through my veins in tingling anticipation.

I finally get to go to Faery.

My dreams are coming true.

Aunt Dalia turns toward me. "Are you sure you have everything you need?"

No. How could I be when I've never been? I know the basics. Technology doesn't work there, some kind of interference from the magic of the world. They'll give us some dresses and jewelry befitting the role we're trying for. But those won't be ready until their tailors can measure us and such, so we're left to our own fashion choices until then—hence my suitcase filled with some of my nicest outfits. I packed my makeup and my favorite perfume, but I have a feeling they might want us to use fae versions of those too. We'll see.

If I didn't know better, I'd say my aunt is stalling. But that's so not like her. She's never been one to say no to a party, which is what we're going to. Humans and fae alike will be gathered to see the women presented before the king for The Choosing.

Despite my uncertainties, I say, "Of course."

I refuse to give them any reason to believe I can't do this or that it'll be a disaster. They already think that, what with my inexperience and being my mother's daughter. It's in everything they don't say, the silent looks they share, and the way their gazes cut to me. After all, I wasn't trained for this, and I'd bet my pinky finger some of the women I'll be up against were. It's not uncommon in gifted families to groom a child to send to Faery, especially if they have more than one with the gift.

Pretty sure that's what my aunt and uncle intended with Selena, but their desire only shoved her further in the opposite direction. I guess that's the thing about putting all your eggs in one basket: sometimes you drop that basket and then you're fucked.

Or they would be, if not for me. Even if I didn't want to go, I don't have much of a choice. I don't doubt that Uncle Matias would pull back his support of my family if I didn't abide by his wishes, and there's no way I'd let that happen.

"Well then." Aunt Dalia gives me a tight-lipped smile, but something in her eyes shines a little too bright. "Let's go."

I blink at her for a moment, still in disbelief that those could possibly be tears in her eyes, before I paste on a smile of my own and step through the circle of trees with Selena at my side.

CHAPTER 2

I HOLD MY BREATH and act like I've done this a hundred times, like it's not my first venture into Faery.

You just have to want to be there to go through the door, I've been told. It sounds so easy. I never expected it to actually be so simple in practice. But one moment, I'm stepping across the grass under the boughs of the trees, and the next, my shoe lands on stone.

The warmth hits me first, like a blast of humid August air that curls around me like a blanket fresh from the dryer. Breath lodges in my throat, despite my mouth gaping open.

I pull away from Selena and turn in a circle, wide-eyed at the world around me.

We're still in a forest of sorts, but the trees soar twice as high as before. Nor are they green and lush like I'm used to. These trees have thick, coppery trunks that pulse with an inner light, almost like they're on fire. Leaves of purple, crimson, and gold hang from spindly branches. Vines of rich brown twirl around them, looping and hanging like a tropical jungle. Here and there, bright pink blooms the size of dinner plates dip their petals toward the ground.

Selena bumps her shoulder into mine, knocking me from my reverie. "Pretty impressive, right?"

"No kidding, I just— Wow." I do my best to rein in my wonder and not look like the stunned newbie human that I am. I'm probably the only person here today who hasn't seen this before, and acting like a fish out of water isn't likely to earn me any points toward becoming the king's bride.

While I know my mom isn't gifted and couldn't have seen this, I'm starting to suspect my dad told her all about it when he was alive and that's probably why she never wanted me to come. She knew if I'd seen something like this in person, I wouldn't have been able to not dream about it and want to see more. Right now, I have to fight the urge to run up to the nearest tree trunk and inspect it to see if I can understand how it glows from within, pulsing like it's burning when the forest surely can't be on fire.

A number of people—no, fae—wait around the large clearing we stand in. Large pieces of flat, white stone with dark purple moss in between create a mosaic landing of sorts. Two white marble pillars mark an exit leading to a worn dirt pathway through the trees, though no one seems to be walking it as far as I can see.

A pair of fae come toward us, both wearing tunics of crimson marked with a golden flame in the center—the same outfit worn by all the fae present in this moment. This, I know. It's the symbol of the Court of Fire. Nearby, Uncle Matias hands off our luggage to fae male who vanishes with them, there one minute and gone the next. I blink at the spot where he was standing, trying to wrap my head around it. Logically, I know what he did. He shifted, the fae method of moving from one place to another through space in moments, but to see it firsthand is something else.

Suddenly, Aunt Dalia is in front of me, smoothing a lock of hair behind my ear before taking my face between her palms.

"Be calm. Smile. Do your best," she whispers.

I can't help but nod along. She's told me the same thing at least a dozen times over the last twenty-four hours, as if somehow those three things will make all the difference.

"Good," she adds, that hint of glassiness returning to her eyes. She turns and steps to my side as the fae reach us.

"We're here to take you to the throne room," the taller of the two says.

This, I'm prepared for...sort of. We expected they'd shift us there to save time, right into the waiting throng of fae where the contestants will be presented for the king and officially entered into the tournament for his hand. Despite knowing what comes next, my stomach still turns over and twists in on itself. My fragile grin becomes hard to hold, and it'd be a lie to say I'm not second-guessing everything that led to this point.

Even so, I somehow manage to take the skirts of my dress in hand and flare them out like some kind of fair maiden from a storybook as I give a little curtsy and reply, "Thank you."

Humans may have advanced out of this archaic greeting and formality, but the fae have not. And I didn't spend endless hours poring over coven records with Selena not to know the basics.

The guards show no reaction to my greeting, stuck as they are in their rigid formality. Maybe I shouldn't have bothered. No one else in my party did. But I'd be a fool to think the competition hasn't already started. Anything and everything I do could be to my favor or my detriment, depending on who sees it and tells someone—say, the king—about it.

"Join hands with one another," one guard instructs as they come to stand between me and my aunt. "Do not let go until we reach the throne room."

I cling tightly to the fae guard's warm hand, my muscles taut in anticipation. The world around us blurs. A little squeak catches in my throat as the trees become one mass of blended colors. The hot and humid air constricts around me. The crimsons, purples, and other darker shades of the vibrant forest slide away like water splashed on glass until only golden tan shades remain. Then other colors rush back in, and the air around us seems to pop like a balloon.

In less than a handful of seconds, we've traveled from the doorway to Faery to a massive, domed chamber. Pillars of cream-colored stone streaked with golden tones soar up to a glass roof. Hallways venture off in various directions. More fae guards linger about their thresholds. Before us stands a set of double doors two stories high that have a subtle glow and pulse within like the forest we just left. They must be made of the same wood, which manages to keep a bit of its magic long after harvest.

"Welcome to the royal palace," the guard says as he releases my hand and steps away.

I all but gape at my surroundings. And this is where I'll be living during The Choosing. At least, I assume it is. A grin pulls at the corner of my lips. It should be a nice change from the cramped house I share with my mother and brothers. Even the marble floors are streaked with golden veins that catch the light and glimmer like little flames rushing under our feet.

"The throne room is straight through here," another guard remarks with a gesture at the doors.

"Thank you," I reply.

"Yes, thank you," Uncle Matias echoes with an air of dismissive superiority that scrapes against my nerves.

But there's no time to focus on him. Two other guards stationed near the double doors are already pulling them open, a wave of sound rushing out to greet us.

Selena grabs my hand and gives it a little squeeze.

"Here we go," she whispers.

Here we go, indeed.

I stand a little straighter, taking in the mass of people—human and fae—beyond. Either more attendees arrived than expected or they plan to cram us in like sardines.

The room is far from small, stretching what must be over half a football field from the doorway and bearing similar characteristics as the antechamber we stand in, right down to the glass ceiling that lets in a flood of afternoon light to dance across those in attendance. It's the far side, however, that holds my attention as we enter. An empty throne sits on a raised dais with steps leading up to it. It's so high that the king would sit above the heads of all those standing before him, though he's nowhere to be seen at the moment. That on its own would demand attention, but it's the sight beyond that I yearn for a closer look at.

There is no far wall. Instead, it's open to the elements. Dark green plants spotted with reds and oranges creep in at the edges, but beyond that, in the distance, are hills of golden sand stretching to the horizon.

The sand sea.

I've learned about it. Read about the great sand sea as big as our Sahara. But reading about it and seeing a glimpse of it are two entirely different things as I'm quickly learning.

In my reverie, Uncle Matias has managed to launch into a bout of praise for the fae, putting on airs for anyone close enough to hear.

"Come on." Selena takes my hand and pulls me deeper into the crowd. "Let's get a drink." She halts at one of the many tables overflowing with various foods and filled glasses of sparkling beverages

"For someone who has no interest in living in Faery, you sure seem to appreciate it," I remark.

She shrugs before plucking two champaign flutes off the table and passing one to me. "I don't have to want to live there to appreciate what it has to offer. Being here for a few hours is tolerable. Being stuck here maybe forever?"

Selena gives a dramatic shiver.

Forever... Right, because that could happen. Not that the king has any real reason to pick someone like me. Even so, the thought turns my excitement on its head. As much as I've wanted to be here, to visit and see this world, the thought of *forever* is terrifying. I take a healthy sip from the glass, expecting the crisp bubbliness of cheap champaign and nearly choke as a symphony of flavor dances over my tongue. It's sweet, fruity, divine...and nothing like what I expected. I nearly moan as the liquid finally slides down my throat.

I really *have* been missing out.

I go to take another sip, but Selena lurches forward and stops me with a hand on my arm. "Whoa! Not so much so fast."

"You think I can't hold my liquor?" I raise my eyebrows at her, suddenly feeling bolder than a moment ago.

"Oh, I know you can," she says with a wink, probably remembering one of our many nights out. "But fae alcohol is different than ours. Stronger. At least for us. I'm sure I told you that, right?"

"Oh." I frown at the glass in my hand. She probably did. I'm sure it's in my notes somewhere, actually, but with everything else on my mind, I forgot about that. "Probably shouldn't have taken half of it in one go then." Especially not if I want to impress the fae and not make a fool of myself, and my family, all before the contest ever starts.

She cringes. "Probably not."

"Maybe I'll just..." I look for somewhere to dispose of the glass.

I spy a cluster of empty glasses on a tray and add mine to it. With something that delicious in my hand, I'd be tempted to sip it again. Even now, I feel a little pang of loss having given it up, but it's probably for the best. I have my burst of liquid courage, and it will have to be enough.

Selena and I wander through the crowd, scoping out the competition, as it were. The potential candidates are easy enough to pick out in their elaborate gowns, fanciful updos, and flawless makeup. They've clearly put in the effort to be prepared. Unlike me. I pull my bottom lip between my teeth as I eye a stunning brunette whose neck is totally going to be sore by the end of the night from turning up her nose at everyone around her. Her stance is no doubt planned, letting the high slit on one side of her dress expose her leg and show off her red-bottomed designer heels.

I nearly roll my eyes at that extravagance. I may not have a lot of experience with the fae, but I'm pretty sure they don't care about human brands. After all, they're giving us each our own fae wardrobe, which Aunt Dalia implied was because human clothes aren't up to fae standards.

If the king has any sense, he'll see right past the woman's pretty looks and see the arrogant attitude already hanging about her like a cloud.

But then, that's never a guarantee when men are concerned, and she has no trouble getting their attention, if the swarm of fae around her are any indication.

"Cora." Selena bites out the name. "Just ignore her."

When preparing for The Choosing, my uncle theorized on who my competition may be and may have used his connections to find out some of them early too. So even though I haven't met the other women who will be my competitors, I recognize a few faces as we wander the crowd.

Alexis, a stunning Black woman with rich brown skin, stands out in a gown of gold that looks like flowing metal. Her black hair is shaved on one side, the other longer and all smoothed to one side. With her tall, athletic build, she can pull off the look with style and might be an early favorite, if not for the subtle frown on her face and crossed arms.

"Maybe she's saving her smiles for the king?" I suggest.

"Or maybe her family chose a different competitor after all?" Selena muses.

Though how anyone could compete with her, I'm not sure. If the king favors an athlete, she'd win for sure...and I'd be out of luck.

Her stance loosens a little bit as a curvy, petite blond with pale skin and a smile as bright as her ruby gown comes to stand beside her. Familiarity tingles at the back of my mind, but I can't place her name. Neither can Selena when I ask her.

Commotion rises behind us, like a swell of sound gently rising from the crowd until the wave catches us in its thrall and has turning toward it.

"Is it him?" a finely dressed woman nearby squeals.

My blood runs hot and cold at once. "The king?"

Breath catches in my throat as I glance at the dais and the man who hadn't been there a few moments ago. Though I guess he's not a man exactly.

I step in his direction, stretching on my toes to see around the people in front of me. And what I find is stunning. Warm golden skin, dark auburn hair falling past his ears to brush against his shoulders, and a jaw that's strong but soft all at once. It might be some trick of the light, but I'd swear a soft glow radiates from his eyes. It's hard to tell from so far away. What I can make out of his attire is just as refined as the regal angles of his face—a fitted crimson coat stitched with gold that glimmers as bright as the circlet woven through his hair.

He scans the crowd, managing to look both bored and intent all at once. His gaze passes right over me. But then he doubles back, and I'd swear our eyes catch and he stares at me. Though *stares* might be an understatement. It's like he reaches across the room and demands all my focus on him.

A hot flush spreads through my chest and races up the back of my neck. This is the Court of Fire, and suddenly I'm sweltering, though I don't think any fae magic is to blame.

"Whoa." Selena steps into my line of sight before turning me away. "Is that a little drool I spy on your lip?"

I blink rapidly, sucking in a breath as a small shiver flows over my skin. Right, this is a game of sorts, and while catching the attention of a royal is the goal, there's just one little problem.

That wasn't the king on the dais but his younger half-brother, Lysandir.

Uncle Matias had given me copies of portraits of the royal family and key advisors to study. After all, my competition would know them and might even have relationships with some of them, depending on their family's influence and their time spent in Faery. I'm already way behind, and the less I can let that show, the better.

When I'd held Lysandir's portrait, something had spoken to me. Maybe it was that, unlike Vasilius, the king, Lysandir didn't have as much of that cocksure arrogance to him. He seemed...approach-able. I liked that and immediately thought that maybe he could be an ally in my quest to win his brother's hand.

After all, a guy's brother probably knows him as well as anyone, and he might be more inclined to take his advice than, say, some stuffy advisor or his stepmother. But that's just a hunch. I'll have to get to know them all to figure out my strategy, and goodness knows I'm going to need one. Uncle Mathias's suggestion of playing up being the shiny new human in Faery will only get me so far. Yes, I'll likely be a curiosity since I haven't been at court, but that alone won't win me the crown.

"Whew, yeah, I'm blaming the wine for that one." I turn and head toward the edge of the room and the balcony beyond, suddenly desperate for some fresh air.

"The wine, huh?" Selena waggles her eyebrows as she catches up with me.

I manage a shrug as I keep walking. "Nothing wrong with looking."

"Right. For like the next hour."

Chapter 3

A s I'd hoped, the air on the balcony is a touch cooler, and a slight breeze does wonders at calming me down.

"Exactly." But even as I say it, I find myself turning my head to glance inside at the dais.

My shoulders droop a little when I find it empty. I kind of hoped I had his attention somehow, but maybe I was just imagining things.

Either way, I'll be introduced to the royal family soon enough. As part of the opening ball, all the candidates will appear before the royal family one by one and declare their intention to compete for the king's hand. The king will accept each one, inviting them to try to be his queen. It's all a formality, or so I was told, part of the ritual that begins the competition, but that brief moment and presentation will be more important for me than all the rest. It will be my first impression, my first introduction. God help me if I trip on my dress and fall or something. Knowing my luck, that could totally happen. At least I don't have some long speech to memorize. I just have to say a few simple words and perform a ridiculously formal curtsy straight out of the history books.

Yeah, good thing I didn't keep drinking that wine.

We wander back inside a few minutes later, lured by the fae music. Uncle Mathias finds us there, drops some comment about looking for us everywhere, and shoos us toward the dais.

"It's almost time for the presentation," he says while expertly weaving us through human and fae alike in search of a closer spot.

My chest grows tight, and suddenly I wish I *had* kept drinking the wine.

A hush rolls across the assembled. My uncle appears not to notice—either that or he ignores it—but for me, the change in tone and mood is impossible to miss. Even the hypnotic music quickly falls away to nothing. Hostage of the sudden quiet, I follow the direction of the crowd's attention toward the dais. All thoughts vanish from my head.

Standing front and center is a male whose presence I could never miss or mistake, even without the golden crown reaching toward the ceiling in wavering points with the rubies slotted into it. In person, Vasilius, King of Fire, is even more regal and imposing than the portrait I studied, and that's saying something. The art alone was mesmerizing. Vasilius's strong, square jaw is tilted up as he regards the assembled, a half smile playing about his lips. The hair that falls around his shoulders is a shade brighter than Lysandir's and even more varied with streaks of gold and burnt umber that make it look like living flame. And then there's his stature, tall even for a fae and broadly built in the action-hero sort of way that screams rippling muscle and bulging biceps, even if I can't see much of his golden skin with the pristine attire he wears—similar to Lysandir's and yet somehow more, though I can't say exactly how their outfits vary. Maybe it's simply the way the king fills it out.

A flush creeps up my neck.

This is the man I'm supposed to marry.

Share his life, his bed.

I squeeze my thighs together to stifle the sudden warmth there. Being queen certainly would come with perks if I got to wake up next to that every morning.

The king is not alone on the dais. Lysandir is back, standing just off to the king's side and a few steps back, next to an older woman wearing a crown as well. She must be his mother. And though the little I've learned puts her age in the nineties, from this distance, she still seems strong and hale, even leaning a bit as she does on what might be a cane—it's hard to tell from my vantage.

Two lines of fae guards in their full crimson regalia descend from the wide dais into the crowd before the king. I stretch onto the tips of my toes and lean around the people in front of me to try to catch a glimpse of whatever they're doing.

"What are they up to?" I whisper.

Uncle Mathias steps up next to me. "Preparing for the acceptance ceremony."

Now that he says it, I realize the guards have been moving people back to make a wide-open space before the dais.

"Are you ready?" my uncle asks, barely a whisper.

It's time then.

In minutes, I'll enter the contest for the king's hand.

I pull my shoulders back and give a stiff nod. "As I'll ever be."

"Good," he replies. "Let's move closer to the front."

Aunt Dalia has joined us, and the four of us continue to weave through the crowd until we're almost to the edge of the open space before the royals. The press of bodies is thicker here, so much so that I can barely move without touching someone and my head is swimming from the riot of perfumes I've drifted through to get here.

No sooner are we there than the king lifts his hand, calling for silence. Not that he needs to. The quiet is so unnaturally oppressive already no one in their right mind would break it with more than the swish of fabric, click of heel on the marble floor, or breathy whisper.

The king's smile broadens before he lowers his hand and begins. "Thank you all for coming today."

His voice is rich and warm like the air of his court, the kind that's pleasing to the ears and feels like it should be heard over a glass of whiskey while seated near the fire.

"My dear mother, your Dowager Queen Elaine, wishes to see me wed to a human bride before she departs this plane." He shifts his attention to her, and though I'm no expert, the affection shining in his eyes seems genuine, nor did I miss that he called her mother rather than stepmother or something else, though she's not the woman who birthed him. From what I've learned, his own mother passed many years ago, but the king still seems to have found affection for his late father's third bride, the mother of his brother, Lysandir.

"To honor her wish, we have invited the noblest families of our human friends to send a daughter of their house to enter The Choosing, continuing the tradition that our court has followed for generations. These women will reside here in the palace until my mother, my advisors, and I have determined which one will make the best queen." He leans in, almost like he's telling a joke. "And who will hopefully provide a few heirs for our great court."

This elicits a roll of quiet laughter from the crowd and an awkward chuckle from me. Kids. Of course that would be part of the deal. I shake my head, trying to clear the sudden surge of unease making my bite my lip. But that's what this contest is. Not just a crown. It's marriage, kids, a new home, and entirely new life in a new world.

I wanted that, didn't I? Didn't I dream of it once?

I wrap my arms around myself. But I'm no one, really, not like some of these women, who have probably been preparing for it their whole life. There's no way I'll win. In fact, I'll be lucky if I'm not the first one sent home. Once the shiny newness of me wears off, I'll be done for if I don't find some other way to stand out and claim the king's attention.

"However, there is one change we must make to The Choosing." The king's expression grows serious, earning an answering chorus of whispers. "The Unseelie have grown in power recently, endangering the Seelie courts and going so far as to kidnap the human mate of the King of Air."

It's news we've heard. Even me, on the fringes of coven society. Such a thing is a headline for the ages. A mate, a partner, especially a human one, would be one of the most beloved and protected people within the court, yet the Unseelie kidnapped her. Faery is supposed to be safe. A place where humans are treasured and given gifts and an easy life in exchange for the fact that our humanity gives power to fae magic. No human expects to be threatened or taken by boogiemen in the night. It's simply unheard of. Or it was.

"We cannot be too careful with the safety of our human friends," the king is saying when I focus back on his words. "Especially one who may be a future queen. As a result, any woman who enters into The Choosing shall be bonded to me until my chosen is crowned."

This is new information to the crowd, eliciting a rush of replies, even a few barks of outrage.

"I know." The king raises his hands, calling for quiet, which settles much more slowly and uneasily than before. "Such bonds on humans are an old and ill practice. Forbidden in this court."

"Surely the wards will keep them safe," some brave individual calls out.

Vasilius focuses his gaze on the direction of the sound. "So the Court of Air believed too, but the Unseelie have a null, a powerful one. Wards are nothing to a null. However, our guards know of this threat and will be on alert. We all will. But the bond is a further precaution to make sure none of these beautiful ladies are taken if this Unseelie threat should slip past our notice."

He pauses, giving time for the rationale behind his words to sink in, and the weighty silence seems to have its effect as people look to one another, a few nodding in resigned acknowledgement.

A bond is...inconvenient for most. But for me, it might be a good thing. Even if I'm the king's last pick, I get to stay here until the competition is done and the queen is selected. I can enjoy Faery, experience it like I've always wanted to, and no Unseelie null is going to steal me away.

"But that's not all," the king begins again, drawing all attention back to him. "We cannot bind all humans to me. It would be improper and require too much power. It pains me to say it, but I cannot guarantee the safety of any humans who reside here. You will be a target to the Unseelie. They need humans more than ever to revive their magic, and their new so-called king will no doubt have his subjects trying to acquire them by any means necessary. Our human friends are always welcome here, but for your own safety, I recommend you return to your world until this threat is dealt with. And deal with it swiftly we shall."

He raises a fist in the air, fire swirling around it a brilliant display of reds and golds. Guards around the room echo the gesture, igniting the air with a flurry of sparks and color. The fire vanishes as he lowers his arm back to his side.

"The timing is far from ideal, but we do what we must for the future of the court." He looks to Dowager Queen Elaine and gives a nod.

My chest grows tight. She must not have much time left, despite the look of health clinging to her aged form. Why would they bother to hold this competition now unless they didn't believe they had time to delay in fulfilling her last wish?

"With that, we shall call forth the human houses and allow each great house the chance to have one daughter enter the competition to become my queen. If any wish to decline their invitation given the circumstances, we understand." The king shares another look with Elaine before nodding to a dark-skinned fae with pale silver hair who has stepped to his side.

This fae—a top advisor, Uncle Mathias reminds me—shares more of the details about what will transpire. When a daughter of the house is formally accepted by the king, she will be bound to him on the spot, the king using his magic with that of his advisors to create a temporary bond that should release upon the choosing of his queen. I don't miss the careful wording. *Should* release. Because I have a feeling they're unsure, a sympathy that Selena shares in whispered confidence.

"I told you not to back out on me, but you totally can if you need to," she says as the first of the houses is called upon, leaning in close enough and whispering so her father can't hear. "We can run away together. They can't make us enter if we both refuse."

But I can't. I won't. I've come this far, and I won't be seen as a coward. Not now.

"I'm doing it." The answer is as much for myself as her. It'd be a lie to say there's not a part of me screaming to turn and run right now before I make a terrible mistake, but I'm nothing if not stubborn. Besides, it's not just me I have to think about. My mom and brothers need my uncle's support. Mom mostly. My brothers have been excelling in sports, and college scholarships look promising. But Mom? I'll do whatever it takes to keep her in my Uncle Matias's good graces.

No, I committed to this, and I'm going to see it through.

Houses are called forward. Young women representing the named house kneel before the king. They're bound to him with a display of magic that resembles golden strands of light being wrapped around their wrist before winding around the king's as well. Only one house declines the invitation, an older woman stepping up before the king and layering on an apology so thick that the king looks more exhausted than disappointed when she finally retreats.

"House Rivera."

The pronouncement rings through the room, sounding more a condemnation than an invitation.

I swallow the sudden knot in my throat.

"That's you." Uncle Mathias has stepped to my other side and takes my hand firmly in his, like he planned to drag me up there if I changed my mind. Actually, he probably would.

But the last thing I need right now is to make a scene, so I paste a pleasant smile on my face and walk with him to edge of the circle of onlookers, fae and humans alike parting to let us through. There I leave him and continue alone. It's easier now as I stare at the king, focusing on his strong jaw, his upturned lips, and the ruby dangling from one pointed ear.

His presence beckons like the symbol of his court, warm and inviting, and it's entirely too easy to curtsy, bow my head, and recite the words I practiced over and over in my head in preparation for this moment. "I am Mira, daughter of House Rivera, here to pledge myself as a candidate of The Choosing. May I—"

"No."

The sudden exclamation steals the rest of my speech and pulls a loud gasp from the crowd at my back. I snap my head up just as Lysandir jumps off the last step of the dais to stand beside the king.

"What's the meaning of this?" the king snaps at his brother.

But Lysandir isn't look at him, only at me. Blazing shock and fury scald me where I stand. I can't help but wobble as I right myself from my curtsy and stare in horror between the brothers.

"This woman has never been in Faery before today." Lysandir regards me like a bug to be squashed. "Yet now she wants to try to become your bride, the Queen of Fire?"

"This is true?" the king cocks his head to the side as he appraised me.

"It is," the prince replies. "There are other candidates here. The competition will not suffer for the lack of one more."

My hands ball into fists. I'm not some rotten apple in the bowl to be tossed into the yard.

"Let me explain." Uncle Mathias's footfalls are heavy behind me, but I throw out my arm to wave him off.

"I will explain," I say.

I'm done letting men talk about and over me. I take a step closer to the king, who stares at me with his arms crossed over his chest.

My uncle halts in my periphery. Lysandir finally yields his attention, and I stare him down in defiance before turning my focus back to the king. It's him I have to convince. It's his hand I'm trying to win after all. The pause gives me a moment to leash the fury wanting to spill off my tongue toward the prince. I'll deal with that later.

"It's true," I start. "This is my first day in Faery. However, I have long wished to come here and be among your court. It's been a dream of mine since I was a child and first learned that I held the gift and could see fae. But before I was of age, my father passed away unexpectedly." Just thinking about it causes my throat to try to close up. I suck in a deep breath before continuing. "My mother did not handle it well. My younger brothers either." Or me, if we're being totally honest. I was lost for a long time. "They needed me. It was my duty to help my family, to care for them, and to be the best daughter I could. I put aside my desires to support them for as long as I could, but when we learned you were seeking a queen, I could not miss the opportunity to follow my dreams and prove my worth."

In the pause where I gather the rest of the thoughts trying to force their way out, the king nods, urging me to continue, so I do.

"I am Mira, daughter of House Rivera, here to pledge myself as a candidate of The Choosing. May I bring honor to my house and the best of myself to your court and your people," I add, finishing out the portion of the entry pledge I was unable to complete before the prince's interruption. "I believe I have qualities that would make a strong queen. I think my time caring for my family has uniquely prepared me toward that end, as I have much experience putting others before myself as a good queen should. I ask for your permission to attempt to prove myself to you in The Choosing."

The king's crossed arms fall loose. He gestures to me as his expression smooths out into a smile. "Why would I reject such a pledge?"

Lysandir takes up the mirror of his brother's former stance. "It's still most unusual. There is nothing in our records—"

"And why should there be?" the king replies. "Only the names of those who compete are recorded, not the circumstances around their entry. Much about this Choosing is unlike those of the past."

The dowager queen rises from her chair and steps forward with the aid of her cane, waving off the fae who steps up to assist her. Both brothers turn as if they sense her movement. She folds both hands over the top of her cane and leans onto it, her heavy crimson dress swirling around the bottom of it almost like it has a life of its own.

She pins me with a gentle look at odds with her regal appearance. "Let her enter if she is so determined."

Lysandir whirls toward me. "Mira."

The way he says my name is a plea, but for what, I can't say. To quit? To leave? But that makes no sense, and there's no way I'm quitting now, especially not since the dowager gave her approval. She spoke in favor of no one else—not that anyone else had this kind of issue—but I still have to believe that's a good thing.

"Do you find some fault in her, my brother?" The king's boot taps on the ground as he waits for an answer. "Other than being new to court?"

The prince stares at me, and I hold my breath, waiting. The king may have asked the question, but I'm desperate for the answer.

Lysandir's gaze locks with mine. "No."

Breath slips from my lips in a rush. *No.* And he can't lie. No fae can outright. My brows pinch together. *Then why?* I mouth before I can stop myself. At least I didn't speak it aloud.

Lysandir pinches his eyes closed as if in pain and turns away, returning to the dais with heavy steps.

"Lady Mira Rivera." The king holds out his hand to me. "I accept you into The Choosing."

The grin on my face now is genuine as I place my hand in his. His touch is warm and softer than I imagined, yet there's no doubting his strength as he clasps my hand in his and his advisors hurry down the stairs of the dais to surround us.

I don't know if my uncle remains nearby or if he retreats to the crowd. My attention is not for him, only for the king whose presence and acceptance has me glowing from the inside.

The advisors begin the binding spell, and I can't help but gasp at the tickle of golden magic that winds around my wrist like spider silk. The glowing threads circle me a few times before they wind the same strand around the king's wrist, right over a golden tattoo of leaping flames encircling his arm. The working glows brighter before tightening. Just when I expect to feel it cinch around my wrist, the magical threads vanish into my skin, leaving a warm tingle in their wake. Where once was just tanned skin, a tattoo like the king's but smaller now encircles my wrist.

I am bound.

There's no turning back now. No rejecting me. I will prove myself worthy. I will and show everyone who doubted how wrong they were. It's those feelings that bolster me as I beam with pride at the king and bask in his glowing appraisal.

The thing is done, and I curtsy once more before turning away to return to the crowd. But as I raise my head, there's one other I can't help but search out and find—Lysandir. He doesn't look at me. If I had to guess, I'd say he's trying very hard not to as he stares at the wall, his face half turned from mine.

He's a quandary. An enemy? He surely doesn't want me to win his brother's heart and become queen, but why? How did I make myself so repugnant to him so fast?

Like a dark cloud, he shadows my moment of glory, and finally I turn my back on him.

CHAPTER 4

ALL OF THE KING'S candidates are presented in a line before those in attendance. Before, I was easy enough to overlook in the crowd. I'm not anymore. Every fae wants to meet and dance with a human woman who may one day be queen. Every human wants to size me up and see what threat I pose to their preferred winner. It's a dizzying swirl of names, faces, and mindless conversation until my feet are killing me, my throat is dry, and between not eating before the presentation due to my nerves and not eating after due to the attention, I'm starving. I would seriously do some outrageous things for a cheeseburger.

If every day is going to be like tonight, I may have made a huge mistake. The other candidates I've seen seem to be faring better than me, a few like Cora even seem to radiate with energy from all of the attention.

For better or worse, the royals left shortly after we were presented to the crowd. It's unfortunate I can't work to make a better impression on the king tonight, but maybe it's best I didn't have to face his brother again.

I nearly weep when my family finally lead me off to the side and shoo away those who try to trail after us.

"You have everything you need?" Uncle Mathias asks.

It's a purely routine question. There's no going back now, and I don't need much anyway. Technology doesn't work here, room and board are covered, and the fae even promised to outfit us—probably because they scorn our poorly made human clothes.

"I hope so," I say.

"Don't forget to write to us. You have to let me know how it's going, okay?" Selena says.

"Of course."

At that moment, a fae guard walks up and clears his throat. "Lady Mira?"

"Yes?" I say as we turn toward him.

The crimson and gold of his uniform are a perfect complement to his umber skin and dark brown hair that is pulled back in a ponytail and hangs past his shoulders. "I'm Tharin." He grins and bows at the waist. "I'll be your personal guard for the duration of your stay. When you are ready, I will show you to your room."

"Oh." The word slips from my mouth before I can stop it. Of course it makes sense that we wouldn't just wander around on our own, especially not with the Unseelie threat, but it still takes me off guard. "Nice to meet you."

I begin to offer him my hand but think better of it and curtsy instead. Fae don't seem like the handshake types.

"Looks like I'll be just fine," I say to my family.

Selena pulls me into a crushing hug. I receive far more formal ones from my aunt and uncle. Though they'd considered staying, with the Unseelie threat and the king's recommendation to leave, it looks like they'll be going directly back to Earth. With promises to write and let them know of my time in Faery, I leave and follow Tharin.

The palace is a wonder.

Halls spiral off in various directions, all bright and lit with glowing fae lights that reflect off the pale and golden marble. Large, open archways serve as windows, letting in pleasantly warm air even though it's night. Despite the size of the place, none of it feels dark or cloistering, especially given the multiple large courtyards we pass. It's hard to tell in the dark, but each one I've seen seems to have a different theme color—be it fountains and plants in shades of blue, a courtyard of mostly golden sand, or another of the same tall trees with trunks that glimmer and glow red and orange like the embers of a fire. The whole palace reminds me of a living flame—bright, sparkling, and with plenty of air to let it breathe.

A few minutes later, we reach a long, enclosed hallway spotted with tall, wooden doors along each side. Guards stand at varying intervals near some of the doors. The lights here are dimmer, as if someone has purposely turned them down for evening.

"All entrants in The Choosing have private rooms in this wing," Tharin says. "There will be guards on watch at all times to ensure your safety."

It should be a relief, but the idea of being so closely monitored threatens to make my skin crawl. Gifted are never truly free. I rub the bond around my wrist. Not in our choices on Earth and not really in Faery either.

Tharin stops in front of one of the doors. "This will be your room. Your things should already be inside along with some re-freshment."

He opens the door and pushes it wide with one arm while standing to the side.

Before I'm able to take in the cavernous space beyond, my attention snares on a tall, fair-skinned fae who jumps up from a chair near the back of the room. She rushes forward and drops into a deep curtsy, her even paler hair slipping over her shoulders.

Tharin enters and comes to stand at my side. "Your attendant, Fia."

And here I thought I'd have the room to myself.

She raises her head and practically bounces on her toes. "I'm excited to meet you."

Her eyes glitter in mirror of her statement.

"You as well," I echo, though truthfully, I'm not sure how I feel about it. After the evening, all I crave is privacy, and the thought of having to chat with and entertain yet another person I don't know has a headache building behind my eyes.

"Fia will see to anything you need and make sure your rooms are ready for you each day."

"Rooms?" I echo.

"Oh yes." Fia stretches taller, twisting her hands together in front of her. "Your bedroom here." She gestures to the room around her. "And your attached bathing chamber. These rooms are specifically reserved for visiting guests of importance, and who could be more important that a potential queen? I've already set out some bathing oils and robe, some food, pitchers of water and wine, a night dress, some slippers. I even thought to get a few books spelled for humans to read." She beams brighter than the flames the king conjured earlier in the night.

"Thank you, Fia," I manage, still reeling from her enthusiasm in the wake of my exhaustion and uncertainty.

"If there is anything at all you need, please tell me. Or even if you wake in the middle of the night, one of the guards can alert me, and I will come right away." She's stepped nearer, leaning in a bit as if to inspect me more closely.

I have to fight the urge to step back or drop the tentative smile on my aching cheeks. "I'd just like to rest for now, thank you. Alone, if that's okay."

"Oh." She rocks back onto her heels. "Of course. I will return in the morning to help you dress for your meeting with Her Highness the Dowager Queen Elaine." She scurries around me and heads for the door but stops, looking back once before vanishing through the partially opened exit.

Once she's gone, I turn back to Tharin, who whispers under his breath, "Overly enthusiastic, that one."

Understatement. But there's something more important I need to know. "I'm to meet with the queen in the morning?"

He nods. "Yes, all of you are to be escorted to her private sitting room for lunch. Breakfast will be provided in your rooms, as you may need rest after the excitement of this evening."

Thank goodness for that. If they wanted me up and going at dawn, I certainly wouldn't be at my best.

"I'll be here when it's time," he adds.

"Thank you." I've said it a lot today, but I do have a lot to be thankful for. Plus, being kind can only help me here, I think. "Is there anything else I should know for tomorrow?"

His amused expression softens a bit. "Your confidence in front of the king was impressive. Hold on to that."

Confidence huh? Can't say I've always had a lot of that, but maybe my spite from this evening will fuel me through the coming days. My gaze drifts away from him, jumping around the bits of the room I can see—a four-poster bed complete with thin, gossamer curtains draped down from the ceiling, a large dressing table, a wardrobe, and a massive, arching window covered with more flowing fabric. Hopefully, it doesn't rain much or there are shutters. Otherwise, the marble floor is going to be a slick mess, to say nothing of the humidity. My suitcase has been set beside a bench at the foot of the bed, as promised.

"Unless you need anything else, I shall leave you," Tharin says.

"Sounds good," I say and immediately catch myself. That's probably not how a would-be queen should talk. "I appreciate it," I add. "Good night."

Finally, I'm alone, and a deep sigh slips from my lips as I take in the dim room lit by more of the glowing and flickering orbs I spied on my walk through the palace. They're fae lights of some kind, though certainly not electrical ones like we have at home.

I don't bother unpacking my things and instead opt for the fae night dress that was laid out for me. It's softer anyway. But I do take my time in the bathing chamber, savoring the fall of warm water that flows from the ceiling into a large, stone basin, some kind of spa-like fae shower-tub combination. The little vials of soaps are heavenly, and whenever I do write, I'm going to have to ask why no one has smuggled these back to Earth because, my gosh, they're divine—pure scents of flowers and fruits that leave my skin clean, soft, and pleasant smelling.

It's a peaceful experience, until I lay in the bed to try to sleep and memories of the prince's attitude toward me leave me tossing and turning. Multiple times, I start to look for my phone, but of course it's not here and wouldn't work if it was. It's the weirdest thing not to be able to distract myself with nonsense or even send a text message. Anything to not be trapped with my thoughts. But no such luck. I could read the books, but the mattress is so incredibly soft that I can't find the will to rise.

It's the king, Vasilius, who matters. He's who I should be focused on. I close my eyes and focus on the king's face, the warmth of his hand, the radiance of the court. And yet, the last thought I have before falling asleep is the memory of a certain prince's face creased in pain after he failed to get me ejected from The Choosing.

CHAPTER 5

I'M AWAKE LONG BEFORE the sun filters in through the pale, gossamer curtains that hover over the windowpanes. After the night before, I should be exhausted, but the adrenaline coursing through my veins has me anything but. We get to meet with the dowager queen this morning. My second chance to make a good first impression, and hopefully there won't be a certain prince around to spoil it.

The fanciest oil lamp I've ever seen sits on the side table, and I light it, letting out a soft gasp as buttery light fills the room and dances along the walls. It's much brighter than it should be, but doesn't hurt my eyes either, likely some advantage given by the fae glasswork. At least they thought to provide these for us since we can't control the magically influenced fae lights. They should brighten on their own with the day, but right now they're barely visible glowing dots around the room like the dimmest of fireflies but the size of ping-pong balls.

There are numerous things the other women may have packed, though I'd wager clothes, jewelry, and cosmetics are high on the list, despite the fae promising to supply us with those. I, however, packed something far more important.

I pull the stack of notebooks out of my suitcase and spread them out across the bed. They're all the same brand and size but in varying colors, each packed with notes, reminders, and conjecture on the fae. Of course there are plenty of blank pages in each too, as well as an entirely blank notebook to fill with everything I learn while I'm here. Not to mention colorful pens, tabs, sticky notes, and of course some stickers. The stickers aren't strictly necessary, but I couldn't help myself. If I do something, I do it big, and what's bigger than this?

Already my mind is swirling with notes I want to add to my collection, tidbits about the flavor of the wine and additional details on King Vasilius that no portrait could adequately capture, like the warmth of his hand, the light calluses there, or the way the gold flecks in his eyes sparkle up close. Some of these notes are just for me, diary entries to capture my experience here for all time. Other notes will be for Selena, bits to add to her ever-growing database of fae knowledge she's working on for the gifted.

I'm hard at work when a soft tap comes on the door.

"Come in," I call, but whoever it is has already cracked the door.

"Oh!" Fia exclaims before sliding through the narrow space and closing the door behind her. Her hair is tied back in a long braid behind her head. With her pale form and the limited light filtering in through the windows, she almost looks ethereal. "I came to wake you and help you get ready, but I see you are already up and dressed."

I smile at her from my perch on the bed, surrounded by my books and pens in what probably looks like an absolute mess of things but suits me just fine. "I've been up for a little while."

Truly, the whole having an attendant thing is a little weird. It makes sense that royals would have help—they do in my world anyway—and one of us will be a future royal, but it's an adjustment for sure. My brows pinch together. A misstep maybe? Should I have let her help me get ready? I give my head a little shake. Can't worry about that now.

"Is there anything I can get for you?" she asks helpfully. "You'll be having an early lunch with the queen, but I could bring you something now? Help with your hair if you need. Not that it needs help," she adds quickly.

To be fair, I didn't do anything with it other than brush it out, letting the dark waves hang around my shoulders. I didn't plan to either. Yes, we're to meet with the queen, but I also want to be seen for myself, not just some made-up version of me.

"I think I'll be fine," I say. "I don't need anything this morning."

I'd swear her shoulders drop, and she glances at the ground for a moment before smiling at me and giving a shallow bow. "Summon me if I can be of help."

It's impossible to miss the note of disappointment in her voice. *Damn, I can't have that.* "Actually," I say before she can fully turn back toward the door. "Do you know if there is any coffee available?"

From my studies, the fae don't favor it the way humans do for whatever reason, but maybe they'll have some anyway since they planned to have humans in residence.

"Of course!" Her whole body appears to brighten and lift. "I should have thought of that," she mutters, half to herself.

"It's fine, you couldn't know that I—"

"I'll get some and be right back!" She whirls toward the door and is halfway out before she stops and turns. "Any milk? Sugar? I hear some humans like that. Or a little... Oh, what is it called?" Her whole face scrunches up as she searches for the word.

I save her the trouble. "Just the coffee. Thank you."

"Right away!"

The door trembles in her wake, and I can't help but give a little laugh as I settle back into my studies. Good thing the doors seem to be pretty soundproof or she might have just woken half the hall.

The coffee may have been a bad idea. Between the caffeine boost and my nervous anxiety, I'm a barely contained mess in a dress by the time our meeting with Elaine rolls around. I put on a good face of course, and I know I look good—this modest navy dress never does me wrong. It might be an odd move not wearing the court's colors on the first full day, but it's a sure way to stand out.

Fia didn't say anything about it, so it can't be major faux pas. She seems determined to do everything to perfection, and I have a feeling she expects the same of me and would stop me from doing anything too bad, to save face herself if nothing else.

When it's time to go, we all meet in the hall. My instincts haven't disappointed me—the other women are all in vary shades of red or gold.

Cora doesn't miss a beat, eyeing me up and down with a disapproving smirk. "Forget the court colors already, Mira?"

The comment slices through the chatter and pulls attention toward me like a magnet.

But I half expected this from her.

"Not at all," I reply in my sweetest voice.

Standing out is my strategy. My best one. The king hasn't shown much interest in humans? Then I'll show him one he hasn't seen before—me. It seemed to work in my favour last night...other than Lysandir's protest. Just the thought of him dampens my spirit, so I push it away.

"Hmm." Cora purses her lips. "I suppose poor choices are to be expected from unknown white trash." She turns, giggling with the stick-skinny blond at her side. Katherine, probably the youngest one here, who clearly has found the wrong role model.

My hands ball into fists at my side, but I stretch my grin wider. As a waitress, I've had a lot of experience dealing with rude people, and I summon it now.

"I'm only part white," I say politely, trying not to show how much their barbs sting.

Cora whips her head toward the woman at her other side, a gorgeous Latina named Gabriella. *Oh yes, look to another non-white person for confirmation. Totally cool.*

"Mira *Rivera*," Gabriella says with a look that says my heritage should be obvious.

My mom is basically as white as they come. For a while, I thought maybe that was why my uncle didn't like her. But no. As I learned from my father before he died, my uncle identifies as gifted first, Texan second, and Hispanic third. And with as long as my dad's family has been in Texas, we really are as American as anyone. It wasn't Mom's coloring that knocked her down in his esteem, just a different part of her genetics that she had as little control over.

Gabriella shakes her head and walks away. We haven't met before, but I tried to pay attention at the ceremony last night and remember first names at least. Gabriella's shiny, dark hair is even longer than mine and brushed to absolute perfection. Not a strand is out of place where it hangs down over the back of her knee-length crimson cocktail dress. With her rich skin tone, the color does wonders for her.

Cora rolls her eyes and mutters, "Whatever," before turning away with Katherine in tow.

Before anyone else can engage me, we're ushered off as one big group of women and guards toward breakfast. It shouldn't take all of our guards to see us there—seriously, one would do—but it seems they're not taking chances with our safety, even if this is overkill.

The room where we meet the queen is impressive even by fae standards. It's circular, high columns holding up a domed roof with a wide, circular opening in the center. That alone would let in plenty of light, but half the room has no walls, instead opening up to a courtyard beyond, that side of the roof held up by thick columns spaced evenly apart.

The courtyard beyond is one I had spied the night before, albeit from a different perspective. Golden sand covers the ground, spotted with large gray rocks and twisting eggplant-colored trees, like some fae version of a Zen garden.

The room itself is lacking the dining tables I expected. In my mind, this was going to be some kind of formal affair straight out of a historical drama. Not so. A few tables filled with foods and drink stand around the edges of the room, but the center is covered with rich rugs and spotted with huge pillows in varying warm shades. The queen herself already sits in the one chair in the room, a grand wing-backed thing covered in plush-looking crimson cloth—velvet maybe.

Some of the other women are openly confused by the setup. One even whispers something to her guard.

If it weren't for the importance of the moment, I might laugh. The dowager queen will have us on the floor around her feet like school children. Maybe that's the point. Though she's yet to smile, I don't get the impression she's trying to make us think lowly of ourselves, and from what I've learned, she isn't arrogant or superior in nature, though she has every right to be given her rank.

"Welcome, ladies." Elaine doesn't rise, but I imagine it may be hard for her to do so, especially given that her cane is propped on the little table next to her chair, which already holds a plate of food and a crystal glass filled with pale golden liquid. "Not what you expected, I'd say." She gestures to the pillows. "Help yourself to some food and find a seat."

We do as we're told, most in near silence. I don't think this is how any of us expected things to start out.

The pillows are clustered into little groups, and I end up taking one near Bailey. Selena had helped me gather notes on my potential competition, and I vaguely remember some bits about her. She's in her early thirties I believe and has a maturity I can appreciate. Plus, she's the only other one who appears to have brought a notebook. She gives me a shy smile before opening her black leather journal and smoothing out a page, her little plate of food completely ignored on the floor by her side.

Once we're all seated and introduce ourselves, Elaine drops into a speech. "One of you will become queen, and that is no small thing. Not only will you be a bound to the king in marriage and, fates willing, grant him children, you will also be a constant presence in his life, and it better be a positive one. Encourage him. Support him. Even reprimand him when he needs. And he will."

A few women still and look at one another. Even I have to admit, it's frank words for the first day.

"Surprised?" The queen angles her head, nonplussed. "At my age, there isn't time to waste words. Vasilius may not be mine by blood, but he is my son in all ways that matter. I wish the best for him and intend to see that he has a capable queen by his side before death takes me. And while he has many strong qualities, he can be impulsive, reckless, and hot-tempered. You will need to help balance that."

Impulsive. Reckless. Hot-tempered. I write, underlining each one.

"A pretty face is not going to win you this crown, and it's not only my son you must impress. The counsel and I will also be sharing our opinions as time progresses, and I trust that Vasilius will take our words into account when making his choice."

Katherine openly pouts and pulls up the neckline of her gown that exposes more of her cleavage than I'm sure Elaine cares to see.

"Now that you understand that," the queen says. "I thought I would take the time to tell you more about my reign as queen, particularly the early years."

The queen's tales are riveting. To me anyway. Some of the others? Not so much. Cora has a serious case of resting angry face, and Zoe stands up and stretches enough times that I'm surprised she doesn't drop into a full-out yoga session in the middle of this morning chat. Granted, we all have to move a little. My legs start to fall asleep more than once.

The queen pauses for questions as she's done a few times already, and Grace raises her hand. Her blond hair is as bright and sunny as her disposition. Some might discount her for her curvy figure, but with the almost roguish grin Vasilius gave her when accepting her into the competition the night before, I'd say it's a nod in her favor.

"Can you tell us more about The Choosing from your year?" Grace asks. "What was it like for you?"

Queen Elaine might have been the former king's third wife, but she was the first selected via The Choosing. The first two were love matches, though only the second resulted in any children. Children are rarer for the fae than humans—probably due to their long lifespans—and even more uncommon among human and fae pairings. However, any children born of such unions always have especially strong magic. It's one reason the fae royals tend to favor human mates. In fact, any of us who are not selected to be queen could probably easily find a different match here...if we wanted to. It's what's expected, human daughters to the fae in exchange for gifts to help our families on Earth prosper. Gifted families have made the exchange for generations. Even so, the thought of being essentially passed on to some other important fae makes my breakfast churn uncomfortably in my stomach.

If it was, love, maybe, but how could it be when I'm here for the king? Early in her speech, the queen made it clear we are here for Vasilius and shouldn't seek attentions elsewhere.

"Well, that was quite some time ago," Elaine begins in answer to Grace's question. "My memory is not what is was..." An unfortunate side-effect of residing in Faery. Human memories of Earth fade quickly in the fae realm, and her arrival was likely blurred into that. "But I will say," she continues, "that I believe humans nowadays to be more free with their attentions than was expected of us. To put it plainly, if you think the path to the crown lies in Vasilius's bed, you'd be mistaken. Such intimacies should only be shared between the king and his chosen."

A few women glance away. Cora, undeterred by the queen's prim demeanor, straightens her upper body and raises her hand. The queen nods at her.

"How would you suggest we attempt to see if there is mutual interest then?" Cora asks.

I nearly snort. As if that's the only way to develop intimacy. Not that I've had a lot of experience on the matter but still.

"Surely relational compatibility is important in a marriage," Cora adds, putting a better spin on it.

"You will have time to get to know one another. Some little intimacies would not be amiss, but nothing that could compromise the future of the royal line, however unlikely. If you find that you—"

The words become a muted droning as my senses focus in on a new and strange sensation, almost like the soft pressure on my back of someone staring at me. I glance both ways, but no one else seems to notice. Or if they do, they give nothing away. I can't very well just twist around without it being noticed, but paying attention under the weight of this feeling is impossible.

My attention snags on the notebook open in my lap and an idea jumps to life. I *accidentally* let my pen roll off, and as I'd hoped, it slides down a silken pillow and onto the soft rug to my left. As I move to gather it up, I glance behind me and freeze.

A figure leans against the curved back wall, arms crossed and one booted foot braced against the curvature. With the dark auburn hair falling past his shoulders and strong physique, I have to blink a few times to make sure I'm seeing things correctly. It's not the king, who I've half expected to make an appearance at any moment, but Lysandir. His gaze slides to me, and I whip my head back toward the front, cheeks blazing.

Of course he would show up. I squeeze the pen so hard it almost snaps. Does he plan to try to embarrass me again somehow? I've thought about that moment more over the last few hours than I care to admit. It should be his brother occupying my thoughts, not him, but I can't for the life of me figure out what I did to make him try to stop me from competing for his brother's hand. I'd never even met him before, for goodness sake!

The weight of his stare leans on me like a tangible force. I'm tempted to turn back around just to scowl at him when the pressure lifts and his voice rings out.

"These ladies," he says, "are attempting to become his wife, Mother, not a mildly friendly companion."

A few women gasp and turn as he stalks around the outside of the circular room, snatching some kind of fruit off a table on his way by before tossing it into his mouth. Others break into smiles or simply sit up a little more. In fact, of everyone I can see, I'm the only one frowning.

"Lysandir." The queen's stony expression breaks to from that of a stern school teacher into beaming motherly affection. He's her only child by birth, and her youngest, though he's still sixty years old. The age is boggling when I think about the number, especially since he looks around thirty at the absolute most, but fae ages are like that. In youth, we age the same, but once a fae reaches maturity, their aging slows down considerably in relation to their power. The stronger the fae, the longer the life.

"I thought I'd see if you needed me." He comes to stand at the side of her chair.

The queen dolefully gazes up at him. "Everything is well in hand."

He nods once then turns toward us. "Ladies. I wish you good luck in earning my brother's affections—and those of my mother." I'd swear he stretches the words out, taking time to meet every-one's gaze but mine. "Her happiness is quite important to me, as you can imagine." Lysandir places a kiss on the top of her head, and she gives him a playful swat. "Since you do not need me, I shall see you later."

He exits not through the door he came into but walking out into the courtyard and disappearing from view. We're quiet enough in the wake of his departure that I swear I hear Gabriella give a wistful sigh.

"Well now," Elaine says, her stoic expression returning. "Where were we? Oh yes—"

But I'm still staring after Lysandir, waiting for him to come back and finish whatever he was there for. It can't have been just that. I keep my attention half pinned to the spot where he vanished beyond the wall. Some advisors come and go, making their introduction. But Lysandir doesn't return, and neither do we receive a visit from the king.

CHAPTER 6

W E SPEND THE AFTERNOON taking turns with the fae tailors who will be designing our wardrobe for the duration of the competition...and hopefully after. It's a weird feeling being measured this way, but pointing out colors and styles I like? Having someone suggest shapes, styles, and fabrics that would best suit my body type? That's amazing. A bubble of giddy excitement lodges itself in my chest and doesn't abate. It probably won't until I get to see what they come up with, and it may not even then. Perfectly tailored clothes—fae clothes with their impossibly soft yet sturdy and vibrant materials—are a luxury I've never had.

When we're not with the tailors, we all hang out in a large and luxurious parlor of sorts. Fine furnishings like something out of a French castle provide numerous seating options. A table is set with snacks and drinks. There are even a few fae board games and pleasant fae music performed by a trio of musicians in the corner. Still, the lack of windows makes the room a bit stifling—that, and the lack of any kind of direction. This rooms is ours to enjoy, but we're supposed to just...what? Hang out?

Each time the door opens, everyone stops and looks. But thus far, it hasn't been the person I'd guess we're all waiting on. The king. And the longer the evening wears on, the more certain I am he's not going to show.

"It's got to be close to dinner," Grace laments with a pout. "Do you think we'll dine with the king?" she asks no one in particular. She's stretched out on the sofa, her bare feet nearly brushing Alexis's leg where she sits on the other end, though Alexis—or

Alex as she likes to be called—doesn't seem to mind. The two are friends and have been for years from what I've gathered. Grace's discarded flats sit side by side next to her end of the sofa.

"I doubt it," I grumble. If so, I'm sure they would have ushered us off to be dressed and primped or something, but that hasn't happened.

Adeline occupies the chair next to mine and across from the sofa that Grace and Alex take up. "Well, let's see," she says. She closes the book she was reading and pulls something from her pocket. It's not until she flips open the little brass cover that I realize what it is, a pocket watch. Her lips draw thin before she frowns. "It's later than I thought."

"That thing works here?" I lean over my armrest to get a closer look.

"It does." She pushes a lock of dark brown hair behind her ear before leaning closer, her often shy countenance bright with excitement. "It's been in my family for generations and is purely mechanical, not like the electric ones made today."

"That's clever." Grace sits up and leans toward us.

"It is." Adeline nods. "I wish I could take credit, but it was my grandmother's idea. She used it when she visited Faerie in her younger days. She said it helped her retain a sense of normalcy."

Grace gives a wistful sigh and flops back onto the cushions. "I do already miss my phone. I feel so...detached."

I nod along in echo of her sentiment. I keep finding myself searching for my phone and having a moment of panic before I realize it's not lost, simply not here at all. I tried to wean myself off of it before the competition, but it was just so dang convenient. And addictive, let's not forget that.

The door to the room opens, and we all turn. A guard holds it open as several fae enter carrying large platters of food.

"I'd guess that's dinner." Alexis shoves to her feet with a sigh. "I'm outta here."

"Alex," Grace calls after her, but she just stalks toward the door.

"We can just go?" Adeline asks, watching her leave.

Alex says something to the guard at the doors and walks out, her own personal guard separating from where she'd been leaning on the wall and hustling after her.

I shrug. "I guess so."

And if she's going, so am I. I've been grazing on the assortment of foods in the room all afternoon and have no appetite for anything else. Besides, I might go a little crazy if I have to sit here any longer. Conversation dried up an hour ago, and I didn't think to bring a book in here with me like Adeline.

I stand and gather my notebook from the side table.

"You too?" Grace pouts. I do feel a little bad that we're all abandoning her. Adeline has already gone back to her book. But if the king isn't coming, nor anyone else, I'm wasting valuable time I could use for something else...if they'll let me.

"I'll see you all tomorrow," I say.

Tharin isn't one of the guards hanging out in the room, but I'd wager he's somewhere nearby, probably even more bored out of his mind than we are.

"Giving up on the king already?" Cora quips as I pass by her chair, not bothering to look up from where she idly paints her nails. I swear she's been working on the damn things for over an hour.

I halt and turn to her, waiting until she finally bothers to look at me. When she does, I grin. "Hardly."

I don't wait for a response before striding to the door.

The guard doesn't even stop me. Two others linger in the hall with Tharin.

"Lady Mira," he says as I approach.

"Are we allowed to go other places in the palace?" I ask. "I was hoping someone could show me to the library." Best not to make any assumptions. "If we're allowed to go there, that is."

Elaine might not have remembered much of anything about the competition she won due to that damnable effect Faery can have on human memory, but I'd bet it's recorded somewhere, probably many somewheres. The fae keep excellent records, and I've heard the Court of Fire's capital library is breathtaking.

The hint of a grin pulls at the corner of his mouth like I've said something funny. "Of course. And an excellent choice. I would have suggested that, had you asked." He gives a sweeping gesture toward one end of the hall. "Right this way."

The walk to the library passes quickly, a few turns, a long hallway, and then we're there. Thank goodness for that, because everywhere we go, the fae we pass stare at me like I'm an A-list celebrity. I suppose I might be if I achieve my goal, but the feeling is still odd and uncomfortable, especially after a life of blending in as best as I could back in my world.

Tharin shows me into the library, and the sight that unfurls before me roots me in place just inside the threshold. It's not just big. It's huge. Bookshelves soar up entirely too high in a room that's probably three stories tall. A balcony walk rings the room about halfway up the wall providing access to higher levels. They even have those moveable ladders on rails. Fae lights float near the ceiling like giant firelights, illuminating the place in a pleasant, dim light, soothing yet bright enough to read by.

"Incredible." I gape, turning a half circle to take it all in.

"It is quite lovely."

I glance over and catch him smiling as he eyes the place, as if he's seeing it in a new light.

"Is there a particular section you're looking for?" he asks.

"I hoped to learn more about previous Choosings." Though now that I've seen this place, I really want to see every inch of it.

"Ah." His brows rise. "An apt subject. The head scholar has probably left by now." He leans in as if to whisper a secret. "She prefers mornings." He winks. "Though I think..." He trails off, glancing down some rows to my left. "I think you may find some helpful books over here."

He leads me to a few rows into the heart of the library. Oddly, we only pass one other fae, but maybe that's because it's dinner time. We turn down a row of books, and Tharin stops near the middle.

"You might find what you're looking for around here. The books spelled for humans are marked with this symbol." He taps a finger on the spine of a book, right over a crimson diamond.

"Well, that's helpful," I say. And it will narrow things down quite a bit since only one in a handful appear to bear that mark, at least in this section.

"Would you like me to stay with you?"

"No thank you," I reply too quickly. I'm in desperate need of some breathing room. Not that I'm a recluse, not really, but being around people all day—especially so many of them—can drain me. "It's a library," I add to soften my response. "I'm sure I'm safe. Nothing bad ever happens in a library."

I don't miss the way he's suddenly taken aback, his brows scrunching. He clearly isn't used to humans and our ability to lie, however benign that lie is. Something *bad* almost certainly has happened in a library at some point.

"Ah," he says after a moment and shakes his head. "You humans and your strange statements."

I guess it is strange to him. "I'll let you know if I need anything."

He nods. "Then I'll wait outside."

When he finally leaves, it feels like someone has loosened the fit of my dress and I can breathe again. I'll probably have to get used to being around people constantly if—no, *when*—I become queen, but for now, it's a relief to have a moment alone.

I select a few books with promising titles that bear the crimson diamond and settle into a vacant seating area between two curved bookcases. The first one I look through is interesting but entirely too old to be relevant, though the book itself looks hardy without a bit of the brittle, delicate pages I'd expect in a human book. I've just opened up the second when a voice startles me from my inquiry.

"What a surprise to find you here."

I nearly jump out of my skin as I twist around in my seat and spy the intruder.

Lysandir. God, of course it would be him.

He's dressed the same as earlier today wearing an impeccable vest of crimson and gold over a pale shirt tucked into black pants. He's the picture of refined yet casual, almost like a businessman who has shed his jacket, loosened his tie, and had just slid up to the bar for a drink.

"Same," I snap before I can think better of it.

His brows rise. So does one corner of his lips.

"You decided not to wait and see if my brother planned to pay you all a visit this evening?" He crosses his arms and tilts his head to the side appraisingly.

I close the book with a thump and settle it in my lap. "I assumed he wasn't coming."

"No, most likely not." He lets his arms fall free before striding toward the seating area. "He's occupied with some urgent news this evening."

I stiffen, sitting a little straighter as he comes around the back of my seat and claims the chair next to mine as if he plans to settle in and sit for a while. At least it's good to know that the king isn't avoiding us on purpose. Maybe the rumors about him not being interested in humans are wrong after all. A girl can hope, right? If he's busy with something important, that's totally reasonable.

"And you're not needed with him?" I refuse to look him in the face. Doing so, this close, does something in my chest that I don't really care to analyze right now.

"He already has my advice." He frowns and looks away. "Not that he'll heed it," he says a little more quietly.

Interesting. "And so, you thought you'd stalk me down instead?" I prod. "How did you even know I was here?"

The hint of a smirk lifts one corner of his lips. "I heard you." He taps his ears. "Fae hearing is quiet sensitive, mine more than most."

Of course it is. I bite the inside of my cheek to avoid saying so out loud. "And to what do I owe the pleasure of your company?" I ask, only a little bit sarcastically. "It can't be to ask me to leave again because of course you know I can't."

I raise my wrist for emphasis, the binding mark on clear display.

"No, quite the opposite." He leans back against the cushions, appraising me. "I'm glad you're here."

I rear back like I've been struck. That makes no sense at all.

"So, you've come to apologize then?" These aren't things I should say to a member of the royal family, Vasilius's brother for goodness sake, but I can't seem to help it. The words just keep coming and show no signs of slowing down and my cheek already stings from trying to hold them back. Of course all the patience I've honed at my job decides to abandon me in my moment of need.

He opens his mouth like he might actually apologize but then closes it, his lips settling into a thin line. "I cannot do that either."

Can't. Not won't. I don't miss the clever wording. He's not sorry, though the reasoning or lack thereof is enough to drive me mad.

I'd always heard that Lysandir was not like his brother. A bit quieter and more introspective. Slow to act and measured in his words. But his actions toward me have been anything but. He has unique gifts too, even for a fae, including the ability to sometimes glimpse things in the future, but no one ever told me that list included making things as awkward as possible for unsuspecting human women.

"May I ask you a question, Lady Mira?"

At the use of that title, I cross one leg over the other, sitting up more primly. "I do believe you just did."

A huff of air slips from his nose. Lysandir rises from his chair, and despite the little smirk on his features, a tiny thread of panic in the back of my mind warns me that I might have taken it too far. A potentially damaging move for my goals. Instead, he lifts the chair with seeming ease, despite its hefty bulk. It's the twin of mine, which didn't move a bit when I sat none to delicately, and I'm pretty sure I'd have to throw all my weight against the back just to slide it across the ground, forget lifting it.

He settles back into the chair, but this time he's staring straight at me. "You've never been to Faery before, correct?"

"That's right." There's no way he forgot that little detail.

"So why this desire to marry a male you've never met?" He leans forward, settling his elbows on his knees, his hands draped over one another between his spread legs. "Unless your focus isn't him but the crown?"

I flinch. Damn if he's not right though. It's not just about the man, but also the title, horrible as that is. Granted, I've had plenty of time to learn about the king, to appreciate his qualities and daydream about his portrait. I *am* interested in him. But it's the crown my uncle wants me to secure. It's my family name that I'm supposed to improve.

There's no way I can say that to the prince though. He'd hate me even more than he already does.

"Are you saying it's impossible to develop affection for someone from afar?" I ask, deflecting. "Can you not hear about them or read about them and develop an appreciation and admiration for them?" Vasilius isn't perfect. No fae or human is. However, he leads his people well, is strong, handsome, respected—all admirable qualities. And then there's Faery, a dreamland that actually exists. "Maybe so much so that you feel compelled to venture to a new land that you've always longed to visit anyway, just to see if they could be your perfect match?"

"Then why haven't you?"

"Why haven't I what?"

"Visited before." He tilts his head, and that long, dark red hair slips over one shoulder. "If you longed to visit Faery, why not come?"

My lips purse of their own accord. Because before I could run off on my own, Uncle Matias spotted an opportunity: an unmarried king on the throne with an aging mother who wants him wed to a human. The certainty of a Choosing was too much for him to resist. So, he decided I'd enter for our family, and he already had the perfect leverage in my mother and brothers.

"You never answered my question," I say instead. "It's rude to ask another without answering mine first."

His settles back into the cushion chair, his gaze never leaving mine. The silence that hangs between us is even heavier than his stare, so much that I think he won't answer. The weight of it presses on my chest and makes me fight the urge to squirm or get up and run away.

"Yes, Mira." The way my name rolls off his tongue, so full, rich, and deep, has a pleasant warmth crawling up the base of my neck. "I do think it's possible to love from afar. To be so enraptured by the thought and dream of someone that you'll rush headlong into something in desperation just to brush the edge of your imaginings." His fingers flex on the cushioned armrests as if he's holding himself still with effort. "Is that love? Or obsession? Perhaps an emotion caught somewhere between?"

Suddenly I have a feeling we're not talking about me anymore. His answer is too deep, too well thought out, as if it's something he's mused entirely too many times. I swallow the tightness in my throat and tear my gaze away, staring at nothing on the bookshelf behind him.

"You see, Mira." His name calls my attention, demands it. "Love can be a beautiful thing. But sometimes it's coated in so much desperation and longing, and that it can drive someone to do quite reckless things."

He shoves himself up from the chair and stalks to mine in two quick steps, so fast I barely have time to gasp before he's right in front of me, filling my vision. His imposing figure towers over me. Subtle spicy notes cling to his masculine scent that envelops me like a warm blanket. And then he's leaning down, his palms coming to land on the edge of the armrests, his legs nearly brushing mine where they're half curled under me on the chair. I don't breathe—can't. He's everywhere, stealing every rational thought from my brain.

"Should I worry about you doing something reckless, Mira?"

My body goes hot and cold all at once. My God. If he stares at me like that a moment longer, I might do something reckless, and it won't be something that will earn me any favors with Vasilius.

Someone clears their throat behind me, and Lysandir retreats, stepping back as if he hadn't just been inches away from me.

I whip my head around to find Tharin standing a few feet away. A bit of the tension stiffening my spine retreats.

"I am checking in to see if you need anything," Tharin says.

Lysandir surely won't do anything with him here, and the wash of sanity that has returned with him is enough to ground me too.

"My prince?" Tharin asks, looking from me to the fae male who's retreated to his former seat, one leg crossed over the other in a casual pose that I might assume he's been in for a while if I hadn't just seen otherwise.

"No, thank you." Lysandir waves a dismissive hand. "I seized the opportunity to get to know one of our candidates a bit better."

That's what you're calling it? I glance in his direction, and though his attention is fully focused on Tharin, I'd swear I can feel the weight of his regard, the challenge to say anything.

"I'm happy to stay here with Mira and escort her back to her rooms later if you have other matters to attend to," Lysandir continues.

I'm on my feet so fast I nearly drop the book still cradled in my arms.

"That's all right," I force out in my calmest voice. "I was just about to retire back to my room. Maybe I can take this with me?" I hold up the book.

Tharin gives Lysandir a reproachful look, surprising, given his station, before addressing me. "Of course," he says. "I will show you the way." He turns to Lysandir and gives a bow. "My prince."

Lysandir nods in return, and we turn to leave. But just before we round the bookshelf out of sight, his voice catches me and pulls me to a standstill. "Goodnight, Lady Mira. I look forward to speaking with you more."

My teeth slam together, and I inhale a sharp breath. *Be courteous. Be calm.*

I turn toward him slowly. "Goodnight, Prince Lysandir."

CHAPTER 7

I'M AWOKEN BY A steady thump at the door and the sound of someone entering my room. When I crack my eyes open, light floods in through the windows.

"Good morning, Lady Mira." It's well past dawn, but Fia is entirely too perky for how exhausted I feel. "I trust you slept well."

Terribly, actually. Two nights in Faery and both of them spent lying awake replaying my interactions with a certain fae prince who has gotten under my skin in all the worst ways. Yesterday I was still able to wake refreshed and excited about the day—call it adrenaline. Today...not so much.

However, as I sit up in bed, I catch a whiff of something that improves my mood considerably. Fia carries a small try which bears a covered plate and a large mug of what must be coffee.

"You remembered," I remark as she sets the tray on my desk, moving aside the book I borrowed and barely touched in the process.

"Of course." She gives a quick curtsy before picking up the coffee and bringing it over to me. "I let you sleep late. I hope you don't mind."

"Not at all." I take the warm mug and inhale a deep breath of the steam. That alone is a lift. The first sip nearly burns my throat, but it's worth it, so worth it, for the way it instantly livens me up.

"I thought it wise because you may have a late night tonight." A wide grin stretches across her pale face. "You're all invited to dine with the king, and we've been told he may ask to spend time with some of you afterward." She all but squeals with glee. "Isn't that wonderful?"

Now, that perks me up even more than the coffee. "That's great news."

Finally, we can start this competition in earnest. Instantly, my mind shifts into planning mode: what to wear, how to get the best seat, topics of conversation.

"Do we know what kind of dinner it is?" I ask.

"A formal affair in the high dining room, which is the real reason I woke you. The tailors are here, but they're not done with everyone's clothes. They've brought what they've been working on so that you can pick your favorite for this evening and they can get it finished for you. They've already met with several of the others this morning."

Which means I'm behind. I slip out of bed, nearly spilling a wave of coffee over the rim of the mug. My bare feet land on smooth tile warmed by the sunlight coming through the near window.

"I'll see them now," I say. "Is that all right?"

Her eyes widen. "Let me get your robe first."

Fair. Greeting the tailors in an oversized T-shirt and sleep shorts probably isn't a great idea. I *did* bring some nice lingerie sleep-wear, but honestly, it's for appearances only—if needed. As Fia hurries back with a long robe of crimson silk, I reluctantly set the coffee aside. It'll have to wait.

We spend the next hour or so with a team of three who have me try on each outfit, not only to let me choose one for the evening but also to confirm that everything fits to their high standard of perfection. Mixed with beautiful gowns are a few more casual outfits too—flowing pants and tops, a few so shear I'm amazed I can't see the mole on my hip.

All of the dresses are gorgeous, which doesn't make picking one any easier. I avoided red during our brunch with the queen, seeing it as the obvious choice and wanting to stand out instead...not that Vasilius showed up. I'm sure several of the other women will wear some bright shade tonight too, but maybe more of them will change it up. In which case, it might help to favor the court colors. Maybe? My head almost hurts from overthinking it—as I'm prone to do—so I eventually just pick a lavish crimson-and-gold dress with flowing sheer sleeves and move on to inspecting the rest of the clothes.

"Are these yoga pants?" I say, lifting black pair that look suspiciously like ones I almost packed but are much softer and light as air.

"Oh, yes, I added those for you," Fia says. "Some of the other women asked for some, so I thought you might like them also. A few women even went to the gardens to practice this morning, or so I heard. It could be a good opportunity to get to know them better. And who knows, maybe the king will even decide to stop by." She winks.

I smile in return. "I like your thinking."

It *is* a good idea. Besides, I'll need something to do with my time if we have more idle days like yesterday.

The day passes quickly between fittings, a few self-guided walks around the nearby areas to get my bearings, and an ill-advised drop by our parlor, which earns a snide comment from Cora about hiding my face all morning followed by giggles from Katherine. I don't dignify it with a response, preferring instead to chat a bit with Adeline and Grace, who confirm they did in fact practice yoga that morning and invite me to join them tomorrow.

Fia finds me long before dinner and insists on getting to work transforming me into what she calls "an enchanting vision the king won't be able to ignore." Her words, not mine. While I don't exactly lack self-esteem, her confidence could put anyone to shame. Though the more she works her own practical magic on me, the more I believe her. My hair is smooth and soft yet crafted into artful waves and partially pulled back to perfectly accent my face. The makeup she's applied is light and airy, highlighting and enhancing more than hiding or changing the way I look.

"You're incredibly good at this," I say after she rubs some cream across my lips that leaves them rosy and slightly glistening.

A bright flush rushes to her cheeks. "Thank you, Lady Mira."

"Honestly though, I'm sure not every fae is this talented."

Sharp teeth pull at her bottom lip, and she glances away. "No. I'm better than most."

Just what I thought. And lucky me for having her help. "Why choose to be an attendant for The Choosing competitors then? Surely there are high-ranking fae who would dearly love your services."

Her normally bright enthusiasm fades into sullen silence as she dips a brush into shimmering powder. She takes her time stirring the bristles through the glittering substance, and I worry I've made some faux pas.

Finally, she turns to me with the brush and says, "Close your eyes."

I comply, and she dusts the brush across one cheek then the other, down the slope of my nose, and a quick flick across my brow.

"All done."

My skin shines, radiant with just a little extra bit of shimmer in the areas accented. The effect is subtle yet masterful. "I love it."

I touch the tip of one finger to my cheek then inspect it, expecting to see some of the powder on my hand, but it's still clean.

"It'll come off with this." She holds up a crystal vile with pale blueish liquid. "I'll leave some in your wash room."

She goes about straightening up her various brushes, jars, and creams, and I expect she won't answer my question from before.

But then she says, "My family has been lower class for generations, living out in the southern jungles, but I was never satisfied with that."

Fia halts her clean up and turns to me, not quite meeting my eye, a shy look on her face. There's more, but she's holding back.

"Go on," I prompt.

She gives one short nod. "I worked hard at my skill and even found I could infuse some of my magic into my powders. That last one I applied is my own creation, hints of cool fire worked into fine sand. The high court loves it, and I was able to move my entire family here due to my success."

"That's amazing!" A self-made woman if there ever was one. "I knew you were talented. But then why work as an attendant at all?"

Her gaze flits away again, and she lowers her head a bit before looking back at me from under her lashes. "They like my work but not always me. They know where I come from and my family, and so many of the court still see me as less. But being an attendant for a potential future queen? That, they respect. And if you do become our next queen..."

Fia looks away again.

She doesn't need to continue. Attending to the queen, being the one who helped her win the crown in a way, would elevate her status and reputation even more, probably bringing her as close to royalty as she could hope to come herself.

I rise and grab her hands where they're folded in front of her. Fia gasps, her head snapping up so that she stares at me, her lips slightly parted.

"I understand. I've dreamed of coming here for years, and I know all about working to make one's family proud and helping them rise in life. I'll do my best, for both of us." I squeeze her hands. "Even if I fail, I will make sure everyone knows how amazing you are."

"You would do that?"

"Of course. Just keep bringing me coffee in the mornings." I grin.

She giggles. "I can do that."

When it's time for dinner, we're all ushered there as one big gaggle of women like we were for our meeting with Elaine the other morning. Though given that most of us are wearing dresses with voluminous skirts that nearly or do brush across the ground, we're a long procession. Red and gold are still the dominate colors, but I can't regret my choice. The front plunges down in a wide V-neck that ends between my cleavage and rises to my shoulders, where flowing, sheer sleeves drape over my arms down to the wrist. But it's the skirt of the dress attached to the fitted bodice that's the real show stopper. It's made of layers of sheer material, like the sleeves, but they're varying shades of crimson, yellow, orange, and gold and cut in various triangular patterns so that the whole thing looks like a flame that dances as I move.

Over the top? Possibly.

But given it's our first dinner with the king, I mean to stand out.

Tharin gives me an appraising look as I pass by him at the doors to the dining room. His grin and nod say I've chosen my attire well. And thankfully, he hasn't mentioned anything about the night before.

The dining room is massive. It could seat a hundred easily with room to spare, but tonight it's only set with one long table in the center of the room. High-backed chairs painted or gilded in brilliant gold have their curved legs sitting upon a crimson rug the same shade as the cushions on the seats. The table itself is a dark ebony wood with golden place settings and tall bowls with flames seemingly hovering above them as a strange, magical candelabra.

But the real breathtaking part is the view. One long wall opens to a balcony, the heavy drapes pulled back and tied between each of seven archways giving a perfect view of the sun setting across the sand sea.

Standing in the center archway is King Vasilius, resplendent in a tailored coat of crimson and gold and dark pants tucked into black boots with golden accents. He wears his crown today, the rubies and his auburn hair gleaming in the sunset glow and adding to his ethereal aura. No one, human or fae, could look upon him like this and think him anything less than a king.

"Ladies." He spreads out his arms in greeting and gives a slight bow of his head. "I'm glad you could all join me for dinner. The dowager queen will be joining us as well."

Not his brother? I wait for that addition, almost sighing aloud when it doesn't come.

Several of the women have already rushed up to the king without invitation, crowding in around him and peppering him with questions and compliments. Katherine literally grabs his arm, and though she doesn't seem to notice, I don't miss his flinch or the way he subtly pulls away from her touch before thinking better of it and pretending like the visceral reaction didn't just happen. I guess she's not his type, which is good news for me.

"There will be plenty of time to talk," he says over the din of women vying for his attention. "Please, choose a seat."

Fae stationed near one side of the room move into action, placing themselves behind the rows of chairs on either side of the table, ready to pull them back for us like servers at a high-end restaurant. The two largest chairs—one at either end—are unattended. Spots for the dowager and the king.

Cora nearly knocks Gabriella down in her rush to claim a seat at one end. Adeline hurries just as quickly toward the other end. They've presumed the same thing as me, though I'd wager none of us know which side will be the king's versus the queen's. I land a space just off the middle. Hopefully, I'll be close enough to the king to catch his ear and participate in conversation, no matter which side he sits on.

We've barely taken our seats when the main doors open and Elaine enters, accompanied by a guard. Vasilius, like the king he is, breaks away from the two women who linger near him rather than claiming a seat and rushes to her side. He's the picture of gentlemanly grace as he leads Elaine to her seat on Adeline's end. The beaming smile he gives her, so full of love, might make my knees weak if I wasn't already sitting down. Maybe his relationship with his stepmother is the reason he hasn't shown much interest in human women before. Maybe he just hasn't found one that can compare. She does set the bar high.

But I've always enjoyed a challenge.

"Thank you all for joining us this evening," the king says once he claims his seat. "One goal of The Choosing is for me to get to know you all better. While I have many pressing demands for my time, I will endeavor to arrange time with you all as well in the interest of finding the best human queen for the court."

While he talks, servants slip into the room on near silent feet carrying plates of food—a colorful array of vegetables with a pale violet soup sprinkled with petals for this first course—which are set upon the charger plates in front of us. It smells divine, and I have to fight the urge to grab my silverware and dig in.

"With the help of my advisors and my dear mother..." He pauses to acknowledge her and allow us all to do the same. "Some activities have been planned over the next few days which should allow us the chance to get to know each other better."

"The group dates begin," Grace whispers at my side while fighting back a grin.

Across the table from her, Alexis rolls her eyes and mouths, *You watch too much TV.*

It really does feel like the opening episode of a reality show though or maybe the second, since the acceptance ceremony was grand—and scandalous on my part— enough to make a worthy episode on its own.

"In addition," the king continues, "I will be asking each of you to spend some time with me one-on-one."

That elicits a murmur of excitement around the table.

"I can't wait to spend time *alone* with you tonight," Cora announces, as if it's some foregone conclusion that she'll be first. The implication in her words isn't lost either, at least not on the dowager, who gently clears her throat, not that Cora notices.

"We shall see," the king says. "But don't worry, each of you will have your time."

"Likely several times," Elaine adds with a pointed look at her stepson.

"Indeed." The king lifts his fork before gesturing to the table with his other hand. "Shall we begin?"

Dinner is long, almost painfully so, yet my chances to jump into the conversation are few enough. Most of the women near Vasilius try to dominate the conversation by talking about themselves. He's polite enough, nodding along and offering the occasional smile between small mouthfuls of food, but anyone paying attention can tell he's bored. Oh, he tries to hide it all right, but even the best actor can only disguise their face for so long. Between the course of grilled fish and the subsequent one of a roasted bird that could almost pass for chicken, Vasilius and Elaine switch seats, allowing him to pay some attention to the other half of the table.

When Gabriella pauses her assault of questions to take a long sip of wine, I cut in with one of my own.

"What would you be doing right now if you had your choice, Your Majesty?" I ask.

The fork he'd lifted halts halfway to his mouth. His brows pinch slightly before he lowers the utensil, a slow grin spreading across his features.

The obvious answer would be he's right where he wants to be, but that would be a lie. I know it, and so does he.

I blink at him innocently, but his growing smirk says he's caught my game.

Conversation dies down as everyone awaits his answer. His eyes hood slightly before he says, "That might not be proper conversation for the dinner table."

The accompanying wink stirs up a mess of butterflies in my stomach, but now that I have his attention, I'm loathe to give it up.

"Tomorrow, then. If you could choose any activity for us to do with you tomorrow, what would it be?"

He sets down the fork completely and crosses his arms as he reclines back in the chair. "Who says I haven't planned tomorrow's outing?"

"Have you?" I tease before hiding my grin behind a small sip of wine.

"I did not," he confesses. "Tomorrow, we'll be visiting with some of the younglings who live here in the capital."

A few of the women let out excited gasps and turn to one another. The revelation makes my smile falter for the briefest moment. Kids are cute, sure, but my experiences with them amount to all of about nothing. Well, other than playing with my younger brothers. But I was still a kid when they were little, and those memories are dim. I have a feeling that kicking their butts at video games isn't going to help me. Damn. I really should have volunteered or babysat or something before coming here. Hopefully, they'll be older fae kids because, if we're talking babies, I am so screwed.

"But if I could choose anything..." He trails off, thoughtful, waiting until all the attention is back on him. He soaks it in like a sponge but never fully looks away from me. "I do love a good duel or melee."

Adeline squeaks in fright where she sits wide-eyed at his wide.

Across the table from me, Alex slaps her hand down, causing the dishes to rattle. "Now that, I could get behind."

Vasilius shifts his attention to her. "Perhaps we should make this happen after all, then."

"Absolutely. I could best all of you, hands down." She sweeps her pointed finger to encompass the whole table.

Honestly, I don't doubt it. She's all lean muscle with the build of a marathon runner and could probably knock half these women to their assess in two seconds flat. Well, except maybe Zoe, who leans from her seat next to Cora.

"Do we get our choice of weapons?" Mirth gleams in Zoe's green eyes. "I've had years of fencing lessons. You don't have a chance if I get a saber in my hands," she taunts Alex.

"I'm in," I add. I probably wouldn't win, but I doubt I'd be the first one out either. Plus, if it would make Vasilius happy, then why not?

The king chuckles. "I'm not sure my advisors would like it if there was a risk of you all getting injured."

"Or me," Elaine adds with a loud sniff. "There's no need for women to beat at each other with swords."

Zoe cocks her head, thoughtful. "You don't think women should defend themselves?"

The dowager notches her chin higher. "Not with swords."

Grace barely muffles her huff, and though I try to keep my features neutral, I can't help but agree with the sentiment. What an antiquated way of thinking.

It's Bailey who breaks the awkward silence that follows, her soft, even voice snaring attention in a rare display of outspokenness. "I wonder if Wren thought the same thing before she was taken."

Wren, the current consort and likely future queen of the King of Air. Selena has been her number one fan lately and told me everything she's learned about her. Apparently she's been a major topic of conversation among the coven too. A gifted human from a family that wasn't on our radar, stealing the heart of a king? And not only that—she was captured by the Unseelie, taken right out of the Court of Air amid hundreds of fae including the king. A traitor was involved they say, but still, if there could be some in the Court of Air, there could be in Fire too. As long as the Unseelie have a null, as long as there is tension between the Seelie and Unseelie, is anyone truly safe?

"You're all bound to me," Vasilius says, holding up his wrist, which bears multiple overlapping bands of magical ink like a twisted bracelet. "They can't take you away. I will not make the same mistake as the King of Air."

"For the duration of The Choosing," Bailey says. "But what about after?"

Because Wren had been bound too, and the very day that bond released, the Unseelie snatched her. Whoever becomes queen could be a target, as would any other humans who stay. That's why he suggested our families return to Earth after all.

All traces of mirth vanished from the king's face. "That's one more reason why the Unseelie threat will need to be dealt with soon."

His attention settles on Elaine, unspoken words passing between them that thin the dowager's lips before they wrinkled with distaste. Maybe that is the business that has kept Vasilius busy recently.

"Enough talk about that." The king turns to the attendants waiting near the side of the room. "Bring out dessert. Let us have something sweet to wipe away such dark thoughts."

Chapter 8

T HE NEXT MORNING, FIA wakes me early so I can join the others for yoga. The halls are still quiet, most of the residents in their beds, as I wander through the pristine halls of gilded marble toward the garden. When I reach it, the sky has started to lighten, the first rays of sunlight still blocked by the palace walls and the soaring trees with their dark crimson trunks that spear out of the large courtyard to the sky. Dew glimmers on the grass, and each breath I inhale of the cool morning air clears out some of the lingering wine fog that I awoke in. Thank goodness I don't have a hangover.

Two guards stand near the threshold and gesture silently to where Adeline and Zoe stretch on mats set up in a flat, grassy area.

I slip off my shoes, grab a rolled mat from a nearby stack that has been set out, and make my way barefoot to join them, leaving a little trail of footprints through the mossy grass.

"Good morning," Adeline whispers with a smile.

I echo her greeting in my own quiet tones and receive a nod from Zoe, who presently has one foot braced in her hands where she stretches it up behind her in a half-arc.

It's been too long since I've done yoga, and all but the basic movements elude my memory. It'll have to be enough. First though, I take my time stretching out on the mat.

I'm convinced it'll just be the three of us when a chorus of giggles slips out into the peaceful morning. They aren't disruptive though, making themselves at home among the plumeria flowers and crisp air. Grace and Alex make their way out into the court-yard, stopping to shed their shoes and grab a mat just as I did.

"Is this all of us then?" Alex asks when she reached us.

"I think so," Zoe replies with a shrug. "If not, they can join in when they get here."

Grace and Alex add their mats to our line. Five human women in a quiet fae courtyard. I wonder what the fae will say if and when they inevitably venture out this morning and find us here.

"Um..." Adeline looks between me on one side and Zoe on her other, where she sits on her legs atop the mat. "I've only done this with someone leading the poses. Would anyone feel comfortable doing that?"

Thank goodness it isn't just me. Unfortunately, I can't help her.

"I will." Zoe finishes her stretch. "I used to teach a course at the local gym." She moves her mat into position in front of our line and takes a seat with the soles of her feet pressed together in front of her. "What level are you all?"

"Um..." Grace muses.

"Beginner is good," I say. "At least for today."

Zoe grins. "Beginner it is."

She leads us through a series of movements as the sky brightens fully into morning. A murmur of activity picks up inside the palace, slipping out into the garden, but I hardly notice. The poses we work through both test and relax my body and let me mind slip into a blissful state unlike any I've had since arriving in Faery.

Lysandir didn't make an appearance at dinner last night, thank goodness, but what would have been a successful meal ended on a sour note. By some poor stroke of luck or fate mocking the rest of us, Cora was picked to stay and have another glass of wine with Vasilius after the rest of us left. Cora with her innuendo, high-pitched laughter, and obvious flirting. Just the thought of it nearly sets my teeth on edge. I suck in an especially deep breath and blow it out slowly as I sink into downward dog pose.

Maybe he was just getting the worst out of the way first.

We finish off with child's pose. I lay there, relaxed and peaceful, until a weight settles between my shoulder blades. My brows scrunch. It so insistent, it almost feels like someone poking me. I wiggle and swipe at my back, trying to dislodge a bug or whatever it is, but nothing is there.

The feeling leaves, only to return against a minute later. I swat at my back again but nothing. I grit my teeth and unfurl from the pose. The other women still rest calmly, finishing the routine. A few guards linger around. Others have passed by. Bailey sits cross-legged on a bench nearby, an open book in her hands.

None of them are what I'm searching for. I'm sure of it. I begin to roll up my mat when the feeling comes again. I look back over my shoulder, and my heart lodges in my throat.

The king has come to watch us. He looms on a second-floor balcony near the railing. That's who I felt. Almost like my spirit is already attuning to his.

I turn back just as quickly, pretending I didn't see him sneaking a peak. If he wanted us to know, he would have announced himself. I set to rolling up my mat again. A few others have risen and are doing the same, but they don't seem to know who has joined us. The most delightful scent wafts by on a breeze. Coffee.

A sweet and satisfied ache fills my muscles as I get to my feet and look toward the source of the scent. Fia stands next to the guards watching us, a large tray balanced between her hands with a few steaming cups.

I hazard a glance back at the balcony. My stomach drops. The king is still there...except not. From a distance and at first glance they look so much alike that I didn't recognize the figure on the balcony.

It's not Vasilius but Lysandir.

His attention is focused on me, and I've stared entirely too long.

I snap my head toward Fia and make a beeline in her direction. I drop my mat on the pile as I pass by.

"Don't tell me you're a mind reader too," I say to Fia as I take an offered cup. The liquid nearly burns on the way down but not nearly as badly as the back of my neck. I hazard a glance back at the balcony, but it's empty now.

She laughs. "You did tell me to bring you coffee every day."

"Still, this is above and beyond." I gesture to the tray and additional cups. Two small bowls are present too that I hadn't noticed before—cream and sugar. I don't favor either, but she really is prepared for anything.

She shrugs as best she can with the tray still in her hands. "I thought the others might want some too."

"Oh, and we do," Grace croons as she arrived at my side. "We really do."

Grace takes hers black. But Alex adds sugar until the little bowl Fia brought is nearly empty.

"So much for relaxing," I say, brows raised at her cup.

"I like it sweet." She takes a long sip, her eyes rolling in pleasure. "Besides, we've got that thing with the kids in a bit. I'm going to need *all* my wits for that."

"Not a fan of kids?" I ask.

Alex shudders. "Smelly, loud, never still."

"Just like you." Grace pokes her in the side.

"Hey!" Alex swatted at her. "I do not smell." She sniffs at her armpit. "Okay, well maybe a little."

To be fair, I do too. Yoga might be relaxing, but it never fails to make me sweat. "I think we all do. And we should probably get cleaned up before we spend time with the king."

That, and I can not handle another run in with Lysandir if he's headed this way.

"Excellent point." Alex sighs. "But I'm taking this with me." She wraps her hands a little tighter around her mug before heading inside. Grace follows her.

I'm about to leave when I notice Adeline talking to a guard. He holds rolled-up yoga mats in his outstretched arms, waiting as Adeline adds another to the pile. She picks up the last two and says, "I'll carry these."

He shakes his head. "I wouldn't ask you to carry them, Lady Adeline."

"You're not." She grins. "I'm offering. You have too many already. Besides, I'd like to walk with you." His sandy cheeks flush, but he doesn't argue with her.

"Coffee, Adeline?" I offer as they passed by.

"Oh." She tears her eyes away from the guard, seeming to finally notice Fia and her tray. "No thanks." Just as quickly, her focus shifts back to her companion, and she says, "Lead the way."

I watch them go, marveling at the seeming friendship that's developed between her and her guard already. Or did they know each other before? My brows pinch. She has visited here often. Either way, it's a reminder of how behind I am, of the connections some of the others have that I don't.

"I'll take these back and then come help you get ready," Fia says, breaking me from my reverie.

"Eh, bring them to my room. I'll drink them."

Her eyes widen. "All of them?"

I wink. "One can never have too much coffee."

She shakes her head but keeps her rueful demeanor. "If you insist."

Chapter 9

Whenever I envisioned meeting the fae children, I always placed us in a classroom of sorts. Somewhere educational and indoors where we'd sit at little tables and talk to the kids while they worked on art projects or something.

Instead, it's about the opposite of that.

We meet in a lush inner courtyard similar to the one we performed yoga in this morning, except this one is a little more open with a large, grassy oval in the center, the outsides smattered with bushes and trees, including some that look like especially tall palms. But where the palm trees I've seen on trips are tall and narrow with all their fan-leafed fronds draping from the top, these have branches that jut out from the trunk as well. Perfect for climbing, and the fae kids clearly think so too.

Two of them are high up in the branches. A distressed fae male shouts up at them from the ground, demanding they come down that instant.

Grace snort with laughter as Alex mumbles, "I told you kids are trouble."

Maybe so, but they're clearly having a good time. As are many of the others already gathered in the wide, oval space. One group of kids plays a soccer-like game with three balls of varying sizes, though I don't see any goals. Little ones crawl in the grass near their caretakers, all of whom wear a similar uniform to the shouting man's, consisting of a tunic and pants in a sandy-colored material that shimmers in the light.

"Eh, they'll be fine," Cora says, gesturing at the young ones in the tree. "It's important to let kids have some fun in life. Actually..." A fierce grin breaks across her face. "I might join them."

To the surprise of...well, probably all of us, Cora rushes toward the tree.

"Cora!" Katherine whines, but it doesn't stop her. Cora doesn't even bother to acknowledge her friend.

"At least we'll get a break from hearing about her date. Dios mío." Gabriella rubs her temples like she's fighting off a headache, and I can't blame her. I was tired of hearing about it in the first two seconds, and from the expression on Gabriella's face when I walked out of my room and into their conversation in the hallway before coming here, I have a feeling she's been forced to endure much more than me.

"You don't really think they kissed already, do you?" Zoe asks no one in particular.

My smile transforms into a grimace. "I hope not."

It's hard to say. I wouldn't put it past Cora to go for the first kiss, even if she had to steal one, just to get a leg up on all of us. Plus, she made it clear enough that she's willing to use all her wiles to get what she wants, even if Elaine discouraged such things.

"I didn't get a kiss," Gabriella pouts. She'd had a breakfast date this morning, one that didn't go as well as she'd hoped, it seems.

The fae younglings stop and stare at Cora as she advances toward the tree. Some of them finally find the rest of us where we're gathered near the edge of the courtyard. Squeals of joy and conversation break off as awareness rolls through the gathered fae like a wave and they turn toward us. A few of the little ones back toward one of the many caretakers. I guess they teach stranger danger here too, and a gaggle of human women aren't something they see every day. Truthfully, humans and fae don't look that different. They're generally taller with more lithe figures, but that's not always the case. They also have just as much diversity in their hair and skin colors—more, actually. We're a bit dull and ordinary by comparison.

Some of the younglings, especially the older ones who look around six or seven in human years, leave their little groups to rush toward us, beaming with excitement.

I generally like kids—part of being an older sibling—even if I don't have much experience with little ones anymore. But even I brace for impact as they advance, rather than dropping down to welcome them with open arms and excitement like Bailey and Adeline.

We weren't given any specific instructions for today. Not yet anyway. Spending time with the younglings, that's all. But when it comes to excited young ones, instructions aren't necessary and would probably be cast aside in moments anyway.

The kids take the lead as the more outgoing ones pick their favorite human and lead them off toward various activities. Bailey and I get corralled by the same group and talked into building towers out of blocks of some foamy substance that manage to be light and soft yet sturdy enough for construction at the same time. In fact, erecting a tower and jumping into it to knock it down seems to be the favored game.

Bailey is a natural, and the kids seem to know it, swarming about her, taking her hand, and immediately climbing in her lap the one time she sits down.

"You're really good at this," I say, adding another block to the masterpiece in progress.

She pushes a few strands of brown hair that have fallen loose from her braid behind one ear and glances over at me. "I come from a big family." She shrugs one shoulder. "When you're the oldest of about a dozen siblings and cousins that always hang out together, you have to be good with kids."

"So many," I say. And yet, I'd heard there weren't many gifted in her family line. Strange for that to be the case when they're so prolific. Yet more and more gifted families struggle to pass on the gift these days. Some have had the gift skip the latest generation completely.

"They're a handful, especially my cousin's twins." She shakes her head. "I swear, one of them would have found a way to get hurt by now, even with how soft these blocks are. And don't get me started on the teenagers…" She gives me a meaningful look.

I grimace in return. "*That* I know something about."

If fae teenagers are even half as moody as human ones, then I'm glad it's just the younger ones we're spending time with today. Bailey and I add a few more blocks near the top, and the younglings deem it complete.

Askar, a fae youngling with seemingly boundless energy, jumps into the latest tower with Kispet, whose black hair is tied back in braids entwined with silver ribbons. They go down together in a heap of blocks and giggles as Bailey and I cheer with the other kids around us and their caretakers. Apparently, this game is safe enough, where tree climbing wasn't. When the two boys finally come down, they have to sit on a bench for a little while and miss some of the fun, though from the way I saw them whispering and gently shoving one another, I gather they find joy no matter the situation.

I've just started to place the beginning blocks of a new structure when a familiar brush of sensation sweeps across my back. Askar's giggles shut off abruptly. His golden eyes fly wide before a toothy grin breaks across his face. There's no time to even glance around before he's up and sprinting past me.

My heart stutters a little in my chest when I finally see who he did. Vasilius and Lysandir walk side by side toward the oval, slipping between the outstretched fronds of the odd palm trees. They're not dressed like royals today, or rather, they're not in the formal attire they've donned before. The brothers are similarly dressed in loose pants and flowy tunics, not all that different in color from those worn by the caretakers. Geometric designs are embroidered in slightly darker thread along the edges and give a more refined look. The ends of the pants are tucked into brown boots laced up their calves, and though the long sleeves of the shirts and their flowy material hide most of their muscular statures, a small split in the middle top of the shirt gives just a hint of what lies beneath. And people say low-cut shirts on women are tempting. I nearly snort. A low-cut blouse has nothing on that tease of golden muscle.

In fact, with their attire, it looks like they're here to...play.

I wave at Vasilius, hopeful he'll join us, but his gaze slips straight over me and settles on where Zoe and Gabriella play a ball game with a number of younglings. Damn.

He breaks off from his brother, striding toward them with de-termined steps while a handful of younglings trail in his wake. I watch him with wistful longing until Bailey whispers, "Don't look too forlorn. We've got company."

"Who—" The question catches in my throat as I look in the direction she bobs her head. With all my attention on Vasilius, I'd managed to lose sight of Lysandir. Just my luck that Askar certainly didn't.

"Look who I got, Lady Mira!" Askar raises his and Lysandir's joined hands as he leads the prince near. The boy is absolutely beaming, chin raised with pride like he's just dug up a diamond from the dirt.

I force a smile for Askar's benefit. Poor little guy can't know that Lysandir seems to like me just about as much as I like him, as in, not at all.

The kids in our group squeal with glee. Even the caretakers seem to have brightened up with genuine joy and excitement. Two little girls dance around the prince as he nears, and he has to quickly sidestep to avoid tripping over one of them. But he doesn't seem to mind. The opposite actually—he laughs and ruffles the hair on top of her head. In fact, his whole face is lit up as bright as the kids.

"Prince Lysandir." I dip a little curtsy. Bailey echoes me and does the same.

He waves his hand. "There's no need for that on my account." To the kids, he asks, "What are we working on here?"

I'm sure he already knows, but he smiles and nods along as some of the younglings explain the game. Askar does most of the talking, finally releasing Lysandir's hand so that he can gesture in broad motions about the things we've built.

"Miss Mira and Miss Bailey are great builders," Kispet pipes in.

"I'm sure," Lysandir replies with a wide grin at Bailey and, to my surprise, me.

In fact, it doesn't even look the least bit forced, which shocks me enough to make me sit back down on the grass. To my continued bewilderment, Lysandir sits on the grass a few feet away, his legs crossed in front of him.

Askar all but climbs into his lap as he asks, "Can you tell us about the tournament? You said you'd tell me about it, but you haven't yet."

Bailey looks up from where she's helping one girl with a block. "We're going to have a tournament?"

Lysandir shakes his head and opens his mouth to reply, but another boy answers for him. "No, the tournament in the Court of Air!"

I've heard of it of course. Most up on coven news probably have, even though our coven has limited ties with the Court of Air. Still, it's a rare thing for a human to participate, much less win, to say nothing of the fact that it was the King of Air's mate, Wren. Or rather, I guess she wasn't exactly his mate then but is now. Anyway, it should have been the biggest news of the year, but with the happenings involving the Unseelie court, the supposed rise of an Unseelie King, and two previously untracked gifted families now having members as consorts of Seelie royal courts... Well, it's been one hell of a banner year.

"Ah, where to start?" Lysandir muses, as if setting in for a long tale. He tips his head toward the sun, basking in its light.

The younglings all move to sit near the prince, a few so close they're touching him, though he doesn't seem to mind. He even pulls Askar into his lap and says nothing when a young girl leans on his knee.

"The Court of Air was not eager to let an outsider compete in their tournament," Lysandir begins before pausing for dramatic effect. "But I can be quite convincing when I need to be." His gaze flicks to me for the briefest moment, and something does a little flip in my chest.

"Did you fight your way in?" one of the boys asks as he leans in eagerly.

"No. That would not have earned me entrance," Lysandir replies. "I explained the benefits of positive relations between our courts to one of their senior advisors, but I don't think that's what you all want to hear about. You want to know about the challenges I competed in, right?"

A chorus of agreement follows from the kids, and I have to admit, he's piqued my interest too. The little girl Bailey was helping has given up all interest in blocks and joined the others, so Bailey settles in near me to listen as well. Lysandir takes his time telling the kids about the competition—the feats of skill, bravery, and even luck that he participated in. As he talks, he gestures with his hands and pitches his voice up and down, even changes his tone completely to voice a few of the others he encountered. I'll give it to him; he's a great storyteller and even better with the kids.

Even so, I can't keep my gaze from wandering across the oval toward the king. He does something I can't quite see, and all the nearby kids cheer for him. He seems to eat up their attention, shifting into a pose that elicits more applause. Zoe and Gabriella both buzz around him until he moves from their group onto another with Katherine and Grace. He hasn't even bothered to look our way.

"What did you plan to ask for if you won?" one of the kids asks.

I glance back at the prince just in time to see his smile abruptly fade. He looks away, down at the ground before giving himself a little shake so subtle most of the kids probably miss it. "I saw something I would change if I could."

A few of the kids gasp.

"In one of your visions?" a little girl asks. Others clamor for more details.

Seelie fae magic is linked to the power of the court itself and the territory in which they reside. Some skills are court specific, but others manage to appear at random throughout the various courts. Fae histories say it's a result of how the ancient queen Aine split her powers ages ago, back when there were just Seelie and Unseelie. She felt her power and life force fading but could not decide which among her children should inherit her magic when the time came. Rather than leaving it up to the magic to decide and because she loved her children dearly, she split her powers among them and faded away.

Fae scholars argue over whether she simply did not section off some of her powers and thus they went to all courts or if she intentionally planned it. I suppose we'll never know, and it doesn't really matter. But one of the rarest magical gifts to appear among the fae is the gift of foresight. Some fae blessed with it may only get a few visions in their lifetime, but Lysandir with his royal blood, is powerful, and so is his gift.

"Do your visions always come true?" I ask.

The kids stop and look between us.

Lysandir blinks at me, a hint of surprise in his features before he nods. "Yes, the ones that have the chance to be fulfilled. Not always how I expect or in exactly the way I see, but yes."

It must have been something truly terrible then, whatever he saw, to make him go to such length to try and change it.

"You won't tell us what it is?" Askar groans.

"Not today." He pats the boy on the shoulder.

Askar looks up at him with big, golden eyes. "Tomorrow?"

Lysandir laughs and moves the boy off his lap. "Not then either. Now, who is going to show me this game you were all playing?"

The suggestion has the kids dropping the topic and rushing back to the blocks. Bailey and I are put to work along with the prince building the biggest structure yet, a castle-like thing longer than me and so tall I have to reach on my tiptoes to place the very last block.

"Almost..." I slowly slide it on top of the tower where the kids instructed, but every inch I move it makes the darn thing sway like it's going to topple over and destroy the creation. The kids would hate gravity knocking it down instead of them. I stretch higher onto the rounded toe of my flats. Finally, it settles. "Got it!"

The kids cheer. One of them knocks into me before I'm fully back on the flats of my feet, and I stumble. My shoes slip on the grass, and I'm about to go head first into the blocks when something solid wraps around my middle and pulls me back. I barely have time to gasp before my momentum shifts and I fall back against a solid chest.

"Careful." Lysandir says. A lock of his hair brushes against my cheek, and my breath hitches. "Wouldn't want to bring it down before they're ready."

His strong fingers flex on my side, and my whole body flushes. One moment, he was a few feet away, and the next, he moved impossibly fast to pull me back from falling into the tower, his arm around my middle.

It takes effort to remember to breath, and when I do, my senses swim with the scents of sandalwood that reminds me of spice cake.

His arm unfurls from around me at the same moment I pull away, putting much needed space between us. I shake my head to clear it, sucking in another breath that thankfully doesn't smell only of him.

"That, um..." I stammer, unable to quite look at him, but there's no hiding the flush creeping up my neck and cheeks. "Thank you."

He nods his head in my direction. "You're always welcome, Lady Mira."

My gosh, how can such a simple statement feel like so much more? I busy myself righting the blocks. But Lysandir does the same just a few feet away, and I can't help but feel some kind of weird energy leaping from my skin toward him and distracting me so thoroughly that I manage to knock over the beginnings of the tower I'm working on.

One of the younglings squeaks in disappointment, and I rush to repair the damage. I stack a final block before proclaiming, "There, all better."

But instead of cheers, a hush sweeps over the little ones who stare at something just past me.

"Lady Mira," a deep voice says.

I freeze at the unexpected voice. My already off-kilter insides give a little flip-flop.

Suddenly I wish I wasn't kneeling on the ground, probably getting grass and dirt all over the legs of my stretchy, fae pants. I whip my head around, craning my neck up to take in the tall form of Vasilius where he beams down at me. Damn, he's a sight. The sunlight catches just so on the lighter highlights in his hair, giving them extra shimmer and accentuating the upturned corners of his lips. It's a good thing I'm already on the ground, or I might just go a little weak at the knees.

"Your Majesty," I say after what's been entirely too long of a pause. And from the mischief dancing in his eyes, he knows it too.

He offers a hand to help me up, which I gratefully accept. So warm and strong. Maybe it's a Fire Court thing, but the way his touch is soothing and disorienting all at once is truly something else.

"Would you like to join me for an early lunch today?" he asks.

A little laugh catches in the back of my throat. As if I would say no.

"I would love to." I beam up at him. This is it, the moment I've been waiting for. A chance to get to know him better and build something between us.

"This way then." He gives my hand a little tug.

"Oh!" My eyes fly wide. "Right now."

Duh, Mira. But I should at least... I look around at our little group.

"Have fun." Bailey beams and gives me a little wave as if she truly doesn't mind that I have the next date with Vasilius. I guess we'll all get a turn eventually, but I doubt I'd be so chipper if the situation was reversed. The younglings give a chorus of goodbyes, even a few comments about how much fun they had.

Lysandir is the only one not saying anything, a completely blank look on face. Ouch. He really doesn't like me around his brother.

I do my best to ignore him and focus on the younglings instead. "It's been nice playing with you all today."

"Thank you for keeping her entertained," Vasilius tells the children who positively glow in response. Actually, I think one of them might literally be giving off the hint of a glow. Or maybe it's just the way the sunlight hits him.

"Should I change first?" I ask Vasilius, overly conscious of the fact that he still holds my hand.

He shakes his head. "This is fine. As long as you don't mind that I don't change."

"Not at all." In fact, the idea of a casual lunch is perfect. Much better than some stuffy formal dinner where we're stuck at opposite ends of a ridiculously long.

"Excellent. Let's be off." He holds out his other hand to me, and I stare at it in confusion. "Ah," he says, reading my expression. "We'll need to shift there."

"Oh?" Now that's interesting.

"I know it can be a bit disorienting for humans," he continues. "But we'd miss lunch if we walked all the way."

My confusion has already faded, replaced by a wistful excitement that tingles in my veins. "It's fine. I'm excited actually."

"Oh?" He cocks his head, and I bite my lip at the mimicry of my earlier comment.

Vasilius flexes his open hand in invitation, and this time, I take it, forming a little ring between our bodies as we face each other.

"I'm ready." I nearly bounce on my toes.

The corners of his mouth lift. "Don't let go."

"I won't." But the words aren't even out of my mouth before the world around us starts to warp and shift, the air constricting like suddenly being stuffed in a too-tight sweater.

CHAPTER 10

I CLING TO VASILIUS as we shift to a new location. Colors spin and blur. And then, just as suddenly, the pressure around us pops, and the world stops moving. Seconds have passed, but we're in a completely different place, though we're likely no too far from the palace.

A roof shields us from the midday sun, but the view spreading out around us is still blinding. Sunlight shimmers off dunes of sand that fill my vision from one edge of my periphery to the other. There's a literal fae king in front of me, one I've dreamed about for years, and yet all I can see is what's *past* him.

"The Dune Sea," I whisper in awe.

The sight pulls me in. I drop his hands and move to the edge of a gazebo of sorts. A railing of pale wood at the edge of the stone platform is all that separates us from the dunes. A strong wind would be enough to brush the sand right over my feet. Finally, I tear myself from the sight and look around.

Vasilius stands with his arms crossed, but he's still smiling, so me totally ignoring him in favor of the view can't be too bad of a misstep. Besides, I'm sure he expected some bit of surprise, given that he didn't even tell me where we were going, and this is... There are few words for it. Stunning? Incredible? Awe inspiring?

The land behind me is sand as far as I can see, but behind the king, I can see this gazebo is at the edge of some large structure. A covered pathway occupied by several fae guards connects us to it. In the center of our structure is a small table set for two, covered platters already at each place setting. A fae male pours a bubbling golden liquid that I'm guessing is wine into two glasses.

"I take it you like the location?" Vasilius lifts one brow.

"It's incredible." I glace back again at the Dune Sea, unable to resist its pull. I never thought it would be hard to pay attention to the king during my time with him, but this may put me to the test. Turning back to him, I say, "Thank you for choosing me today, for bringing me here."

"You're welcome. I'm glad you're pleased." He holds out a hand to me again. "Shall we dine?"

A weightlessness fills me as I cross the space to him and take his hand. This could be our life, our future. Suddenly, the fact that my uncle somewhat forced me into this doesn't seem so bad. There are certainly perks, maybe a lifetime of them.

Lunch passes both too quickly and far too slowly. I poke at the food, trying to pretend I'm still eating just to prolong things, but I haven't actually taken a bite in a while. This should be the part of the meal where awkward get-to-know-you conversation has shifted into something genuine and exciting that leaves my skin tingling with anticipation and the actual meal itself a footnote in an otherwise exquisite date. Or that's what I'd hoped for.

It must be because I started the conversation wrong, asking Vasilius what he liked to do when he wasn't busy being a king. I had no idea he was going to spend the whole time regaling me with stories of hunting fae beasts through the wilds of the court.

Oh, I want to be interested, I really do, but I can only hear about slaying various vicious beasts for so long before the meal turns from exquisite to nauseating and it takes everything I have to focus on the words coming out of his mouth. I want to learn about him, truly, but I wanted him to get to know me as well. There's no back and forth, little time for me to try to jump into the conversation, and every time I manage to get in more than a smile and nod, things boomerang back to where they were with Vasilius telling stories like he's the one trying to impress me.

Maybe he is? My smile falters just a little at the thought. He's a king after all. Most people probably just want to hear about him and play to his interests. I *should* do that, right?

Vasilius wipes at his mouth with all the grace of his title before setting the cloth aside. "So, what do you care to do with your time?"

I blink at him. *Me?* I almost ask, so surprised by a question finally tossed my way. "I've always loved to dance."

"Ah, a dancer!" He raises his glass and takes a sip. It's his second, or maybe third, glass, though the fae wine doesn't seem to have any effect on him.

I wish I could say the same for myself. I was so nervous and excited that I downed half the glass right after I sat, and boy, was that a mistake. The effect was quick, leaving me flushed and my head spinning just a bit. The king's proximity sure doesn't help matters. Maybe it is a good thing he's done most of the talking up until now because I'm really not sure what would have come out of my mouth half an hour ago. Since that first unfortunate sip, I've left the wine alone and the food has managed to balance me out a bit.

"Not professionally or anything," I add. "I loved it though. The way the music just seemed to take control of my body. I took lessons for years and was in a number of local performances, including several where I was the lead. Performing for a crowd was absolutely thrilling."

It started as a fun hobby. My mom was a beauty pageant queen and wanted the same for me, and you can't win the big contests without a strong talent. The beauty pageants didn't stick. They weren't my thing. But the dancing did, especially after my dad died. It was my sanctuary, a place I could lose myself and forget about being sad for a little while.

I probably shouldn't have entered so many dance contests. Trying to disappear to Faery if you have any measure of fame or notoriety in the human world? Messy and complicated. It was reason I shied away from the pageants—I already knew I wanted Faery in my future.

"You must have quite the skill then." The remaining liquid in Vasilius's glass swirls as he rotates his wrist in little circles.

"I'm sure it's nothing compared to fae dancers," I say in a show of modesty. Fae are naturally graceful, and with their longer lifespans, they have plenty of time to develop way more skill than me.

"Well." He sets down the glass. "I know a way we can find out."

The suggestion takes a moment to slip past the bit of wine still slowing my thoughts. And in that moment, I want to test it, to see if I still have any skills and if I measure up to the fae.

"You... You want me to dance? As part of a show or something?" I ask.

"I'm afraid I don't have much of an audience to offer." He sweeps an arm wide to gesture to the area around us, where only a few guards linger nearby. "I'd like you to dance for me. Consider if more of a private performance."

"Oh!" A flush creeps of the base of my neck. He can't have meant *that* kind of performance, but leave it to my mind to slip right into the gutter. "Here?"

He arcs a brow. "Why not?"

Dancing after a full meal isn't ideal, but I can. My clothes aren't half bad for it, though I'll have to lose the shoes. A smile breaks across my face as I push up from my chair.

"Why not, indeed?" At least his attention will be on me this time rather than lost in a tale. "I'll just need a moment to stretch."

I slip off my shoes and walk toward the open area of the pavilion so that Vasilius will have a good view. There should be enough space for me to dance without knocking into things as long as I stick to the center of the space. No long leaps for me today.

"Of course." Vasilius slides his chair back from the table and angles it to face me. The look on his face is pure indulgence dripping with intrigue, and gosh, I hope I don't make a fool of myself. "Please, take your time."

Moments pass filled only by the whisper of breeze across the dunes and the heavy press of Vasilius's regard as I move through a series of stretches. Somehow, the idea of dancing before a packed crowd feels infinitely more appealing that this solo performance for an audience of one—or a handful if I count the guards, though their attention isn't quite so distracting as their king's.

"Okay." The one word sounds entirely too loud as I clasp my arms behind me in one final stretch. "A solo performance for you, my king."

The use of his title has Vasilius's grin stretching wider. That's the last thing I notice before I force my focus inward and let my gaze rest on everything and nothing at once. A full orchestra begins to play in my head, the song just as moving as the last time I performed to it a few years ago. And then I'm moving, letting muscle memory lead me in a series of flowing steps, my toes pointed, my arms stretched out to the tips of my fingers.

Growing up, I spent a lot of time with my mother, but I wouldn't call it quality time. Usually, she was busy hustling me and my brothers to school, dance lessons, a pageant, the boys' sports matches, or some other appointment. When she wasn't on the move out and about, she was on the move at home, convinced that the house was never quite clean enough or decorated as well as it should be. There was always something to do, a necessary task to make the house as immaculate as she could, probably to make it appear like we were better off than we were. We were never poor. Not by most people's standards. But it always felt like she was trying to measure up to prove worthy of being part of a gifted family. Maybe if she worked hard enough, she could truly fit in among the likes of Uncle Matias and Aunt Dalia with their wealth and high-society airs

Despite Mother's need for perfection in everything and her drive toward that, there was one thing she made time for that we both enjoyed: *Dancing with the Stars*. We never missed an episode. It was a ritual in our house, almost a religion. Looking back, it's obvious why I picked dancing as my talent and threw myself into the lessons. I was always impressed with how the best performers seemed oblivious to the millions watching or the way the pros managed to move with such power and finesse.

I try to imitate that now, keeping my chin high and my expression carefully neutral. I feel the beat of the movement in my memories and let it push me along, throwing myself into the movements, keeping them crisp and powerful. After a minute, I can almost forget where I am and who I'm performing for. I'm not in some gazebo dancing for a fae king whose hand I'm desperately trying to win. I'm alone in my parent's basement with its too-bright lighting and slight musty scent as I twirl across the laminate floor, listening to the music play on my phone where it lays on an old wooden chair. I remain there for the rest of the song, the railing of the gazebo, the table, and my audience of one a hazy presence beyond the one I've constructed in my mind.

The music draws near its end. I'm on my knees, head curled down, when the final note blares and I reach up for the sky, my body stretched up as far as I can from the anchor of my knees. I hold the pose, breathing heavily.

A loud, slow clap jerks me back to the moment, the scene and song vanishing almost completely from my mind as I turn my head just slightly to see Vasilius rise to his feet as he continues his applause.

Finally breaking form, I push wayward hairs out of my face and rise before giving him a sweeping, dramatic bow.

"Very good." His deep voice makes me acutely aware of the sweat now dotting my neck and chest. "It was quite powerful. I could feel the emotion of it even without any music. Very well done indeed."

"Thank you, Your Majesty." My chest swells with pride at his admiration. And it's not false praise. It can't be given, that fae cannot outright lie. If my performance had been horrible, he wouldn't be able to claim it otherwise.

Vasilius holds out a hand to me, and I cross the space between us and take it. Strong fingers curl around mine before he draws it to his lips and places a kiss upon its back. That act, his warm lips on my skin, sends a jolt straight to my heart that slides downward, settling low in my abdomen.

"I may have to arrange a show after all," he says. "Perhaps you'd enjoy performing with some of my dancers?"

"I'm not sure you'd find my skills so appealing then." I lower my eyes. Side by side with the fae? There's no way I'd be seen as anything but clumsy and awkward, especially since I'm sure we'd be using their music.

A soft laugh fills the air between us as he lets go of my hand. "Give me some credit, Mira. I believe I am a decent judge of skill. Besides, I wouldn't want to see any of my potential brides, or any of our human guests, shamed before the court. What good could come of it?"

He has a point there. "Maybe some time," I concede. "If you think you would enjoy it."

"I believe I would, if only to see you dance again."

The richness of his voice does something to my insides, leaving me awash in a sea of feelings and my knees a little weak. I'll definitely dance for him again if it earns me another reaction like that.

"Unfortunately, it will have to be another time," he continues. "There is something that requires my attention, but I thank you for sharing this meal and for the performance."

"Of course, you must be very busy," I say, trying to hide my disappointment. "You'll be taking me back, then?"

He shakes his head and my shoulders droop in response. "My guards will shift you back."

Vasilius gestures to them and two advance.

I guess that's it then. "Thank you for a lovely meal and for choosing me to spend it with." I dip into a low curtsy and rise, expecting... I don't know what. But Vasilius is still just standing there, a mildly pleasant expression on his face.

"I'll just get my shoes..."

Get your shoes? I chastise myself as I turn and practically flee to where I left them next to my chair. *Great way to end the date, Mira, just great.*

CHAPTER 11

T HE NEXT DAY WE are led as a group to the council chamber around mid-morning. I'm dressed elegantly, if practically, in an outfit I've nicknamed my fae business suit. My crimson dress is fitted through the bodice and upper thighs but flares out where it ends around my knees. The golden blazer over the top is a perfect match for a few golden threads woven through the crimson, and Fia even found me a pair of shimmering gold-colored heels. If this doesn't scream "dressed for a council meeting," I don't know what will. It's a more mature, sophisticated look than the dresses worn by some of the other women today, but that's exactly what I'm going for.

"Mira, you're finally back," Gabriella remarks as she falls into step next to me.

"She was at yoga this morning," Zoe says to her. "Which you'd know if you came. Offer is still open."

Gabriella all but rolls her eyes at Zoe, who stalks ahead with her long-legged stride.

I smile. I'm sure it looks like it's for Gabriella, but the grin is totally for me. After my lunch date, I was able to slip back into my room without being seen and decided I'd just stay that way. I asked the guard who shifted me to keep it quiet also, and it seems he listened. Why let the others know the date ended right after lunch? There was nothing else on our schedule for the day, so my presence wouldn't be missed by anyone, but my absence would certainly be noticed by the competition. Hopefully, they were all stewing over wondering where I was and assuming it was with Vasilius.

A few asked at yoga this morning, but I carefully dodged direct questions, just remarking on the beautiful date and the flowing conversation. They didn't need to know that it was mostly one-sided either. I may have also thrown in a few extra yawns...just to give them something else to chew over.

"How was the date? Was it just you and Vasilius? Did he kiss you?" Gabriella fires one question after another as if she can't get them out fast enough.

The corners of my lips stretch higher as I let a beat of silence pass, then two, while I take in the wide-eyed and expectant look in her brown eyes. "Yes and yes."

"What!" Gabriella screeches, causing a few of the women and even one of the guards to jump. "You kissed him too?"

"More like he kissed me." On the hand. But totally still counts.

Ahead of us, Cora whips her head around to glare daggers at me, never breaking her stride.

"I can't believe it." Gabriella gives the most dramatic sigh I've ever seen. "I'm so behind already."

That gets Grace's attention. "It's not a race."

She shrugs, her long hair sliding off her shoulder, as we round a corner and stop in a circular antechamber with a high-domed roof made of colorful glass that paints the otherwise white marble space in a kaleidoscope of colors. I'm not the only one whose head tips back, drawn by the artful display of light to its source above us. It's absolutely gorgeous, if a little disorienting, and instantly I have the desire to dance there under the colorful barrage. Yesterday was the first time I'd really danced in months, and it seems to have reawakened something in my spirit that I'd let fall asleep. All morning I've been flexing my toes and hearing a hum of music that's only in my head. If nothing else comes out of this contest, it's nice to have recaptured that spark of joy in my heart.

"You're not worried?" Gabriella implores, dragging my attention back to her.

"Nope." Grace lifts her chin in a show of confidence. "No offense, Mira."

I shift my notebook to one hand and lift the other in front of me. "None taken."

Her comment didn't feel like a jab toward me at all. Rather, she has that inner confidence going, and I admire that. Grace might be her name, and she has plenty of that, but poise and confidence are hers in spades.

Someone ahead shushes us, and we all quiet down as the double doors leading into the chamber are pulled wide. The inside of the room is the opposite of the antechamber and most of the palace for that matter. The walls, floor, and ceiling are all stark white marble, and there is not a window or piece of artwork to be seen. Arced tables form a wide, empty circle with chairs spaced around them on one side facing toward the center. And they're already occupied. The advisors rise from their seats, as does another figure I'm momentarily surprised to see, though I shouldn't be. Lysandir's gaze flits across the crowd of us before landing on me and stopping. My breath catches, and my chest grows tight. *Why would he...* But then he's moved on, looking at someone else, so maybe I imagined it.

"Come in, ladies," Dowager Queen Elaine says. I hadn't seen the dowager queen beyond the press of other women in front of me, but her voice is unmistakable. "Please have a seat, any open one you like."

The center table is mostly full, but behind it sits another circle of chairs, these without a table. It's the spectator section, and apparently, that's what we are today. Too bad we don't have a seat at the main ring, though Elaine's presence is an indication that one day one of us will.

Several women rush forward, trying to snag a spot as close to the king's seat as possible. But I do the opposite and aim for one straight across from him. Why be behind him out of sight when I can be right in his line of vision the entire time? Zoe has the same idea, and we end up side by side.

"Have a seat," Vasilius orders, forcing the last few women silently fighting over chairs to pick one and sit.

Everyone takes a seat but him and Elaine. And though he's the king, it's clear his seat at the table—literally and figuratively—is the same as everyone else's. There's no special place at this round table, and it makes me think a little bit about King Arthur and his knights of the round table. So many legends in our world are influenced by fae traditions. Not that most people know that of course. But as the story goes, those without the gift heard tales from those with it and had to make sense of them somehow, so what better way than tales of human accomplishment?

I've heard about the Court of Fire's tradition of the round table and including many advisors and royal family members in the dealings of the court. It's as close to a democracy as the fae get and one of the reasons I so admired Vasilius from afar. Anyone who can be born to power and yet share it can't be too terrible. The jury is still out on whether this tradition actually did inspire the Arthur story, though, or if it happened the other way around. Maybe they fed and fueled each other. We may never know.

"Thank you for joining us today. Mother?" He sits, leaving her standing alone and leaning on her cane.

"Welcome, ladies. As you can see by my presence here, being queen is more than a title. It carries responsibility beyond being the king's companion." She takes her time looking around the room, meeting our eyes one by one. "You will be looked to as a voice of authority within the court, a source of knowledge and guidance for the king and others. Today, listen. Learn. And in the next meeting, you will all get to participate and share your voices."

Once the queen takes her seat, the advisors are introduced. It's a formality—we should know them if we've done our research—but I appreciate the refresher all the same. Stony-faced Avara, Captain of the Guard with her sharp features and straight pale hair that falls past her shoulders. Advisor Danai with her flawless ebony skin and youthful features. In human years, I wouldn't put her past twenty-five, but fae appearances rarely tell a true story of age since the strength of their magic prolongs their life well past human years. She must be quite powerful indeed. There's Efthymi, pleasantly plump and sharing the same coloring as the king. If I remember correctly, they're related. A cousin maybe? Memnon is one of the few advisors who smiles at us and seems genuinely excited we are there. In fact, his piercing blue gaze is almost a little disconcerting as it hops from one of us to the next with a level of intensity that make me squirm in my seat.

Finally, there is Lysandir, brother of the king.

"And seer, don't forget that," Vasilius remarks when Lysandir gives little more than his name, title, and relation to the king. "His insights have proven valuable on many occasions. Too bad he can't just tell me who should be queen, eh?"

A few hesitant laughs filter out into the quiet, but they are awkward things at best.

"And deny you the opportunity to find your bride yourself?" Lysandir responds, the comment caught somewhere between humor and seriousness.

Vasilius shrugs. "It would make things simpler."

Lysandir frowns but doesn't push the matter and takes a seat.

"Well, on to business then," Vasilius orders.

Business, it turns out, is much more boring than I expected. No wonder half the advisors looked grumpy when we arrived, and frankly, still do. I've written little in my notebook, and I'm starting to think that maybe some of the others who didn't bring one won't be at as much of a disadvantage as I previously thought. Still a bad move on their part not to be prepared though. So far, most of the things they've discussed have been disputes between various citizens and families, which could primarily be resolved by being fair and equal.

"As our next topic," Memnon begins, "we really must discuss the Unseelie."

Now *that* gets my attention. I lift my pen from the cluster of flowers I've been slowly doodling and sit a little straighter in my seat.

Vasilius gives a nod for him to continue, and Memnon wastes no time. "As we discussed previously, activity near the Forest and Air Courts has slowed significantly since their conflict some weeks ago. We know now that they were trying to incite a war between the two courts with the aim of weakening them and making them easier targets, but those efforts came to naught. Since, our scouts have spotted more and more bands of Unseelie moving near our own borders. There was even that incident a week past where they attempted a breach."

Someone gasps. I feel my own breath hitch. We knew there was trouble, but an attempted breach on the Court of Fire? That's certainly news, at least to us, though no one around the center table is surprised. They clearly already know. They've discussed this before.

"That doesn't leave this room, ladies," Elaine says, her aged voice ringing with strength.

She doesn't wait for our acknowledgement. It's expected.

"It's only a matter of time before things escalate further," Memnon continues.

"But to what end?" This from Avara. "We're not weakened like the Court of the Forest or off our guard like the Court of Air. They cannot hope to attack us through force alone. Our forces would destroy them. It would be foolish to toy with us."

"There must be a reason," Danai says.

"Curiosity? They may not know our strength," says Elaine.

"They'll learn of it quickly enough if they try our borders again," Avara replies.

Through it all, I watch Vasilius take in one party then the next as they speak, his head propped on fist with his elbow holding up his arm like a post. The casual posture belies the intensity in his gaze.

"They're likely testing us, checking for weakness and seeing how we react." Efthymi nods along while they speak, as if their conclusion is the only right one, though I have to admit it makes sense.

"And so we should react with force!" Memnon's voice rises with fervor. "Let them know we are not to be trifled with. They are the worst of our kind, and we cannot allow them to gain further strength."

"That's probably what they want." Lysandir's voice is the opposite of Memnon's. Calm, assured, and pitched so that everyone has to be quiet in order to hear him speak. "The Unseelie have been divided for an age. The Court of the Forest already made the error of giving them reason to unite, and we've seen what happened as a result. If we give them more cause, we're inviting a war we do not want or need. From what I've gathered from my contacts in the Court of Air, the Unseelie King is not as brash as many of his kin and will know he cannot win through force. There's a deeper game at play here, and we risk losing if we move too quickly."

Memnon slams his palms on the table and rises. "So you'd rather we sit around and become prey? They have the sword! They could use it against our wards."

That gets Vasilius's attention, and he shoves to his feet, leaning on the table with both of his palms pressed against it.

"That's enough for now." His deep voice is edged with just enough command that no one dares move, much less speak. "Let us think on it for now and continue to gather information. The coming days may bring us more insight."

Memnon grumbles and wrinkles his pointed nose but says nothing further. The next few topics are much less exciting, and more than once I catch Lysandir looking my way.

Everyone seems to like him. Hell, I always liked and admired what I'd heard about him. So, if he's against me, it's going to be trouble. I have to figure out a way to get on his good side.

But why *does* he dislike me so?

Is it possible he had a vision that included me?

The new possibility has me squirming in my seat. What if he did see something about me? Though, I'm not sure what I could do that would inspire such distaste that he'd try to kick me out of Faery the moment I arrived. It's not like I'm here to be a spy, take them down from within, or some other nonsense. Maybe I should ask, but I'm almost afraid to know the answer.

I muse on that throughout the rest of the meeting, impatiently waiting for the chance to improve my odds.

CHAPTER 12

T HAT EVENING, BAILEY HAS her date with the king. Elaine visits with us for a little while, which involves a lot of the women trying to be on their best behavior and even a few very fake personalities coming out to play that fall away the moment she leaves. After that, the rest of us are all left to our own devices, which entails a whole lot of nothing in the parlor.

We're not supposed to speak about what we learned in the council meeting, which means no debating it with each other where the guards can hear, but sitting around isn't getting me anywhere either. It's not going to be enough to say something like "War bad. Peace good." I need thoughtfulness, reason, and insight. Worse, I'm not really sure which way Vasilius leans on the topic. He showed no preference one way or another before the conversation started toward an argument rather than a discussion.

Eventually, I seek out the library. If nothing else, maybe I can glean more insight into the history with the Unseelie and how their unfortunate circumstance came about. Living in a dead and ever-dying land is certainly a bad situation, and that can make anyone desperate.

I head toward the history section I'd found useful before and stop short just as I turn around the bookcase.

"You again." The comment slips out before I can think better of it.

Lysandir looks up from the book he's reading and has the audacity to grin at me. God, that look alone makes my chest burn, though maybe not in the way he intends.

"Mira, what a pleasant surprise." He pushes a tendril of crimson hair back behind one pointed ear. "I wondered if anyone would decide to do a little research on their own after today's discussion."

"And so you decided to lay in wait, as it were?" I clutch my trusty notebook closer to my chest.

He nods once. "Something like that. Though I'm glad it's you."

I nearly laugh out loud. "Why is that?"

"I have something I'd like to ask of you." He waits in silence. Careful, patient, unmoving, save for the occasional blink of his eyes.

He's going to make me ask, damn it. I don't know why that bothers me, but it does.

"And what would that be, my prince?" I ask in the sweetest voice I can muster.

There's a subtle widening of his eyes before he mouths "my prince", but another blink of his eyes and it's gone. "I want us to start over. To see if we can forget what happened in the throne room and begin anew as if it never occurred."

Of all the things he could have asked, that one surprises me. My brows pinch and lips purse as I wrestle with the request. "You want me to forget that you called me out in front of the entire court and tried to prevent me from entering the competition to become your brother's queen."

Saying it aloud makes it sound even more ludicrous.

"Yes." As if it's such an easy thing. When I don't reply, he adds, almost like it pains him to say it, "It would mean a great deal to me."

I'm curious—I can't help it—so I walk to the little seating area and drop down into the chair across from him. "Why?"

God help me, I have to know.

"Several reasons." Lysandir leans forward, elbows on his thighs, book closed in his lap and long forgotten. "For one, you could be queen someday soon, and if you are, I want us to get along."

Should have thought of that before, I think, but hold my tongue.

"Secondly, I want to get to know you better." He leans back. "Since you are a candidate to become my brother's bride, it only makes sense. After all, he won't make that decision alone. He's relying on feedback from those close to him. As his brother, it's my duty to advise him."

And there it is. Something that rings with more truth than the first statement, though they're undoubtedly both true since fae cannot lie. Didn't Elaine even say that she and the advisors would be helping him choose? After all, there is a lot of time when he is not, and cannot be, around us. Just this afternoon, Elaine spent time with us again. She dropped some helpful tidbits about her life, but I'm sure her purpose was just as much about getting to know us and observing how we interact than anything else.

"Ah, I see," I reply with only a little bit of sarcasm. "So, you're trying not to let your judgement be clouded by whatever initial dislike of me you had so that you can advise your brother without bias?"

There's a subtle shake of his head that I almost miss.

My lips press thin, holding in the question that's been stewing in my head since the council meeting. Call it frustration more than courage, but the pressure in my chest isn't letting up and I have to know. "You're a seer, right? Let me guess, you saw something about me that made you dislike me?"

He shakes his head more clearly this time. "I've never disliked you, Mira."

The response takes some of the wind out of my sails. I was so convinced that had to be it.

"Right, well," I stammer. When it he says my name like that, all calm and full of something I can't name, it does something to my head and almost makes me lose my train of thought. "You certainly have a funny way of showing it."

"I know," he admits, raising his palms in the air. "Which is why I hoped we could start fresh and that I might be able to get to know you better without the cloud of that first meeting hanging over us.

Perhaps a peace offering?" He picks up the book in his lap and hands it to me.

The lettering on the title shifts before my eyes, becoming readable. Someone has spelled this fae book to allow humans to read it. The shimmering golden ink of the title reads *The Fall of the Unseelie Court.*

Lysandir leans in again, this time whispering like we're friendly confidants. "I thought that you, or whoever might seek out knowledge in the library, might be interested to learn more about the last Unseelie King and his sword. A weapon known not only for its prowess in battle but its ability to do the otherwise impossible, like slice through wards."

My lips part in surprise. Not just at the knowledge, but that he's sharing it aloud. Granted, he's whispering, and the library is once again quiet tonight but still.

"There's a reason it's troublesome that it's been found and is being wielded by this new king." At my incredulous look, he adds, "Don't worry, you're not sharing anything you're not supposed to. I'm the one talking."

Clever man. I can't help it when the corners of my lips quirk up at that. Still, all this is a bit out of the blue. "This isn't some trick?" I say, lifting the book for emphasis. "You really do want to help me?"

"It's no trick." He scoots a little closer, nearly sitting on the edge of the cushioned seat. "I'm curious to see how your mind works and what you might advise."

"Oh." The book is suddenly heavy in my lap. "It's a test then, not a gift."

"Can't it be both?" He cants his head to one side. "But I did mean it as a gift, and I'll prove it to you. If you'll let me, perhaps I can show you some portions of this particular book that I found interesting? We can even discuss them if you like." He holds out his hand.

For a minute, I just stare at it. It doesn't seem like a trick. He does seem to want to help me, and it makes sense that he'd want to get to know me better and test my wits to see if I'd make a good queen. But I still can't reason out our first terrible interaction.

I pass him the book. He grabs it, but I don't let go.

I lean in, matching his whispered urgency. "If you don't dislike me and you want to help me, tell me why you did it. Why make a spectacle of me in front of everyone?"

His fingers tighten on the book, his skin paling from the pressure, though he doesn't move to jerk it away. All his attention is focused on me, his gaze so intense I have to fight every urge within me to look away. A hint of light flares from his eyes, and finally, he breaks first, glancing away.

"I told you before, it's strange that a woman wanting to be queen wouldn't visit Faery before now." He gives the book a gentle tug, but I still don't let go.

"You did, but it's more than that. There's something else." I know it deep in my bones, and saying it aloud only solidifies that certainty. "You're always calm and collected, a voice of reason. Or you have been every time I've seen you except that moment. So, what else was it? What did I do wrong?"

A deep sigh slipped from him, the kind that moves his whole upper body. "You didn't do anything wrong, Mira. Nothing at all."

Nothing? I release the book, confused as ever, the fight going out of me like a full balloon that someone forgot to tie and just let go of.

"Someday, I'll tell you everything. But not yet. Just know, it has nothing to do with me disliking you or thinking you unworthy to be queen."

So, there is something. Or was.

I ball my hands into fists in my lap. "Please—"

"Patience." He tsks, slipping back into the calm and easy demeanor he presented earlier. "I promise you'll know in time."

I scowl at him. "Has anyone ever told you that you're absolutely infuriating?"

A small huff of laughter slips through his lips as Lysandir moves over to the table and sets down the book with a soft thump. Finally, he looks back at me over one shoulder. "Only you. Care to join me?"

There's a challenge in his raised brow and the mirth sparkling in his eyes, and damn it if that just makes me want to accept it all the more. Whatever secret he's keeping, he was right on one score: His brother listens to him. I need the prince as an ally, not an enemy, and if starting over really means that much to him, then I have to try, for my benefit if nothing else.

I don't really think before popping open my notebook to the same page I took notes on during the meeting and jotting down a few of the tidbits Lysandir points out.

To be honest, analyzing the book and discussing it with him for the next hour or so is easier than I expect, almost comfortable. Almost. And when I shove away the embarrassment that was my first night in Faery, I can forget that I dislike him and swore to loathe his presence. I can even forget that he's a prince and is probably only being nice to me to make up for being an ass and to report on my worthiness to his brother. It's a lot to not think about, but at the same time, it's easy. He makes it that way, stripping away all pretense and treating me like a person, like a friend.

"So, the Unseelie King's sword can repel magic and shatter wards with a single slice, in addition to being a formidable tangible weapon all on its own," I speak aloud as I write, finishing the line with a quick little sketch of a sword. "Anything else?"

When I glance back at Lysandir, he's looking past me, straight at my notebook and the lines of shimmering blue ink. He doesn't say anything for a moment, and in the silence, I consider the hundred horrible things he might say mocking my hobby. My neck burns with imagined indignation. Retorts rise to the tip of my tongue, ready to be hurled back at him.

"That's lovely." He looks up, meeting my sharp gaze.

With that one honest look, he knocks the breath from my lungs. My shoulders slump, and my arm relaxes—I don't even remember tensing up. It's only then that I notice our arms are almost touching where they lay on the table near one another, and actually, that might be his leg I feel under the table and not a chair leg.

"Umm..." I make to brush my hair behind my ears, though it hasn't fallen loose from my pony tail, and scoot a little to the side in my chair. "Thank you. I like to use color. It just brightens things up and makes them a little happier. Why use black ink when you can have all sorts of colors, right?"

A tiny laugh slips out, and I slam my lips shut to stop my rambling.

My habit of journaling started after my father died, when I needed all the little escapes that I could find. Selena got me a pack of glittery gel pens, and suddenly everything I wrote literally sparkled with bits of joy. But my notebooks have always been just for me, my secret little treasure.

His grin only widens. "Agreed. And it's nice to see you taking this seriously and keeping notes. Many of your fellow competitors didn't today."

"Their mistake," I reply.

"Exactly. It's not something everyone would notice, but I did. It's nice to find others who are serious about their studies. May I?" He tips his head toward the book.

Despite the compliment, my gut reaction is to snatch my book away and tell him not only no but hell no. God, if he saw my notes about his brother? Or him? I might just die of embarrassment.

Lysandir gives a small chuckle. "Never mind. I know a rejection when I see one."

I wince. "It's just...personal, you know?"

He points to the little floral divider I'd sketched during the meeting. "I was mostly interested in the colors and designs like that one you have there at the top."

Pulling it between my teeth, I bite my bottom lip. "Okay, a quick peek."

I hold the notebook up and make a show of quickly flipping from one page to the next and maybe skipping a few pages around where some of my more sensitive notes are. When I reach the end,

I snap the notebook shut with a little too much force and wait, holding my breath for whatever reaction comes next.

Lysandir leans back in his chair. "Quite the rainbow of colors. I especially like the one that seemed to change color as the page moved. You did that with a pen? Not magic?"

"Just a good ole prismatic." I set the notebook back on the desk. "Did humans even have magic like that once? If we did, we certainly don't anymore."

There are some older coven members who can do little things, charms and whatnot, with limited effect. My generation can do even less, barely enough to know that magic still exists in our world. It worries the elders more than anyone cares to talk about, at least openly. Magic started to fade first, then the gift, showing up less and less in our family lines. The fae *should* be worried about it, though with the gift popping up outside the covens, maybe it's just some weird changing of the guard.

"A pity about human magic," he replies. "Some fae can make letters shimmer like that though."

"Oh yes, my attendant Fia does something similar with cosmetics. She infuses them with her power to add extra sparkle and shimmer. I have a little bit on my eyelids right now actually." I close my eyes and tilt my head to make sure he can get a good look in the dim light of the library. Though with his fae eyesight he can probably see just fine.

When I open them again, he's angled his body more fully toward me, his hand on the arm of the chair. He lifts that hand, as if reaching for me but quickly drops it back into his lap.

"I noticed" is all he says.

A fluttering starts in my chest, completely unexpected and igniting a soft burn over my heart. Was he just going to...

Lysandir clears his throat. "I don't think I saw red in your notebook. Or orange for that matter. Averse to the court colors?"

Changing the topic...right. But if it will erase the weird feeling moments ago, I'm for it, so I roll with it.

"There was plenty of gold," I say. "I love the way it shimmers. But you're right about the red. In the human world, red is typically used to point out errors or mistakes. I've always found it a little jarring to use when taking notes."

"Ah, most unfortunate for our court to be the color of error."

I shrug. "Or maybe humans are the weird ones using red that way."

He hums in agreement, casting a glance down my form them back up again before straightening in his seat and turning back toward the table. "Now, where were we?"

Ah, yes, because we were discussing the Unseelie. Probably a more useful topic than my choice of pen colors.

Lysandir leans forward, his long hair sweeping over one shoulder, the crimson strands catching the light and almost glowing the color of red wine. It's apparent that he's at ease here, comfortable in a way he was not in the council chamber, where he sat straight and still for most of the session. Not that I was staring at him of course, but he was hard to miss since he was squarely in my line of sight.

On the topic of sight...

"When you see the future," I ask, "can you pick what you see?"

Asking the question flipped a switch, changing him from calm and relaxed to stiff and serious all in a breath. "It's not quite that easy. Some visions come to be on their own, unbidden. Other times, I can meditate on a question and seek wisdom from the magic that flows through all of Faery, but I do not always get an answer. Even when I do, it's often vague at best, a momentary vision or even just a feeling. That can be helpful in some things, but when it comes to complex questions like our enemy's plan, I have been able to glean little."

"Ah, sorry to pry. I just thought maybe that would be more helpful than a book, but I suppose if it was, you'd have done it already."

The tension eases out of him, and his lips quirk up in a half grin. "Smart girl. Histories don't give exact answers either, but they do let us know what's happened before and can give us hints toward the future that can often help more than any vision."

The way he says it, the pride that resonates in his voice, isn't just that of someone repeating a saying. It means something to him—history, books, all of it.

"You enjoy studying the past," I surmise.

"I do. I enjoy learning quite a bit. Most of the time, I end up doing it alone, but it's nice, having someone to discuss things with who is actually interested in them." He gestures to the book and my notebook, to us.

"Your brother isn't interested?"

"Does my brother seem like the studious type to you?" He arcs a brow at me.

No, I can't see Vasilius spending his time in libraries. Or reading at all really. The idea of Vasilius curled up with a book just doesn't work. "He's mentioned he likes more active pursuits like dueling and hunting."

Lysandir nods. "Exactly. He can appreciate books when they serve his purpose, but generally, if something needs to be researched, it's left to me or a member of his council."

"There's no one else you can study with? Close friends or lovers?"

My gosh, I did not just say that aloud. Lovers? I could smack myself in the forehead. What business of mine is it who he spends time with? None at all. But the question just slipped out, and there's no taking it back.

"No current lovers." He draws out the response, humor dancing in his eyes and his head tilted to the side in question, letting his hair slide around his pointed ear.

Of course he'd choose to respond to that part first. I could sink through the floor right here and now.

He glances away. "I gave my heart to someone long ago, and she has yet to return my feelings."

"Oh." It's a pitiful reply, but from the way his voice drew quiet at the end and he wouldn't quite look at me, it's clear he doesn't want to talk about it. Though it would be interesting to know who claimed such a man's heart and why she doesn't return his affection, especially given that he's a prince and quite pleasant to look at.

"As for friends..." He shrugs, glancing back my way. "I have a few who are close, but it's not something that comes easily for me, not when I know that many would try to become my friend simply for the privileges it offers."

My traitor heart aches for him. "You think they'd befriend you just because you're a prince?"

The smile he gives me doesn't quite reach his eyes. "I know they would. Still, I have managed to find some. Unfortunately, they don't share my love of books." When I don't immediately reply, Lysandir asks, "So, what do you like to do, Mira? When you're not writing colorful notes?"

He shifts in his chair, his leg brushing mine, and I nearly jump out of my skin. My heart kicks up its rhythm, and my ribs feel like they're both expanding and crushing in toward my spine at once.

"Dance," I squeak, if only to cover the way the sudden touch just twisted me up. "I like to dance."

But his touch shouldn't do that. It's Vasilius that I'm here for, him that I'm trying to impress, his queen that I'm supposed to become. And all of the sudden, sitting here with Lysandir, our legs brushing and only inches between us, feels too intimate. Maybe he's just curious about me, just doing his duty to his brother, but for me, it suddenly feels different than that. In any other circumstances, I'd be excited, overjoyed even, to be talking with a guy about books and journaling and my damn prismatic pens.

But this is Lysandir. The confusing, infuriating prince who tried to keep me from being here but then says he never disliked me and that it would mean a great deal to him to start over. He can't lie—I know it like I know the sun rises—but something is wrong and quite possibly it's me.

I danced for Vasilius. I'm supposed to be getting to know *him*, sharing myself with *him*, not through some proxy.

All at once, I stand up, nudging the table hard enough to shift the books and send the chair sliding back in the process.

"Mira?" Lysandir half rises too, his look of curiosity shifting into concern with his pinched brows and higher volume.

"I'm sorry. It's getting late." I snatch up my notebook and pen from the table. "I should go. Maybe I can borrow the book to read later?" I glance at it, decide waiting for it is a horrible idea and running away would be much better, and turn to do just that. "Never mind, I can look at it another time."

"Mira." He touches my arm, and I go absolutely still, the entire world funneling down to that searing touch. "Is this about my question? About dancing? If you didn't want to share—"

I pull away from him and take another step back for good measure. "It's not."

Not really. It's about who I danced for, about who I should be wanting to share with, about the way my heart swelled with glee at his question in a way it never did with his brother. Thoughts race one after another as fast as my hammering pulse, and I might just hyperventilate right there if I don't get out right this moment. A full-on panic attack is brewing like a hurricane inside me, and I need space to sort it out before it goes full cat five on me.

"Thank you for sharing the book with me. I appreciate it. It's just a busy day tomorrow, and I need my rest. I didn't sleep well last night, and I don't want to be half asleep for anything, you know?" Lies. So many rambling lies.

He's still standing there, hand outstretched right where it had been when he'd touched my arm. Slowly, he lowers it to his side, and I catch the quick clench of his fingers into a fist before they loosen again.

"Should I walk you back to your room?" he asks.

"Nope," I squeak, far too loudly. "I'm good. I'm pretty sure the guard that escorted me here is still outside. Poor guy. I've left him standing there so long. It really would be rude of me to stay longer and leave him out there, so I'll just have him show me back."

There's a little bob of Lysandir's throat as he swallows, his gaze sliding down my form and back up again. And damn it if my heart doesn't do a weird stutter at that too.

"Good night then," he says.

"Night!" I give an awkward quick wave and too-bright smile, clutching my notebook to my chest like armor with my other hand before I twist sharply on my heel and hurry toward the door.

CHAPTER 13

IT'S FINE. I'M FINE. It was quiet. We were alone and vulnerable. Of course I would feel something for him after he confessed to not having many friends. Who wouldn't?

I've told myself that over and over—when I laid in bed last night, when Fia helped me get ready this morning, and even now as I sit in the garden with Bailey.

She gives me the softest nudge with her elbow, jolting me from my spiraling thoughts. "You're still half asleep this morning."

Not asleep. Distracted. A little half laugh slips from me.

"Good thing I have this, then." I lift my steaming mug of coffee and take another sip.

She, on the other hand, is wide awake, despite an evening date with the king. Awake and practically glowing. Another soft sigh falls from her lips as she looks out across the dew-covered grass.

"It was that good of a date, huh?" I say.

Her smile widens, and she takes another sip before answering. "It really was. I didn't expect it to be, but...yeah."

Gosh, the girl is lovestruck. "And you two just...talked?"

It's hard to believe, especially after the one-sided date I had with Vasilius. But maybe Bailey likes to listen? Maybe that was ideal for her? Or maybe her date was just wonders better than mine. Maybe I messed up somewhere and the king doesn't want to get to know me? I squeeze the mug a little tighter between my palms. I can't help but relive every moment of that lunch and think about how or what I could have done differently. He liked the dance though. I know that was true enjoyment on his face at the end.

"He told me all about Faery, about being king and the burdens of the role that a queen would share with him." Bailey looks at me, her brows pinched. "I think so many women see a title like queen and get stuck on the sparkly gowns, the wealth, the privilege. But there's so much more than that. Those are perks, no doubt, but it's real work too, and Vasilius needs someone who can walk beside him and help carry those burdens. In some ways, it's a lot like looking after my younger siblings back home. Always someone screaming for your attention, many needs to be met, lots of people depending on you, day in and day out." She shakes her head, blowing out a long breath. "It's exhausting."

"They sound more like your kids than your siblings," I joke, but her eyes darken, and I wonder if I've made a huge misstep.

But then she gives a little shrug, and her smile returns. "They are, I guess. I moved back in a few years ago to help my mom care for them since she was getting older and it took a lot out of her. I guess that's what happens when you just keep having babies until your body is too worn out to do it anymore. My parents firmly believed in having as many kids as possible to continue the gifted bloodline."

She gives me a sideways look that says much. One of *those* families.

"They had me early, so I'm a lot older than the rest of my siblings. Sarah is the closest to me in age, and she's only twenty-one. Dad still works a lot to try to support everyone, so it's just Mom taking care of the kids and the house and everything on her own. Even with my helping out, it's a lot sometimes."

"So why come here then?" I ask. "To get a break from the kids?"

Bailey glances over one shoulder then the other, maybe to see if anyone is listening, before scooting a little bit closer. "I actually didn't want to come."

"What?" Now that's a surprise, especially coming from such a large family that could have sent someone else to vie for the king's hand.

She shakes her head. "I've only been to Faery a few times. I'd never even met Vasilius. It was supposed to be Sarah. She's younger, prettier. If a little helpless."

No kidding, if she's not helping out with all those siblings.

"But she fell in love"—Bailey makes little air quotes—"last summer and couldn't stand to be parted from her boyfriend." She tips her head, looking over at me down the slope of her nose. "He's a few crayons short of a full box. Probably took too many hits playing football, but there's no changing her mind when she's set on something. So, when she adamantly refused to come, threatened to run away and never speak to the family again if they made her, I volunteered to go in her place."

"No cousins or anything that would have fit the bill?"

"Not the right age, boys, or already married." She lifts one shoulder. "I figured I'd come and give it a go. It was a good excuse to dress up and do something new, experience the wonders of Faery. But I'm glad I came now. I think Vasilius might need me more than my family does." She winces. "Not to say that they don't need me or the others wouldn't be a good choice either."

I force a laugh to lighten the mood. "It's fine."

Sort of. Maybe. The twinge I felt in my chest was jealousy all right, but not the kind it should be.

"You two really didn't get up to anything more last night?" I prod.

It should be weird, talking about dating the same guy. It is a little. And though there's a heaviness in my chest as I wait for her response, it's not the crushing weight it could be.

Bailey looks away from me, out over the garden. She raises her coffee mug, stares into its depths, and whispers, more to it than me, "We kissed."

The color rising on her cheeks says it wasn't just a kiss on the hand.

Now my stomach twists in on itself. I'm behind. My family expects me to become queen, has pinned their hopes on it. Hell, it's what I've been focused on too. Maybe I'm an idiot, but I thought it would be easier.

Maybe getting Lysandir on my side really could help? If the brothers are as close as they seem, it definitely can't hurt.

"So long as that's all." I wink, trying to make it a joke. To be fair, she probably thinks my kiss with him was more than it was, and I'm not about to correct that now.

"I don't think any of us want to defy the dowager," she replies with a meaningful look.

I give a fake shiver. She may be on in years, but she still has the ability to make anyone feel two inches tall with a few well-placed words. A true queen if there ever was one.

"Speaking of," Bailey says, "brunch with her starts in a little bit."

"Ah yes." I sip at my cup. "I wonder which will be more exciting, that or tomorrow's council meeting?"

"Perhaps we should start betting on it," she replies with a grin.

"Maybe we should."

CHAPTER 14

W HEN WE ARRIVE AT the council meeting, the circular table has been expanded to allow room for all of us as well. We're spaced out between the advisors and members of the royal family. Advisor Danai gives me a look as I open my journal, her attention catching on the colorful lines of text, one dark brow rising. I wait for scorn, but the hint of a grin forms in the corner of her mouth before she focuses her attention back toward the open center of the wide-ringed space.

Vasilius looks particularly resplendent today in a loose, cream-colored shirt with golden accents that shimmer in the light. A split in the center of the neckline lets part of it fall open, teasing the muscular chest below. His sleeves are rolled up, baring his equally impressive arms. It's distracting to say the least. Maybe that's part of the test—who can pay attention to the topic at hand with a handsome god-like king showing off his prowess?

In fact, everyone seems a little more relaxed today. Well, everyone who isn't in the competition and there to be judged by the others around the circle.

The discussions start off easy. How to resolve a dispute between two parties where one is clearly in the wrong. Suggestions on what to do with an excess harvest.

But it doesn't stay that way.

"Now," Vasilius begins, "we need to talk about the Unseelie."

The word chimes through the room like a discordant note, echoing back on itself. If there were any windows in the room, I wouldn't be surprised if a cloud didn't decide to block out the sun simply for effect.

"Avara," he continues, "please share this morning's update with everyone else."

The Captain of the Guard rises to her feet. She fills the silence with her presence, her sheet of pale hair barely moving as she slowly takes us in. "Late last night, we intercepted a band of Unseelie that crossed over the border after a breach was sliced through our wards."

A few quick intakes of breath precede the damning silence that follows. Adeline openly gapes. But it's only us women who appear surprised. The others must have already been informed.

Grace recovers first. "I thought the wards protect us from Unseelie?"

"They do," Avara replies. "Weaker Unseelie are kept out. The strong ones can sometimes move past them, but we always feel it, those of us who have attuned to them, our king especially." She nods toward Vasilius. "It has been a rare occurrence with the Unseelie, at least in our territory."

"You said, sliced," I clarify. My gaze drifts to Lysandir, who gives the briefest of nods. "Like by the Unseelie King's sword?"

"Mmm, someone is well-versed," Elaine muses.

The praise bolsters me, and I count it as a win. *Thank you, Lysandir.* He really wasn't kidding about helping me out after all.

"That's right," the captain says. "We weren't sure his sword possessed such power yet, since our last reports from the Court of the Air stated the Unseelie King had been able to fully recharge it. The cut through our wards was slow and sloppy, but effective none the less."

"What did they do once the ward was breached?" Alex asks, leaning onto the table.

"Good question." Avara nods toward her. "Their aim once inside our wards was unclear. The band of Unseelie that slipped through did not go far, perhaps because we were on them quickly."

Katherine wrinkles her nose. "What did they hope to accomplish?"

It's a fair question, though her tone is more derisive than inquisitive.

Avara looks to the king. Vasilius glances around the circle.

"What do you all think they hoped to accomplish?" he asks.

"Was there a city or a settlement nearby?" Zoe asks.

"None," Vasilius replies. "This happened along a stretch that is mostly uninhabited."

Zoe leans forward, hands clasped in front of her on the table. "Would they have known that though?"

"We're unsure the extent of their current knowledge of our terrain. They would have known the locations of our cities at one time, but whether their records remain intact is uncertain."

Adeline clears her throat. "Is there anything valuable there? Natural resources?"

"Nothing significant," Vasilius supplies.

"What about—"

"They're testing response time," Cora says with confidence.

It's a smart answer. A good one, as much as I hate to admit it. She glances between Vasilius and the captain, waiting for one of them to confirm her assumption.

When no one immediately replies, she continues, "They had to know you would feel the breach. The Unseelie did not go far. Probably so they could flee back through it once you all arrived, which also supports that they were not looking for anything in particular. There wasn't a city or resource nearby to draw them. It has to be a test."

Vasilius smiles. "Very good."

I could kick myself for not thinking of it first.

Memnon rises to his feet. He was the one who had been so strongly anti-Unseelie the last time. Not that anyone was pro-Unseelie, but his opinions were a little stronger than some of the others. "So, now the question is—what do we do about their little foray into our lands? Surely such a thing cannot be ignored."

He stares at Vasilius, awaiting a reply.

But the king is unruffled and turns the question to the rest of us. "Ladies?"

A debate erupts over whether to go on the offensive or defensive. Katherine is a clear offensive proponent and keeps steering the conversation that way, though most of the women and myself prefer a defensive approach.

"If the Court of Fire attacks the Unseelie, people will get hurt. That's for sure," Zoe says. "But if you all don't, then maybe they'll just leave you alone too." She's not always the brightest bulb, but I murmur my agreement.

Bailey raises her hand. Elaine is the first to notice and encourages her to speak.

"Prince Lysandir," Bailey starts, "you see the future at times. Have you been given an insight on what the Unseelie plan?"

All attention in the room focuses on him. I assumed if he had, we would have heard about it already, but it's a fair question.

After a moment, Lysandir says, "I've meditated on the Unseelie's intentions toward our court several times over the past weeks, but each time I've seen only the same brief vision, flickering flames."

"Fire like the court symbol? A campfire?" Grace asks.

He shakes his head. "I wish I knew. I simply see flames no matter where I look, nothing else."

Adeline clears her throat. "Fire could be a good thing."

"A sign of our victory," Memnon adds, though Adeline frowns at that, as if it's not what she'd meant at all.

Lysandir turns his palms up over the table. "Only the fates can say, and they did not. I have no more than that."

"But it's got to be a good thing, right?" Katherine presses, tossing her long hair over one shoulder. "This is the Court of Fire." An unspoken 'duh' lingers in the wake of her words.

"Visions are not always that clear," I say. "If Lysandir, who has seen it himself, is unsure what it means, how can we think to know any better?" I hold his gaze across the room. "We can learn more by looking at the past than we can from uncertain visions of the future which we might misinterpret. The past is set. The future is not."

Lysandir goes eerily still, his gaze boring into mine as if seeing me in a new light.

Advisor Danai picks up the thread where I left off. "The past, even recent days, has shown the Unseelie to be unpredictable."

Lysandir blinks and the look is gone. He shifts focus to the woman speaking at my side.

"No one expected them to try to incite war between the courts," Danai says. "It's too subtle for the brute force we've seen them employ in ages past."

"The Unseelie King has not been able to fully recharge his sword and has done no more than make this one cut in our wards, right?" I ask. Several advisors nod. "So, it would stand to reason that he doesn't have what he needs to empower it further and hopefully cannot hurt the court more than he has already."

"Unless that changes, the Court of Fire should be safe from the Unseelie threat," Danai says at my side.

"Except they have a null," Avara points out.

"One," I argue. "Only one."

"A powerful one though," the captain replies. "The Unseelie King's sister, from what we gather."

"And therefore, he won't want to endanger her with some reckless mission," I say. My brothers and I aren't exactly close. I wish we were. Things were different when we were younger, but the older they get, the more time they spend together and the less with me. It doesn't hurt that they share the same hobbies and are really close in age. But even not being that close anymore, I would never send them into danger in enemy territory.

"She already snuck deep into the Court of Air. You think she would not do the same to our court?" Memnon says.

I purse my lips. He has me there.

Thankfully, Grace runs with my idea. "To what end? We are bound. Safe."

"Who can say what such monsters plan," Memnon sneers.

The debate continues, threatening to devolve into more of an argument again. The proponents of taking action are few, but they sure are loud.

"Maybe it would be best to save any military action until after The Choosing concludes?" I suggest when there's a pause.

Vasilius leans back in his chair. "And why is that?"

I'm not sure if it's a test or he genuinely doesn't like my suggestion. I risk as glance at Lysandir, who gives an encouraging nod. Bolstered by the idea that I haven't totally screwed up, I glance back at the king and continue, "Because anything that risks lives should get your full focus and attention, and that might be hard to give when you're still getting to know all of us so that you can make another important choice."

"Mmm," the king muses. "You all can be quite distracting."

A flush races to my cheeks at the look in his eyes.

"But a worthy suggestion and a wise one. I cannot go far from you all, given our bond." He raises his wrist. "It keeps the Unseelie from taking you all, but it also restricts my movements and keeps me close. Trying to venture into Unseelie territory would be extremely difficult for me, maybe impossible with all of your bonds pulling me back to you."

Vasilius slaps a hand on the table. More than a few women jump at the sharp, unexpected sound.

"Enough talk about Unseelie," he says. "Let's debate a more pleasant topic—what activities to include in our upcoming garden party."

Several of the women perk up just as many of the advisors groan. It may be a tiring council meeting after all.

Chapter 15

Y OGA HAS BECOME AN almost daily routine, and something I find myself looking forward to. It's the one time of day when the other women feel just like friends and not competition, and I'm finding I like that more and more. Making friends wasn't something I gave much thought to before coming here, but now that the sprouts of possible friendship are starting to grow, it's one of the best parts of The Choosing. Not that any of us are besties or anything, except Grace and Alex, but they came here that way. There's potential though, and that's something.

This morning, I felt Lysandir watching me again. I spied him on the balcony as we moved and stretched and surprised myself wishing he'd come down to our level where I could speak with him. I never did get to thank him for studying with me before the council meeting. More than that though, I enjoyed his company even more than that of my new potential friends. Maybe he could be more than just an ally if I play my cards right.

It's for that reason—well, and the wealth of information available—that I spend the entire afternoon in the library. Alex had a date this morning. Katherine is on one now. I won't miss time with the king. I've filled a few pages in my notebook with details about magical fae objects when I get the little rush of feeling along my spine that I've been hoping for.

I'm not even surprised when I turn to find Lysandir headed my way. I give him a little wave and smile, which he returns. A leather-bound book is clutched against his chest.

"More research today?" he inquires, pulling out the chair next to mine and taking a seat at the table where I have books spread out before me, my green gel pen resting on my notebook.

"It can't hurt. And there's only so much time I can spend listening to gossip about fashion and celebrities from back on Earth."

"Not to your interest?"

"No, not really." Not at all. "Actually, I was hoping I'd meet you here."

"You were?" He blinks, looking almost dumbfounded.

I hold back a little laugh. He actually looks kind of cute when he's confused. Not that I'm looking... Though no one could say he's unattractive, not by any means. Between his strong, balanced features, lean muscle, and stunning dark red hair, he's many a woman's dream come to life. But that's something I try not to focus too hard on. I'm here for his brother after all.

"Yes, I wanted to thank you for your help here before, and during the council meeting. I did better because of you."

He shakes his head and scoots in his chair. "I didn't do much. It was you who put the information to use. And the points you made were very strong. Those were yours, not mine."

"Still, I appreciate it. I was convinced you hated me there for a little while." I push a wayward strand of hair behind my ear, and his gaze snaps to it, lingering after I drop my hand.

"I don't hate you, Mira." He leans in closer. "I'm sorry you thought that."

I nod. "I know that now. I don't suppose you'll tell me what the nonsense that first night was about yet, huh?"

A half smile twitches at the corner of his mouth. "Not yet."

Of course. I nearly sigh with disappointment. Lysandir grabs my open book and slides it closer to him.

"What have you been reading about today?" he asks, even as he takes in the open pages.

"Fae objects of power," I say. "The Unseelie King has his sword, and that weapon presents a great threat. But what if we could find an object to counter it?"

"Ah." He flips through the next few pages of the book before settling on one. "Then you'll want to learn a bit about the spear." He slides the book back to me and taps the open page.

I lean in. "The Spear of Shielding."

As I read over the details on the page, Lysandir opens the book he brought. Except, upon closer inspection, it's not a book at all but a notebook.

"You brought a notebook."

He slips a pen from his pocket and taps the end on the open page. "It's wise to be prepared. You never know what we'll discover."

I bite my bottom lip, hiding the goofy smile trying to break out across my face. A fae prince taking notes. Who would have ever thought.

"Did you bring a red pen?" I tease.

He laughs. "I didn't, though perhaps I should acquire one."

Tension builds in the silence as we stare at one another, and only then do I realize how close we're sitting. I scoot back a little in my chair and drop my attention to the open book, anything to try to ignore the warmth building in my center.

"So, the spear." He shifts his attention back to the book as well. "It's an object of protection and one we have in our possession. It is always held by the Queen of Fire, so my mother possesses it now."

"Oh! That is helpful. Though a spear is an object of protection? That seems strange."

A soft murmur of agreement slips from him. "It is, I suppose, yet the spear allows its wielder to protect those near them."

"Very handy in battle." Though Elaine certainly isn't taking the field if there's a conflict. Maybe she would give it to someone else, then? I start to ask about it when someone clears their throat nearby.

I look up to spy Tharin advancing.

"Prince Lysandir. Lady Mira," he says.

"Yes," we echo in unison.

I'd swear he grimaces, but the look is there and gone so quickly that I start to second-guess it.

"The king has requested all the women of The Choosing return to the parlor," Tharin says.

I push to my feet in a rush. "I thought he was on a date. Did something happen?"

"It seems the date has ended. He has something to discuss with you all, though I do not know the details of it."

Sounds like Katherine's date probably didn't go as well as she hoped if it's done already. Can't say I feel too bad about that one. Some women I've grown fond of. Her and Cora? Not so much.

I quickly close my notebook and pick up my pens. "I should—"

"I'll return the books to the shelves," Lysandir offers.

"Thank you. I appreciate it." I offer him my best winning smile.

He shrugs. "Don't want you to be late to meet my brother."

Ouch. Right. The comment shouldn't sting, but it does.

Tharin isn't helping, staring at me like I've been caught doing something inappropriate. We were just reading and talking.

I turn and head toward the door.

"The library again?" Tharin asks.

"It's a public place," Lysandir replies.

Tharin sighs. I've missed something, but I don't know what. Should the prince not be in the library? And come to think of it, the two seem more familiar than I first thought. The whole walk back to the parlor—which isn't that far—I consider asking Tharin about it but never do.

When we get there, it appears I'm the last to arrive, as the others all sit around the seating area, Katherine and Gabriella on either side of the king who has claimed the center seat of the couch. He looks almost uncomfortable with how close they are, basically pressed up against his sides. Maybe Katherine's date didn't go so poorly after all.

"A ball?" Katherine all but squeals. "I love balls!"

"Yes," Vasilius gives her a wary look. "It's tradition in The Choosing to host a ball, and we have extended the invitation to several of the other Seelie courts as well."

This earns a round of excited whispers and comments.

I come to lean on the edge of Grace's seat.

Vasilius looks at me. "I look forward to showing off all of my lovely candidates to our neighbors who attend."

No doubt he does. It's a strong statement to make to the other courts, especially the ones that don't have relations with as many human families—if they attend, that is.

"But that's not why I'm here this evening," the king says. His countenance dims. "You all have been privy to the concerns we've had regarding the Unseelie of late."

He pauses, waiting as we acknowledge him.

"We originally invited your families to attend the upcoming ball as well. The question is whether we should let them come, given that they are unbound and we cannot guarantee the Unseelie, particularly their null, will not try something."

That sobers everyone up. It would be nice to see Selena again. But if it put her at risk? I'm not sure.

"You mean our family members are at risk of being stolen by the Unseelie if they come," Alex says plainly.

Vasilius grimaces but nods. "It would be a significant risk for the Unseelie to take, given all the fae who will be in attendance, but we cannot guarantee they will not seek to take advantage of so many humans present if they become aware of it."

"But it's a small risk, right?" Adeline asks. "You don't really think they'd get all the way here from the border, do you?"

"I would hope not," the king says. "But the risk is not zero. I promise that my warriors will be present and alert throughout the event. And we will ask that the families not stay here in Faery to limit their risk."

"You want them to come," I say.

Vasilius looks at me again. He's quiet for a moment before he says, "I do."

And it makes sense. Even more humans present will show off the glory of his court, and that's the whole point of the ball. Well, that and probably seeing how we interact with the other courts or what they think of us. It would be foolish to assume it's not another test or chance to evaluate us.

"If you want our families to come and are taking precautions to keep them safe, then they should be invited," Zoe says. "If they are worried, they can choose to stay home."

"I don't know." Grace shares a look with Alex before blinking dolefully at the king. "Maybe it would be best if they don't come."

"Why is that?" Katherine retorts. She grabs the king's arm, and I don't miss the way he subtly jolts at the touch. "King Vasilius will keep them all safe. They wouldn't dare try to harm those under his protection."

"Wishful thinking," Alex says.

Katherine huffs.

Vasilius frees himself from her grip and stands. "Think on it this evening. Tell your attendants your wish in the morning, and I shall use that to make my decision. For now, I have things to attend to." He gives us a slight bow.

"Aww," Katherine whines.

But he doesn't give her a backward glance as he leaves the room.

CHAPTER 16

T HE KING ELECTS TO invite our families to attend the ball. I'm not surprised. No one seems interested in spilling their vote, so I don't know if his decision aligns with ours but assume it probably does. Lying in my bed last night, thinking about my mother and brothers, I realized how much I missed them. Selena too. I could do without seeing my aunt and uncle, but the others? Yes, it's a risk. Something bad could happen. But bad things can happen just walking up the stairs, driving down the road, or anything else. If I could see my mother, I wouldn't want to miss out on that chance because of fear. Not that I can, since she's not gifted, but I wouldn't want to deny others feeling the same way the chance to see their parents or loved ones. So, I gave Fia my vote of yes and didn't doubt it later.

Thinking about my family also reminded me why I'm here: to become the queen, to win the king's heart and his hand. I wish I could say I feel like it's going well, but I'm not sure. The king has seemed pleased enough with me in meetings, he liked my dancing, and he did kiss my hand. We haven't yet shared a more passionate kiss like Bailey alluded to, but the keyword is *yet*.

Today, we're attending a party in the gardens, and I intend to use it to my advantage. I refuse to lose out on becoming his queen and disappoint my family simply because I didn't try hard enough. I won't let Uncle Matias say I didn't represent us well or didn't do enough for him to keep caring for my mother and brothers. It may be an awkward event again with all of us trying to get his attention, but I'm determined to find a way.

When the sun is high in the sky, our guards shift us all to a garden I haven't been to before. Situated near what must be the edge of the capital city, given the glowing forest that's visible beyond a high stone wall some distance away, the space puts every botanical garden I've ever visited to shame. A wide, grassy oval dominates the middle of the space, large gurgling fountains with dancing water on either end. Beds of roses, sculpted bushes, and more of the court's famed glass sculptures surround the oval, interspersed with walking paths and spotted with benches. Trellises give bits of shade here and there, and off to one side stretches a hedge maze, the walls too high for anyone to see over. A large tent has been erected in the middle of the oval, tables and chairs spotted underneath.

Fae in fine, flowing clothes of all colors wander the space, most chatting in small groups. A few notice our arrival and openly turn to stare.

"Wow, this is just like my cousin's wedding last summer," Katherine replies, wandering ahead of our group into the garden.

"Oh, I'm sure." Alex rolls her eyes and whispers, just loud enough for Grace and me to hear where we flank her.

Grace covers her laugh. "It does feel like something out of a movie though. 'Oh, excuse me, Your Majesty, while I spin my parasol.'" She mimics the action and a British accent. "'I think I dropped my handkerchief. Can you pick it up for me?'"

"Don't let the king hear that," Bailey admonishes.

Vasilius must be here somewhere, but I haven't spied him yet among all the others. Given how expansive the gardens are, the towering hedges, and willow-like trees draping long branches, it'd be easy for him to be obscured from view.

Cora practically elbows past and comes to stand with her hands on her hips, surveying the scene. "It does have a Bridgerton feel to it."

We all give her a sideways glance.

"What? I watched the show." She shrugs. "Every season." And then she turns, her nose in the air, and strides toward the tent like it was erected just for her.

"Do you think that's where she learned to act like a spoiled rich girl?" Grace whispers, though not too quietly.

"Act?" Alex asks with a laugh. "More like came by it honestly."

It's tempting to seek out Vasilius directly, but I'm sure at least half the other women plan to do the exact same thing. I'm better off waiting and chatting with some of the other fae. Actually, the best would be if I could make Vasilius envious and get him to come to me, but that's probably hoping for too much.

No matter what, I plan to find time to steal him away today. Maybe we'll slip into the hedge maze, or maybe I can even get him to take me somewhere else where we can be alone. He needs to know that I want to be his queen, and if he's already sharing real kisses with the others, then I need him to have one with me too, even if I have to initiate. What's that old song? Something about the truth being in his kiss? Maybe it'll be the spark we need to get things rolling.

I join a lawn game similar to bocce with a number of the fae in attendance. I'm terrible at it, though they have the courtesy not to mention that. Whether from experience or natural fae grace and skill, these fae can land the little balls exactly where they want them to go, and mine... Well, I'm lucky I haven't hurt anyone yet.

"It's your turn, Lady Mira," one of the males says with a smirk, having just placed his ball within about two centimeters of the target. As if I could beat that. My best bet is to try to knock his away, though at this distance, that's going to be a challenge and he knows it.

"Well, I'll just have to give it my best then." I give a little laugh and flash a blinding smile. Trying to be social with people I don't know is its own kind of hell, but hey, I'm trying. The little flute of fae wine I sipped earlier helps too. I'm not above liquid courage, especially where crowds are involved.

I step up to the line and look over one shoulder to where Vasilius was a moment ago, hoping to snag his attention. My fake smile slips away. *Drat.* I have no idea where he went off to.

"Mind if I join the next round?" says an unexpected voice.

I whirl toward it, my heart giving a fervent thump against my ribs. Lysandir meanders through the nearby fae, the sunlight catching on his long hair, which he's left unbound to fall around his shoulders. The outfit he's chosen for today is very similar to the one his brother wore the day before with a loose, white tunic whose sleeves are rolled up to his elbows and a slit at the top that shows off a hint of tanned chest more sculpted than I anticipated. Not that I thought him unfit, not by any means, but he's less obvious about it than his brother. More the scholar than the fighter, but damn... All I can do is blink. He's not the royal I was searching for, but my mind trips over itself in his presence anyway, rending me momentarily speechless.

The nearby fae I've been playing with titter with excitement.

"We'd love to have you join, my prince," one female replies, her eyes practically sparkling with mirth.

"Well, Lady Mira?" His nose twitches, humor lighting in his features like he knows exactly what his sudden appearance has done to me.

"Of course," I reply with a nervous laugh. "I'm about to lose this round anyway."

I turn and toss my ball toward the target, completely forgetting that I was going to knock my opponents out of the way. It lands an embarrassing three feet away.

"See?" I gesture toward it. "My team lost, so now we can start again."

"Hmm." He grips his chin, his thumb underneath while the knuckle of his pointer finger runs across his lips in a way that's utterly distracting. "Can I be on your team for this round?"

I laugh. "So eager to lose?"

The other fae I was playing with work to collect the little balls and targets and bring them back so that we can start a new round.

"I think you have potential," he says. "Besides, have you ever played this game before?"

"No. We have something similar in my world, but I only played it a few times." Once actually. Someone brought it over to my aunt and uncle's house during a get together, but we only played a little bit before my aunt lamented we might leave divots in her perfectly manicured lawn. I almost roll my eyes thinking about it. She gets bent out of shape about the most random and ridiculous things.

"I'll partner with Mira for this round." Lysandir holds out his hands to the returning fae, and they pass him the four little balls for our team.

Lysandir takes his place at my side as one of the fae males set out the targets. I barely notice where they're placed. Tingling warmth radiates from the side closest to him, almost like we're magnets being pulled together. I pounce on my feet, the wide heels of my shoes sinking into the grass.

"The trick," he says in a whisper, "is to throw the ball in an arch so it stays where it lands and doesn't roll away. Unless, of course, you go second and decide to try to knock away your opponent's ball. Then a hard and direct roll is best."

I turn my head and crane my neck to look up at him. The gentle breeze blows his hair, a few strands brushing against my cheek due to his nearness. With it comes his scent, a heady mix of leather and spice that has my toes curling.

"You make it sound so easy," I say.

"Sometimes the simplest things are the hardest, but I like a good challenge." A hint of amusement twinkles in his eyes, and I don't think we're talking about the ball game anymore.

I step back, putting some much needed space between us. Spending time with him in the library was comfortable. Easy. This is... I don't know what this is.

"Well then," I say, "why don't you show me how it's done?"

His lips quirk up in the corners, and he steps up to the mark. With three balls balanced in one hand and the one he plans to use in the other, he gives it a toss. It sails through the air in a perfect arc, landing with a soft thud. Right next to the target.

"Show-off," I mumble.

"Would you like some help?" he offers once it's my turn.

I glower at him. But then I remember that getting on his bad side isn't going to earn me any points with his brother, so I relent with a sigh. He did help me with preparing for the council meeting after all. Maybe he can work some magic here too.

"Sure, why not?" I say.

He drops two of the balls and passes the remaining one to me. Our fingers brush in the process, a little jolt zipping up my arm at the fleeting connection. *Weird.*

"Okay, so—" he starts.

My breath hitches as he comes up behind me, cupping my hand with his so that our arms are flush with one another. Butterflies erupt in my stomach.

Lysandir leans in, his hair brushing my cheek. "Pull your arm back like this." He does it for the both of us. "Now, when we go forward, let go of the ball the moment I release your hand."

Such a simple instruction, yet it feels like a monumental task that I'm bound to screw up. "Um, okay."

"Here, let's practice. I'll tap your hand instead of releasing it this time."

He swings our joined hands, tapping his fingers against mine when we're about forty-five degrees past my legs. "There, just that speed. Are you ready?"

"S-sure."

Gosh, did I really just stutter?

We swing the ball back again, and this time, when he releases my hand, I release the ball and slam my eyes shut. I suck in a breath. Hold it.

"Excellent." His heavy palm lands on my bare shoulder, and my lids fly open. I twist to look at him, blowing out the breath I was holding. Lysandir grins down at me, still touching my shoulder. "Look at that, right near the target."

Is it? I turn back to the game.

"Wow." Only an inch or two away. It's far closer than I ever managed on my own.

A loud, slow clap comes from somewhere nearby. Those near us step back and give a little bow.

"Very nice," Vasilius says.

In a flash, Lysandir's hand is gone, and the warmth of his nearness vanishes. I twist around, nearly getting tangled up in the skirts of my dress.

How long has Vasilius been there? It can't have been long, but his relaxed stance says he didn't just arrive. He crosses his tanned arms, his loose cream sleeves once again rolled up to his elbows. A piece of crimson clothing somewhere between a cape and a jacket hangs off his shoulders, the edges secured by a golden chain that drapes across his collarbone.

"Somehow my brother seems to be better at finding my bride candidates than I am." He laughs, others around him following suit.

Candidates? Plural? My brows pinch, and a hint of jealousy flares in my chest. Who else has Lysandir been hanging out with? Not that it's any of my business or that I should care. Of course he should be getting to know the others—that only makes sense—but my body's reactions rarely have anything to do with reason.

Lysandir somehow finds a way to put more space between us without moving, which only makes the flush creeping up my neck burn hotter.

I force a bright smile to my face. "Would you like to join us, Your Majesty?"

When Vasilius glances toward the balls, his smile drops.

I immediately switch tactics. "Or maybe we could take a walk, just you and me? I'd love to see more of the gardens."

"Then by all means, let me show them to you." He extends his arm in a courtly gesture, and I loop mine through it.

"Thank you for the instruction," I say to Lysandir over one shoulder.

No emotion crosses his face as he nods our way. "Anytime, Mira."

I turn my attention back to the king. "Shall we?"

CHAPTER 17

W HEN YOU'RE ON THE arm of the king, everyone notices. It's a truly unnerving feeling, having so many people watch me, their whispers chasing in our wake. When I used to enter competitions, people watched me strut across the stage, but that was different. Then, I expected it, planned for it. Here, during what should be a casual and companionable stroll, it's an annoyance at best, a distraction at worst.

I want to pay attention to Vasilius, truly I do, but my ears catch fragments of words from those we pass and my brain keeps trying to cue in on those instead of whatever he's saying.

"Do you think we could have a seat over there?" I interject when he stops to take a breath.

A little wooden bench sits near what looks like a massive weeping willow tree, its branches draping over to sweep against the ground. It's not exactly private, but it's a little more concealed than most places—other than the nearby hedge maze. But people can follow us through the maze or pretend to be meandering on their own but stay on our path. Under the willow tree, no one can get that close to us without making it obvious they're trying to eavesdrop or directly seeking our attention.

"Why not?" he replies and leads me over to the little bench.

It's a cozy setup, which is perfect for what I have in mind. Vasilius alone takes up half of the space, and I don't bother spreading out on my side, instead brushing up against him and staying there. From the way his face lights up, he doesn't seem to mind. It's a far cry from how he reacted to Katherine and Gabriella being all over him in the parlor the other night. Maybe I'm not doing so poorly after all.

"I'm honored that you came to find me." I touch his arm, just the briefest pressure on his sleeve.

"Of course. I planned to spend some time with each of you today." He adjusts himself on the bench, angling his body more toward mine. "Did you enjoy the game? I noticed you playing it earlier too."

"It was all right," I reply. "Though I'm not very good at it."

"Oh?" One auburn brow arcs. "That last throw was excellent. You may have won that point if you'd stayed."

The flush that rises to my cheeks is entirely real. "Thank you. I had a lot of help." And here we are, talking about his brother. I need to alter this conversation and fast. "Though, I'm happy to give up a win to spend time with you."

He chuckles. "I'll remember that."

"I hope you do," I say honestly.

We talk about everything and nothing for a moment, and I savor it, eating it up like the refreshing cool breeze that drifts by.

When I spy a natural opening in the conversation, I take it. "I think it's wonderful that you're inviting some other courts to the ball."

"Oh? Eager to meet other fae, are you?" It's a tease from the glimmer in his eyes, but there's a slight barb in the words that I have to shove down and push away.

"Only so much as it's good to know one's neighbors, so to speak. But I think it could be a really good thing for the Court of Fire to have them visit. It's a chance to show how comfortable and competent you are in your reign. I know the courts have not mixed much in the past and relations have not always been good, but you could change that and create a new dawn for the Seelie fae."

"A new dawn," he muses while rubbing his chin. "I do like the sound of that."

"And maybe it could be nice to have closer allies, especially if things with those-who-shall-not-be-named go poorly?"

A strange look crosses Vasilius's face before he tips his head to the side and asks, "Those-who-shall-not-be-named?"

"Sorry, it's kind of a joke from my world." I briefly touch his leg before retracting my hand and bunching the fabric of my dress in my fingers. I drop my voice into barely a whisper. "I was referring to the Unseelie."

"Ah." His eyes darken. "Them. You'll be safe here, Mira." He pats my leg, and I nearly jump out of my skin at the unexpected touch. "Bound to me, they cannot take you away."

Not like they did the King of Air's mate.

He doesn't say it, but it lingers unspoken between us.

"I know you'll keep us safe." It's hard to imagine a threat out there with how calm and pleasant things are in the Court of Fire. Especially today, here in the garden, it's as idyllic a setting as they come.

He leans back with a sigh, closes his eyes, and stretches his arms out along the back of the bench. One brushes along my shoulder in the process, and I sit a little straighter, my abs tensing.

"If only all of my advisors had your confidence," he laments.

"They wouldn't be very good counsel if they always agreed with you though."

A light huff of air escapes through his nose. Vasilius turns his head my way and opens his eyes. "I suppose not."

"It must be hard to be a king." I lean in to him just a little. "Trying to balance everyone's expectations and still do what you think is best in your heart."

"You have no idea." He sighs. "Speaking of, it would be nice to stay here and relax, but I still have a few others I need to spend some time with."

"Oh." My stomach drops straight to the ground. "So soon?"

"I do wish I could stay here longer," he adds, sitting up a little in the seat. It's the rebound I need, the boost of courage for what I'd planned.

"Before you go…" I place my hand on his leg and leave it there this time as I pull my bottom lip between my teeth. "You see, I've been hoping…"

"Yes?" He leans in, mirth sparkling in his eyes. That outstretched arm of his curls in just a bit, urging me closer, and I go, leaning in until his scent fills my nose and my heart tries to pound straight through my ribs.

"Can I kiss you?" I blurt.

The corners of his lips curl up into a blinding smile. "I believe I would enjoy that."

I swallow and lick my lips. "Ah, good." My pitch rises as I sit a little straighter. "I'll just…"

I lean in all too awkwardly, a nervous laugh climbing up my throat. *Shit. It was supposed to be natural.*

Vasilius laughs, and before I have the time to consider whether it's at me or with me, he tugs me closer, cups my cheek with his free hand, and leans in to place his lips against mine.

My hand falls to his shirt, which does nothing to hide the rigid planes of muscle below. He's so warm, his spicy scent filling my nose. His lips are against mine, and at that moment, I feel…

Nothing.

Absolutely nothing.

Well, that's not entirely true. I feel like a teenager just learning to kiss again, all awkward and unsure of how I'm supposed to move and wondering if my breath smells bad. But the butterflies that I just *knew* would be there, that have been there the few times we've touched before?

They fall still and silent as death.

Vasilius gives a little groan of pleasure. His head tilts to the side as he moves to deepen the kiss, the tip of his tongue flicking against the seam of my lips.

My eyes are wide open—God, why are they open?—but his are closed, as if he's enjoying this, as if he feels something, even if I do not. And he's the king. I'm supposed to want this.

I *do* want it. Or I did.

I'm trying to become his wife, for goodness sake. I have to want him.

So, I part my lips, close my eyes, and try to enjoy the kiss, to forget that he's a king and there are probably people watching and just enjoy sharing this moment with someone. And maybe, for a brief moment, I'm successful. But the next thing I know, he's pulling back, his hand falling away from my face, and I can finally breathe again.

I pry my eyes open again and force a smile to my face. Vasilius looks me up and down with his hooded gaze, his attention so strong it's almost a caress in itself.

He has to know it wasn't great, right? Maybe he's just good at faking it?

"Well now," he says, "I will certainly remember that."

I force my smile wider and tuck a strand of hair behind my ears before glancing away. Remember it in a good way or a bad way? I want to ask, but don't.

"Thank you," I whisper, at a loss for words. All I want to do is run and hide, but there's no hiding from a king. Not to mention that it would go against my plans.

Damn it all to hell, how am I supposed to keep going with them now?

Vasilius takes my hand in his and places a kiss on the back.

"Of course," he says, exuding all his gentlemanly manner. Finally, he rises to his feet. He says something else by way of farewell, but I completely miss the words. They're drowned out by the pounding of my pulse in my ears, the panic rising in my brain, and the effort of keeping my smile in place.

Distantly, I watch him leave, counting the seconds until I can flee.

The number is entirely too low when I stand and make a beeline for the hedge maze, doing everything in my power not to run and not to look back.

CHAPTER 18

I TURN DOWN A path in the hedge maze, not looking or caring where I go.

"This is going great. So great," I mumble, my voice squeaking more than I'd ever admit.

I want this, don't I? I was so excited to get to Faery. And the prospect of marrying a king, becoming a queen? I was genuinely thrilled about it. Who doesn't want to be a royal? Yes, my uncle kind of shoved me onto this path, but it's one I wanted to go down.

I want to be here.

Entering this contest, winning it, could fix everything. As queen, I'd have more than enough money to support my family for generations. Check the box on keeping Mom and my brothers taken care of, as well as pleasing Uncle Matias and Aunt Dalia. Selena would be taken care of too. I'd get to stay in Faery, the world I've dreamed about all my life. I'd marry a great man who is handsome, respected, and powerful. *I* would be respected and powerful, not just some poor girl on the outskirts of the coven who doesn't fit in anywhere. It's the life I've dreamed about for years. It's what I want.

"But what if I don't want it?" I fling my hands down in exasperation as I round another corner, the hedges a blur of color in my periphery. I hardly notice them, or anything, beyond my thoughts racing one after another.

It's not like I didn't try. He was only going to pick one of us anyway, right? So, it's okay if it's not me. No one can say I embarrassed the family name. Hopefully, I'll still get some gifts or something to support the family. Maybe they'll even let me stay, you know, far away from here, where my uncle can't find me and call me an embarrassment or something? *Yes, Mira, excellent idea.*

I let out a groan and drop my face into my palms.

Damn it, this is not how things were supposed to go.

It was supposed to be magical. Fireworks and all that. He was supposed to realize he wanted me, I was supposed to want him, and we would live happily ever after like in a fairy tale.

A bird call snares my attention, and I glance up, taking in the bright blue sky above. One breath after another fills my lungs, calming some of my racing thoughts. I didn't know I wasn't going to feel anything. How could I know that?

"Maybe the feelings will come?" I ask a bird as it flies by. "Just because there's nothing now doesn't mean it can't be something, someday, right?"

But even as I say it, I know it for the lie it is. The king is not mine. He never will be. There would have been *something* there. The little sparks I'd felt around him wouldn't have faltered and gone out so completely.

"Not the kiss you'd hoped for?" says a deep voice.

The sudden question has me nearly leaping out of my skin. As it is, I spring off the ground, nearly falling in my haste to twist around. I might have screamed, had a gasp not lodged itself in my throat.

Lysandir stands in the middle of the pathway. His crossed arms are the only thing that belie the apparent carefree ease with which he stands there, legs spread, taking up far too much space.

"You." I fill the word with all the accusation I can muster. "Why are you here?"

"You appeared to be in distress, so I followed you to make sure you were okay."

Distress! I almost laugh at the nonsense of it all.

"I'm fine. Perfectly fine," I blurt.

His brows pinch, head twitching in apparent confusion before a look of clarity sparks in his eyes and his features smooth out. He sighs. "You humans and your lies."

I'm not lying, I want to say. But I am. I so am.

A hard look settles over his features. One hand lifts like he might reach for me, before he drops it again. "Mira, did my brother do something to you?"

Heat rushes to my face. I want to sink below the dirt and hide. "How much did you see?"

"Enough." He crosses his arms. "Kissing someone you hope to marry shouldn't leave you like this."

"Shouldn't it?" I ask, voice filled with bite. "When I know that he's probably kissing all the other women too?"

Lysandir winces at that. The small tingle of satisfaction I feel isn't nearly enough, but it's something.

"Still," he continues, "a kiss should make you feel something but not—"

The calm tone of his voice raises my hackles.

"The only one making me feel anything right now is you," I snap. He doesn't deserve my anger. Distantly, I know that. But all my walls are crumbling, and he's the only one nearby to fling the debris at.

"I was going to say, happiness. Joy. Pleasure," he replies with that same annoyingly even tone. "Not..." He gestures toward me. "So, what did he do, Mira?"

"He just kissed me, okay? Nothing else. He was perfectly respectable." A bit too much.

Lysandir crosses his arms again. Something flickers across his features that I can't decipher. "So, it wasn't him then, but your reaction to the kiss?"

The words land like a shove to my chest, and I step back, lips thin.

"Just leave me alone, okay?" *Let me wallow in peace for goodness sake!* I turn on my heel and hurry back down the pathway, as fast as I can go and still call it a walk. I don't need to look behind me to know that Lysandir follows. I can feel him. I always feel him, like he has his own kind of gravity that inevitably pulls me toward him.

I turn a corner, not slowing down. The path forks just ahead, and I make another quick right, hoping to lose him. Another two steps and the path splits again, so I make another sharp turn.

My feet skid on the dirt pathway as I come to an abrupt stop, taking in the sight before me. The narrow path has opened into a circular space with a fountain in the middle and a few benches around it, varying trails leading off in two other directions.

But that's not what has my eyes flying wide.

Adeline is locked in an embrace with one of the guards. His hand is fisted in her hair, tilting her head back so he can kiss her neck. A soft moan slips from her pink lips.

Adeline. Sweet, innocent Adeline, kissing someone who is decidedly not the king we're supposed to be wooing. It's against the rules. Treasonous. But beyond the shock of seeing her like this, there's a little thought whispering in my ear that's louder than all the rest.

You're not the only one.

Her cheeks are flushed, eyes closed in pleasure. But they could open at any moment, and she's at the perfect angle to see me standing there gawking like an idiot. It's not me she needs to worry about though.

I rush back around the corner, encountering Lysandir just a few steps from coming upon a scene that he *can't* see.

"Mira?" He looks me up and down, a question in his eyes as well as his words.

Without thinking, I wrap my fingers around his upper arm and try to haul him with me as I move past. "Let's go this way."

But I might as well be trying to move a tree for all that he budges.

"What..." He stares at my hand on his arm like it's an alien thing then back toward the direction I'd just come from.

Another ungentle tug and his attention whips back to me.

His gaze narrows. "There's something there."

Shit. Maybe they're done. Maybe he wouldn't see anything too damning, but every instinct in me screams that's not the case. He rolls his shoulder, trying to pull free from my grip, and I panic.

"Lysandir." I practically jump in front of him, blocking the way back. "Please."

There's a moment of hesitation, a slight widening of his eyes that makes me think he's listening to me. But then he glances past me, and my stomach drops straight to the ground.

So, I do the only thing that I know will stop him.

I grab his face with both hands, stretch up on the tips of my toes, and drag him down until I smash my lips against his.

The reaction is instant. My body jolts like I've been shocked. My chest constricts like my ribs are trying to reach my spine, and there's a sudden wobble in my legs that wasn't there a moment ago.

The kiss should be nothing. A distraction. A con.

But God, it feels like I've been knocked down by a wave and swept under. And those are Lysandir's arms wrapping around me, holding me up and cradling me like I'm something precious. At some point, I closed my eyes, and I open them, catching sight of his soft lashes along his closed lids. Something caught between a sigh and a moan rumbles amid our kiss, and he pulls me tighter.

Like he feels something too. Like this isn't a farce.

Like I'm not bound to his brother and trying to become his bride.

That thought douses me in ice, and I pull back, breathing hard and head spinning. Lysandir lets me go but not fully. His strong palm still rests against my lower back, the touch firm and possessive in a way that melts something in me.

But it shouldn't. It's not him I'm supposed to want, damn it.

Lysandir's eyes flutter open. The pupils are blown wide, leaving his eyes dark. His chest rises and falls, and all his attention is glued to my face.

"Mira."

The way he says my name has my insides flopping over themselves. He fills it with so much—heat and fire that have nothing to do with his magic. I can almost understand why women swoon.

A crunch of gravel and rustle of the hedges are the only warning before Adeline and her guard round the corner, but it's enough. Lysandir drops his hand and steps back so quickly I nearly fall, and do end up leaning back against the hedge, its stiff branches poking into my back.

"Oh, hello!" Adeline's voice is a little too high. "We thought we heard someone else here."

The giggle that comes out is so forced and off it's a dead giveaway for her nerves. The guard doesn't look at us, instead keeping his eyes averted toward the ground like a scolded kid caught stealing a cookie. Or in this case, a kiss.

Look more guilty, why don't you?

I recognize him now. Erymis, the guard assigned to her. He's the same one she often talks to after yoga. I thought it was just friendship, but clearly I was way wrong.

I shove off the bushes, wincing as a branch scrapes my forearm. "I just got a little overwhelmed at the party and Prince Lysandir walked with me to make sure I was okay." I spear him with a glance that dares him to say otherwise. "Very gallant of him."

"Oh, me too." Adeline shoves at her hair as if that could fix the section at the back that the guard thoroughly mussed. "Erymis kept me company. It was so nice of him."

Erymis studiously avoids looking at us and gives a little bow. "Since Lady Adeline has companions once more, I shall depart."

His words still hang in the air when he vanishes.

"Erymis ..." The dejection in her voice is so clear it's a wonder Lysandir hasn't mentioned anything about it. In fact, he hasn't spoken a word, and I've been too nervous to even look at him.

"Walk with me." I slide my arm through Adeline's and tug her alone like we're two Victorian ladies on promenade.

Lysandir falls into step somewhere behind us. If not for the steady feel of his gaze leaving tingles down my back, I might have thought he'd stayed behind. But no such luck. Every step back toward the party, all I can think about is our kiss. It's marked me like a scarlet letter across my chest, haunting me with the thought that somehow everyone will know what I did.

"Why are we going so fast?" Adeline asks.

The question drags me back to the moment, and I slow my pace. I hadn't even realized I was dragging us along like a champion speed walker.

"Don't you want to see the king?" It's a cruel jab, and I regret it the moment it's out.

Adeline flinches and pulls away, coming to an abrupt halt. "How much did you see?"

I drop my voice to a whisper. "Too much. And you should be glad I kept Lysandir from seeing it as well."

Said fae prince has stopped further back on the path, giving us some semblance of privacy, thank goodness.

A deep flush colors her cheeks below her freckles. "Mira, I can explain."

I sigh and loop my arm through hers, turning her back in the direction we were headed. "You don't need to. I won't tell."

Her head snaps toward me. "You won't?"

"Not a word."

"But why?" She leans her head back, almost like I've slapped her, as if this act of decency is some kind of trick or deception. "You could damn me." Her whisper is almost a hiss. "Destroy my chances."

"You're interested in someone else." I shrug. "That's no big deal."

She stares at the dirt as we walk. "It is here."

The reply is so soft I barely hear it.

And damn, don't I know it. The back of my neck burns at the memory of what I just did, the feel of Lysandir's lips against mine that I can't erase no matter how I try to block it out.

We round a corner, sounds of the party growing louder, and Adeline quickly looks up and over at me. "And what were you doing in the maze?"

"Taking a moment to breath, as I said."

She cocks one brow. "With the prince?"

I attempt a shrug with our linked arms.

"He followed me. Apparently, he's good at that." I shoot a glare over one shoulder before we make another left.

"Wrong way," Lysandir calls from behind us.

I jerk to a halt, more annoyed than I have any right to be. How can I long for him in one moment and loathe him the next? Adeline and I turn around and head down the other side of the split in the path.

"Thank you," I reply with a little courteous nod.

Lysandir gives a little bow and sweep of his arm in return, which I swear is a mocking gesture meant to get under my skin. Bastard.

Finally, we make it out of the maze, and Adeline sucks in a deep, steady breath as she takes in the many fae milling about. Her arm tightens on mine.

"You promise you won't tell?" she asks, leaning in so only I can hear her.

"Promise."

She untangles from me but then takes my hand in hers and gives a little squeeze. "Thank you. For that and...understanding."

More than you know.

The moment she hurries off, the air around me grows thick and tense. I'd swear the temperature rises too—and this is the Court of Fire, so maybe it does. It wouldn't surprise me if Lysandir's presence alone could affect that. Or maybe he only has that effect on me.

Tension coils around my chest, leaving it tight and hollow all at once as he steps to my side. In his hand, he holds the thick green stems of two massive, red flowers. A sweet, heady scent wafts from them, only addling my senses further. If you could drug someone with a whiff of a flower, this one would do it.

"Take these." Lysandir holds them out to me.

They might as well be snakes for how terrifying the offer is.

"You're giving me flowers? Here?" *In front of everyone?* I stare at him wide-eyed. My God, he really does want to paint a scarlet letter on me.

"Hurry and give one to your friend." He practically shoves the stalks at me. "Fae sense of smell is much greater than a human's. These are pungent and will help cover the scent."

"The scent of what?"

Lysandir stares at me hard, his face impassive and still save for a blink of his eyes. The answer hits me square in the chest.

"She—They weren't—" I blurt.

But he knows.

Damn it all, he knows exactly what they were doing, despite my attempted distraction.

"Please." I reach for him, dropping my hand just before I grab his sleeve. His gaze snaps to it, eyes widening as he follows the path of my hand as it drops. "I promised. You can't tell."

His gaze snaps back to my face, his form still cold and impassive like the fae royal he is, other than his eyes which swirl with emotion.

"Please." The readiness with which I'd drop to my knees and beg him shocks me. "Don't give her—them—away. For me. Please."

His throat bobs, the only sign of emotion in his features. Finally, his impassive façade cracks, and his shoulders droop on a sigh. "I won't."

The single phrase releases the noose of panic from my neck.

"No one will hear of it from me." His stance loosens, and he rubs the back of his neck. "But she has to be more careful. Keep her distance for now, disguise the scent."

I nod. The advice is for her, but I can't help feel like it's more for me than anything. And with that, all the emotions of moments ago rush back, flooding me with a fire that makes me want to char to ash right there.

"What I did, back there in the hedges... I—" I want to say I'm sorry, that I regret it, that it was a trick, but the words don't come out, almost like the magic that binds the fae to truth is trying to hold me to it as well.

"You wanted to keep me from seeing whatever you saw."

My lips wrinkle themselves up then flatten out. It's true. I did, but hearing him say it sounds so callous. And what I felt in that moment was anything but that.

He steps closer, and I suck in a breath, but there's almost no air to inhale.

"I won't tell anyone about that either." His hand closes over mine where I clutch the stems.

The touch has me nearly jumping out of my skin, and from the way he stiffens and his hand tightens on mine, I know he feels something too. But any hesitation is there and gone in a flash. He guides the flowers up until the soft petals brush against my cheek then across my lips.

The party disappears as I stare into his eyes of molten gold, the crimson blooms a slow blur of movement at the bottom of my vision.

"To cover the scent." He releases my hand, and I let the blooms drop down to my chest.

Because I can't have his scent on me. Because someone might know, might suspect. I don't have the heart to tell him Vasilius could already smell him on me, had already commented on it earlier. At least he didn't have reason to suspect it anything other than innocent assistance in a yard game.

But what we did in the maze... It might have been impulsive, a tool to distract, but the lingering effects are anything but innocent.

"Thank you." It's all I can come up with before I turn and hurry after Adeline.

Staying with Lysandir a moment longer, the strange blooms flooding my senses, would have led to disaster. Because there's one thing I know with certainty as I search for my friend.

Kissing Lysandir was everything.

Magic and heat and a force all its own.

It's what kissing Vasilius should have been but wasn't and I know deep down could never be. The rush of feeling in that moment, the way I can still feel his lips against mine and taste him on my tongue, has to mean something. It does mean something, the thing I've been trying to deny for days and can't any longer.

I've gone and fallen for the wrong fae royal.

CHAPTER 19

F IA BRUSHES MY CHEEKS with some of her special shimmering powder that literally leaves me glowing. "Lovely." She smiles at me in the mirror and sets down the brush. "I think you're ready for luncheon with the royal family."

If she notices the fragility in my forced grin, she doesn't comment on it. I am not ready. Can anyone be ready to go to lunch with two men they kissed the day before? Especially when the one you can't stop thinking about *isn't* the one you're supposed to be wanting and kissing? Oh, and their mother will be there. Let's not forget that awkward tidbit.

"If I'm not, it won't be because of your artistry." I turn my face this way and that. My insides might be a twisted-up mess, but I can still appreciate the wonders Fia works. "You do such an incredible job every time. Seriously."

"It is my job." She winks. "Besides, nothing is too good for the potential future Queen of Fire."

The false smile falls right off my face. Right. That. I can't bear to tell her that I'm pretty sure I'm not going to be the queen. Even if Vasilius picked me, could I tell him yes? I shake my head and push the thought away.

"On that note, have you heard anything?" I ask instead. "Any rumors about who the king might be favoring?"

Fia plops onto the tufted stool near my chair. "Well," she starts, leaning in conspiratorially, "the king has had more dates with Bailey than anyone else." Her voice falls to a whisper, not that there is anyone else in the room to hear us. "It's said she's quite taken with him too."

That, I know for sure. She's been moon-eyed and sighing for days.

"Although," Fia says, voice rising again, "some of the other attendants think it's just a passing fancy, but that might be wishful thinking, hoping that their contender will win the crown. I've heard good things about you too though. You're definitely in the top five." She giggles.

"That's good to hear," I say, only because I know it's what she expects to hear. I should be pleased, but the emotion doesn't come. If anything, the news makes everything I'm feeling worse.

"Perhaps today will improve your standing even more," she continues. "It's said the king plans to spend more alone time with at least two of you before the ball. And then there's the ball itself! It'll be such a good opportunity to be seen with the king. All of the advisors will be there, nobles from other courts, even several royals, if the rumors turn out to be true. They'll all get to see you with the king and see how good of a match you would make. That'll be important, you know. If the advisors think the other courts favor you, it will influence who they advise the king to choose."

Many of the women are excited about the ball, but the looming event fills me with dread. Mingling with many fae and humans I don't know? Not my favorite. Knowing that our families have been invited and I'll likely have to confront my uncle again after realizing how much I no longer want to win the crown? Dreadful. The only bright spot will be if Selena comes, but even then, I know I'll be a center of endless attention, even more so than the opening ball where at least I was somewhat unknown for much of the time until the presentation. This time, everyone will know exactly who I am and who I may become.

"Don't be nervous." Fia pats my leg. "I'll make sure you're the most stunning candidate there. You'll be renowned throughout the Seelie courts."

A little humorless laugh slips between my lips.

"And your family should be there too," she says. "Won't that be nice?"

I'm sure my uncle will be. He won't miss the chance to make sure I'm behaving myself and doing my damnedest to win the crown. All of the human families are invited. It should be safe enough. After all, why would the Unseelie dare to attack an event with so many powerful Seelie fae present? That's assuming they could even get this far into the territory at all, which everyone seems to think is unlikely. Plus, it doesn't take a genius to understand why King Vasilius and the rest of the Court of Fire would want so many humans present when their rivals come to visit.

Humans are power. Our spirits fuel fae magic, and so the more of us around, the more of a show of strength it is. To say nothing of the king showing off all the human women vying to become his bride. His has his pick—a far cry from some of the other courts, where humans are rare. Why on earth members of our coven don't defect and try to appeal to those fae is beyond me. Loyalty, I guess. Tradition? Still, if Uncle Matias really wanted to raise our family's status and wealth, you'd think he'd strike up an alliance with say, the Court of the Forest, where humans are a rarity. Surely, they'd shower a human family with wealth if a member or two decided to live with them. He could have pawned me off there—packed me up the moment I came of age and sent me away. I'd have gone, probably, despite my mother's outcry.

My chest squeezes tight at the thought of her. I miss her. I really do. My brothers too. Since none of them have the gift, they can't come to visit me, and I'm bound to the king, unable to leave, until this competition is done. Mom's letters have just seemed sad. Supportive in her way, but the undercurrent of loss and longing is still there.

I should write to her, send something back with my uncle, though what to say is always a struggle. *I'm doing great, Mom! Don't worry.* It'd be true, but it doesn't feel like enough and is a far cry from the promise that I'll be back soon, which I know she wants but I can't give. This is my life, and I'm finally living it. Even if I don't win the crown, I don't see being in a rush to move back home. A visit? Sure.

But after kissing Lysandir... I'd really like to see where that could go.

"I suppose—" I begin but am saved from further response by a knock at the door.

"Come in," I call.

The door creaks open and Tharin fills the entry. A small, thin box is held in his hands.

"A gift for Lady Mira," he says, but for some reason he doesn't look happy about that.

Fia gasps and leaps to her feet. "From the king?"

Tharin fully enters the room, closing the door behind him. "No," he says as he crosses the room to us. "This comes from Prince Lysandir."

If it wasn't for the makeup Fia had just applied, I'd probably have turned as red as my dress. If anyone has any suspicions about something between us, this is *not* going to help.

"The prince?" Fia looks as wide-eyed as I feel.

Tharin comes to a stop in front of me and holds out the box. "Lady Mira?"

"Thank you." I take the shimmering gold box and set it in my lap. It snares my full attention. A curiosity and damnation at once. If the box had just appeared in my room, I'd be giddy. That fluttering joy is in there somewhere, but my nerves swallow it up.

"Why would the prince send a gift?" Fia asks, clearly skeptical. God help me, I don't have a good answer for her.

God doesn't answer, but Tharin thankfully does. "He must favor or admire her," he replies. "And don't you think that's a good thing, Fia? Whoever will be our future queen should be well-liked by the rest of the royal family, wouldn't you agree?"

Despite the words out of his mouth, it doesn't feel like he agrees with them. Does he not like Lysandir? But the other night in the library, I'd have sworn they seemed familiar with one another, more than just casual acquaintances.

"Oh! Well, of course!" Fia twists my direction. "Then this is a great turn of events!"

She nearly vibrates with enthusiasm, but it's to Tharin I glance. His lips twitch up in one corner. He knows, damn it. Somehow, he knows and yet still managed to lead Fia to a different conclusion with a few clever suggestions that I have no doubt he thought up before coming in here.

"Well, Lady Mira. Why don't you open it?" He doesn't seem the type that wants me to be uncomfortable or thrust into an awkward situation, but he's certainly making a show of this gift.

"Might as well," I reply.

The box isn't tied up with ribbons or sealed any way that I can tell, so I grab the lid and slowly tug it off. Fia stretches on her tiptoes and leans in for a better view—not that she can't see perfectly from where she's standing just two feet away.

Inside are three long, skinny tubes of varying colors fitted down into a silken pillow of sorts. Each one narrows to a metallic point at one end.

My breath catches.

Not tubes. Pens. He got me pens.

I pluck the center one from its cushioned holder and hold it up to the light. A shimmering substance, this one in varying shades of green and gold, fills the glass chamber.

"What are those?" Fia asks.

But I ignore her and swirl around in my chair toward the desk, careful not to spill the box and its precious contents. I gently set it on the desktop and grab a piece of paper. My heart races as I touch the tip to the page and write the first thing that comes to mind: Lysandir.

Tharin chuckles behind me. "Pens. Though it seems Lady Mira figured that out quickly."

Lysandir's name shimmers in tones of sparkling gold and green that blend effortlessly as the pen shifts from one color to the next at random.

He didn't just get me pens.

He got me special fae, metallic pens, like the ones he'd mentioned in the library.

Emotion burns at the corners of my eyes. I pull my lip between my teeth, holding it in. It's so simple and so thoughtful at the same time. Between his reaction to the kiss and this gift, one might think he was trying to win me away from his brother. But that can't be right. Fae just like to give gifts. Everyone says that.

Still, it fills me with a deep warmth that I know will linger just as long or longer than the feel of his lips on mine.

"Should I tell the prince you appreciate the gift?" Tharin asks.

I stare at Lysandir's name on the page, suddenly embarrassed at my choice of words for testing the pens. I add a comma after his name, a short and swirling "thank you," and then sign my name, like I'd meant to write it as a letter all along. I quickly fold it up and hand it to Tharin. "Yes, please pass along my thanks for the thoughtful gift."

With care, I set the pen back in its box so that I don't clutch it to my chest like the treasure it is and give myself away further.

"Do you have any other letters you would like sent?" he asks.

Guilt swells again at the thought of my mother and brothers. Selena too.

"None today," I reply.

Maybe I'll write tonight. Not maybe—I *will*. I need to. I have to send something home with my uncle for my mother. I could use my new pens. I glance at them on the table, my spirits lifting.

Yes, I think I'll do just that.

Tharin nods. "I will pass this along to Prince Lysandir."

I really need to figure out what he knows and how. And why his moods on the matter are all over the place.

"I'm sure she can do that in at luncheon in just a few minutes," Fia remarks.

I barely hold back a sigh. If rumors are spreading, things could get really awkward really quickly, and I might be just about to walk into an epic disaster.

CHAPTER 20

I F MY STOMACH DOESN'T settle, I'm not going to be able to eat a bite at this luncheon. Actually, I'll be lucky if my breakfast doesn't end up all over the floor or in a flower pot. Adeline slides into step beside me as the guards guide us toward wherever we'll be dining. The look in her eyes might make a lesser person wither, but I have nothing to apologize for.

One of her brows arcs up.

I give a slight shake of my head. Of course I didn't rat her out.

Her shoulders lift in a visible sigh, and she turns more fully, mouthing a quick *thank you*. The other women chat quietly or marvel at the soaring stained-glass windows along one wall that send a kaleidoscope of colors dancing over us and the otherwise pale marble hall.

I really would love to know what she's thinking, entering a competition to marry the king and then falling for a guard, one who's suspiciously absent today.

Not that I'm one to talk.

Two double doors are pulled open at the end of the hallway. Through the women in front of me, I catch sight of a long table, high-backed chairs lining its sides. The sight makes me skip a step and nearly halt as my heart pounds against my ribs. The urge to turn and fake an illness is strong, but Adeline slips her arm through mine and pulls me along.

"Nervous about seeing *him* again?" she whispers.

If anyone overheard her, they'd probably assume she meant the king, but I know better. So does she. I really don't think she saw

Lysandir and me kiss, but the similarity of our situations wasn't completely lost on her.

"Of course not," I reply.

She pats my arm as if we're closer friends than we really are. "It's okay. I always am, even though I want to see him."

My brows pinch. She makes it sound like things have been going on far longer than the days we've been here. That can't be, can it? Though how much do I really know about these other women? The answer leaves me feeling hollow. I've seen them as one thing—competition. An obstacle to be overcome so that I can make my family proud and live out my dreams of spending time in Faery. But not all of them are new to this world like I am. Some may have visited for several years. Didn't my uncle say as much? That I might have an advantage because I was a fresh, new face? Adeline herself talked about visiting before and how her pocket watch helped her keep some sense of normalcy. Maybe she has had a thing for her guard far longer than this competition, but it still doesn't help me understand why she'd enter—

The answer resonates through me like the deep sound of the doors closing behind us as we enter the room. What if she didn't have a choice? What if her family forced her into entering much like mine did?

There's no time to contemplate it further as the tittering picks up and I spy the reason why. Vasilius beams at the gaggle of us where he stands next to Queen Elaine. Light pours into the room—or large balcony rather. Though a high roof covers our heads, the walls, save the one we entered through, are a series of open archways that let the light and warm air pour in. While the king looks pleased, the dowager's expression is more shielded, and she leans heavily on her cane. But I don't take the time to ponder that as I scour the room searching for another face.

I stretch on my toes, leaning side to side, and though I spy some of the king's advisors who I did not expect to be here, I can't see Lysandir.

"Absent?" Adeline whispers, finally releasing my arm.

The breath that had been lodged in my throat slips out in a sigh, and even I'm not sure if it's relief or longing.

"That could be...good?" she adds.

For her, maybe. And probably for me too. At least I'll be able to pay attention, but something about it leaves a stinging burn on my chest.

Vasilius welcomes us all, as do the others, but his smile is a little too broad, his words careful. The little bit of relief I savored evaporates as he gestures for us to take a seat at the table. We have assigned seats this time, probably to save us from the near brawl that threatens to break out as the women scramble to see who can sit closest to the king. After what Fia told me earlier, I'm not surprised when I see that Bailey is one of the ones sitting at the king's side.

Good for her.

In fact, I'm rather glad to have a seat near Elaine and farther from the king. It makes things far less awkward after yesterday.

"Before we begin, you'll have noticed that our party is a little different than planned," Elaine says, her strong, clear voice in sharp contrast to her aged appearance. It's easy to see why she has such respect from the court, not to mention the king. No matter the effects of age and her human fragility, she carries herself with dignity and authority—it hangs about her like a cloak that she never needs to take off. "My son, Lysandir, is absent today, and I feel you should all know why."

My stomach bottoms out. Adeline stares at me hard from across the table, and even though no one else turns their gaze from the dowager just a seat away from me, it *feels* like they do. I grip the seat beneath me so hard that I feel a fingernail give way against the wood.

"The Unseelie have breached our boarders and harassed a set-tlement," Elaine says.

Gasps ring out around the table. I blink, my brows knitting as some of the tension loosens from my shoulders. The Unseelie? Of all the things I expected, that was not it.

"Was anyone injured?" Zoe asks.

"What happened?" Grace asks at the same time.

Elaine raises a hand, calling for silence. "Prince Lysandir and Captain Avara are investigating with a squadron as we speak, but know that we will not let such atrocities continue."

Investigating. I shift in my seat. It implies the attack is over, but if they sent someone with his authority and a whole squadron of guards, it cannot be without risk.

"The ball," Gabriella says. "Will it be safe for our families?"

"The Unseelie would be foolish to attack while the other fae delegations are present, and we'd feel their presence at our wards far before they could ever hope to make it remotely close to the capital," Advisor Danai says with calm surety.

A round of murmured agreements follows, but I'm far less concerned about the upcoming ball than whatever Lysandir and the others are facing presently.

"Is the conflict ongoing? Prince Lysandir, and the others," I tack on quickly, "are they at risk?"

"The conflict with the Unseelie is always ongoing," Advisor Memnon grumbles from his seat next to Adeline. A bang of his tightly clenched fist on the table rattles the dishes. "We should take the offensive. Stop them before they can cause further harm."

Advisor Efthymi lets out a dramatic sigh and leans back in their chair as if they've heard this speech a million times.

"This is hardly the time for a council discussion," Elaine says. And though her voice never rises is pitch or volume, the rebuke is clear enough for Memnon to snap his mouth shut and frown toward the other end of the table.

"Indeed," Vasilius echoes. But his voice lacks the softness of his mother's, as does the hard look in his gaze as he stares across the room at nothing. "But I should be there to deal with them myself. To show that the Court of Fire is not to be trifled with."

"Why aren't you?" The table falls deathly silent at Bailey's question.

Vasilius twists his head to stare at her, expression unreadable. A beat passes. Then two. I can't help but sink back in my chair, bracing for the worst.

A huff of air slips from his nose, and the king's features even out into a half smile that's only for her. Thank God it was Bailey who asked and not anyone else. The thick bubble of tension seems to slip away as several of the women's gazes dart between one another before settling back on the king who has yet to speak, caught in a silent conversation with the woman at his side.

I'm starting to think they don't intend to let us in on it when Vasilius raises his arm and taps on the binding marks encircling his wrist. "Remember our bond? If I were to shift to the edge of my territory, for example, you would feel a strong tug on your bond mark that would persist until I returned. But for me, bound to you all, the pull would be excruciating."

When he initially bound us, I never considered that—that the protection the bonds offers us might have a negative consequence for him. Surely, they thought through that beforehand, but I wonder if they regret it now.

"So, I cannot go. Not unless you all go with me," he finishes.

And there's no way he'd take a bunch of human women into a war zone.

Bailey's brows scrunch. "But if it's for the good of the court..."

Vasilius shakes his head before finally turning to look at the rest of us. "My brother and Captain Avara are capable of dealing with the incursion for now. They'll see that things are set right and our border is resecured."

What's probably supposed to be a reassuring grin breaks across his face, but it does little to settle my nerves.

"But," he begins once more, this time with a pointed look at his stepmother, "once the ball is over, we may need to move to a city closer to the border so that I can address this threat myself."

Elaine gives a dramatic huff. "Enough on that." She claps once, the sound ringing through the open space. At once, fae servers snap into motion, bringing platters of food and pitchers of drink toward the table. "Let's move on to happier topics, shall we?"

Conversation picks up. Food is scooped onto my plate. But I can't summon much appetite for either. One thing is for sure, it's going to be a long luncheon, but for entirely different reasons than I expected.

CHAPTER 21

F OR THREE DAYS, I don't see Lysandir. We receive little news about the Unseelie attack, other than there were limited casualties and the wards that protect the court have been restored.

Worse, I have another one-on-one date with the king. It was as painful as I feared, trying to pretend to be into him and enjoying myself when most of my thoughts were with his brother somewhere at the edge of the territory. The king invited me to watch a performance by some fae dancers. Thoughtful, actually, though as I feared, they're definitely better than me. At least we didn't have to talk much though—or rather, I didn't have to hear more hunting stories.

At the end of the date, when he leaned in for a kiss, I successful faked a yawn and managed to ask enough questions to distract him from trying again. If I were to go simply by logic, I probably should have kissed him. It was expected. It's weird that I didn't. But I just couldn't bring myself to.

I twirl one of the pens Lysandir gave me between my fingers, watching the ink shimmer in the light from the fae lamp on my desk. I'd started to write in my notebook. Stopped. Started again. And then stopped once more when it became clear my thoughts were a jumbled mess not deserving of being written down.

Did Lysandir get my thank you letter yet? Does he know how much I like the gift? Probably not. When I cornered Tharin earlier and asked directly if Prince Lysandir had returned, he told me that he hadn't, but not to worry, that the prince was capable and would be fine.

My cheeks flame at the memory. He had the nerve to smirk about it too, like he knew exactly what I was asking and why. A good guard should be observant, but I could use a little less inspection on that front. Though if he suspects something, at least he hasn't told anyone about it. That I know of anyway.

A knock sounds at my door, and I jump in my seat. The pen slips and nearly clatters to the tabletop before I grab it at the last moment. *Lucky save.* I sigh to myself and place it back in its holder.

"Come in!" I call to whoever is at the door. I expect Fia or one of the guards, but that's not who enters.

"Hey, Mira," Grace calls in her cheery voice as she saunters into the room.

"Evening," Alex says before closing the door behind her.

It's after dinner, but these two aren't dressed for bed. The opposite actually. My brows pinch as I take them in. Grace's hair definitely wasn't that perfectly wavy earlier this evening, nor was she wearing the gorgeous, flowing gown she has on now, which flutters with the colors of sunset. Alex's heels give her a few extra inches—not that she needs them, tall as she already is—and her sleek one-shoulder romper screams of a night at the club.

But I know I didn't get the date wrong. The ball is tomorrow. Vasilius has been busy greeting arrivals from the other courts, and we've all been tucked carefully away in the parlor, bored out of our minds. Hence why I retreated early.

"What are y'all up to?" I ask as Grace plops unceremoniously on my bed, bouncing a little on the edge of the soft mattress.

"Do you want to ask her, or should I?" Grace asks Alex.

The latter crosses her arms and leads against the post of my canopy bed. "This was your idea."

"Well"—Grace wags a finger at her—"if we're being accurate, it was really Cora's idea."

"Cora?" I rock back in my seat. Not the person I would expect Grace and Alex to be going along with. In fact, I was pretty sure they disliked her as much as me. Did something change?

Grace shrugs. "Okay, so I don't normally like her, but this totally sounded like a good idea, and you know how boring things have been lately."

That I do. "So, what is it?"

She glances at Alex again, and when she remains silent, Grace continues, "We're going to crash a pre-ball party!" She squeals. "Aaaand we thought you might come with us?"

"To a party," I echo, slightly dumb founded. "We're allowed to go?"

At this, Alex finally unfurls her arms and leans off the post. "Apparently so. There was one last night for early arrivals, and Cora, Katherine, and Gabriella all went."

"It's a good chance to meet other fae. They'll be mostly Fire Court, but there might be other courts too. We got the impression this is a regular thing." Grace talks with her hands, moving them around in front of her like an orchestra conductor. "Anyhow, we can't all marry the king, so it can't hurt to meet other fae and keep our options open, as it were."

"Better than our families demanding we return after this is over," Alex mutters.

Grace winces. "Right. If we have connections here, it's easier to argue staying."

"The fae want humans here. Why would they ever kick us out?" I ask. It makes no sense.

In fact, it's a wonder they don't just outright demand that we all stay and pair us off with other powerful fae after the king has taken his pick. It would make sense for the good of their court. Though I suppose that could offend humans, and that's the last thing they want to do. Piss off gifted humans who could withdraw their willingness to come and turn off the tap on their magic, just like was done to the Court of the Forest generations ago? No fae wants that.

I'm still stewing over the possibilities when Alex speaks again.

"The fae wouldn't. Never. But families like ours..." She looks at Grace, and something passes between the two of them. "I'm sure you have an idea of how they can be. 'Everything for the good of the family, the coven,'" she says in a fake deep voice. "'If you can't secure a good match in Faery, then return here and continue the line.'"

Grace sighs, her normal spark suddenly dim. "I'm not sure how it is for you, but my family didn't want me to come here. They wanted a cousin of mine to come instead. Pretty, graceful." She sneers. "Skinny."

"So, if you don't land the king, they'll be disappointed and insist you return?" I ask.

She huffs. "I don't think there's much chance of him picking me, but if we make a good impression and some of the other fae are interested, at least we should get to stay." She glances up at Alex, who nods, solemnly. "Anyhow—" She shoves off the bed, her tone turning light again. "Do you want to come? Solidarity in numbers and all that?"

Would Uncle Matias demand that I return if I fail to woo the king? He'd be disappointed for sure. He might take that out on my mom and brothers—financially anyway. But if I could catch Lysandir's eye, if the prince possibly feels just a little bit of what I do, could that soften my uncle's ire? A prince is still an amazing catch, right?

My mind picks that moment to taunt me, reminding me of something I've been trying very hard to forget. Lysandir mentioned already having feelings for someone, even if said woman hasn't returned them. If he's loved for so long, would there be room for someone else? He definitely kissed me back, but it's possible to kiss people you don't care for. I would know.

The truth is, I don't know how Lysandir feels. I can hope all day. I can want and pine and all the things, but who knows when I'll even get to see him again. The king could make his choice tomorrow, and this whole thing could end.

And even if he doesn't, Lysandir's heart may already belong to someone else.

"All right, let me get changed," I say.

Grace claps her hands and bounces in place. "See? I told you Mira would come with us."

CHAPTER 22

I F SOMEONE WOULD HAVE told me months ago that the fae had night clubs, I'd have laughed my ass off. That totally wasn't covered in the coven's records. It didn't fit any of my imaginings either, which were mostly painted in my mind as magical, willowy settings with soaring ceilings, colorful flora, and tall, graceful fae floating about like celestial beings. And truthfully, a lot of Faery has been like that. But tonight, I've learned that Faery contains multitudes, and some of them aren't that different from the human realm at all.

Drinks are free for humans—an especially dangerous temptation when they're all glasses of bubbly fae wine that are way stronger than the human variety—the lights have been turned down low, and well-clad fae mingle on onyx floors shot through with ribbons of crimson. The room would be spacious if not crammed with people. The low ceiling doesn't help the feeling either. In fact, it's the opposite of many rooms here, in that it's more contained and enclosed with solid walls, save the far one which leads onto a terrace and down into one of the many courtyards.

True to what the others said, the guards don't stop us from coming, though Tharin gives me a disapproving look and follows closely after us. He's been lingering against the wall the whole time we've been here too, along with another of our guards. I suppose they want to make sure no one gets too cozy with the king's potential brides, which is totally fair.

If Grace and Alex were worried about finding an interested fae, they shouldn't be. It doesn't seem to matter that we may be the king's intended. Many of the fae here are more than eager to spend time with us. And honestly, it's exhausting. The endless questions are like a job interview that never ends. I've also taken way too many sips of the damnable wine in an effort to avoid talking, if even for a moment.

"I'm going to get some air," I say the moment the fae female I've been speaking with opens her mouth to ask yet another question.

"Oh but—" The male next to her begins.

"I'm sorry." I paste on the best smile I can. "I'll be back in just a little bit."

Or never.

Thank God humans can lie. It's so helpful. I don't want to bail on Grace and Alex, not when they seem nearly as uncomfortable as me. But I do need a moment, or I'm going to scream. Or say something entirely un-queen-like. I'd have to be a fool to think that an outburst here wouldn't make it back to the king or at least the dowager. The dowager certainly gives the impression of knowing everything that goes on in this place, no matter how minute.

Is that what I'd be expected to do too, if I became queen?

I nearly shudder as I sidestep another fae who reaches for me, a question falling from their lips that I don't stop to hear.

The terrace beckons, offering the illusion of peace. An image that's quickly broken when I step beyond the walls of the room and out under the night sky. The press of bodies is thinner here, but there are still a number of fae around, ones who immediately notice the human who has stepped into their midst, even though I'm not the only one.

Cora stands amid a cluster of fae, a drink in hand, and the laughter on her face drops right off as she takes me in, her features morphing into a scowl.

I'm not here to steal your spotlight, I wish I could say. How she manages to enjoy so much attention, I'll never know. Maybe that trait would make her a good queen. She certainly would never fade into some man's shadow.

I turn abruptly and head for the flight of wide marble stairs leading down into the courtyard.

Lush, green vegetation spreads out before me in the expansive open space, tall bushes and trees soaring toward the sky and offering shelter and privacy to the various portions of the space. The oppressive blanket of sound that had surrounded me is quieter here. Bits of conversation drift down into the courtyard. The hum of distant music weaves through the night. But it's so much quieter. For the moment, I can breathe again, especially since it doesn't appear that anyone followed me down the steps—yet.

Though that's bound to happen if I keep standing here, so I move off into the foliage. Thank goodness for wide heels that fit like a dream and don't sink into the grass.

I'm not alone out here either though. Laughter rises nearby, at least half a dozen voices by the sound of it. I sigh. Of course some of the fae would have migrated down here too. Can't say I blame them.

I'm about to turn and head in a different direction, when the laughter quiets down and someone says, "I saw several of your humans enjoying the gathering tonight."

I skid to a halt. *Your humans?* The fine hairs on the back of my neck stand on end. There's only one fae they could mean.

"So, I've heard." A deep chuckle follows.

My heart pounds against my ribs. That's definitely Vasilius. We'd been told he was busy welcoming guests, but I suppose that was hours ago.

"And to think you choose to be here with us instead." More laughter follows.

A wise woman would leave. I've heard enough to know this conversation isn't meant for me, but it's certainly about me, or partially me, and that thought reels me in like a fish. How can I *not* listen in? Quietly as I can, I creep nearer through the courtyard.

"You're not at all worried someone might take an interest in one or two?" someone asks.

"Who would dare when they could be mine?" Vasilius asks, though the question is entirely rhetorical.

Something hard settles in the base of my stomach as I draw near, careful to keep to the shadows. Multiple someones would dare apparently. Adeline's lover Erymis, and then Lysandir... Hell, if Vasilius knew I kissed his brother, he may lose it. My cheeks flame. The lingering taste of the wine on my tongue turns sour. Lysandir may not have initiated the kiss, but he wasn't the first to end it either.

"Though, I suppose," the king drawls, "I'll have to settle on one eventually."

"Do you though?" comes a female voice, a little giggle following the wake of her words.

The sound stabs through my center. It releases something foul that slithers around in chest and demands appeasement.

Light spills from around the hedge ahead. I ease up to it and peer through a thinner area of the branches. The sight beyond knocks the breath from my lungs. Vasilius sits on a wide stone bench, a lithe fae woman with bronzed skin and dark hair draped across his lap. One arm is curled around her back, holding her close as she traces a longer finger down the curve of his jaw. A handful of others look on, unfazed by their king's actions.

What in the fucking hell?

"You can't tell me you find any of them more beautiful than me," the female croons. Her dress—if you can call it that, given the limited material—is all open on one side, held together with bits of ribbon that do nothing to hide the curve of her breasts, her ass.

The king smirks, his gaze dropping from her face to her breasts and the peaked nipples I can see from here. "Ah, but can you give me power? You know that bonding a human is necessary to reach my full potential."

"Let's not forget powerful heirs," a male says, raising his glass in mock toast. Others mutter their assent. I recognize this male's attire, the clothing that mark him as the king's personal guard. Looks like their relationship is as much personal as professional.

"And my mother insists," Vasilius adds with a half shrug.

The fae female pouts. "Just because she insists doesn't mean you have to settle for less."

A dark look crosses Vasilius's face, and he slides out from under the woman. She gives a yip of protest, nearly tumbling to the ground.

"A human is more, not less," he says, "even if it goes against my...inclinations. I will do my duty."

Duty. That's all this is to him.

I'd heard the rumors that he wasn't drawn to humans. Fia mentioned as much too. It's not a secret. But hearing it from his own lips? Seeing him openly flirt with some fae woman while supposedly dating all of us to pick a bride?

I think I'm going to be sick.

I stumble away from the hedge and hurry in the opposite direction.

There's no love between the king and me. I knew that before. But the others? Bailey? My heart clenches at the thought of her. She might love him, and I thought...

God. Is it all an act? Is every smile, every kind word from the king, every moment he spends with us a lie? Duty? Is that really all? Some task he must complete?

An open hallway leading into the palace looms before me. It's not where I entered from, but I hardly care. It's away from the courtyard, from all that just upended my evening.

"Mira." The harsh, masculine whisper causes me to skip a step.

Without slowing, I twist my head back toward the voice. Tharin stalks after me, silent as a ninja.

"Wait." The word barely teases my ears.

But I don't stop. I can't. If I do, it will all become too real. Just seeing him—someone, anyone—has my emotions tumbling after one another and getting tangled together until I'm not sure if I'll laugh or cry or something else.

The clack of my heels on the marble accompanies me once I reach the hallway. It's empty at this hour, a strange comfort, though I have no doubt Tharin follows behind.

As if my thoughts summon him, he says my name again, louder this time.

I turn a corner, pressing onward, though I have no idea where I'm headed. This part of the palace is new to me. My destination doesn't matter, as long as it's away from the courtyard and the king.

"Your quarters are the other way," Tharin says. "Let me show you back. Or shift you."

The hallway ends in a T-shaped intersection just ahead, pathways branching off right and left.

I look back over my shoulder as I plow ahead. "I can't. I just—"

He halts. Tharin's eyes go wide.

"I need—" I smack into something firm and bounce backward.

But it's no wall that reaches out and grips my upper arm to steady me. The scent that envelopes me makes my head spin more than the wine I drank earlier in the evening, and in that moment, I know who it is before I see him. My heart skips a beat. My chest swells, and I grab a fist full of his shirt to steady myself. The moment I lift my face toward his, all the emotion of the evening crashes into me full force, and tears burn at the corners of my eyes.

"Lysandir."

"Mira." The sound of my name is somewhere between a gasp and prayer. He cups my cheek, turning my face as if searching for injury. "What happened?"

"I—" The single letter cracks from my throat, and I can't force anything out. All I can do is stare at him, caught in the heat of his stare that starts to blur beyond the tears that threaten to form and fall.

He drops his hand from my cheek, and his attention snaps past me. "Tharin?"

Distant conversation and laughter grow louder, signaling others coming our way. The sound makes me take a half step closer to

Lysandir. The irrational urge to bury my face against his chest and sob is nearly overwhelming.

"Not here," Tharin replies.

"Her room." Lysandir gives a little nod.

His other arm comes around me to hold me closer. That's all the warning I have before the air constricts, the hallway melts away, and then suddenly we're standing outside my chamber.

CHAPTER 23

T HE GUARDS STATIONED IN our hall leap to attention and step forward.

Tharin raises a hand to ward them off. "No need. Lady Mira is unsettled, and the prince would like a word."

Said prince has already released me, opened the door to my room, and is ushering me inside. Tharin follows us and shuts the door behind him.

I don't wait for them to speak or ask me questions. Numbly, I walk to my bed and plop down on the edge. My teeth dig into my bottom lip, the sharp bite of pain centering me and forcing the tears away. The fae lights are dim, and no one bothers to brighten them.

A little voice in the back of my head is screaming about the awkwardness of the situation. *Bed. Prince. Room. Dark.* But it's barely a whisper compared to everything else.

"Well?" Lysandir says.

From the sharpness of his tone, I know the question isn't directed at me. I don't even need to look up. And I don't, focusing instead on one deep breath after another.

"Some of the women decided to attended a party. I went along to keep an eye on things, of course. At some point in the evening, Mira ventured into the courtyard. There, she…" He trails off, and I can almost feel the tension radiating from Lysandir in the pause. "The king was there with some of his close companions. Male and female."

Lysandir bites out some curse I'm unfamiliar with.

"Indeed," Tharin replies. "I may not have caught all of the conversation that Mira did, but in the parts I heard, your brother made clear his dedication to his duties as king, despite what he may personally prefer."

Another curse slips free, this one even more edged.

"I was attempting to convince Mira to let me bring her back here when we stumbled upon you."

Literally. I huff air through my nose and glance up at the men.

Lysandir has a hand clasped over his eyes, fingertips massaging his temples and ruffling his auburn hair. Tharin's face is grim, but his stance is casual, not what I'd generally expect of a guard in front of his prince.

With a deep sigh, Lysandir drops his hand. "I'll have a discussion with my brother."

Tharin nods and glances toward me, his head canting to the side. "Should I leave you?"

The prince looks my way, and only then do I realize the question was directed at me. *Oh.* Lysandir makes his way toward me in silence, and a flush burns up my cheeks. He stops abruptly near the corner of my desk. A grin lifts one corner of his lips.

"I see you got my gift." He runs a finger over a piece of paper where I'd doodled a few random designs before realizing I wasn't in a state to write anything.

"I sent a thank you note." I eye Tharin.

"Which was delivered." He raises his hands in surrender.

A huff of breath catches in Lysandir's throat. "If you gave it to Tharin, I'm sure it's waiting for me in my quarters. I haven't had the chance to look at much since I returned this evening."

Oh, lovely. He just got back, and I had to run right into him with my problems. I'm sure that's exactly what he wanted.

"I think we should be fine on our own," Lysandir says to Tharin. Then he glances at me. "Unless Mira disagrees."

I swallow, my throat suddenly dry. He intends to stay? Warmth spreads out from the center of my chest. That little voice whispering in my head from earlier is suddenly so much louder.

Bed. Prince. Room. Dark.
Alone.
"We're fine," I whisper, unsure what else to say.
"Let me know if you need anything." He and Lysandir hold one another's gazes, some silent communication passing between them. Then Tharin looks at me. "Either of you."
The moment he turns to leave, the atmosphere in the room turns thick and full. It's harder to breath, even harder to think. It takes everything I have not to squeak or leap away when Lysandir takes a seat on the edge of the bed just a foot away from me. The tension jumping between us is palpable.
His shoulders hunch on another sigh. "I should ask you not to speak to the others about what you witnessed tonight."
Should...
"But?" I ask into the heavy silence.
He shakes his head. "I'm not sure, exactly, but I don't want to demand that of you."
"Oh." A risk, to be sure. I could undermine his brother in a few words. Send this competition into chaos. And yet, he won't ask me not to share it?
"Though..." He winces. "Perhaps you could wait until after the ball tomorrow if you do tell any of the others?"
Right. Because upsetting the competition is one thing, but potentially causing a scene in front of the other courts could be absolutely disastrous.
"I will. Or won't." My brows scrunch. "I won't tell anyone before the ball. I can promise that."
"Good. Thank you." He visibly swallows, tension radiating from him. "I'm sorry you had to stumble upon that tonight. I wish you could have avoided such revelations."
"It's..." Not okay, exactly. That wouldn't be right, but I can't regret it. "I'm actually glad I did."
"Glad?" Lysandir rears back like I'm a snake about to bite.
My head bobs. "It was shocking. Uncomfortable. It...hurt. But I'd rather know than continue on in ignorance believing that the

king might really fall in love with one of us or is doing this because he truly wants a wife. I'd heard rumors. I think many of us have, but having it confirmed... Well, it puts things in a different light. But I'm still glad I can see that rather than walking in blind, you know?"

He's silent for a minute, staring at nothing, before he looks over at me. "Knowing the truth isn't always easier. You know about my visions." He leans back on his palms, one placed on either side of him. When I nod, he continues. "Seeing the future, the truth of what's to come, is often a lot harder than not knowing. Once you know, you're stuck with it. You can't pretend it could be some other way. Well, I suppose you can try, but you'll always know the truth deep down. It would be just deluding yourself." His voice drops to a whisper, and he glances away again. "Hoping for what isn't and what cannot be."

I have the sudden urge to hug him, but that would probably be inappropriate. He's a prince. I could end up marrying his brother. And then there's that awkward kiss and the fact that he literally told me he already has someone he cares for. I swerve my thoughts in a new direction. Besides, I don't know if he's a hugger.

Right. Because that's the reason, Mira.

"You're not wrong," I say at length. "But I still think a hard truth is better than ignorance."

Lysandir shifts, and I'd swear his fingers inch closer to mine. When did I even drop my hand to the covers?

"I don't know," he says. "There are many times I would love to be ignorant. Just for a little while. If pain or disappointment is inevitable, I'd like to be able to enjoy the happy moments before them without the cloud of the future hanging over me."

Like it hangs over you now? Something does. Maybe his time pushing back the Unseelie.

"Surely not everything you see can be bad?" I say.

He looks at me then, really looks, like he's trying to see beyond my body and into my soul. I look away, suddenly regretting my question.

"No, Mira," he says. "No, it's not at all bad. Not at all."

"Then you have happy things to look forward to as well, right?"

He smiles but closes his eyes and drops his head. His hair is loose this evening, and some of it slides over his shoulder to shield part of his face. The barest hint of a pointed ear pokes through the tresses. He pulls his arms in front of him and braces his elbows on his thighs as he leans forward.

It's strange, but the darkness brings out as many variations in his hair as the light, accenting the darker strands and giving a depth to the color that makes me yearn for a red pen despite my dislike of them. Not red. Crimson. Burgundy. Something darker yet rich and full of life.

Lysandir clasps his hands in front of him and looks over at me. "I suppose I do."

Another ache pulses through me. Why, oh why, does he look so sad? Because of what I learned about his brother? Something else?

"We were told you were dealing with the Unseelie these past few days," I say. "Was it terrible?" *Is that the reason for your pain?*

I want to know. No, I need to know. More than anything, I want to find some way to soothe whatever is troubling him. It calls out like a wound in need of healing, and something tells me he doesn't have many people to tend to him. He's shown me care and concern. I'd be a fool not to do the same, my personal feelings aside.

"Terrible?" he says. "I've seen much worse. This raid was quick. They seemed to be after information rather than trying to cause real damage or loss of life."

I lean in, intrigued. "What kind of information?"

"Some of the fae the Unseelie cornered and interrogated were asked about whether there were any unbonded humans nearby."

My skin turns clammy. "Were there? I mean, they didn't take anyone, did they?"

"No." Lysandir shakes his head.

I nearly sigh in relief. To be taken by Unseelie... I shudder. It's too horrible to consider.

"The humans that come to live here typically have little trouble finding a willing partner," he says. "In fact, most unbonded never even leave the capital before they secure one. I'm sure you haven't missed the interest you all receive at events." A lopsided grin flashes across his features. "You probably aren't supposed to know the details of the Unseelie raid. At least not yet."

I make a gesture of zipping my lips, which earns a slight huff of laughter. It would raise way too many questions if I just happened to know things about enemy attacks that the other women don't. I'm not foolish enough to give myself away like that anyway, but I get the sense he's not insulting my intelligence, just covering his own bases.

"After we secured the border, we tracked them back into their territory, and—" He cuts off with a shake of his head. "We didn't find much. I should be disappointed. My brother sees it as a failure. But such offensives fit more with his interests and skills than mine. I'm..." He swallows again, a hint of color rising to his cheeks. He flexes his arm, showing off the lean muscle there. "Vasilius and I are different in many ways, but in one thing we are aligned. We do what we must to fulfill our roles and protect our court. Even if it's not what we want."

The pain in Lysandir's eyes as he looks over at me is all too real.

Fighting goes against his nature, just as marrying a human goes against his brother's. But both do their duty. They put the court first, no matter what they want.

It's the most natural thing in the world to place my hand over his and give it a squeeze. The moment we touch, a thrill rushes under my skin. Lysandir jolts, and I think he might pull away. But he doesn't. The shock in his expression fades as he stares at the place where we touch.

"Mira..." He turns his palm over, and his fingers curl around mine.

It's so simple, almost innocent, but that touch is everything. My heart swells until my chest aches. My stomach twists in on itself. And the grin that rushes to my face makes all the hurt and uncertainty of the evening fade into nothing.

"I..." I bite my lip, hesitant to break the moment, and then force the words out. "I'm sorry you had to deal with that and that I brought it up."

"Don't apologize." Strong fingers twine through mine. His grip tightens. "Not for something like that. Your thoughts, your questions, are safe with me." *You're safe with me.* He doesn't say it, but I feel it in the warmth of his skin against mine. I hear it in the echo of his words as they twist through the recesses of my mind.

It'd be so easy to lean in and lay my head on his shoulder. Or better yet, kiss him again. I've imagined it way more times than I have any right to. It's an effort to stop myself from giving in to the pull tugging me closer.

So, I fill the void with words instead. "I love the gift, by the way."

His head cocks to the side. "You do?"

I barely stifle a laugh. There's genuine wonder in his eyes. How could he possibly believe otherwise?

"Gorgeous, glittering pens?" I raise my brows, glancing toward the item and then back to him. "You've seen my journals."

The hint of a smile pulls at his lips. "I have."

"So you had to know I'd love it. How could I not?"

One shoulder lifts in a shrug. "It's not jewelry or gems or—"

"It's perfect." I squeeze his hand. "I'd much rather have something lovely that I can use all the time than something I'd be too nervous to wear because I'd worry about breaking it or losing it."

He chuckles again. "I'll have to keep that in mind."

My face flushes hotter. I wiggle in my seat, suddenly all too aware of the mattress beneath us.

Lysandir pulls his hand away from mine. My heart lurches then plummets. But then he shifts to face me. My breath catches as his leg brushes mine.

"Mira. I..." He pauses. "There's something I need to tell you."

I tense, my chest hot and tight. This is where he mentions that his heart is taken. That I'm in a competition to marry his brother. That we can't possibly be together.

A stiff knock sounds at the door. Lysandir all but leaps off the bed, moving a few steps away so quickly that it steals my breath.

I blink, still staring at the spot he was a heartbeat ago.

It takes a moment for my brain to catch up, to switch from everything that was just happening to the sound that had the prince fleeing my side. When I turn to look at him, he's breathing heavy, chest rising and falling as he stares at the door like a monster might burst through at any moment.

The knock comes again. The familiar pattern of beats is one I've come to recognize—Fia.

Lysandir glances my way, his earlier surprise tamed into neutrality.

"Should I?" I mouth. Maybe he wants to vanish first.

But no. He nods. And suddenly I feel like I've slipped back into my teenage years to that time my mom caught me with a boy in my room and the door closed. We really were just friends, not that she ever believed that. He became public enemy number one at our house and until his family moved away a year later.

"Come in," I call.

Fia opens the door and bounds inside with her usual enthusiasm before freezing mid-step and nearly tumbling over. "Oh!" Her eyes widen and she drops into a bow. "My prince."

"This isn't what it looks like," I stammer.

"The door," Lysandir commands at the same time.

"Of course." Fia whips into action and closes it. "I'm so sorry, Prince Lysandir. I did not mean to interrupt, only Tharin mentioned that Lady Mira had returned to her room and might need something before she went to bed for the night."

A frown tugs at my lips. But Tharin knew that Lysandir was here. Unless he expected him to be gone already.

"Was he incorrect?" She glances at me. "Should I come back later?"

"No, please stay," Lysandir sighs and shakes his head. "He was simply doing as I asked. Lady Mira was unsettled earlier this evening, and I wished to make sure she was all right. Now that you're here, please see that she has what she needs."

The words lack feeling. The warmth and closeness of moments ago has vanished.

I will Lysandir to look at me, to explain, but he doesn't. Instead, when he turns and bids me goodnight, it holds nothing more than the mild pleasantries one might reserve for a new acquaintance. The last of my own goodnight still hangs in the air when he pulls open the door and leaves without a backward glance.

"Well, that was odd," Fia comments once he leaves. "I thought after the gift he sent that perhaps he had shown a particular interest in you. Was I wrong?"

Yes? No? I thought so too, but... The words stick to my tongue, refusing to come out. I swallow.

"I'm not sure," I say at last. For a moment there, I was so sure my interest was returned. But then he'd pulled away, he'd tried to say something before we were interrupted. What?

"Oh." Her shoulders slump and she frowns toward the door. It's only then I realize I'm wearing the same expression.

Does he care for me? Or is he as good an actor as his brother?

Chapter 24

DESPITE THE EXHAUSTION WEIGHING on me, the emotional toll of the evening keeps me awake far longer than I'd like. Thankfully though, I don't miss anything sleeping most of the morning away since it's the day of the ball.

I run into Grace and Alex at a casual lunch in the parlor. Grace is quick to point out how I ghosted them last night, but surprisingly, Alex steps in to my defense.

"Can you blame her?" She bumps her shoulder into Grace's. "It was awful. Don't feel bad, Mira. We left right after." She pops another piece of fruit into her mouth with a shrug. Discussion closed.

It's not long after that when Fia shows up at my room to help me get ready for the ball. Ridiculously early in my opinion since it doesn't start for hours, but Fia will hear none of it and is determined to take her time making me shine. Quite literally in fact.

The woman in the mirror is jaw-dropping. I almost can't believe it's me. Fia's cosmetics highlight all my best features, managing to even add sparkle to my eyes, or maybe that's just the awe and wonder shining through. My long, dark hair is curled in perfect waves and pinned back just so, letting it flow around my face and shoulders but be tamed and constrained all at once. Tiny crystals woven into my hair on near invisible strands catch the light and make me shimmer and shine. The quarter-sized garnet on a thin chain around my neck doesn't hurt either. But it's the gown that's the real showstopper.

"I knew this would be perfect for you," Fia says in triumph as looks at my reflect in the mirror. She was right, so right. The idea of something so unique gave me pause. But she pushed me toward it, and I'm so glad.

The crimson fabric darkens to near black where the bodice stops just above my breasts, a small slit giving an extra peak at my cleavage which the almost corset-like top has pushed to new heights. The skirt of the gown is so mesmerizing I can't stop twisting this way and that just to watch it move. Tones of gold and orange rise like flames from the bottom hem as well as the layer beneath the sheer top fabric. Little crystals, like the ones in my hair, catch the light, giving the whole thing the impression of being a dancing flame every time I move. Short, gold heels complete the look, peeking out here and there when I move.

I'm a living tribute to the Court of Fire. No one present will doubt where I belong.

The sun is just dropping below the trees when we are all shifted by the guards to an area just outside the palace.

"I'll never get used to that," Bailey says with a wobbly smile as soon as we arrive. She's resplendent tonight in a blood red gown accented with shimmering gold and jewelry to match.

Of everyone, she seems to be the most genuinely in love with the king. Oh, Cora and Katherine are good at acting like it. Even now, Katherine gives a dramatic sigh and laments about when we get to see Vasilius, but it's too much—too forced. Hopefully the king sees that, though maybe it would do him some good to marry a pretender after what I learned last night.

Still though, I hope he notices Bailey tonight. More than that, I hope he picks her in the end. He may just be doing his duty, but I can't believe everything I've seen between them is false. There's a hint of something, a seed that could grow if given time, and Bailey has the patience and demeanor to water it and watch it bloom.

The ball is to be held in a large, open space bordered on one side by the palace, another by the glowing trunks and lofting branches of the trees that glow with inner fire and a long arcing curve of what a guard informs us is the glass menagerie. In a way, it's a tribute and symbol of the Court of Fire all on its own, with towering works of art made of glass, interspersed with a variety of flora and fauna spotted around meandering pathways and gurgling fountains. A large glass butterfly in a rainbow of colors spreads its wings out wide as three cars at the nearest edge. It beckons, begging me to wander and take in the stunning sights I can catch mere glimpses of, but that's not why we're here.

The massive open space before us has been decorated grander than any celebrity wedding. Fae lights of varying colors drift around in the dimming sky like string lights cut loose and given lift to float on their own. Long tables already filled with food and drinks are set up near the sides, and smaller ones covered in shimmering fabric are dotted around, presumably for people to eat and mingle. Various fae rush about, adding things to tables, adjusting decorations, and such. Others, based on their breathtaking attire and casual stance sipping drinks or chatting idly, are clearly guests who have arrived early.

Savory scents waft our way, causing Gabriella's stomach to rumble. She gives a little embarrassed squeak. A few women giggle.

Zoe claps a hand on her shoulder. "I was too nervous to eat much either," she admits. "Hopefully we get to eat soon?" She inclines her head toward a nearby guard and gives her a pointed look.

"Of course," the guard replies. "Should I have a few plates brought over?"

"And risk a stain on my gown?" Katherine remarks, like we've suggested something ridiculous.

I shrug. "A snack would be nice."

A few others murmur in agreement.

"Well fine," Katherine snips and tosses her hair. "You can all stuff your faces and smell like food. *I'm* going to find the king."

"He'll be joining you all shortly." Tharin's booming voice just behind me causes me to jump. He steps around toward the front of our group. His uniform is more elaborate than usual, with golden stripes marking the crimson fabric of his shoulders and an extra halo of light shining off the flame emblem in the center of his chest.

I squint at a few of the others then back at him. Everyone guarding us holds an elite ranking, but compared to the others, he has a few more marks on display. It reminds me of someone else, though I can't place it at the moment.

"In fact, let's go ahead and move over there." He points to the far side of the space, where a short dais has been erected bearing three thrones, the one in the center much larger and more ornate than the other two. A wide pathway of fitted marble stones bisects the area from where we stand to the far side. In the center, it bulges out into a wide circle—a dance floor I suspect, given the fae musicians tuning their instruments not far from one side.

"You didn't tell me you were in charge," I remark to Tharin as we cross the space.

He smirks. "You never asked."

I barely stop my eye roll, instead voicing the suspicion that has taken root. "What did I do to get assigned someone of your status to watch over me?"

"Who says I was?"

"I do." I refuse to believe it's random.

"Perceptive," he remarks.

Our little group reforms near the edge of the forest. Pillars of cold flame create a border of sorts. Guards linger beyond, as they had near the palace. If I had to guess, I'd say they ring in the entire space, keeping watch to make sure the evening goes off without a hitch. A few stand closer to us, and my attention snags on one in particular, the head of the king's personal guard. He was one of the others with the king in the garden last night, but that's not all that makes me draw a short, sharp breath. His uniform insignias bare a startling resemblance to Tharin's.

I turn back toward Tharin assessing him in a new light. Pieces click into place. "You're the prince's personal guard."

It makes so much sense. Too much. I should have seen it earlier, with the way he and Lysandir were so familiar with one another, though why he dressed like a regular guard before tonight's ceremony, I can't explain. I can't remember if he dressed this way during the opening ball. There was too much else on my mind that evening to pay attention.

Tharin winks at me. "As I said, very perceptive."

But why is the prince's personal guard watching after me? I could see it at first, since he was unsettled by my being here. But surely that's changed?

A whisper of magic tingles across my skin.

Tharin's attention shifts to open space toward our left. "They come."

No sooner have the words left his mouth than Vasilius, Lysandir, and Elaine appear along with a cluster of guards and advisors.

My focus goes unerringly to the prince. He looks so much like he did the first night I saw him that it's almost unsettling. I prefer the more casual prince that I've gotten to know rather than this stiff, formal version. Not that he looks worse. The opposite. He's absolutely devastating, a glow of power leeching from his skin and giving him an otherworldly air.

Lysandir's gaze snags on mine, and my heart flip-flops in my chest. The smallest hint of a smile touches his lips before he turns to respond to his mother.

Commotion picks up as several of the women close in on the king. His eyes widen briefly, and I have to stifle a laugh. It's funny how a little knowledge can shift my perspective so thoroughly. Knowing what I do, I can pick up the little hints of panic and revulsion he's done such a good job of hiding.

A kinder person might feel bad for him, putting duty above his own preferences, but I can't summon the feeling at that moment, the revelation too fresh.

"Ladies." The king spreads his arms wide. "I'm glad you're all here this evening."

I frown. *Just because we make you look good?* I shove the mocking thought away and plaster a smile on my face. I told Lysandir I wouldn't disrupt the ball, and I won't.

The prince tends to his mother, helping her over to one of the smaller thrones beside the king's. The sight warms my heart and transforms my smile into something genuine. If only my mother could be here tonight. I'd love her to see me like this, to know that I'm holding my own and putting all those years of pageants to some use. I may not win the crown, but at least I haven't embarrassed the family. And maybe, if my gut is telling me true, I might be able to let her know I have a connection with the prince. Just thinking about it makes my chest squeeze tight. It's new, fragile. Uncertain at best. I'm almost afraid to even think about it for fear of making it untrue or finding out he was just doing some duty like the king. Or that whoever stole his heart long ago has it irrevocably.

"I will need you all here with me when the other fae royals make their entrance, but before then, I do have a little surprise for you all." Vasilius gestures behind us toward the area where we came in. A number of other fae have filled into the space, most sipping drinks and chatting with one another. My brows scrunch as I try to deduce the surprise.

After a moment, Adeline squeaks and bolts toward a small group of figures making their way toward us.

Human figures.

Her family.

Zoe and Katherine take off next. Gabriella is not far behind, racing with far more speed than I would ever expect toward an older woman who to whom she bears a striking resemblance.

I bounce on my toes, shifting as I search for familiar faces. My uncle will be here. I have no doubt of that. I only hope he isn't alone. Even Aunt Dalia, flighty as she can be, would be a welcome balm to the barrage of questions he'll have for me, not to mention terse reminders about why I'm there and my duty to the family.

Duty. I sigh.

It's become a master of us all.

Then, I see her. Selena wears all black, of course, but the bright red lipstick and subtle blonde highlights in her hair are new. The sight of her breaks the bonds holding me still, and suddenly I'm one of the women rushing down the pathway toward her approaching figure.

We've gone longer without seeing or speaking to one another, but seeing a familiar face, one I love, brings all the emotion of the past weeks to a sharp point that stings at the corners of my eyes. I've never felt quite so light as she calls my name before pulling me into a tight hug.

"It's so good to see you." Her grip tightens to bone-crushing before loosening.

"You too," I reply.

"And us, I hope?" My aunt gives a too-bright smile.

And it is. It genuinely is. Even my uncle with his immaculate air and superior demeanor is strangely comforting. In a world where most everything is strange and new, they're not. They're home, and I didn't realize until this moment just how much I've missed it.

"Yes, you all too." I hug them each before pulling away to poke at my hair and make sure it's stayed in place. My aunt stands a little straighter, as if she's surprised by my actions.

"We hope all has been well." Uncle Mathias inclines his head, making it a question as much as a statement.

I swallow a sigh. It wouldn't be him if he didn't get straight to the point. "Of course. We've been treated exceptionally well, as I stated in my letters," I remind him. "And I've been honored to spend a good bit of time with the royal family."

"Hmm," he muses, a sharp contrast to Aunt Dalia's exuberant remark at my response or Selena's eye roll. She's no stranger to my uncle's layered conversations.

"Your mom and brothers are doing well, by the way," Selena says.

If I thought I was light and floating a moment ago, I'm really drifting away now.

"That's the best news," I reply. It really, really is. I'd almost been afraid to ask.

"They miss you of course, but they're proud too, I think." She shrugs one shoulder and offers a genuine smile.

We don't have much time to catch up before guards are ushering us back to the king and moving the thick crowds that have formed back to make a pathway between the entrance and the dais. The sky is painted in shades of dark pink fading into dark blue, leaving the floating fae lights to illuminate the encroaching night. The way they reflect off the creatures I can spy in the glass menagerie almost make them look like they've come alive. I try to shift my body so that I'm not looking at them as I come to stand with the other women in two arcs on either side of the pathway in front of the dais.

The music changes. Spectators quiet down and turn toward the entrance. At my side, Selena covers her mouth to stifle a giggle, and I grin, wondering if she's thinking the same thing as me, that this is entirely too much like a human wedding.

Vasilius, Lysandir, and Elaine all rise in anticipation of receiving their guests.

The procession begins, and it only takes a glimpse to know which court is presenting themselves first. The King of the Forest, Rivenean, looks like a druid knight from one of my brothers' video games come to life. Golden leaves adorn his shoulders like scales, dripping down over the deep green of his attire. Tall, brown leather boots hug up his calves, and even his hair is adorned with a twisting crown of golden branches spotted with emeralds. But it's not him that I give my focus to. I'm much more curious about the women at his side, his consort and soon-to-be-bride, as we understand it.

Lia Ashmore. A human, just like us. It's still baffling to me that she didn't know until recently that she was gifted and now is the future Queen of the Court of the Forest. To say Uncle Matias was a little frustrated by that turn of events is putting it mildly. Not that he would have endorsed anyone from our coven going to the Court of the Forest, much less trying to win the heart of their king. That would have been disloyal to the Court of Fire in his eyes—and that of the elders—and we couldn't have that. Maybe it's the idea that there are more gifted humans out there just waiting to be found, that we're not as special as he'd like to believe. Either way, it's impossible not to feel some kind of kinship with this young woman I've never met.

In many ways, her outfit is a mirror of the king's. Her gown of dark emerald almost looks like a living carpet of soft moss dotted with small flowers that glimmer in the light. A short, decorative cloak is draped around her shoulders, baring the same golden scale-like leaves as the king's and bound with a clasp resembling branches. More golden leaves dot her wavy, brown hair, and a small crown of gold and emerald graces her brow.

They stop at the foot of the dais, not far from us, and give a little bow to the royals. A train of forest fae—based on the colors of their attire—halt in their wake and bow more deeply.

"Welcome, Rivenean, King of the Forest, and your ensemble." Vasilius's voice booms over the assembly. "Thank you for joining us at this celebration."

"We are honored to be here after many years apart," Rivenean replies. "I hope that this will be a new start for our courts."

"Indeed," Vasilius inclines his head. "I look forward to speaking with you more soon." Confirmation and dismissal. The Court of the Forest has been mostly isolated until recently. Something about age-old feuds and lack of trust between Seelie courts. It's nice that Vasilius invited them, that maybe old bridges are starting to mend.

Next comes the Court of Water. Of all the courts invited, this was the one most expected to accept the invitation, and the king's advisors were not wrong. Opposing elements, they may be, but relations with the Court of Water have been pleasant and steady for a long time, or so my research showed. Balanced, one might say. The Queen Mayania leads the procession with her daughter and heir. The sight of them literally takes my breath away. Maybe it's their long navy hair or their similar gowns that appear to be woven of iridescent scales that shimmer in a rainbow of colors. But it could also be the way that water droplets appear to hang suspended in the air around the queen. Any way around it, they're truly a sight I won't forget.

The last court to be presented is the Court of Air. I'd be lying if I said this isn't the one I'm most curious about. After all, this is the court Lysandir visited to try and earn his wish, one I still don't know the details of. And he lost, to the human woman who now walks at the side of the king. Wren.

I hazard a glance over my shoulder at Lysandir. His gaze is fixed squarely on Wren. The wide smile he grants her as she approaches causes my stomach to clench. My body doesn't seem to care that he's not mine or that she's definitely with the King of Air. Reason has nothing on jealousy. Could she be the woman he gave his heart to? Though he made it sound like it was a long time ago, and the competition where he met her wasn't long ago at all.

It probably doesn't help that she's wearing a navy dress with a slit at the front that plunges far lower than mine or that the light, gauzy material of the skirts of her dress hint at the shape of her long legs beneath. And that's to say nothing of her shining golden hair and the broad grin she gives Lysandir in return that lights up her whole face.

Compared to the other kings, Sigurd, King of Air is more restrained in his attire, all well-fitting dark grays, navy, and hints of silver in a long coat that ends past his hips and breeches tucked into boots. Honestly, his outfit isn't too far a cry from my uncle's. His crown is simpler too, just a silver band, but it's the confidence he wears like a second skin that gives away his title. He doesn't need an elaborate outfit to impress, and the hint of a smirk on his lips says he knows it too.

After the introduction of the visiting royals and their courts, each of us are introduced and curtsy before King Vasilius and then once more before the crowd of fae. If having us all lined up in front of the dais wasn't obvious enough, Vasilius has made it clear to everyone present that his court doesn't lack for humans—or bride candidates.

It's a bit of a slap in the face to some of the other courts, the Court of the Forest especially, given I've heard they had a startling lack of humans before the king found Lia and she discovered a stone that can open doorways to the human realm—something else the Court of Fire doesn't seem to lack. But at least they're here and the courts are talking, so maybe some good will come of it.

Presentation complete, the celebration moves into full swing. Harmonious music played by the fae band fills the air, weaving past the immediate flood of conversation to tickle my ears and ensnare my body. It's impossible not to feel its melody resonate in my chest as it beckons me to move to its beat.

I'm caught there in its thrall when Vasilius unexpectedly steps before me.

"Would you care to join me in a dance?" he asks.

Me? Dance? I blink at him as the words sink in. My smile is genuine as I drop into a curtsy and reply, "Of course."

Check this out, Uncle.

If he had any doubts about how I've represented our family, this should smash them to pieces.

CHAPTER 25

T HE SONG CHANGES AS the king leads me down the marble pathway toward the wide circle where a few others have already started to dance. Fae and humans alike part for us. I raise my chin and channel all of my thoughts into looking like a queen and not tripping. Even the other royals look on.

The king's hand on my lower back is warm as he pulls me into his embrace, as is his smile. I can almost forget the secret I learned the evening before. He really is a very good actor.

A slow rhythm leaves us in close quarters, my chest nearly brushing his crimson coat and the golden vest underneath. At first, I stare up at his face, trying to give the impression of being enamored in hopes that the crowd believe it. With the magic pouring off of him this evening and the feel of his body close to mine, it's hard to keep up the act. I feign embarrassment and shift my gaze away out toward the crowd.

I catch sight of my uncle—hallelujah!—who gives me an encouraging nod. Yay for checking that box. My cousin is even less subtle with her two thumbs up.

Vasilius turns us slowly with the music, and I catch sight of something that almost has me skipping a step. Lysandir stands next to Wren from the Court of Air. She says something, and he throws his head back with a laugh. I nearly stumble a step, despite the fact that we're barely moving. He's so relaxed with her, so at ease... Hard to do with the King of Air glowering at him from Wren's other side, but he still manages it.

"You're close with the other courts?" I ask Vasilius.

He stares at something over my shoulder and blinks rapidly before glancing down at me. "The other courts?" His head cants ever so slightly to the side. "Not particularly. The Court of Water is an old ally, but close?" He shakes his head. "We could do better in the future though, don't you think?"

"Of course," I say. "That's a great idea."

And one I hope he follows through on, no matter who he chooses as queen or whatever else happens.

"I only ask because, well…" I slide my gaze back to his brother, and Vasilius follows it.

"Ah. Yes, my brother has been a strong advocate for expanding our relations with other courts, particularly since he ventured to the Court of Air to participate in their tournament." Vasilius tsks and shakes his head. "A prince, participating in a foreign tournament for the chance at a wish from the cauldron. Though I suppose the friendship he developed with the king's human lover is a boon for us."

Friendship. I cling to the word. Though the topic of the competition brings up an entire litany of questions that taunt me so thoroughly I can't help but voice the one that shouts the loudest. "Do you know what he planned to wish for? If he won?"

Vasilius adjusts his hold on me. We're closer than before, his nearness more unnerving than anything. It takes effort to focus on each word when he finally speaks. "That's the thing. It had something to do with his fated mate."

"Mate!" I squeak. "He has a mate?"

He chuckles in return. "Not yet. He said he saw her in one of his visions. She must have been truly horrible for him to want to change her future or his." He hums to himself. "Both of them, in a way, I suppose." He shrugs amid the dance.

Mate. Lysandir has a fated mate? Or will? A humorless laugh slips from my lips.

"Horrible. Yes, she must be," I say in an effort to cover my reaction.

"My brother seems to think fate is set, but I prefer to think we choose our own destinies, don't you?" Vasilius continues, as if what he's shared isn't all that significant. Maybe it wouldn't be if I was as invested in him as I should be, but it's his brother that's woven his way into my heart, one who is apparently already fated for someone else. And loves yet another. Or maybe the same woman?

The whole night suddenly seems much darker.

"Yes," I reply, feeling a bit numb. "That's a much more optimistic perspective."

The song draws to a close. Vasilius releases his hold on me, and for once, I'm reluctant for him to let go since he was the only thing keeping his comments from knocking me on my backside.

I go through the motions.

Smile. Curtsy.

Katherine is already there inserting herself in front of the king and asking for the next dance, which he accepts.

I wander off to the side of the dancefloor, heedless of my direction and the few fae who try to get my attention. Instead, I narrow in on a server with a tray of crystal flutes bearing bubbling liquid that resembles pink champaign. I grab one and take a big sip, savoring the sweet flavor and the bubbles that dance across my tongue.

"Hey! Look at you, getting the first dance with the king!" Selena throws her arm around my shoulders, causing the liquid in my glass to slosh precariously. She stares at me for one beat then another, before her expression drops along with her arm. "But you don't look excited," she says just above a whisper. "*¿Qué pasó?*"

"It's..." I break off, my gaze shifting around us as various fae close in like they might want to chat with us or at least overhear what we're talking about. That won't do. Not at all.

I slide my arm through hers and turn us toward the glass menagerie. "Walk with me."

If there's anywhere we can be slightly more alone, it's there.

CHAPTER 26

While the crowds are still thick, I ask about her and home. The new blond streaks in her hair? Something she tried for fun but won't keep. The red lipstick is staying though. It's her new favorite color. My brothers are racking up the sports accolades, and college scholarships look promising—thank God. And Mom has been baking up a storm. Selena swears she's gained five pounds thanks to her snickerdoodle cookies, but I can't see it.

The farther we walk, the more the crowds disburse, and I'm able to feed her some details on the competition in short whispers. The king has been fine. I'm not his favorite, but not the least favorite either. I've represented the family well. All good facts she can tell my uncle later when he grills her. Because he totally will.

Selena nods along through the updates, nonplussed.

"So have you two..." She waggles her eyebrows and nudges me.

I roll eyes in return. "The dowager is a little old-fashioned and gave us strict no-sex rules." That I don't think anyone has broken. "But I did kiss him."

"And?" She leans in, giving me a serious look. "I need details."

"It was..." I shrug.

She cringes. "*Ay!* So, he's a bad kisser. Not looking forward to that for the rest of your life?"

Decidedly not, but I didn't drag her out here to talk about a lackluster kiss. I pull in a deep breath. "The thing is..." I lean in to whisper directly in her ear. "He's not the only person I've kissed."

"*Santa mierda!*" She screeches then claps her hands over her mouth.

"Selena!" I look around. Thankfully, no one seems to be nearby.

She grabs my arms and practically pulls me down onto the nearby bench. "Mira. Seriously. Oh my God."

"Yeah, I know."

She drops my arms now that we're seated, and I bury my face in my hands.

"You can't leave me hanging." Selena shakes me. "Dish. Now. Right now."

I peek out from behind my hands. "You cannot tell your dad."

"Psh." She blows air through her lips. "Of course not. He'd blow a gasket, and *I* don't want to deal with that, much less have it come back on you or your mom. Your secrets are safe with me." She holds up one hand. "Scout's honor."

I drop my hands and give her a sideways look. "You were never a scout. And isn't that Boy Scouts anyway?"

She shrugs. "You get the point."

Yeah, I do. And I trust her more than anyone. So, we have the quietest conversation possible about Lysandir. I tell her everything, from our first terrible meeting that she witnessed, to our encounters in the library, seeing him play with the kids, him teaching me yard games, the kiss I can never forget, last night, and finally what I learned about from the king moments ago.

"Damn." She leans back when I finish. "I thought we were headed straight for a *happy for now* ending there for a minute, and you have to go and drop the whole *mate* bombshell."

"Selena!" I hiss.

She swats playfully at me. "You worry too much. We've seen all of—what?—two people come by? We've got to be at the back of this place. Besides, no one knows who I'm talking about."

"Still."

"Fair enough." She holds up her hands in surrender. "But damn."

I lean back on the wooden bench with a sigh. "Exactly."

We're silent for a moment, staring at the giant glass beastie nearby, which looks like a cross between a hippo and tiger, all striped and generously proportioned.

Selena looks over at me. "Maybe there could be a little fling in the future?"

Until his mate shows up. She doesn't say the last part, but she doesn't need to.

"A little hard to do that when..." I raise my wrist and tap my bond mark.

She shrugs one shoulder. "After?"

It was always going to be after anyway, wasn't it? It's not like I could be hooking up with the prince behind his brother's back, especially not in Faery where everyone's sense of smell is ridiculous and there's a little thing called a mark, a magical mating bond, that can appear if two people are intimate with one another. Pretty sure that would be impossible to hide and very damning.

"Maybe," I say at last. If the future was always leading there, why does it hurt so much to admit it now? "He mentioned liking someone else from long ago, though I hoped—"

Selena flings out her hand and grabs my arm. I fall silent. Then I hear it, a small laugh, the crunch of footsteps after.

We sit quietly, waiting for them to move on. Though I suppose we actually should be getting back to the celebration before we're missed. I'm about to suggest as much when some of the approaching people's conversation catches my attention.

"You're really sure what you've seen cannot be changed?" a woman asks.

"What I see always comes true, in one way or another, and this vision was quite clear."

I jolt in the seat and clasp my hand over my mouth to stifle a gasp. Lysandir. But who is the woman? I pull my bottom lip between my teeth, angry at myself over the jealousy that immediately flares in my chest. *Not yours, Mira.*

Selena gives me a funny look.

I drop my hand and mouth, *Lysandir.*

It takes a moment to sink in, but I know the second it does. Her eyes widen, her mouth drops open, and she hikes a finger behind us toward the backside of some large glass animal that the bench is positioned against. I nod, straining my ears to listen. Both of us shift in our seats, turning to look behind us.

Two figures draw still, their silhouettes visible beyond the colorful translucent glass. With any luck, they won't be able to notice Selena and me, especially if we hold still.

"Then don't you think you should just tell her?" the woman asks. "Or your brother?"

"And surrender to fate?" The sorrow in Lysandir's voice is so deep it makes my chest ache.

Her. Oh God. Has he already met his mate? Is that what he was trying to tell me last night?

The woman crosses her arms. "It sounds like you're doing that already."

"Yes, he's good at that." Tharin? I can't see him, but that's definitely his voice.

A low, growling, grumble echoes from beyond, raising some of the fine hairs along my arms.

"So touchy." The woman walks away, her silhouette disappearing.

"I just..." Lysandir's head drops. "I kept hoping to find a way around it, but I feel like I'm running out of time."

"So why aren't you out there spending what time you have with her then?" the woman asks.

I suck in a breath and turn fully in the seat. My stomach plummets, and my shoulders sag. Not his mate. Not the horrible woman he wants to get away from. They're talking about the one he gave his heart to. Someone he must care about a great deal. She's here. Tonight.

"Because that will lead to more pain and heartache for everyone involved." The bitterness in Tharin's tone is sharp as a blade.

"You talk about her like she's a curse," Lysandir snaps.

"Isn't she?" he retorts.

Something hard slams against the glass structure in front of us. A crack rushes down the surface in front of my face. I let out a startled screech. Too late, I clap my hand over my mouth. In horror, I turn to stare at Selena. Her eyes are wide, a hand over her mouth as well. Did she scream too or just me?

But it doesn't matter. One or both, it's enough to condemn our eavesdropping.

Tharin is the first around the corner. Fae light reflects off his drawn blade. With a quick scan of the area, he zones in on us, blade lowering.

A heartbeat later, Lysandir rushes around the corner, a stunning woman on his heels. And not just any woman. It's Wren, the beautiful consort of the King of Air.

Lysandir skids to a halt, his eyes widening.

Shit. I don't even know what to say, where to begin.

Tharin sheaths his sword before crossing his arms to stare at us—or rather, me. "You have a bad habit of listening in on conversations in gardens."

A flush of embarrassment races up my neck to my cheeks. *Just call me out, why don't you?* What I wouldn't give to be able to shift away like some of the fae can.

"Your fault for talking in a public place," Selena replies with impressive casualness.

Wren tips her head to the side and glances at the men. "She has a point."

Tharin frowns, but Lysandir doesn't seem to hear her. In fact, he hasn't reacted to a thing anyone has said since they appeared. He's just continued to stare at me, that same look of barely muted horror etched on his features.

"Mira." My name falls from his lips like a prayer, but I can't image how he could be the embarrassed one in this situation. He's not the one literally sitting here hoping to vanish.

"Oh!" Wren's head whips around. "*You're* Mira?"

The words are so full of meaning that it takes me a moment to digest them. But it's the look in her eyes that makes everything slam into place with jarring awareness.

I shift my attention to Lysandir. He grimaces, his eyes closing as he tilts his head down. His hands ball into fists at his side before releasing, his eyes flying open as they do, his gaze focused solely on me. A glow flares from him, bright then gone, like his resolve slipped for the briefest moment.

Oh. Oh God.

"You... I'm..." I stammer, taking a step back, as puzzle pieces crash into me so hard they threaten to steal my breath.

"Mira?" From the corner of my eye, I see Selena step closer.

But I don't turn. I can't look away from the male in front of me and everything that's suddenly, painfully clear, like fog rolling back to reveal a graveyard.

Tharin mutters some curse and turns away.

"It's me. You were talking about me. I'm your..." *Mate.* The last word sticks, bitter, dirty, and hard as a rock on my tongue.

His mate. The one he didn't want. The one he entered a deadly competition to be freed of.

No wonder he tried to be rid of me that first night and prevent me from entering the competition.

He doesn't want me here. He never has. Any feelings, any emotions... It's just been biology, fate. Nothing real, nothing meaningful.

My legs no longer want to hold me up, and I wobble. Lysandir races forward, reaching for me, but I recoil. The motion has me careening back, falling, but the damnable man is faster, managing to scoop an arm around me and pull me to his chest before I tumble to the ground.

The warmth, strength, and gentleness of his hold make my body into a traitor. It wants to stay there, to cling to him, to bury my face in his chest and cry.

But my mind is screaming. *Mate. Unwanted mate.*

Maybe he can hear that, or sense it, because he lingers for only a moment, just long enough to steady me on my feet again before stepping back. It's only when cool air rushes between us that I can breathe again, that my body remembers how to move on its own.

Bits of quiet conversation float around me, but the first words I make out are my cousin saying, "Maybe we should give you two a few minutes?"

"Yes." Lysandir swallows. "But not here."

We're lucky enough that no one else has stumbled upon us, but someone could be listening. In this maze of a place, it's hard to tell, and fae hearing is so much better than a human's. The last rational part of my mind reminds me of that. It may be the only thing keeping a leash on my tongue and all the questions and accusations I want to fling at the prince. Keeping them in only makes my skin burn hotter and the tears trying to form at the corners of my eyes sting more.

It's Wren of all people who rushes up to me and takes my hands in hers. It's entirely too comforting, given that we haven't properly met. "Tell Tharin that you have a headache and need a few minutes before you return to the party."

My brows draw together and I blink at her. "What?"

"He can't lie." She looks over her shoulder at Tharin, who now stands at Lysandir's side just a few steps away, then back at me. "But you can tell him something that he can tell others, should they ask about where you've gone. Right?"

He sighs. "Seems like we're too far in to go back now."

"Then you can have a moment." This time, she glances over at Lysandir. "And he can explain some things?"

The look she gives him could peel paint. A queen in the making indeed.

That hard stare has softened completely when she looks back at me. "These fae and their secrets." She shakes her head with a sigh, finally releasing my hands to gesture at Tharin. "Go on."

He crosses his arms but nods at me.

"I..." It takes a moment to find my voice. "I have a headache and need some quiet. I'll come back to the party in a little bit?" The words finally spill out of my mouth, but my voice doesn't even sound like mine. I'm a world away.

"Don't worry about me. I'll go back with them," Selena says. If anyone can handle herself, it's her. A techy she may be, but an introvert she is not. "Actually..." she slides up next to Wren like a kid to the ice cream counter. "I've been dying to talk to you."

"Talk while we walk." Tharin ushers them toward the pathway. "Our absence is likely already noted."

I watch them go. The moment they are out of sight, Lysandir extends a hand to me. "Mira."

The watering in my eyes increases. My chest grows tight. But I refuse to cry in front of him. I want to smack his hand away, to berate him for leading me on when he's obviously tried to move heaven and earth to avoid me. But more than anything, I need answers.

So, I take his hand.

CHAPTER 27

O NE MOMENT, WE'RE UNDER the evening sky, surrounded by glass and plant life. The next, we're inside a room. It only takes one breath for me to know exactly where we are. The scent of sandalwood and spice—*his* scent—clings to the space. We stand next to a small sitting area, but it's the sight of the bed with its crimson sheets ruffled on one side a few feet away that makes me dizzy. Damn my traitorous body for wanting him after what I just realized.

Instead of releasing my hand, Lysandir adjusts his grip to try to twine his fingers with mine, and I jerk away.

"What the hell is wrong with you?" I snap.

Apparently whatever leash held me back is gone.

He rears back like I slapped him. "Mira..."

"I'm supposed to be your mate?"

"I-I didn't think you'd be so opposed. Not after that kiss or last night." He shakes his head. "Did I misread—"

This man makes no sense. My hand balls into a fist at my side. "Last night? You think I was faking my interest? It's you who led me on, putting on an act for the humans, just like your brother."

Lysandir snarls, lips pulling back to reveal white teeth. "I am not my brother. I should have realized its him you prefer after all."

"What?" I gape. "I do not! You know what I felt when I kissed him? Nothing. Absolutely nothing."

His lips twitch. He crosses his arms and stares me down in smug satisfaction. "And when you kissed me?"

My mouth goes dry. *Everything. I felt everything.* And now I feel sick over it.

"You led me on." I poke an accusing finger at him. "You kissed me back. You held my hand. You gave me gifts. And don't tell me it was a mistake that you were always there, watching me, seeking me out. Because I'm your mate? It is some biologic thing that made you do that?" I nearly scream in frustration. "You should have just told me upfront you didn't want me instead of acting like that and making me believe you did. Didn't I tell you I'd rather a hard truth than not knowing—"

"Not want you?" Suddenly he's right in front of me, staring down at me. His chest rises and falls. Warmth radiates from him, jumping the narrow space between us. "Not want you?" he thunders. "You're what I want most in this world! You have been for years!"

"I..." My thoughts shut down. Completely. The world tilts on its axis. I'm not even sure I'm in my body any more. All I know is the man inches away from me telling me something impossible.

And then everything rushes back.

"I-I don't understand." I reach out my hands to my sides, trying to grab something, anything, to steady myself. But nothing is nearby, nothing but him, and I can't anchor myself to the thing that's just upended my universe. Nor can I make feet move. "You just told Wren how horrible it would be to surrender to fate. You entered a damnable competition to try and not have me be your mate. You told me you already gave your heart away. You don't want me!"

"Mira." His fingertips graze my cheek, and I shudder. "I want you so badly it hurts."

Holy shit.

I lean away from the touch I crave like life itself. I want it. I want it so much. But I hardly know up from down.

Lysandir flinches and drops his hand but doesn't step back.

"But..." It comes out almost as a whimper.

There has to be something. A shoe waiting to fall and crush me.

"I tried to change your future," he says, calmer now. "Not that you were the woman I was destined to love. My future mate." His voice cracks over the last word. "Never that."

"But the king said…" My mouth falls open in disbelief. *Never that.*

"What did my brother say?" Lysandir's tone takes a hard edge.

What did he say? My brows pinch. It couldn't have been that long ago, but it feels like a lifetime. "That you saw your mate," I say. "That she must have been hideous because you didn't want her or wanted to change things related to her or something."

He huffs air through his nose and looks away. "I told Vasilius what he needed to hear so that he wouldn't question me when I went to the Court of Air to compete for a wish from the cauldron." He glances back at me. "It was the truth…in a way. Enough that I could speak it and he believed it or believed whatever he wanted to, I suppose."

The king was wrong. I cling to that thought like a lifeboat.

"It wasn't that you found me hideous?" I swallow, bracing for the response.

A humorless laugh falls from his lips. "No. Far from it." He cups my cheek. The urge to pull away has vanished. Instead, I lean into the touch, savor it. "You're beautiful, Mira."

Beautiful. How one word can heal so many wounds, I'll never understand.

"Then what did you want to change?" I ask. There's something. Not a small thing. I have to know.

His throat bobs. He swipes his thumb across my skin one last time before pulling away. "Can I start from the beginning?"

"Please."

When Lysandir laces his fingers though mine, I'm eager for the touch. It's connection, its strength, and I need that more than ever. I still feel adrift, lost in a little boat on the seas and at the mercy of the waves. I thought the fog had rolled back and let me see the truth, but it had plied me with another illusion instead.

Now, finally, his hand in mine, this is real. This is true.

So, I follow as he leads me to the nearby sofa, and we sit down together.

Mate. Holy shit. He's my mate.

The revelation plays over and over again inside my head.

It's not a simple thing. More than a partner, a spouse. Some fae think it ordained by the stars, by the spirit of the long-ago queen who blessed the land with her powers. Either way, it's the soul's answering echo found in another. Fated? Maybe. But when someone who can see the future is involved, fated is the only explanation.

Lysandir releases my hand, only to place his palm on my thigh, as if he can't bear to not have the connection or he fears I might vanish. My dress doesn't lack for fabric. Layers separate us. But his touch almost feels like a brand on my skin nonetheless.

"You know about my visions," he says at last.

"That you see glimpses of the future." A very rare talent, even among the magically gifted fae.

"Most come unbidden, some when I least expect them, but every once in a while, when I meditate on a particular thing, I am granted a vision of it as well. A few years ago, I suppose I was feeling particularly lonely." He glances away and then back at me with a tight, brief smile. "I decided to meditate and ask the fates if there was someone I was destined to love and be loved by in return. I did not expect them to answer. They so rarely do. But just when I was about to give up, they showed me a vision. And I saw you, Mira, looking much as you do now, smiling at me."

A whole different type of tear burns at the corner of my eyes. My heart tries to lurch straight out of my chest and give itself over to him. When it doesn't, I place my hand over his and wrap my fingers around his, needing the connection.

His expression changes to something soft, vulnerable, and if I thought my heart was ripping itself out a moment ago, it truly is now. I've never known a man to be so open. My uncle isn't. My brothers certainly aren't. And if my father was, I can't remember. But the show of emotion doesn't weaken Lysandir in my eyes—it strengthens him. He holds such emotion and yet walks through life with such strength and resolve. I force a smile for him, maybe like the one he saw. I can't know, but I try all the same.

"Seeing you, not knowing who you were but that I had such a woman in my future, gave me such hope, such joy. I thought about you often. It should embarrass me to say that, but it doesn't. If I had a hard day, when I was lonely, if I was feeling rejected or overshadowed, I would think about the woman fate showed me who awaited me in my future. You were my light, Mira, the fire that beckoned me on when times were dark."

"Lysandir..." I scoot closer to him. "But you said you gave your heart away long ago."

"I did." He caresses my cheek. "To you."

All this time... It was me. He wanted me. He waited for me.

"But you didn't know me, not really," I say.

"I didn't. But I've had the chance to now. There's so much more I wish to learn and know, but what I have seen, the time I've been able to spend with you, it just confirmed all the things I hoped."

The urge to kiss him, to heal the broken parts he's showing me, is overwhelming. I reach for him, but this time he's the one who pulls back.

His eyes close as if he's pained, and he slowly shakes his head. "But it might have been easier if you hadn't lived up to my dreams."

The comment hits like a dagger to the heart. "What?"

"At first, I almost wanted to dislike you. I hoped that my dreams were inflated and wouldn't hold up because that's not the only time I saw you in my visions."

"Tell me." What could be so horrible for him to wish that? Fingers of dread crawl up my spine.

"When it became clear that my mother was determined for Vasilius to find a queen while she still walks this plane and a Choosing would be the most reasonable method of it since he'd not made a love match, my brother asked me to look into the future and see if my visions would reveal the choice for him."

No! My mind has already followed the thread to its end and roars against what it finds there. I begin to shake my head side to side, but Lysandir keeps speaking.

"So I asked the fates and I looked." His hand returns to my thigh in what's probably meant to be a comforting squeeze but only feels like condemnation. "I saw you, Mira."

"It's not possible."

But the sorrow in his gaze says it is.

"Why would I ever say yes to him? He doesn't want me, not really. I'm not sure that he wants any of us." Though that wasn't always true. Weeks ago, I would have jumped at the chance to be his bride. "Something must have changed. I've changed. I came here aiming to be the king's bride, but that's no longer what I want. I would never agree to marry him now." *Not now that I've gotten to know you. Not now that I know I'm your fated mate.* I grasp at his arm. "Surely, you can't think I'd pick him over you?"

"The fates don't lie, Mira. What I see comes true."

I leap to my feet, unable to sit still a moment longer. "There has to be some explanation, something fate hasn't shown you." I pace, fighting the urge to cry, to scream all my frustration for the world to hear.

All the while, Lysandir watches me like a hawk, that same stricken expression etched into his features.

"What all did it show you exactly?"

He takes a deep breath and braces his palms on his knees. "I saw you standing before my mother on the dais. She placed a crown upon your head and passed to you the Spear of Shielding, making you Queen of the Court of Fire. It's exactly what's planned for whoever my brother chooses."

I nearly fist my hand in my hair before thinking better of it at the last moment. Fucking hell, that's pretty damning. I pace again, like I might outrun the truth he's laid bare.

"That's why you didn't want me here that first night." I stop pacing as the pieces I'd been missing for so long fill themselves in. "You didn't want me to enter the competition because then I couldn't win it and become your brother's queen."

"Yes," he admits. "I even considered throwing you over my shoulder, shifting to the doorway to your world, and tossing you back through. But that would have only made my brother suspicious. If he was aware that I knew the winner of the competition, he would have demanded it from me and chosen you on the spot. My mother would have been appeased, and he wouldn't have had to go through all of this." He gestures around.

Dear God. And I'd have gone through with it too. To please my uncle, to secure a fruitful future for my family. His vision would have come true that night. I return to the sofa and plop down next to Lysandir. The weight of inevitability tries to shove me down through the cushions.

Lysandir cups my face in his palm, turning it toward him. "A smarter male may have stayed away from you. What good could come from falling harder for a woman he could never truly have?" He leans in, his forehead nearly touching mine. "But I couldn't. I'd been waiting for you, yearning for you, and even knowing the pain that lay ahead, I couldn't pass up this opportunity to be near you now, before you become his."

"Lysandir." I all but crumple against him, throwing my arms around his neck and laying my head against his chest. His arms come around me, so comforting and sure. His heart races, his pulse echoing through my body. I could stay like this forever and be content, I think.

How on earth am I supposed to marry his brother when I feel like this? And his brother will expect heirs... I shudder and hug Lysandir tighter. There's no way. It just can't be possible. I won't let it be. A sob nearly breaks free. I bite my lip—hard—to hold it back.

When I've wrestled my emotions under control, I pull back. Not far, just enough to look up at him, to cup his cheek as he had mine, to stare into his eyes and know with a certainty that the words I'm about to speak are true. "We will change fate. Because I pick you. I choose you. I am yours."

Lysandir leans in until his breath ghosts across my lips. "And I've been yours longer than you can imagine."

My soft gasp never leaves my lips before his crash into mine. Their soft warmth is the only feeling in the world, the only thing that matters. My eyes slam shut, and I lean into him, savoring the electric spark that dances across my skin. In the garden, his kiss was tentative at first, then more ravenous. But neither compared to this one. It's a volcano compared to a match. It's passion like I've never known.

His palm cups the back of my neck before sliding down my body, making its way my backside. He lifts me, and I go. And thank goodness the skirt of the dress is wide enough to let me move with him, to settle in a straddle across his thighs. I'd have torn the damn thing without regret, if not. Lysandir groans against my lips as I settle atop him. The sound only makes my chest burn hotter and sends a flood of moisture pooling between my legs.

Lysandir teases the seam of my lips with his tongue, and I open for him. He sweeps inside, deepening the kiss. He embraces me like a man starved. But I suppose he has been. If I'd seen him years ago, if I'd known for so long he would be mine, I would never have had the restraint to hold back like he has.

Part of me wishes he wouldn't have, but the other is thankful. I got to know him first, to build something between us, to want him. If he'd told me straight off that I was his, I wouldn't have believed it. It might have snuffed out any flame before it could begin.

His fingers tangle in the hair at the base of my skull, holding me close. Our kiss turns less fevered, more languid, and somehow even deeper. There are layers of fabric between our bodies, but I still can't miss the hardness between his legs or the rapid pulse that hammers against his ribs. I want to feel it, all of it, every inch of him. I rock my hips, unable to hold still. Maybe it's traitorous, kissing the prince when I'm bound into vying for the king's hand, but I don't care. Nothing has ever felt more right, more perfect.

I can't imagine finding this to lose it or how it must feel for him to have waited so long only to have fate threaten to steal his happiness before he could claim even a taste of it.

Lysandir gently tugs my hair as he breaks from our kiss.

"Mira," he groans.

His eyes have been closed, and when they open, a bright glow pours out to illuminate the area around us in crimson light. That glow, that sign of strong emotion in powerful fae, lets me know just how much our kiss affected him—if the rest of him wasn't proof enough. As the glow dims, I catch sight of his dark, hooded gaze, his kiss-reddened lips. One of my hands has tangled in the silken strands of his crimson hair, mussing it.

"I..." He utters some fae curse I'm unfamiliar with. "I want..."

"Me too."

But we can't. Damn fae marks and sense of smell. It's already going to be a problem. If Vasilius gets anywhere close to me, he'll undoubtedly smell his brother's scent and not just a passing whiff that could be easily explained.

That knowledge doesn't stop the wanting though.

His expression shifts, sorrow leaking into the desire. He sucks in a long breath then shudders. "Fuck," he blurts. "I can smell you."

Impossibly, my body flushes hotter. Pretty sure he doesn't mean my shampoo. I try to squeeze my legs together but only manage to wiggle in his lap and rub against his erection. He groans, his head falling back.

Not helping, Mira.

Reluctantly, I slide from his lap and step away. A few minutes longer in his lap, feeling his heat under me, and I might have done something incredibly stupid. I brush out my skirts, searching for wrinkles, anything to keep from rushing back and kissing him again.

Lysandir rakes his hand through his hair as he stares at me. "How am I supposed to keep from touching you? From kissing you?"

I halt in my efforts and stare at him, feeling every bit of the agony in his gaze.

"From pulling you into my arms every time I see you?" he finishes.

"I know." I pull my bottom lip between my teeth. "I think I understand why Tharin called me a curse."

Lysandir sighs. "He'll be angry with me about tonight."

"You two are close?" I venture.

"One of my best friends. He's my personal guard for a reason."

"And you assigned him to watch after me for the competition?"

He nods. "I did. My brother questioned the assignment that first night, but I used a similar lie as I had with you, that it was strange for you to come here wanting to be queen without visiting before. I told him I was concerned about you. A truth, but I meant it differently than he took it. Tharin was to protect you but also to keep me in check and make sure I didn't compromise you or my visions."

"I don't think he's a fan of mine," I grumble.

A small laugh falls from his lips. "He just worries about me." He sighs. "And I need to take you back to the ball. I'm not sure how long Tharin will be able to explain away our absence." He props his elbows on his knees and leans forward to hang his head in his hands.

I can't say how much time has passed. Probably too much. It is hard to imagine that someone hasn't noticed my absence from such an important event or Lysandir's.

He looks up, his heated gaze threatening to consume me once more. "But all I want to do is carry you to my bed and mark you. Make you mine, if you'd have me."

I would, damn it. In a heartbeat. But somehow, saying that out loud feels like it would make everything worse. I don't need to dangle another carrot we can never reach.

So, I ignore that last comment. "You're right, we should get back."

Lysandir groans and slowly gets to his feet. "I'll get you a flower first."

"A flow—" I haven't finished before he vanishes, only to reappear a minute later with a handful of the beautiful red blooms he gave me in the hedge maze, one of them still with roots and dirt dangling from the stem.

"Oh." I press my thighs together and shift my stance. "That flower."

He holds one out to me. "Just in case."

"These might be my new favorite thing." I take it and offer a sly grin in return as I stare at him from under my lashes.

Lysandir chuckles darkly. "Little temptress."

Once my head is swimming from the nearly overwhelming floral scent, I add my stem to the pile he tossed onto a nearby table. The mess of flowers should be a saving grace, but the sight of them opens up a void inside my chest.

"We'll make this work," I say.

Lysandir looks over sharply at my somber tone.

"One way or another, we'll be together. I'm yours. I promise."

He swallows and holds out a hand for me, which I accept. "It's unwise to make promises you can't keep, especially in Faery."

"Then I'll have to make sure I keep it."

His hand tightens on mine, but silence is his only reply before we shift away.

CHAPTER 28

"**D**IDN'T SEE YOU MUCH last night." Grace plops down on the seat next to me and gives a little yelp when a few drops of coffee splash over the rim of her mug and onto her hand.

I stifle another yawn and sip at my own mug—my second—before responding. "It was hard to find anyone with so many people around." I shrug. "Besides, I wanted to catch up with my cousin and spent a good bit of time with her."

She offers a half smile. "I wish I could say the same. I mostly tried to avoid my family and their endless line of questions. Seriously, I wonder if they even read my letters. Not like I sent that many."

"You all should have focused less on your families and more on the king." Katherine sits a little straighter and raises her chin as if she's already been crowned queen. "But then, I'm glad you didn't because *I* had my focus where it should be and got to dance with him three times."

Zoe snorts as she slides around a nearby chair and drops into the seat. "Only because you threw yourself at him and he was too gentlemanly to say no."

Katherine scowls at her, a flush rising to her cheeks.

"Besides, it's not like you got the most dances." Zoe takes a bite of a banana-like fruit, chewing slowly, triumphantly.

"Oh?" Having missed a large chunk of the party, I completely missed much of the dancing. It's a good thing I got that first dance in so my absence wasn't even more suspicious. By the time we returned, drinks were flowing freely and most people—fae and human alike—had partaken liberally. The party wore on another few hours, which for me, were filled with longing looks at Lysandir from a distance and more conversation with my cousin, who spent considerable time gushing about Wren and all that she'd learned from her. I was all too happy for the distraction and thankful she wanted to talk about that instead of gaping at me wide-eyed and pushing for more on the revelations I shared with her.

By the time I returned to my room, I could barely keep my eyes open, and even my feet had started to hurt—something I believed impossible with the mastery that is fae footwear. Apparently even it has its comfort limits. Still, I lay awake in bed replaying my time with Lysandir, my mind chanting *mate* over and over, until morning light was already creeping in my window.

I managed a few hours of sleep before Fia arrived around noon to help me dress for the day, saying that Elaine asked for us all to meet in the parlor, having some surprise in store.

"Not me." Zoe swallows her bite and raises her hands in front of her. "That honor goes to Bailey. And where is she this morning?" She glances around for emphasis, a hint of mischief in her gaze.

Despite my sleeplessness and the difficulty of dragging myself out of bed, I wasn't the last one here. A shock to be sure. Though I highly doubt Bailey of all people would be up to anything not completely above board. If I've learned anything about her, it's that she's probably the most respectable, color-inside-the-lines one of us all.

Grace sighs. "If it wasn't obvious that she was the king's favorite, it sure is now."

"You can't know that for sure," Katherine snaps, but even her voice holds a bit of uncertainty.

Zoe levels her with a flat look that reads, *Really? Give it up.*

The door opens, and we all sit a little straighter, expecting the dowager, but it's Bailey at last, with Cora at her side, the two locked in what could pass for friendly conversation. They cross the room together, heading for coffee and food.

Katherine nearly gapes, personally affronted by her friend's seeming shift in loyalty.

Grace raises her brows before shaking her head. "Can't beat 'em, join 'em, I guess."

Elaine arrives not long after, informing us that we'll all be able to spend some more quality time with our families before they return to Earth for their safety amid the ongoing Unseelie concerns. But that's not her surprise. The figures who enter after she calls to the guards to let her guests in steal all the air from the room.

Lia and Wren.

They're dressed more casually today but still bear their respective court colors of green and blue, which stand out in sharp relief against the warm tones of the Court of Fire.

Wren casually pans her gaze across the group of us before returning to settle on me. She gives the smallest nod of her head, her smile widening just a bit as a knowing look crosses her face.

All at once, I both yearn to speak with her and wish to be anywhere else. She knows. She knew before I did. There may be nothing romantic between her and Lysandir, but he clearly trusted her enough to divulge a huge secret that he didn't even share with his brother...though there's a damn good reason for that little exclusion.

"I thought it may be helpful for you ladies to speak with others your age who have gone through what one of you will soon experience. That is, being the bonded of a king of Faery." Elaine leans heavily on her cane, but one quick look is enough to wave off the guard who tries to offer her a chair. "I will give you all space to talk without my old ears around."

The dowager queen has barely left the room before the flood of questions begins.

"Did you really not know you were gifted?"

"How did you end up in Faery?"

"What is your court like?"

Lia steps back like we're a pack of rabid dogs, and honestly, we're acting like it. Wren, however, laughs and handles it like a pro.

I had heard she was a bartender before her adventure in Faery, so I suppose she has experience wrangling rowdy groups.

Time slips by in a rush, and before I know it, they're leaving and I've yet to find a way to talk to Wren about Lysandir, as I'd hoped. There was just no good way to approach that topic with all the other women around. Though if Wren's frequent looks and encouraging smiles were any indication, she wanted to say something too but couldn't manage it either.

The rest of the afternoon is mixed heaven and hell. Spending time with Selena? Awesome. Hanging out with her parents and enduring their reminders of how important it is that I represent the family well and such? Misery.

I'm all too happy to retreat to my room at the end of the day, though it'd be a lie to say I'm not disappointed to find my room empty. I know Lysandir is probably busy with the others courts, given that they leave in the morning. I know we're supposed to keep things secret to avoid appearing like outright traitors to the king. That knowledge didn't stop hope though. Going through the rest of this competition, knowing what the future might hold, seeing the man I actually want but having to hold back and pretend I'm interested in his brother instead is going to be a misery.

I collapse back onto my bed with a sigh. It holds me close, beckoning me to rest, so I don't even bother to change or wash my face before I kick off my shoes and slide farther onto the comforter.

The edge of blissful sleep has just started to creep over my consciousness when there's a firm knock at the door. I groan, shoving upright.

It's no surprise when Fia cracks open the door and pokes her head in. "Good, you're awake."

"Just barely," I grumble. She's far too attentive to miss checking in on me, even if sometimes I'd prefer it.

She slips into the room, her customary upbeat skip in her step. "I see you're tired. However, I agreed to deliver this straight away."

A letter sealed with wax is held in her outstretched hand.

It summons me like a beacon, and I nearly rip the thing out of her hands. I've snapped the seal and unfolded a moment later. But as soon as I take in the handwriting, my heart drops. It's far too messy to be Lysandir's flowing and precise script. Actually, it lacks all the smooth and artistic rhythm of the fae handwriting I've seen, which makes perfect sense when I spy the signature at the bottom.

"Wren."

"Yes." Fia's crisp reply gives away her annoyance. "I take it you were expecting a message from her?" She wanders over to my desk and dressing table, reordering the array of things she undoubted already organized earlier in the day.

"I wasn't actually."

"Oh?" She looks over one shoulder. "It seemed like you were."

"I thought it might have been from someone else."

She blinks at me expectant and curious.

"My cousin or one of my family." The lie comes easily.

Dear Mira,

I'm sorry we didn't get the chance to catch up earlier today. I know yesterday was probably a shock, but you seem to have taken it well. I hope you won't hold it against him. Sometimes love makes people foolish. Take my friend Galen, for example. He loved a woman so much he did something truly stupid—kidnap me actually—to try to get back to her.

Don't worry. I made it home safely, and he made it back to her too. And yes, I forgave him because, while what he did was dumb, he did it out of love. He also thought I'd be completely safe, but I digress.

The point is, I hope you forgive a certain someone for keeping secrets. Hopefully we can spend more time together soon.

P.S. Selena is awesome, and I'll be sending her so much stuff for her database.

From Wren

I fold the letter back up and tuck it into my palm. Wren was carefully vague in her letter, probably in case anyone else read it.

I appreciate that she thought to send it, even if the advice wasn't necessary.

I know why Lysandir kept things a secret. Do I wish I'd know sooner? Yes. But I'm surprisingly not aggrieved about it. I know now. We'll figure out a way forward, somehow.

"What did it say?" Fia asks.

"Just some advice," I reply.

An almost feral gleam sparks in her eyes. "Advice on how to win a king?"

"Uh... Something like that."

"Winning over the queen of another court." She gives a wistful sigh. "And this after earning the prince's favor too."

"The what?" I ask far too quickly. The letter suddenly feels damning, though it was still sealed and I have a good feeling she didn't read it.

"He hasn't visited anyone else or paid them much attention either. But don't worry. I've kept that to myself." She makes a sign like zipping her lips. "If the king doesn't pick you, hopefully the prince will." A wide grin stretches across her face.

"Uh..." I grasp for words, not finding them. "I suppose we'll see how The Choosing turns out first."

"Never hurts to have a plan B." She winks.

If only I had her optimism.

CHAPTER 29

I'VE SPENT THE PAST two days looking over my shoulder—and everywhere else—hoping for a glimpse of Lysandir. It's impossible not to worry that he might be ignoring me and that the revelation about being his fated mate was some kind of fever dream brought on by too much faery wine. Doubts eat at me, hammering away at every corner of my self-esteem.

In all my imaginings, I really thought I'd have seen him by now, but nothing. I know he was busy with the other courts, which is the same reason we haven't seen the king since the ball, but still.

I sigh, glancing around at the assembled mass of women and fae where we stand on dew-soaked grass at the edge of the forest. The sun has barely risen, and more than one of companions look asleep on their feet.

"They couldn't bring us coffee?" Grace groans, rubbing her eyes.

It's time for the king's hunt, and apparently those start early. Like, before breakfast early. Not that I'd want to tromp around in the woods on a full stomach, but doing it on an empty one isn't any more appealing.

If there's one thing I know about Vasilius, it's his love of the hunt. I've heard enough stories about it during our dates. A few days ago, he announced we'd join him on one. Since so many of us shared our passions with him, he wants to share his with us. It makes sense from his perspective, though I'm not sure any of us are very excited for the outing.

"There'll be refreshments later," Adeline reminds her. She's entirely too chipper this morning. Probably because her guard is nearby. I've caught more than one longing glance between them already. How does no one else notice?

I stretch on my toes, trying to see above those around us. The king isn't here yet, but some of his advisors are. Apparently as soon as he arrives, we'll be ready to go, which means no Lysandir unless he shows up soon.

"Is everything alright?" someone asks.

I jolt at the sudden question as Bailey comes to stand beside me. She's the picture of calm elegance and looks so natural, with her hair braided back, a quiver of arrows on her back, and a bow in hand. So unlike the rest of us, who look like bad cosplayers. Katherine nearly stabbed herself with an arrow and looked at the bow like a mixed up Rubik's Cube. Zoe outright refused the bow and arrows, saying that she could never hurt an animal, so why bother. In fact, she protested the whole event pretty hard. Her vegan lifestyle and love for animals really could lead to marital problems if she's picked, since the king has expressed his great love for hunting the wild beasts of Faery. Not that it's stopped her from trying to win his hand.

"Um, yeah, I'm fine," I say.

"You've just seemed on edge lately," Bailey replies.

"I guess the other courts being around the past few days and all the recent talk of Unseelie has left me a little unsettled. That's all." I shrug.

Bailey offers a comforting smile. "We're safe here. The Court of Fire is strong, and the king won't let anything happen to us."

The pure admiration and respect shining in her eyes is sweet enough to hurt. She has no idea that the king really isn't into humans. It's a little painful to watch, but breaking her illusion would be even worse. Besides, if anyone has a shot at truly earning his love and respect in return, it seems to be her, and I want that for her; I really do. The sooner Vasilius sees that and picks her, the sooner the rest of us can move on.

Maybe I can help it along, give the king the little shove in her direction that he needs. Could changing fate be so simple?

"Mira?" Bailey's head cocks to the side.

"Yes, you're right," I reply, coming back to the moment. "Of course there's no need to worry. I'll try to relax."

"Good, I think Vasilius would be sad if he thought we doubted him."

Oh good lord, she has it bad. I force myself to smile at her in return. Either I'm good at keeping my thoughts from my face, or she chooses to ignore them. Either way, I'm relieved when magic tingles across my skin and I see additional figures appear out of the corner of my eye.

The king, I expected, but my heart skips a beat at the sight of Lysandir next to him. *He came.*

I doubt I'll get to spend much time with him today. I'm not that lucky, but seeing him is reassuring nonetheless, even more so when his searching gaze lands on me and holds, a small smile lifting at the corners of his lips. That's all it takes. A tiny twitch of muscle and my worries are vanquished.

What a simple mess he's made me.

We're divided up into small groups, each of us women with a guard in case we should wound the creature and be unable to finish it off. Or we hurt ourselves. No one says the latter, but it's obvious. The king joins Alex, much to her apparent shock, though he promises to shift around and spend time with as many of us as he can. The same is said about Lysandir, who joins Grace, and the two advisors joining us Memnon and Avara, who pair with Bailey and Cora and their guards to start. It's both a relief and letdown not to be with Lysandir, though it would likely be suspicious if he'd picked me.

As it is, it'll be just me and Tharin, of course. The hard look he's given me all morning says he'd rather be with anyone else, but I have a feeling Lysandir has probably ordered him to keep an eye on me.

Today, we're hunting a deer-like creature said to have a blazing crimson coat. Such a thing would stand out in a normal forest, but here where many of the trees have bright hued trunks and leaves and several glow with an unearthly fire, it should blend right in.

We'll be lucky if any of us can hit a tree trunk, much less some poor creature. The *honor* of winning the hunt will most likely go to whichever of us is with the king when he inevitably makes the kill. Scouts have already located the unknowing victim and will be shifting us to various points around its location. All we really have to do is follow our guards, stay relatively quiet, and see if we spot the creature before it catches wind of us and flees.

The sun is still rising by the time we're shifted to our starting locations. Tharin and I end up in a pretty flat and peaceful section of forest with limited undergrowth. The cool, crisp breeze is a welcome companion, as are the various pleasant bird calls and occasional hum of an insect. By some miracle of Faery, there are no mosquitos in this world, which already makes being in the woods a million times better than back home.

If Tharin has any idea where the beast is, he doesn't show it. Instead, he's content to follow behind me as I wander aimlessly through the woods, soaking in the sights and sounds of nature. He's quiet enough that I might think him gone if not for the heavy weight of his scowl that's impossible to escape. I don't hear or spy anyone else, which either means I'm going in the absolute wrong direction or we're further apart than expected. It doesn't take long for boredom to set in, and I start humming a soft tune for lack of anything else to do while I wander.

"You're going to scare it off before we ever get close," Tharin says.

I halt, glancing back over one shoulder. He's stopped about ten feet behind me, arms crossed over his chest.

"There's zero chance of me killing it with this any way." I tap the bow slung over my shoulder. It's surprisingly light for its size. If I didn't know better, I'd think it a toy made for kids.

"At least we agree on that."

"Ugh." I roll my eyes. "You really hate me, don't you?"

"No." He drops his arms with a sigh. "I don't *hate* you, Mira."

"But you don't like me." That's obvious enough.

He shakes his head and walks my way. "I don't dislike you either."

"Really?" I arch one brow. I know he can't lie, but his attitude sure fools me.

Tharin stops beside me. "My first duty is always to the prince, and since your arrival, you've complicated that."

That's true enough. "Because you're guarding me and not him?"

"No." He rubs his jaw. "It's safe enough in the court, and the prince is a capable male anyway. But I'd be a terrible guard if I didn't keep him safe from his own inclinations."

The way he looks me head to toe speaks volumes.

Warmth creeps up my neck and rushes to my cheeks, forcing me to look away. "You sent Fia the other night, when he was in my room."

"I did."

The smugness of his tone makes me grit my teeth.

Tharin grabs my arm, and I gasp. He holds it up, the king's bond mark inches from my face.

"Don't forget this," he says. "While you bear it, you are pledged as a potential bride to the king. His and his alone until he releases you." He gently shakes my arm in emphasis. "To be with anyone else is treason."

"And after?"

"If the prince's vision comes true, you'll be more dangerous to him than ever." His lip curls, and he drops my arm like a sack of garbage.

"Why? The king isn't interested in humans. Maybe he'd be happy for his brother and me to be together. One less obligation for him."

"You're a fool if you truly think that." The utter disappointment in his appraisal makes me flinch. "To be bonded to a human is power. That he hasn't bonded a human before now for that alone is mind-boggling." He leans in closer, nearly right in my face. "Vasilius likes power. He enjoys being king. And more than anything else, he does not like to share."

My hands clench into fists. I notch my chin higher in challenge, but Tharin just turns and walks away.

"Then the vision must be wrong," I call after him. "Or there must be a way to change it. I'm already not the king's favorite, and I have no desire to change that. You've seen enough of this competition. Surely you agree. He won't pick me"

Tharin halts. Turns. "You're correct that the king appears to favor Lady Bailey. His advisors have approved her as well."

I suck in a sharp breath. Approved her? As in, this competition may be nearing its end?

He shakes his head. "I see that hope in your eyes. Squash it. For Lysandir, if not yourself. The prince's visions have never been wrong. I won't believe otherwise until the king is wed to someone else and you share a mating bond with the prince."

Two things he seems certain will never happen.

"When both of those things come true, I'll have your apology," I say, refusing to let him have the last word.

"*If* those things ever come true, I'll give it gladly." His expression softens. "Lysandir is my prince, but he is also my friend." He pauses, letting the statement sink in. "I want his happiness as much as my own. More, perhaps. If you could bring him the joy he seeks, the companionship without the risk of betrayal and treason, I would welcome it with my whole heart."

A knot forms in my throat, and I swallow it down, along with the bitter spew of words I'd been forming only moments ago.

Instead, I simply nod in acknowledgement. He returns the gesture.

The tension between us has lightened as we continue our trek through the woods. Anything near us is long gone after our heated debate.

We don't make it far before a pained bellow echoes from the distance. The utter agony in the sound, the way it reverberates through my body, raises the fine hairs on the back of my neck. The birds of the forest go eerily quiet. Tharin pulls his sword from where it's strapped along his back and turns in place, assessing for danger.

I reach for my bow, for any weapon. "What was—"

The sound comes again, this time from a new direction. Closer. Through a break in the tree canopy, I spy something soaring up into the sky. My chest empties out as recognition sinks in.

Fire.

A pillar of fire soars toward the clouds.

I gasp and jolt as Tharin grabs hold of my arm. He tugs me close until I'm practically plastered against his body. His sword is out in front of us, a shield against some unknown foe.

"What is happening?" I implore.

I barely register the tingle of magic across my skin before Tharin jerks me behind him.

"Mira!"

My heart leaps. "Lysandir!"

At the arrival of his prince, Tharin releases me.

I run to Lysandir, but he's already there, pulling me into his arms. Strong fingers weave through my hair and cup the back of my head, and he holds me against his chest, cradling me like a lost child.

"You're okay. You're fine." His palm skim down my back and across my side.

I lean my head back just enough to look up at Lysandir. His eyes are wide and panicked. His chest rises and falls with heavy breaths like he's just run a marathon.

"What's happening?" I all but beg.

"I don't know," he admits. The edge of a quaver lingers in his voice. He shifts his attention to Tharin. "Take her to my mother at the pavilion."

"What?" I gape as he pulls away.

It's trouble. Or something horrible. Both. I don't know. All I know is being apart from Lysandir in this moment feels like the worst possible outcome.

I reach for him. "I don't—"

But Tharin is already there. I barely have the chance to register him taking my hand before the world melts away and suddenly we're standing under a large, open pavilion consumed by frantic whispers and rushing bodies.

"What's happened?" Elaine is on her feet, inching her way toward Tharin the moment we appear.

Nearby, more guards materialize with Adeline and Cora.

"I do not know," Tharin replies to the dowager. "There was a cry I believe to be the king's, followed by a another and a pillar of fire."

I nearly choke on a gasp. "The king?" I stammer. "Is he hurt?"

But no one is paying me any attention.

More magic rushes over my skin. Katherine and Zoe are back now, asking the same questions as the rest of us. Lysandir reappears with Grace in tow. There's barely time for relief that he's back when he orders, "Get my mother and the women inside. Keep them safe."

The last of his command still rings in the air when he vanishes again.

"Tharin?" I turn to him, but his attention is focused on Elaine.

"Bring us to the royal wing," she orders nearby guards. The way she so calmly assumes command would impress even a hardened general. "We'll stay in my quarters. They're heavily warded. It should be safe there."

Tharin finally glances at me, face set with hardened focus. "You heard her."

He takes my hand, and we're moving again.

CHAPTER 30

I N MOMENTS, THE HALLWAY we appear in is full of activity, and we're being shown into the queen's private rooms. They're as grand and lavish as one might expect but not in the ostentatious and cold way that my aunt and uncle's home is. Her quarters exude warmth and comfort, with plush seating, blankets aplenty, and many woven tapestries hanging from the walls. Shelves filled with all sorts of knickknacks take up the remaining space, and a hint of something earthy clings to the air, just like it did in my abuela's home before she passed.

We need all of that comfort right now.

"A few of you go back and make sure all of the women are brought to me immediately," the queen orders. "And find out what's happened!"

The guards rush to obey, their movement a sharp contrast to the rest of us, who stand like frozen pillars near the entrance. I quickly take stock of the women around me. Zoe, Katherine, Adeline, Grace, Cora. Gabriella is here now too. But where are Alex and Bailey?

"Grace!" comes a cry from the hallway. And then Alex is there, wide-eyed and breathing heavy.

"I'm here!" Grace rushes to her friend. "The king," she starts. "What happened?"

Alex clings to the doorframe, as disheveled and panicked as I've ever seen her. All her focus is on Grace, as if she almost can't believe she's there.

"Come in, child." Elaine hobbles forward with her cane, waving off the guards, who always seem to try to help her only to get refused. "Sit. You're safe here."

Alex blinks and nods, but it's clear she's only half here. Her attention darts from one of us to the next as she makes her way to the nearest chair and all but falls into it.

The air in the room is full of tension and unspoken questions. I come and take a seat near her, waiting for the answers I can sense before they're spoken. Alex is never rattled, but whatever happened has knocked her for a doozy.

"I was with the king," she says, her voice barely above a whisper. She glances at the dowager. "Everything was fine. We thought we might have the beast's trail. But all of the sudden, he went eerily still. And then his wrist, the bond mark"—she holds up her own for emphasis—"it started to smoke."

The dowager's eyes close and don't reopen. Some of the strength seems to go out of her, and she doesn't rebuff the guard who eases her toward a chair.

Alex turns toward the rest of us. "He cried out like he was in pain. Then vanished without a word. We heard another cry then saw fire. He didn't return." She hangs her head, shakes it, then look up at Grace. "I worried— I thought maybe..."

Cora rises to her feet. "Where's Bailey?" Unexpected brittleness clings to the name.

Dawning horror seeps through my veins like molasses.

"Where is she?" Cora asks again, her voice rising in a panic.

"Dead."

The single word knocks the breath from me like a punch to the chest. Even more so because of the male who delivered it. Lysandir stands in the doorway, something protruding from his closed fist. Tharin stands just behind him.

His statement was for the whole room, but he stares only at me, a hollow emptiness in his eyes like it's my death he pronounced.

"No," Adeline gasps. Grace lets out a whimper. Even Cora collapses on a sofa and covers her face. Tears come from nowhere to leak down my face.

Lysandir grimaces and cuts his gaze toward the floor.

Dead.

Bailey, who was kind to everyone. Who had a million brothers and sisters back home that she loved and cared for. Bailey, who might be the only one of us who truly cared for the king. And who he may have cared for in return.

No. Did care for.

It was anguish I heard in his cry. Utter devastation. The pillar of fire... It was his rage. Heartbreak.

My nails carve little grooves in my palms. He loved her, damn it! She was his pick. His choice.

"It's not possible," Zoe implores. "It can't be. We're safe here. She—" She claps a hand over her mouth, tears leaking down her face.

"We believed so as well." Lysandir enters the room and comes to kneel before his mother, who has finally opened her eyes. For the first time since I've seen her, she looks her age. Worse, she looks defeated.

Lysandir unfurls his palm. The object he holds looks like the back end of an arrow, but the fletching and make are different than the ones we had.

"That style..." Elaine glances up in horror.

He nods and tightens his fist around it once more. "Unseelie."

The word steals any remaining warmth from the room.

"But the wards," I say. They're supposed to keep the Unseelie out or at least alert of their presence, should they be breached. That's what happened before. We're near the center of the territory. If Unseelie had slipped past their defenses, they should have felt it long ago.

Lysandir rises to his feet. "With all the comings and goings of members of the other courts over the past days, we must have missed something."

"Missed something?" Alex snaps, whirling in her seat. "*Missed* a deadly enemy?"

"Alex—" I begin, rising to Lysandir's defense. She whirls on me, her teeth pulled back in a snarl.

A strong tug on my wrist nearly pulls me from my feet. A few other women cry out. But no one has touched me. Still, it feels like ghost has grabbed me and is trying to toss me across the room.

"What is—" Alex grabs her wrist, right over the bond mark, and suddenly it all clicks.

I snap my attention to Lysandir, a question in my gaze. As suddenly as it started, the tug releases like a snapped rope.

"Vasilius is furious." His gaze dips to my wrist. "He's trying to go to the Shadow Lands."

"But he can't," I say. "The power of the bonds he has with all of us prevent him from being so far away. Just like the power is trying to pull us to him, it's jerking him back to us nine-fold."

A stab of sorrow pierces my chest.

Eight-fold. Not nine. Not anymore.

"Find him," Elaine demands of her son. "Talk some sense into him. He cannot storm into battle during The Choosing, not with all of the women here."

"I will," Lysandir promises his mother.

He turns to me, and once again, his eyes hold an ocean of sorrow. All I want to do is run to him, wrap my arms around his neck, and pull him close. But I can't. Not here. And then he's gone, off to carry out orders.

Tharin steps into the void. "I must ask you all to stay here for now, for your safety." To the queen, he says, "Advisor Memnon was severely injured but lives. Hopefully, we will be able to learn more when he wakes."

"Inform me at once, whatever you learn," she says.

Tharin bows, and then he's gone too.

Sorrowful silence and sniffles accompany us until Cora speaks.

"She was his choice, wasn't she?" Her makeup is smeared, but she doesn't seem to care. All of her spark has gone out. I thought her companionship with Bailey was a recent thing, a front to get closer to the king, but maybe I was wrong. "He was going to pick her."

Elaine swallows. The slight bob of her head that follows is another nail in each of our hearts. He cared for her. He was going to choose her.

But Bailey—sweet, wonderful Bailey—is dead. The king will have to choose anoth—

I cry out. My hand flies to cover my mouth, but it's too late to stifle the sound. The horror of my realization threatens to choke me, and it takes everything I have to pull in one breath or another.

"Mira?" Adeline sniffles and slides closer to me before wrapping her arm around my shoulders.

She can't help. No one can. Because the king's choice is dead. He will have to choose another.

And Lysandir has already seen that outcome.

Chapter 31

T HE HOURS THAT PASS don't lessen the crushing weight of guilt and despair that threaten to break me apart. It's not just that either. This waiting around in sadness reminds me all too much of when my dad died. It was quick too, as heart attacks often are. Fine one minute and gone another. I wasn't even there for it. It's the after that's painful for those who are left behind.

There was numbness first. Shock. Then such deep sadness that I didn't know how I'd ever smile again or how I could even breathe without feeling the pain of loss. I wasn't that close to Bailey. I'd only known her a couple of weeks, but I'd talked to her this morning. She'd smiled at me. Comforted me. And now I'll never have that again.

And I can't help but think it's my fault. That fate destined me for the fae king and had to get her out of the way to make that happen. Even my mother said I was destined to wear the crown. I thought it was just optimistic talk back then, but now?

Now I can't help but wonder what I did to piss the fates off so terribly.

The death toll is up to three. Bailey and two guards—thankfully neither of whom is Adeline's lover. He is safe. For the moment.

The queen seems certain that The Choosing cannot be canceled, not since we are bound to the king. The bonds prevented us from being taken away, which we thought to be the biggest risk from the Unseelie. No one imagined that they would harm a human. It's so foolish, so contrary to their goal of gaining the power that a human could offer them.

We pondered whether it might be accidental, but Tharin, in one of his reports back to Elaine, said Bailey's wound was intentional, the arrow quick and efficient.

At least she didn't suffer. It's the only good news we've had.

There have been a few more sharp tugs on our bond marks. I can almost feel Vasilius's rage mingling with my own.

The head of the king's personal guard arrives to speak with us and the dowager queen. "We're to move you all to Calida at first light."

Elaine smashes the end of her cane against the floor. "He cannot be so foolish as to charge into battle for reckless vengeance. He will start a war that we do not need."

The king's burly guard flinches. "I am sorry, Your Grace. He will not be dissuaded. I have tried, as has Prince Lysandir."

She begins to rise. "Let me speak with him."

"He will see no one. He has left."

"Left?" she asks in disbelief, sinking back into her chair.

He nods slowly, frown deepening. "The king ordered that we not follow him." To us, he says, "Your maids are readying your things for travel. You should rest while you can. All of your rooms have been thoroughly checked for safety, and we've tripled the guard." He snaps his fingers and more guards enter. "We will escort those who wish to return to their rooms."

Several women leave. A few of us remain. I can't seem to make myself rise from the sofa. The presence of others is the only thing keeping a leash on my emotions. If I were alone, nothing would hold them back anymore.

When Tharin returns some time later, those of us who remain look to him for news. "Advisor Memnon is awake," he says.

Some of the tension in the room releases. But Elaine only says, "And?"

"He was not able to provide much information. He saw—" Tharin looks quickly at us before adjusting his stance and starting again. "He saw the beginning of the encounter but was quickly injured and knocked out. A small, targeted attack, he believes. Our investigation of the area confirmed as much. There could not have been more than one or two attackers."

"And you've found them?" she continues.

Tharin swallows.

"No, Your Grace." At the thinning of her lips, he continues, "We have been able to find no trace of them outside of where the attack took place. No physical evidence. No scent. Even that which we found at the site was fleeting—barely detectable, like they found some way to disguise their scent without concealing it with another."

"Some nasty blood magic to be sure." The old queen's voice holds all the venom of a viper.

The mention of it leaves me glad I haven't eaten. An empty stomach is preferable to one turned by the mention of the dark rituals the Unseelie are said to perform, especially now that the magic of their land is all but extinguished.

"And the king?" she asks after a moment. "He has returned?"

The pause before he answers says everything. "No, Your Grace."

With considerable effort, Elaine gets to her feet, hunching over her cane. "Then I must rest and prepare to travel as well."

"Is that wise?" Tharin asks, though his voice is soft, full of more concern than he's ever shown me.

She looks up at him, considering. "Someone must make him see reason. I must try."

They hold each other's gaze for a moment before Tharin nods. "Then I will see the women returned to their rooms so you can rest."

It's only me, Adeline, and Cora—who's been unusually quiet and somber. We go without argument. A quick shift and we're closer to our rooms but not quite there. Night has fallen while we've been cloistered in the dowager's room. Complete darkness looms outside the nearby windows, and I can't help staring at them, wondering what dangers lurk beyond that I cannot see. Not that I need to worry about that, I suppose. My destiny seems set.

"Your hall has been completely warded against shifting," Tharin says by way of explanation. "And we've posted extra guards at all entry points. No Unseelie will get close to you."

We wander toward our rooms when Tharin steps closer to me. "Mira, a moment."

Adeline looks at me in question, almost like she doesn't want to leave me alone, even though her guardsman is one of the ones waiting to escort us to our rooms.

It's okay, I mouth. She sighs softly but continues on.

Tharin and I wait in silence until the others have departed. "Mira, I—"

"I know," I cut him off sharply. "You don't need to say it."

He crosses his arms. "I don't think you do."

"Fate is set. This proves it, right?"

His lips thin, and I expect him to agree with me. Instead, he sighs, his arms swinging free. "I wanted to say that you should not blame yourself. If your fate is set, so was hers."

Tears burn at the corner of my eyes, and I squeeze my fists tighter to try and push them away. "Why not just tell him? End this."

He rakes a hand through his hair. "I vowed not to. And I—" He looks away then back at me. "I doubt the king is in a mood to take a queen right now." Tharin clasps my shoulder. "Rest. Be kind to yourself. For *him*, if nothing else."

I know he doesn't mean the king anymore, though anyone listening might not.

I scowl and open my mouth, prepared to snap at him when he vanishes. Lucky bastard, being able to disappear whenever he wants.

CHAPTER 32

I BARELY REGISTER WALKING to my room or the palace around me. I don't think as I grab the handle of my door, push it open, and step inside.

The first indication that something is wrong is a soft moan and the sight of shadowed movement on the bed in the dimly lit room.

I freeze. My stomach plummets. Anger and jealousy rear up within me until one of the figures sits up with a sharp gasp.

"Mira?" Alex stares at me in horror.

A feminine squeak comes from farther in the bed.

Oh God. All my shock and fury snuffs out in a moment, melted into a tide of embarrassment that has my skin burning.

Wrong room. I'm in the wrong fucking room!

I turn on my heel and lurch back out the door, pulling it shut behind me. In the hallway, I glance around and quickly spot my error. One room too soon.

Grace's room...

One of the guards pacing near the end of the hall stops. "Lady Mira, do you need—"

"We're good," I call, a little bit of near hysterical laughter bubbling out. I'm at my door a heartbeat later, throwing it open, rushing inside, and almost slamming it behind me. I lean back on it for support. My heart pounds in my ears.

What did I just see? I ask the dimly lit room. But I know. They've been close the whole time. Just friends, I thought. After all, they came here to marry the king, right? Didn't they?

A knock reverberates through the door. I yelp, jumping away from it.

"Mira?" Alex calls through the wood. "Can I come in?"

Oh my God. I buy my face in my hands. As if this day could get any worse.

The door cracks open, and I hear another voice, this one barely as whisper. "We just need a minute."

Grace.

Damn it. The last thing we need is the guards getting curious.

"Yeah. Come in," I squeak.

They slip inside and close the door but linger just inside it. Grace's hair is a little disheveled, but otherwise no one could tell what they'd been up to. They're both wearing casual human nightwear—a baggy shirt and shorts for Grace, a hoody and long sleep pants for Alex—but that's not unusual on our hall at night. Awkward silence fille the short distance between us.

Finally, I break it.

"Sorry. I got the wrong room." *Of all the times to not lock the damn door.* I hold up my hands. "I didn't—" *see anything.*

And technically that's true, but we all know that I know exactly what was happening in there.

I sigh. "I won't tell anyone. I promise."

They look between one another, some silent conversation happening. Grace gives a weak smile.

Alex's jaw stiffens, and she twists to look at me. "Why wouldn't you? Tell anyone, that is."

"Why would I?" I counter.

"To narrow your competition."

I nearly snort. Right. Which might be valid if I was a total bitch *and* actually wanted to marry the king, but I don't. Not that fate gives a damn about what I want.

"Trust me, I have no intention of doing that." I wander across the room and sit heavily on the edge of my bed, the weight of everything nearly crushing.

Alex and Grace share another look.

"Why?" Grace asks carefully as she crosses the room to stand near the end of the bed. Her brows are still furrowed, her head cocked to the side. I guess I'd be confused by me too if I were her.

"Maybe I don't want to marry the king either."

"Really?" She looks taken aback. "Though I never said I was opposed to marrying him."

I blink at her, dumbfound. "Huh?"

"I, we—" She looks at Alex, who has come to stand at her side. "We don't plan to leave Faery. Ever."

"Grace..." Alex gives her a hard look.

The shorter woman shrugs. "I think we can trust her."

Alex swears under her breath. "I hope you're right."

"So, you two are a thing? But you also want to marry the king?" Two and two are not making four, but they might add up to a different number. "Like a threesome?"

Alex groans. "Let's just go."

"No wait, seriously," I hop off the bed. "I'm sorry. I'm just confused."

"I'll explain." Grace brushes past Alex to sit on the edge of my bed and pulls me down next to her. "Our families have always been close, which is how we became friends." She smiles at Alex. "And then more than friends. But they're also both super strict about coven rules and such. They stick to the old ways."

She says it as if I should understand, but I don't really.

Alex must realize that because she says, "Gifted daughters have one real use—breeding." She all but spits the word. "Either you go to Faery and make a match with a powerful fae and bare his little magically gifted faelings, or you stay on Earth, make a good match with a gifted man, and bear his kids."

Continue the line on Earth or become a tribute to the fae. It's so old-fashioned, so... backward. But isn't that what my family has done too? If I didn't go to Faery, Selena might have been forced to. And doesn't my uncle dislike my mom just because she's not gifted? Because my father sullied our family line with her non-gifted blood?

"But isn't marrying the king just following through on that?" I ask.

"Sort of," Grace admits. "But the king doesn't really favor humans. It's why he's put this off for so long. When he does take a human bride, I doubt he'll be the picture of an attentive husband. He's not..." Her breath catches. "Well, he did care for..." She breaks off with a sniffle.

For Bailey. I take her hand in mine. Alex drops onto the bed on her other side, wrapping an arm around her.

"Sorry," Grace says after a moment.

"Don't be," I reply. I still feel like part of my chest has been ripped open. Talking about it, thinking about it, makes it much worse.

"We thought," Alex continues for her, "that we'd have a better chance of being together here than on Earth, where our families forbid it. It was run away and try to start a new life with nothing or come here and hope for something better. Either one of us marries the king and uses our influence to keep the other around, meet the king's needs when we have to, but otherwise be together. Or neither of us gets picked but we still earn enough of the king's favor that he'll let us stay and be together, despite what our families might demand after the competition."

"Damn. That's..." Even their most optimistic outcomes seem rough, and I hate it for them. Fighting for a man you don't want just so you can stay with your lover? How awful that must be. "I'm sorry for all that you've had to go through. You should be able to be together because you love one another. That should be enough."

"Maybe since you know about us," Grace says, "you could help?"

"Yes. If I can, I will. But how can I?"

"If the king picks you, use your power as queen to make sure we can stay." She glances over at Alex, her gaze full of love. "Together."

How ironic that fate says I will be. I hate it. I dread it. But maybe I can make something good come from my fate. "I will. I promise. No marriage to some fae or anyone else required."

Grace beams like all their problems have been solved.

"So damn optimistic," Alex grumbles, but I catch the hint of adoration in her gaze as she stares at Grace.

For the first time in hours—days—the tightness around my chest loosens.

"So, you really don't want to marry the king?" Grace asks.

Uh oh. Should have figured she'd remember that. "He's...not my type?"

"Oh. You're a lesbian too?" Alex peers over at me.

"Hey now," Grace scolds her.

Alex ruffles her hair. "You don't have anything to worry about."

Grace huffs but looks at me, waiting for an answer.

"No, sorry." I don't know why I'm apologizing. "More like I like someone else?"

The flush of embarrassment is back again, and I can't seem to make anything come out a statement. In fact, I suddenly feel like I've fallen back in time to my preteen years when I had a sleepover at Selena's house and was too embarrassed to say which member of the boy band I thought was the hottest.

"So, your family pushed you into the competition?" Grace asks. "I was wondering why we hadn't met you before. He's not gifted, I take it?"

This only makes my cheeks flame hotter. She's way wrong, and I should let her run with those conclusions. It'd be smarter, safer, but for some reason I whisper, "The prince."

"Harry?" Grace's brows pinch.

I run my palms down my face. "Lysandir."

Both of them stare at me wide-eyed.

"Well damn," Alex remarks.

"Oh. Oh!" Grace bounces on the bed and looks like she's about to combust with the need to say something more.

I grimace. "Yeah, so maybe don't tell anyone?"

"You keep our secrets, and we'll keep yours," Alex promises.

"But oh my God, we have to talk about this!" Grace grabs my arm and gives it a little shake, her whole body still vibrating with excitement. "I mean, he is always around you, but I thought that maybe he didn't trust you after that whole thing at the induction ceremony." She leans in closer. "Does he like you? Is it one-sided?"

"Uh…" I lean back, trying to put some much needed space between us.

"When did all of this start?" Grace presses. "Does he know?"

The panic welling up in me must be written on my face because Alex gently tugs Grace off me and pulls her off the bed and toward the door.

"Settle down now, kitten," Alex says.

"But I— We—" She gestures between herself and me.

"Later." She urges her toward the door. "Good night, Mira," she says to me.

"Good night." I give a little wave. *And thank you a million for making this discussion stop.*

Grace sighs. "But you have to tell me more sometime. Okay?"

A brittle smile twitches at the corner of my lips. "Um, okay."

"Out." Alex gives her a gentle shove toward the door, and then finally they're gone.

But the minute the door closes behind them and silence settles over the room once more, it doesn't take long for the horrors of the day to slink back through the shadows to haunt me.

CHAPTER 33

T HE MOVE TO A new city is oddly simple and seamless. Given the fae ability to shift, there's no real travel involved. One moment, we're in the capital, and then after a dizzying and stomach-dropping moment, we're not.

The rooms we're assigned here are a little smaller but even more ostentatious, with thick rugs, beds with lush canopies, and furniture could have been plucked straight from the palace at Versailles. Tapestries and glass sculptures make the room more a museum than anything I'd ever call comfortable. Sneezing feels like it could be a dangerous activity here.

Apparently, the city of Calida was once a regular getaway for the royals and upper nobility of the court, and these rooms were decorated to reflect that. Their positioning is strange too, with all of the rooms on one side of a large, circular hallway like spokes on a bicycle tire. Each has a back door leading out into a large courtyard that all the rooms can access.

It seems like a huge security risk, but we've been assured there's no safer place in the city, as the section is heavily warded and no one save the king himself can shift into any of the rooms or the courtyard. Plus, the guards can easily ring in the area to keep Unseelie—or anyone else—from slipping by unnoticed.

Fia is already in my room when I get there, organizing the last of my clothes into a wardrobe taller than her. My dressing table already contains an artful display of her cosmetics, and my desk has been setup just like my old one, right down to the pens I received from Lysandir displayed in their case. For me, it's like I snapped my fingers and my old room appeared here, but I know that's far from the case.

"Did you sleep at all?" I ask Fia.

"A little." She closes the wardrobe. The door gives a soft click. "But don't worry about me."

It's hard not to. I worry about all of us, especially this close to Unseelie territory, and if the king is as mad as they say? It'll be war. Bloody, terrible, and deadly.

Whatever talent I may have had for hiding my thoughts and emotions seems to have been lost in the wreckage of the last few days, because it's almost like Fia can read my mind. She stops just in front of me and cups my cheek. The oddly intimate touch makes my chest swell.

"It may be wrong to say, but I'm glad it was not you." She drops her hand. "Not just because I hope you'll win, but I would be heartbroken if anything happened to you."

My face is still puffy from the tears that accompanied me to sleep. I thought I'd exhausted them all, but somehow, more sting at the corners of my eyes. "You too. I worry that you, that all of us, have been dragged into danger."

On account of me. Because I'm fated for the king, but he wanted another.

I gasp as she wraps me in a hug. When she releases me, she says, "We'll get through this. All of us together."

I so hope she's right.

"Maybe some coffee?" she offers. "That always helps you."

"Sure."

The moment she pulls the door open to leave, Tharin fills its frame, fist raised like he was about to knock.

"Oh? You again." Fia gives him an appreciative once-over. "Do you need something?"

His lips quirk up a little in the corner as he stares at her. The look that passes between them makes me feel like an outsider intruding on a private moment. When did *that* happen?

"I require Lady Mira," he finally says. "I'll return her to her room in a little bit."

I barely hold back a sigh. What now?

Knowing better than to keep him waiting, I head toward the door, but he switches places with Fia and closes it behind him.

"We're shifting?" I ask. "I thought that didn't work here."

"No," he replies. "But I thought the back door might be more discrete."

My brows pinch. "For what?"

"You'll see."

I follow him out the back door of my room and into the courtyard. Morning sunlight slants in at angle, painting the colorful foliage in soft light. A stone pathway weaves from the back door off into the array of strategically placed trees that tower at least two stories high. Dew clings to the grass on either side of the pathway, and I spot doors and windows leading to the rooms on either side of mine before the plant life and curvature of the building blocks my view of the rest.

The stone pathway leads to a central open area with many other paths branching off of it, presumably leading toward the other rooms. Smooth flagstones create a floor of sorts, short mosses and grass filling the narrow spaces between them. A massive glass flame occupies the very center of the space. It catches the sun, the bright colors of the glass shimmering. A few benches and seats are stationed around it, ready for people to gather and socialize.

"Kind of a weird setup," I remark.

Tharin halts, and at first, I think we've reached our destination, but he seems to be assessing the paths, looking for another one. It's then I notice the colorful stones inlaid at the beginning of each one, likely an indicator of where they lead.

He glances over one shoulder. His lips quirk up in the corner. "A former king commissioned this wing specifically," he says. "He was quite fond of parties where people tended to end up in each other's beds. Discretely"—he glances toward one path and then another—"or not so."

There are some things I really don't need to know. "You're joking."

My mind crafts a vision of fae giggling as they steal through the courtyard at night, heading for someone else's room.

"Joking?" A strange look crosses his face. "Ah, you mean lying. No." He smirks again. "In case you forgot, I can't do that, much as I might wish to at times."

I nearly groan. "I shouldn't have asked."

"Ah, but you did."

He heads down another path, and I follow.

"Where are we going?" I ask again.

"I'd have thought a clever woman like you might have figured it out already. Or did you forget why it's me guarding you?"

I skip a step, warmth rushing to my face. Lysandir.

Part of me cries out in joy. There's no one I've yearned for more. But another part is terrified.

All too soon, we're standing before another door. Tharin doesn't even knock before it opens, and he's there.

The Lysandir before me takes my breath away. Gone are the light, casual clothes he favors. Nor does he wear the grand ceremonial attire he'd worn at the balls. Instead, golden armor hugs his form, gleaming where the light strikes it.

My mouth drops open. I barely register Tharin saying, "I'll wait outside."

And if not for the soft shove he gives me in Lysandir's direction, I'm not sure I could have made myself move at all.

Lysandir holds out his gauntlet-covered hand to me, and I take it, letting him lead me into his room. Tharin closes the door behind us, the sound fracturing the hold on my emotions. *He's here. He's here.* But this isn't my usual bookish prince. Golden plate covers his boots, his arms, and shoulders. Thick, dark material hugs him like a second skin beneath. The breastplate he wears bears a bright red flame. Only his head is uncovered, his hair pulled back in a tight ponytail behind his head.

"You're going," I say.

"Yes." His throat bobs. "My brother seeks vengeance. As do many of our court. Someone must check his more reckless impulses, or he won't stop until he's tracked down the Unseelie King himself."

"And that someone is you." Of course it is. I pinch my eyes closed.

Something cool touches my face, and I snap my eyes open. He cups my cheek with his armored hand, tipping my chin up. "I had to see you again before I leave."

Before he heads off to war. To fight. To kill. To do all the things he hates.

"I'm sorry. It's my fault," I whimper.

"No!" He cups my face between his palms and leans in until our foreheads nearly touch. "No. None of this is your fault. Not Bailey's death. Not Vasilius's actions. None of it."

"But your vision..."

"*My* vision," he echoes. "If anyone were to blame, it would be me. But even then, we cannot know that it would change this. If fate is truly unchangeable, if my visions must come true, then what happened to them, what happens now, may have been inevitable as well." A tear leaks down my cheek, and he smooths it away. "Do not ever blame yourself, Mira. Please."

I swallow the tightness in my throat and manage a nod, though I'm not sure I can keep my word. How can I? The guilt still gnaws like hunger that won't be sated. "But if revealing my future can end this, prevent future death—"

Lysandir jerks his head back and forth, eyes glowing with emotion. "He's not in a state to hear it. If we were to tell him now, it would only incite his fury. I won't risk him harming you."

I gasp. "You think he would?"

"I am not sure." He swallows thickly.

If not me, Lysandir could be on the receiving end of his anger. He kept the secret longer. He knew what his brother wanted to know but did not tell him.

"He might punish you," I whisper.

His gaze darts away, and that's all I need to know.

I tighten my hold on him. "Then we won't do it. I won't risk you either."

"Mira." He swipes away another tear and then pulls me into a hug against his armored chest. I wrap my arms around him as best I'm able and burrow closer.

"What comes next?" I whisper. "Do you know?"

"My brother asked me to look into the future, to see what would happen if we invade the Unseelie lands." He pulls in a long, slow breath. "I did, and all I saw was fire."

I pull back enough just to look up at him. "Fire, as in your victory?"

"I don't know. It could be but..." He shakes his head. "It's all I saw when I asked about the Unseelie before too."

It's too vague. He doesn't know. Worse, he's worried. He doesn't need to say it. It seeps from him like tears do from me.

"I'm going to get my smell all over you." I start to pull back.

He doesn't let me go. "I... I should care. But I don't. Not right now." He cups my cheek again. The pleading desperation in his eyes tugs at something deep within me. "Mira..."

I wrap my arms around his neck, stretch up on my toes, and kiss him.

And God, does he kiss me back. The passion, the hunger, steal my sanity.

I want to tear the armor from him piece by piece just to get closer. It's foolish, reckless. This whole kiss could be a horrible mistake. But he's leaving. He's going off to war. He could be injured. He could die. And I would never forgive myself for holding back, for stealing away what could be our last moments because of fear.

So, I kiss him, and I cling to him, and I hold him close, savoring every touch, every breath, until he slowly, gently pulls away.

"I have to go," he whispers before placing another kiss against my lips.

I let him untangle my arms from around his neck, pull my fingers from his hair where they've ruined his smooth ponytail. Tears blur my vision, and I'm not ashamed when a few slip free.

They're his. All of me is his.

My legs wobble beneath me when he releases me and steps back. His hungry stare as he looks me up and down nearly makes me whimper. I have to bite my bottom lip to hold it back. But that might be the wrong thing to do because his gaze snaps to my lips. A glow flares from his pupils, and I'd swear he looks like he might pounce on me like a beast at any moment. But I'm not afraid. Not nearly. I'd give myself over to be devoured in a heartbeat.

"I..." He rubs a down his face. "I have something for you before I must leave."

Lysandir stalks over to a table and rips the lid off a small box. He plucks out a golden chain with something dangling from it.

As he returns, my heart skips a beat. It's not a pendent hanging off the necklace but a ring.

It's hanging from a chain, clearly not an engagement ring or anything of the like, but my lust-addled brain can't compute and screams in shock like it is.

He holds it up, so I can clearly see ornately carved golden band inlaid with red—possibly ruby. "I want you to have this. The ring is too big for you I think, so I placed it on a chain, but its twin to one of mine, a bonded pair."

"Lysandir..." I'm speechless, my mouth gaping open like a fish. "Thank you."

"May I?" He lifts it for emphasis.

I nod. He places the necklace over my head, caressing the back of my neck and down over my collarbone as he brushes my hair out from under it. The ring lands heavy and warm at the apex of my cleavage.

I take the ring before my thumb and forefinger and stare down at it. The design, although a bit masculine, is stunning, with a circle of flames rushing around the band. At first, I only saw the red stones, but there are others too, inlaid within the metal so its smooth when I run the pad of my finger across it.

"It's warm," I say, struck by the oddity.

"With any luck, it will stay that way," he says. The hint of a grin pulls at the corner of his mouth. "I can feel yours now, warming on my finger." He holds up his hand, though of course I can't see it wherever it lies below the gauntlet. "Wear it always, if you will. As long as it's against your skin in some way, mine will warm and let me know you're safe."

"And mine will stay warm if you're safe," I confirm.

He nods. "That's not all. As a bonded pair, the two call to another. I'll be able to find you, to shift to you, while you wear it." His tongue slips out, moistening his lips, and he glances away. "I hope that's all right with you."

Something caught between a sigh and a laugh slips out. "Of course it is."

When he glances back at me, the adoration in his smile nearly makes me melt. "Good. I'm glad. It'll give me peace of mind to know you're safe."

"Same."

His smile dims and he swallows thickly. Just that action, and I feel my heart start to crack. I tuck the ring under my shirt and savor the way its warmth settles on my skin.

When I fear I might crumble, Lysandir pulls me into his arms once more and kisses me which such ferocity it steals my breath. I'm almost dizzy when he releases me.

"Now, I really must go," he says. "But I'll come back to you. I vow it."

A tingle of magic shimmers in the air. A vow. A one-sided fae bargain.

"You sealed it with magic?" I gape.

Lysandir grins before picking up a golden helm and tucking it under his arm. "Only death could keep me away. And I suppose then it wouldn't matter if I couldn't keep my vow."

"And you think I'm going to let you leave after saying something like that."

He huffs air through his nose. "Probably not." He gives a sharp whistle. A moment later, the back door opens, and Tharin enters. "Please see Mira back to her room."

"Of course." He gives a little bow, nose twitching. "Don't forget to fix your hair."

My cheeks heat, and I'd swear a blush rises to Lysandir's cheeks as well.

Tharin wraps his hand loosely around my upper arm and guides me toward the door.

"Please be safe," I say to Lysandir, hoping my words carry so much more than that.

"I'll see you soon," Lysandir promises.

I watch him over my shoulder the whole way to the door, savoring every moment until Tharin closes it and leads me away.

Chapter 34

T HE FAE DON'T BURY their dead—they burn them. At least, that's the case for the Court of Fire.

But we don't have Bailey's body to burn. It was returned to Earth, to her family, along with letters to all of ours, confirming our safety and the king's commitment to keeping us all safe and healthy. I sent one to be delivered to my mom, as well as another to my cousin. I truly don't remember much of what I wrote in either. They were short but full of love. What else is there to say? They'll worry no matter what. I suppose I could tell them the future. That I'm destined to wed the king, so I won't die, at least not anytime soon. But what comes after that? Promising my safety would feel hollow no matter what.

Without a body to burn, the queen orders a ceremonial fire instead. It's purely symbolic, but the small bonfire the guards craft in a wide brazier in the courtyard amid all our rooms might as well be a funeral, for the somberness that blankets us all.

No one speaks much as the last of sunset fades away, leaving Bailey's ceremonial fire as our source of light. But in the silence, in the sorrow, we find solidarity.

The competition doesn't matter right now. How can it? We're just a bunch of women, acquaintances, tentative friends, more in some cases, but the differences that kept us apart, the goal that divided us, no longer seem as wide and impossible to cross. I even find myself standing next to Cora and feeling a weird urge to put my arm around her or give her a hug. I don't, but any anger I've felt toward her is gone. Katherine too.

For now, we're all allies.

Queen Elaine keeps us close to her the next day and the next. Lysandir's ring stays warm against my chest, a little spark of hope that I find myself reaching for and physically clinging to more than I should. It could be problematic if someone notices and asks about it, though I can always lie. Humanity has some advantages.

Our movements are limited, our comings and goings mostly restricted to our rooms and the central courtyard. For lack of anything better to do, or maybe out of the need for some semblance of stability, Zoe declared that she would lead yoga this morning. We haven't done it since before Bailey died. She never participated but watched a lot, and I almost feel like she's watching this morning.

Maybe everyone else feels it too because every single woman shows up. Even Elaine sits on a bench and watches. She occupies one of the rooms. Another belongs to the king, though I don't think he's used it. According to Tharin, neither Vasilius nor Lysandir have returned. And what they've been up to... The dark look that crossed his face was all I needed to know. In some ways, I'm glad he wouldn't tell me.

When we finally rise from the final child's pose, more than one woman has wet streaks on her cheeks, including me.

Elaine waves forward a few fae carrying trays of drinks and little snacks. I almost smile at that. She's really taken to us like a mother lately, seeing that we're eating, watching over us, trying to provide little comforts where she can. When no one else takes up the seat on the bench next to her, I do.

"Thank you for being here with us," I say.

Her features soften a bit as she takes me in. "Of course. I do what I can."

"If you'd be more comfortable in the capital though, we'd all understand," I say. She seems a little out of sorts here, and more than once I've seen her struggle to navigate the cobbled paths—not that she lets anyone help her, ridiculous as that is.

She pats my leg. "That's kind, dear, but I must stay."

There's something in her words I can't help but pick at. "Must?"

Adeline takes a seat on a bench nearby with Gabriella—the two have become closer friends of late.

"Mm hmm." She pulls her cane into her laps and gives it a little tap. "I suppose I should tell you all about my cane."

"Your cane?" Zoe asks. She takes a seat crisscross-applesauce on the stonework near us, almost like a kid waiting for story time.

"Yes. Come. Sit. All of you." Elaine beckons the rest near, and they come. Cora even sits on the ground and doesn't act like such a thing is beneath her.

"I take it none of you have worked out exactly what it is yet," she says, holding it up and turning it slightly in her weathered hands.

A beautiful work of art, the cane has many delicate engravings down its length and widens out for about the top foot before ending in a smooth circle that shimmers and catches the light almost like polished glass but is probably some sort of massive gem.

"It's expensive?" Katherine offers.

"Um..." Adeline muses.

Nothing smart comes to mind, so I keep my mouth shut.

"It denotes your position as queen," Cora says confidently.

"That it does," Elaine replies, focusing on her. "But what else? Why does it do that?"

Cora shifts in her seat, her lips pursing. "The shaft is similar to the Spear of Shielding. I assume it's meant to represent that, since it's the Queen of Fire who is tasked with guarding it."

Is it? I sit a little straighter and shift forward in the seat for a better look. I've studied the spear, all of the sacred fae relics, but I always focused more on what they did and why they were important, not so much what they looked like.

"Very close, dear." Elaine runs her hand down the length of the shaft. "Very close. But it's not I who guard the spear so much as I am meant to use it to guard us all in times in of danger, as the next queen—one of you—will be tasked to do as well."

The answer she's leading us toward rears up before me, and I don't stop to think before blurting, "Your cane is the spear."

Pride radiates from her as she turns toward me. "Very good."

"But how?" Adeline asks, echoing the question in my head. "It doesn't look like it."

All the women have moved closer, some rising from their seats, others leaning in.

The Spear of Shielding. A sacred and powerful fae relic. Right there. A foot away from me. I hold tighter to the edge of the bench to steady myself as the realization tries to knock me off kilter. I've been near it so many times and had no idea.

"The shaft can extend." The dowager traces her fingers over some of the engravings. "A push here. A twist there. And the spear point itself, the real power of the thing, remains, carefully hidden." She taps the top of the cane before running her hand along the wider part of the shaft. "As I aged, we had it adjusted so that it could remain with me should I have need of it, but this"—she taps the top—"can be easily shattered, should the time call for it."

"It's smaller than I expected," I admit, still wondering at design of it and the enchanted point of metal that lingers just underneath a carefully crafted cover of sorts.

"Small things can make the biggest impacts," Elaine replies. "Don't let its size or appearance make you doubt its strength."

The gleam in her eye makes me wonder if she's speaking more about herself than the object in her hand.

"You can still use it?" Adeline has shifted so far to the edge of her seat I'm surprised she hasn't fallen off. But her question is a solid one. Everything I've read says the spear is most effective when wielded by a human bearing a fae mark, or mating bond.

"My mate, my husband, may be long dead, but the shadow of his mark remains upon me still." The queen touches her abdomen, the likely spot where the remnants of his mark still linger on her skin. For it to have lasted so long after death, they must really have loved one another. "I can still wield the spear and use its power to shield us, but the effect is not nearly as strong or wide as it was in my youth when my mate still lived. But you see, that is why I must remain close to you all in this dangerous time. Should the worst happen and the Unseelie reach us here, I can protect you until help comes for us."

The admission strips some of the heat from my skin. She must think it a possible outcome, given how staunch she's been in staying near us. That realization seems to settle in on some of the others too. Grace hugs her arms around herself. Adeline slides back in her seat, Gabriella moving closer to her, her eyes downcast.

"That is why you wish the king to marry," Gabriella says into the quiet that has formed. "So another can use the spear."

"One reason. But I also hoped it might center him. Calm his wilder impulses." Elaine shakes her head, gaze downcast.

"A strong woman can do that," Gabriella says.

"She can," the queen agrees. "And he needs it."

It's too bad he doesn't seem to want that. Or didn't... It's hard to say, given how he's reacted to Bailey's death.

"You could choose for him," Cora says. She holds her head a little higher, and there's no question she's hoping the dowager will select her. Just when I thought we'd truly put the competition on hold.

Thankfully, Elaine is a smart woman. "Not now. Not with..." She waves her hand, not wanting to speak what we all know. "He will return, and we will find a way to move forward."

"So, what should we do until then?" Katherine asks.

The absolute most painful thing that can be asked of anyone. "We wait."

CHAPTER 35

W AITING IS AGONY. THOUGH I try to spend every moment with the other women to escape my thoughts, my mind keeps trapping me in one nightmare after another. What if Lysandir's vision of fire meant death? What if I marry the king because Lysandir dies in this battle, and divulging the truth could have prevented it? Being married and bound to his brother while Lysandir lived would be a torment, but he would be alive. And life... Life offers possibility, whereas in death there are none.

It's that nightmare, the worries and what-ifs, that have me clinging to Lysandir's ring almost constantly. It's the first thing I reach for when I open my eyes in the morning and the thing I'm clutching when I close them at night.

It's stayed warm. So far.

"You've been doing that a lot lately." Grace's gaze dips to where I clutch the ring against my chest.

I quickly tuck it back under the neckline of my dress.

"Nervous habit," I reply. It's true, if new.

"Uh huh." She looks unconvinced. We've become closer the last few days. Actually, all of us have. I even found myself enjoying Katherine's company yesterday, much to my own shock, not that I'm anywhere near comfortable enough to share my secrets with her like I have with Grace, Alex, and Adeline. Admittedly, they all learned them somewhat by accident after I stumbled upon their own secrets, but the knowledge of each other's that we keep has drawn us tighter.

I did finally give Grace a few more of the details she so desperately craved, though not about the ring. No one knows about that, and I'd prefer to keep it that way.

"A family heirloom?" Gabriella asks. She's seated across from us and had been reading, though the book must not be that engaging, since apparently she's spent more time watching us that diving into the pages.

Rain this afternoon forced us out of the courtyard and inside to a large and lavish sitting room just outside the circle of our quarters. Still safe, according to our many guards, including Tharin. I'm not really sure when he sleeps because he's always watching over me these days. Even now, he lingers across the room playing a chess-like game with another guard.

"Something like that," I say.

Gabriella lifts her arm, making the bangles around her wrist clink together. "These were my abuela's. I feel better when I wear them." Now that she mentions it, she has been wearing those every day lately. "It's the same for you, yes?"

I force a smile. "Yeah."

Tharin leaps from his seat, knocking over the game board and sending pieces clattering across the floor. Other guards snap to attention.

The fine hairs on the back of my neck rise. "What is it?" I demand, pushing to my feet. "What's happening?"

Elaine, who has been half dozing in her high-back chair is suddenly alert, the spear clutched tight. Grace grabs my hand, grasping it tightly. Alex all but leaps a table to get to us.

The double doors to the room burst open, swinging wildly on their hinges to slam into the walls with a loud crack.

I jump at the noise, my brain scrambling to recognize the figures that stalk through the doors in golden armor. The one at the front is the most imposing of them all, his muscular form accentuated and given a sharp edge by the hard points of his armor that rise like little flames through his shoulders, gloves, and even his boots. The king has lost his helmet somewhere along the way, and his hair is a wild mess, sweat-dampened bits clinging to his cheeks while the rest of it hangs free. It's not enough to conceal the hilt of the sword strapped across his back. Another two shorter ones hang sheathed at his sides.

Bits of dark red paint sections of his armor, but it's not intentional like the glowing flame on his breastplate.

Blood. He's covered in splatters and mists of drying blood.

A feral, almost possessive gleam shines in his eyes as he stalks forward, taking us in one after another, and I fight the urge to flinch under his piercing assessment. The easy-going male who watched me dance those weeks ago, who danced with me, who sat with me under the willow, is long gone, replaced instead by this fearsome warrior straight out of a nightmare.

God help me if I truly have to marry this man.

"My ladies," he croons. "Safe and waiting for my return."

A dark brown bag marred with darker stains is clutched in one fist, and he holds it up. "I return with gifts, of course."

But the chill creeping down my spine says they're not the kind we want.

"Vasilius!" My heart leaps at the sound of Lysandir's voice. *He's here. He's safe!*

The prince shoves between golden-clad warriors to reach the king. He's removed his helm too, holding it in one arm. The stains on his golden armor—though fewer than on his brother's—have my chest clenching tight. Lysandir appears healthy and whole on the outside, but inside? I nearly whimper, considering the toll he's had to endure.

"Don't," Lysandir implores.

But Vasilius ignores him, his attention never leaving the lot of us who cling to one another. "The Unseelie will think twice before they touch what is mine again, or I'll add the rest of them to my collection."

He upends the bag, sending its contents spilling out onto the rug at his feet.

Lysandir freezes, his wide-eyed gaze snapping from his brother, to the ground, then to me. A thousand words pass between us silently in that moment, but one is louder than all the rest. "Don't."

It's a weird thing about humanity. We have to look at the car crash on the side of the road as we drive by. We cling to stories of natural disasters and bloody conflicts. We search out the worst of things just to confirm its really as bad as we think it is.

Maybe that's why I can help tearing my attention from Lysandir to glance at the floor. To understand why Katherine screams, why Gabriella invokes God, why Grace's hand in mine nearly crushes it, or why Zoe gags and turns away.

The strange assortment of things doesn't register at first. Brown and curled. Sharp and twisting. Small and pointed. They are bits and pieces of a puzzle my mind cannot piece together.

Until it does. All at once.

Horns. Antlers. Bits of fur. Teeth. Shards of bone.

Trophies from the dead. From the Unseelie the king has slaughtered in our name. And there are dozens of them. Hundreds.

"My son," Elaine gasps. "What have you done?"

CHAPTER 36

A LOT OF WHAT happened after the king dumped the gruesome contents of his bag all over the floor is a blur. I can't clearly recall what was said or done. Someone fainted—Adeline, I think. I remember being jostled as someone else knocked into me. I found Lysandir standing near his brother, deep sorrow and regret etched into his features. All his focus was glued to me, pleading. Then the guards were there, ushering us away.

I ended up back in my room with Fia offering things she thought might help—dinner in my room, tea, a bath, a sleeping potion. None of those would help me. There was only one thing I needed, and it was far out of reach until I could convince her to leave me be and let me rest.

It took a while. Worse was waiting a few minutes after she left to make sure she didn't come back and that I was truly alone.

Finally, I push open the back door an inch or so, just enough to peek out. No one lingers in the courtyard that I can see, though much of it is blocked by foliage.

It's quiet out, the other women tucked safely in their rooms.

I quickly slip out the door, close it behind me, and make my way along the cobbled path. My flats are quiet on the stonework, and only the gentle sounds of night birds and bugs fill the air. Such a contrast to the outcry that erupted upon the king's return.

Once I reach the center, I pause, trying to remember which color stone marked the path to Lysandir's room. But every moment I wait just makes me second-guess my choices and has my pulse racing faster at the fear of getting caught, so I pick one and head down it. It *feels* right.

I turn the corner around a particularly thick tree and draw up short. Lysandir has just closed the door behind him and turns to me. Armor still graces his form, and when he spies me along the path, he goes absolutely still almost like he's spied a ghost.

"Mira." The harsh whisper of my name barely reaches my ears, but that's all it takes, all I need. I race across the last few feet of the cobblestones and nearly throw myself into his arms when Lysandir stops me with an upturned palm and outstretched hand.

"Not here. Not like this." He gestures to himself, to the blood I'd tried so hard to forget about.

I nod and quickly follow him inside.

"You were coming to see me," I say once we're secured in his room.

"I was," he admits.

"Without even stopping to change."

A hint of color races to his cheeks, and he rubs the back of his neck. "I should have. But I wasn't thinking. I needed to see you, to know that you were okay."

This man. Less than a minute, and he has me wanting to collapse into a puddle of warm, melty feelings. "You just saw me when you returned."

"Yes." He swallows, gaze darting. "But after what you saw, what you all saw... Not at all injuries are physical."

No, they are not. "It was..."

Disgusting. Horrific. Terrible.

"Upsetting," I say, finally settling on a response. "But I will be okay. You're here. You're safe. The worst of my fears didn't come true."

A fragile smile lifts the corner of his mouth. "You worried about me?"

"Of course." I shove his shoulder, an area untouched by obvious filth.

He glances at that spot then back at me, his gaze suddenly hot and hungry. "I worried about you too," he says. "Every day. Every spare minute."

Warmth spreads out from my chest, and suddenly I wonder if I made a terrible mistake rushing over here. How will I ever stay away from him? I turn away. Because if I don't, I'm going to end up trying to jump on him again.

"Sorry I just rushed over. I should have given you time to change at least." It doesn't matter that he reeks of sweat and worse. I have a feeling I'll want him in any condition, which doesn't bode well for our future, if his visions hold true.

"I'm glad you did," he says.

The heat in my chest sinks lower. "Well, now that I know you're safe, I can give you time to change and wash."

I head toward the door but make it only a step before he says, "Stay."

I stop and look back.

"Please."

I swallow, my mouth suddenly dry. "Okay."

"Wait here. I'll be back in just a few minutes."

Lysandir heads through an adjacent door and into the attached washroom. Our rooms seem to muffle noise from the outside—a nice perk—but not so much from the washroom because I hear the clink and clack of metal as he removes his armor then the running of water for a bath.

Truth is, I'm terrible at waiting. Always have been. My family might think otherwise, given how long it actually took me to get to Faery, but I had reasons for waiting then.

Now, I can think of many more reasons not to wait.

I listen by the door until the water stops and I hear the soft splash of him entering the tub. That alone is enough to create an ache between my legs and almost has me drooling, but I pull myself together. The tub should give him some semblance of privacy if he hates my idea, but I don't think he will.

I crack open the door and step inside.

Lysandir startles, twisting my way in the wide stone tub. "Mira."

My heart nearly stops. I've always found him attractive. From the very first moment I saw him, and even before, when I first saw a portrait of him. No one could doubt that. But what I hadn't fully considered is how he'd look unclothed. And to say that clothes don't do him justice is an understatement. A fine smattering of dark red hair dusts the hard planes of his chest. He grips the edge of the tub, cut muscles of his biceps flexing. His hair is loose and already wet from being dunked under the water. It hangs just past his shoulders, trailing little rivers of water across his golden skin.

"I…" Everything I'd planned to say has vanished straight out of my head. "I thought I'd see if you need some help?"

I fight the urge to slap my hand across my face and duck back out of the room.

Way to play it cool and sexy, Mira.

A low chuckle slips from his lips as he releases the rim and leans back in the tub. "And here I'd planned to bathe quickly."

I nearly whimper at that sound and press my legs together to stifle the ache there. "The water," I say. "I mean, I thought the water could help us. Maybe keep scent off?"

My cheeks flame, and I pull my bottom lip between my teeth. *Why* can't I make a coherent sentence?

"Mmm," he muses, slinging one strong arm along the back of the tub. "I think I'd try just about anything you asked of me right now. Especially if it means getting to touch you."

I stand there like an idiot, unable to move.

He stretches a hand out toward me, the ring that's the twin of mine glimmering in the light. "Join me?"

The slight crook of his fingers beckons me, and I go. But then Lysandir sees something on his arm and frowns. "A moment. I won't have this shameful filth touch you."

Lysandir begins to stand, and I twirl around quickly, giving him privacy. Behind me, I hear the water begin to fall from the spout on the wall again. There's splashing, the citrusy aroma of his soap.

The hot water creates more steam that warms the room and clings to my hair.

The thoughts that float through my mind one after another are likely just as filthy as whatever grime he scrubs off, but somehow, I manage not to turn and stare.

Should have waited a little longer, I chide myself.

The unmistakable sound of someone exiting the tub makes everything in me draw up tight. I jump as he touches the exposed skin of my upper arm, just below where the short sleeves of my casual dress end. Something catches in my middle, tugging me toward the male at my back and his warmth that jumps the narrow space between us.

"Will you join me, Mira?" His breath ghosts across the shell of my ear and sends a shiver down my spine. "Or have you changed your mind?"

"No." It comes out a little squeak. "I haven't changed my mind."

He gives a low chuckle that turns my insides soft and melty.

"Good. Because I want to see you wearing my ring. Only my ring."

CHAPTER 37

LYSANDIR'S FINGERTIPS TRAIL DOWN my arm before he pulls away. My pulse pounds in my ears as I listen to him return to the tub. Only then do I finally move, pulling my dress over my head and slipping out of my underwear.

I want this. So much.

But turning around to face him is still one of the more challenging things I've ever done. I'm no fae—not perfect and willowy in the way so many of them are. Too be honest, I'm pretty average, and despite my love for dance, I've always had some extra pounds I can't seem to shed no matter what. It's all on display now, and I can't help but wonder if I'll measure up to his imaginings. He's had years to picture this after all.

I stand perfectly still, arms at my sides, hair loose and shoved behind my back. Per his request, only his ring on its chain remains on my body, warm and solid against my skin. His gaze is hot and intent, searching every inch of me from my head to my toes then back again. But it's not a quick examination, more a slow perusal, as if he's trying to memorize every curve and dip.

I hold my breath all the while, fighting the urge to shield myself with my arms.

Eventually, he blinks, then scrubs a hand down his face. A curse slips from his lips. "You're beautiful. Even more than I imagined."

"Impossible," I scoff.

But the praise adds a little pep to my step as I finally stride toward him.

"No, Mira. You're a dream come true. Seeing you here before me..." He shakes his head. "Not even my imagination was so generous. And this?" He gestures between us. "After what I saw, I never thought something like this would be possible."

"But it is." I remind him. "I'm here."

"You are."

Lysandir rises from the steaming water, and I force my attention to remain glued to his face. His arm is outstretched to help me into the water.

Don't look down. Don't look down. Don't look down.

I look.

The sight of him takes all the warmth and moisture from my body and sends it straight to my core. Holy shit. A little trail of hair races downward from his chiseled lower abs. His thighs are lean but powerful. But it'd be a lie to say it's not the sight between them that has me so affected. To say he's well-endowed would be an understatement, and I'm treated to the sight of every glorious inch of his hard length. Any lingering doubts about his feelings about me and my little surprise vanish.

When I finally return my attention to his face, a little smirk twitches at the corner of his mouth.

I take his hand and let him help me into the deep tub. Citrus-scented water at the edge of being too hot wraps around me as Lysandir pulls me down into his lap. I gasp at the feel of his chest under my palms, my thighs on either side of his, and his hard length between us, prodding toward my stomach.

"Fuck." His head drops back. A magical glow emanates from him. Lysandir's hands run slowly up and down my sides under the water. When he tilts his head back up, I nearly combust on the spot from the hunger in his eyes. "How am I supposed to keep my sanity after this? Touching you, holding you close."

I pull my bottom lip between my teeth. "Maybe this was a bad idea."

Because he's right. How can I not want more? How could I think this was a good idea when it just reminds me of all the things I can't have, except maybe in stolen little moments like this one?

"No." He pulls me toward him, and I gasp as I slide along his legs, my center bumping up against his cock in the most deliciously tempting way. "We're going to enjoy this moment, Mira. I wish I thought of it myself. I wish I'd had the courage to suggest it myself."

"Will it work?" I ask, anything to distract myself from the feel of him.

At that, he releases me to grab a vial of soap from the side of the tub and pours the entire thing into tub. "Nothing is perfect, but the water and the scents will help. But I still can't—" His throat bobs. "I can't fuck you. I want you, too much, and I think you want me."

I nod enthusiastically, which earns a little grin.

"If we did, I'd mark you." He slides his hand down to my hip, his thumb rubbing little circles on my lower abdomen, right in the area where his mark would appear. "I'd mark you so hard everyone would know that you're mine."

"I wish you could." I lean further on his chest, rocking my hips against him.

I want to be his. Never in my life have I wanted something more. It's ridiculous in a way. I haven't known him all that long, and our beginnings were fraught at best. But ever since he revealed his vision about being fated to love me, I've wondered if my lifelong dream of coming to Faery wasn't something more. Maybe it was fate pulling me to him.

Which makes it all the more cruel that fate seems to want to divide us.

A low rumble leaves him. "Know this," he says. "Whatever fate has in store for us, even if someone else tries to claim you, know that you're mine. And I will always be yours. Only yours."

Lysandir crushes his lips to mine, sealing his words with the promise of his kiss. His fingers tangle in my hair, pull me close, cradling me against him until we're pressed together in the cocoon of steaming water. I wrap my arms around his neck and lean into the kiss. My breasts are smashed against the hard planes of his chest, his cock is a hard shaft between us, and the feel of it—of everything—makes me dizzy. I could happily stay just like this until the water turns cold and my whole body is a prune.

On instinct, I rock my hips, desperate for friction to ease the ache steadily building between my legs. If we weren't already in the tub, I'd be dripping for him, an absolute mess. I grind against his shaft, and Lysandir shudders beneath me.

He pulls back. "I'd have you on me all night, but my resolve is too weak."

"Is it?" I rub against him again, earning a low rumble from deep in his chest and a flare of light from his eyes.

"Yes. And I can already smell you on me."

"Oh." My cheeks flame even as my shoulders drop in disappointment, and I slide back to the other side of the tub.

He reaches between us, tipping up my chin. "I can't fuck you, but there are other things we can do."

A mischievous glint looms in his features.

All at once, my dejection is gone. I grin. "I'm open to suggestions."

"Good girl. Spread your legs for me."

I lean against the curved incline of the tub, leaving only my neck and head above water, and comply. Lysandir's gaze dips to the soap-clouded water.

"I wish I could taste you," he says.

"You could." I arch my hips in invitation below the water.

He looks up at me under his hooded eyelids and leans forward in the tub until he's looming over me. "Someday, I will."

The promise in those words has me pulling my bottom lip between my teeth.

"For now..."

I suck in a sharp breath as he palms between my legs. One long finger runs down my seam, and I whimper in response.

"Let me fill you with my fingers." The rubs my clit, further inflaming my desire. "Let me feel your warmth and imagine that it's my cock slipping inside you instead."

"Yes." I let my head drop back, savoring the pleasure he's already wringing from me. "Yes, please."

Lysandir grips my chin, his other hands still engaged below the water. "Eyes on me. I want to watch you as I fill you."

I nod, staring at him where he looms between my spread legs, his hair dripping water between us as he leans forward, keeping space between us but swarming my senses with his nearness all the same.

He drops his hand from my chin to grip the edge of the tub. And then his finger is sliding inside, filling me up. My inner walls clamp down around the pleasant intrusion, the feel of him, the intimate touch wringing the knot of pleasure within me so tight with just one thrust.

"Lysandir."

"Fuck, Mira." He withdraws his finger, only to return it with another. The metal under his other palm groans. "You're so tight. So wet, so soft, so perfect."

He thrusts slowly in and out, his gaze intent on my face. And with the water concealing us, the delicious friction and fullness of him, it really could be his cock inside me. Each stroke is bliss, and I'm so close already, so desperate for more of him.

It's not fair that he's giving me so much pleasure while holding himself back. So, I fumble beneath the water, searching, until my fingers wrap around his hard shaft.

Lysandir jerks backward, but I don't let go.

"Mira," he says in a strangled voice.

"Let me, please." I slide my palm along his length. "You wanted to pretend it's your cock inside me. You should feel it too." And I want to touch him, to feel him and revel in this moment and the nearness we're stealing.

He curses in the fae tongue and then rocks his hips forward, shoving his length through my grip at the same time he thrusts his fingers back into me. Lysandir leans in to me, our bodies so close but not touching. Water sloshes between us, we share the same air, but other than the intimate parts of us connected under the water, nothing touches. Each movement drives me close to the precipice of pleasure until Lysandir crooks his fingers, hitting that spot within me, and I shatter. I cry out, riding a wave of pleasure and rocking against him. I stroke him harder, my grip firm, trying to draw him with me.

Lysandir gnashes his teeth, growling something that might be my name. My release has just started to ebb when he vanishes. My fist closes around water. Emptiness fills me.

A bellowed groan echoes from a few feet away, and Lysandir is there, cock in hand. He throws his head back as his release spurts onto the stone floor.

I stare transfixed at the sight of him lost to his release, the powerful muscles of his body flexing. He finishes with a shudder that moves his whole body and then looks over at me, breathing heavily.

He releases himself to snatch a towel from a nearby shelf and toss it over the mess. "I'm sorry to shift so suddenly," he says, still panting. "I worried the scent of my release in the water might linger." He grabs two larger towels. "Or worse."

"Worse?" I press my legs together beneath the water.

Instead of wrapping a towel around himself, he carries both to the tub. "Or I'd mark you through the water."

"That's possible?" I gape.

"I'm not sure." He sets the towels down and, to my surprise, climbs back in the tub.

My arousal flares anew, demanding satisfaction despite the last of my orgasm still tingling through me.

"But I couldn't risk it." He grabs two other bottles of scent from the ledge near the tub and holds them up for me to see. "Which do you prefer?"

After we wash for real, somehow managing not to touch—well, no more than semi-accidental grazes—Lysandir changes into new clothes and I redon my underthings and dress. We find our way back into Lysandir's main room, which is suddenly way too small, the massive canopy bed stealing all of my attention. It's impossible not to think about what we could do there if not for the fact that I'm destined for his brother, a male who definitely isn't in his right mind and clearly has a possessive streak a mile wide.

"I can let you rest," I say. "I'm sure you're tired."

Lysandir gives me a sad smile. "Trying to get away from me?"

"No." I scowl at him. His eyes hood, and I look away, crossing my arms in front of myself. "Though, I would if I were smarter."

"You are smart, Mira." He fills the space in front of me, so close but not touching. "Brave. Beautiful."

I stare at him. "You're not helping my restraint."

He grabs a piece of wet hair, running it through his fingers before dropping it again. "You destroyed mine the moment I saw you."

The moment he made a scene to try and get me to leave, to set me on a course that wouldn't have led to the vision he saw.

I sigh and drop my arms. "What would have happened if I'd left that day without entering The Choosing? I'm not sure my family would have ever let me come back."

"I'd have found you," he says. "Some way. Somehow."

But my stubborn self shattered that plan and got myself bound into the contest for his brother's hand in marriage.

"Stay with me tonight." He touches my upper arm. Electricity races under my skin, and I stare at that point of connection. He drops his arm.

"I'm definitely going to end up with your scent all over me if I do that." And more. It was hard enough to resist him before. He clearly has some restraint left, even if it's destroyed as he says, but mine has been ground down to dust, the last of it used up.

He stares at me for a moment longer, maybe debating his words. "I haven't slept in that bed. The sheets won't carry my scent."

"But they'll carry mine after I sleep there."

A soft growl of pleasure rumbles from his chest. "I know."

I nearly roll my eyes. Ridiculous fae male possessiveness. "And if one of the maids notices?"

He shrugs. "I won't let them in."

"Forever."

"I'll burn the sheets."

Now, that does get an eyeroll. "Because that's not suspicious."

"It's the Court of Fire, Mira." He smirks. "Burned sheets aren't that uncommon."

I blink at him, waiting for him to tell me he's kidding, and finally remembering that fae don't do that. "Noted," I say. And then, "And where will you sleep?"

Lysandir looks arounds. "The couch."

I eye it skeptically. There's no way someone as tall as him could find it comfortable, especially not after all he's been through these last days. "It's too short."

"The floor then."

"The floor," I echo. "In your own room?"

"Perhaps I'll just stay up all night watching over you." His eyes darken and he looks away. "It wouldn't be my first sleepless night recently, and this time, I'd have something far more pleasant to occupy my sight and thoughts."

"But that's exactly why you need to sleep." I reach for him and stop just short, dropping my hand. Damn it, not touching, not getting my scent all over him after he just scrubbed it off is so hard.

"And I'll do it much better if you're near. If I don't have to worry."

My brows pinch. "What could harm us here?" When he's silent, I prod further. "The Unseelie?"

He drops his head, hand tightening into a fist at his side. "It would be foolish to think they won't attempt something after the havoc we just wreaked upon them." Lysandir walks to a nearby chair and practically falls into it. He still doesn't look at me when he continues speaking. "He treated it like a hunt, stalking down any group he could find and—"

I crouch near him and take his hand in mind. I know, touching bad, but I can't help it, not when he's hurting. He squeezes my hand in return and makes no move to pull away.

When he finally looks up at me, I'd swear his eyes are glassy with unshed tears.

"It wasn't... They weren't warbands we found, Mira."

Oh God... Everything he doesn't say stirs a burning horror deep within me and I hold tighter to him.

"They were unprepared. It doesn't make sense. They should have known we'd retaliate for such a crime against humans, a potential bride of the king, no less."

"Unless it was a few acting alone?" I offer, weakly.

"Maybe. But to get so far into our territory, to harm a human instead of trying to steal them away?" He shakes his head. "It doesn't make sense with the behaviors we've observed of late. I fear we're missing something or have stirred a nest of buzzacks that will only come back to sting us even worse."

The revelations sit heavy in center, making me want to hunch in on myself. "Lysandir..." I blink at him, lost for words.

"Whatever they plan, I won't let them harm you," he says. There's a ferocity in his tone, but more than that, a vulnerability, the slight warble of fear. "And I can defend you better from whatever comes if you are near me. So please," he leans in close, our foreheads nearly touching, "at least for tonight, let me keep you close."

When he asks like that, I'd give him the world if I could. Though more than anything that this moment, I wish I could hold him close and heal the little broken parts he's been brave enough to show me. Hopefully, I can someday.

But for now I say, "How could I possibly say no to that?"

CHAPTER 38

W E MANAGE TO KEEP our hands off each other—mostly. Ironically, it's only our hands that touch, but it was almost so much more when I removed my bra, forgetting that my hair had dampened my dress and that Lysandir would be able to see absolutely everything. He'd stared at me like a lion about to pounce on its prey. It probably didn't help when I pulled my shoulders back ever so subtly.

He calmed a little and claimed the couch when I tucked myself under the sheets. But both of us were restless, unable to sleep, though I so desperately wanted to. Eventually, Lysandir lay on the floor by my bed with a decorative pillow propped under his head and held the hand that I dangled over one side of the mattress. It should have been so much harder to sleep like that—touching him, holding the hand that had elicited such wicked pleasure in the bath, but I fell asleep quickly then.

It was just after dawn when Lysandir woke me, and though I wanted nothing more than to continue lying in bed, preferably snuggled up beside him, the rational part of my brain reminded me that I needed to get back to my room before Fia or someone else noticed my absence.

"You're not leaving again, are you?" I ask.

"My brother did not say, but I hope not," Lysandir replies. He told me he slept some, but some might have been five minutes for the sleep-deprived look on his face. "Even if he continues his bloody crusade, I will not go unless he orders me to."

Which he might, like he did the first time.

Lysandir opens the door and peeks outside. The sky has just started to lighten, leaving much of the world in soft shadow.

"I don't see anyone," he says from the threshold.

Good. The last thing we need is someone spotting me leaving his room. I join him at the door, lingering in heavy silence. He takes my hand in his. His thumb rubs across my skin in a soothing promise. We stand like that for a while, just staring at one another, savoring the peace of the moment. The birds are just starting to wake up. A soft breeze ruffles the foliage. Once again, I wish I could hug him. Leaving with only a squeeze of his hand feels wrong after all we've shared. So, very quickly, before I can second-guess it, I rise up on my toes and plant a quick peck on his lips.

Color paints his cheeks. He lifts an arm like he might pull me to him but drops it, balling it into a fist. "I'll see you again soon, Mira."

The courtyard is just starting to lighten as I slip out of Lysandir's room and make my way along the cobbled pathway. Dew clings to everything. The crisp air and peaceful aura belie all the horrors of the past week.

At least Lysandir and I were able to steal a precious night together.

Memories of it accompany me down the pathway, distracting my thoughts. It's not until I'm halfway across the central plaza that I realize I'm not alone.

"You're up early," a female voice says.

I half stumble, drawing up short. My blood chills to ice as I look over to find Cora standing a few feet away. She's wearing a cream-colored sleep shirt and soft-looking long pants, her hair sloppily braided over one shoulder, but she's far too alert to have just woken up.

"And isn't your room that way?" She points in the direction I'd been headed, a knowing look on her face.

I turn slowly and give the most casual shrug I can muster. "Couldn't sleep."

"So you decided to try a different bed," she all but spits the last word, stalking toward me. "The king's perhaps?"

The accusation causes me to flinch.

"I would never," I reply in an urgent whisper.

"Oh really? Isn't that the same dress you wore yesterday?" She tsks and gives me a once-over, frowning at what she finds. "Thought you'd gain an advantage over the rest of us by comforting him on his return?"

The tiny part of my head seeing reason screams. *She didn't see you with Lysandir. She doesn't know.* She'd have called me out on it in a minute if she had. She's guessing. That's it. My nails cut little half-moons into my palms as I wrestle control of my fury.

"It sounds like that's what you had in mind," I reply.

She smirks and tosses her braid over her shoulder. "It's not a bad idea."

The thought turns my stomach and not because I have any desire for the king or his crown. The opposite. "You can't seriously want him. Not after yesterday."

"Of course I do," she scoffs. "He's the king. I have to win this competition and become his queen. There's no other choice."

"What do you mean?" I rear back in confusion. No other choice? Of course there are other choices.

"You wouldn't understand." She crosses her arms and turns up her nose. "Cloistered girl with a family who loves you."

"Loves me?" My mother and brothers, yes. And Selena. But my aunt and uncle? I'm not so certain. "I'm not here because they love me. I'm here because my uncle saw an opportunity to better the family name and is happy to use me as a tool to get it."

"Ugh." She sighs in exasperation, letting her arms fall wide. "Don't pretend you don't want to be here. I saw your little per-formance before the king that first night. How you *dreamed* of coming here and becoming his bride."

My cheeks heat. "I did. That's true. But even if I hadn't, I wouldn't have had a choice in coming here. My uncle has provided for my family since my father died years ago. If I didn't come, if I didn't do everything I could to win the crown, do you think he'd still keep a roof over their heads?"

Maybe he would. Part of me has to believe he wouldn't be so cruel as to leave them homeless, but I have no doubt they'll be better off if I make him happy. His love for his brother was unconditional, but the rest of us? It never extended that far.

She huffs. "There are worse things than being poor."

I gape at her, and I'm so furious it takes a moment before I can close my mouth and make it form words. "Spoken like someone who has never had to worry about money a day in her life."

She's oozed money since the moment she arrived in her fancy Louboutin heels.

Cora lets out a small squeal of frustration and stomps toward me. I shift my stance, ready for her to take a swing at me, when she stops two feet away pulls up the bottom hem of her shirt.

"You see this?" she points a manicured nail at her side.

It takes a moment to make it out in the morning light, to notice the slight yellowish tint of the healing bruise on her skin. When I do, my stomach plummets.

"Yeah, that's from my brother." She drops her hem only to tug down part of the neckline, revealing a round mark below her collarbone. "And this, this is from my father—or rather his cigar. He's too good to use his fists."

"I..." I step back, blinking, lost for words. "I didn't know."

"No one does," she snaps and releases her clothes. "And you better not tell. I want no one's pity," she spits the word like it disgusts her. "But you see, I can't lose the crown and go back because they might just kill me."

"You really are determined to marry him."

"I'll do whatever it takes."

The ferocity, the determination in her gaze, has me taking another step back. What wouldn't she do for the crown? To escape that kind of abuse? But to win the crown, she'd need to be the king's pick, and she wasn't.

I swallow the tightness in my throat. "Anything. Like find a way to kill Bailey?"

"What?" The absolute shock and horror on her face fills me with instant regret.

It was a low blow. A long shot.

And I was so, so wrong.

A tear streaks down her cheek, and she shoves it away with the base of her palm. "Think me a bitch all you want, but I would never have harmed her. I *liked* her, okay? She was *kind* to me."

The confession reaches into my chest and pulls back my ribs, exposing my battered heart. Bailey was kind. To everyone.

"I'm sorry," I begin, but she may as well have not heard me.

"She was going to help me," Cora's voice cracks. "She could have the king, and I'd..." She sniffles. "You think I'm that horrible, don't you?"

I raise my hands. "I don't. I'm sorry."

For a fleeting moment, the idea was there. If I hadn't been sleep deprived or shocked by one revelation or another, maybe it wouldn't have been or I'd have shut it down, but in that moment, all I could think about was her anger and desperation and what Lysandir had said about the Unseelie being unprepared and unaware.

"But you said it," she snaps.

"I did." I step closer, my hands still up like I'm trying to calm a spooked horse. "I'm sorry. You didn't hurt her. You would never hurt her."

"I really wouldn't have." She swipes at another tear. "Not her." She starts to sob then, whatever dam of emotions she's held together completely breaking free.

I stare awkwardly for a moment before wrapping an arm around her and guiding her toward a bench. We may not get along—at all—but no one deserves to cry alone, not when they're hurting.

After a minute, she pulls herself together, stemming the tears.

"I'm sorry," she snips, angrily swiping away the tear tracks on her face.

"Don't be. It's my fault."

"At least we agree on that," she replies but gives me a fragile smile.

We sit in silence for a minute, and when Cora makes no move to leave, I ask, "How was Bailey going to help you?"

She pulls in a long breath then lets it out and looks over at me. "It seemed obvious the king was going to pick her. Even I could see that, and nothing I did was turning him from her. So, I decided that my next best plan was to appeal to the future queen for help." She glances off into the courtyard, staring at nothing. "I told her about my family. The hell they put me through. She said that if she became queen—" Cora shakes her head. "If. She was too modest for her own good." Another tear slips free and she brushes it away. "If she became queen, she was going to ask the king to let me stay, even if my family demanded me back for however brief a time. Keep them away too. Maybe the king could find me a good match with a noble or something."

She lifts one shoulder.

I hug my arms around myself. Her wish is like Alex and Grace's. Different but similar all the same. Does anyone want the king for himself? Tears sting at the corner of my eyes. Anyone but Bailey?

What a mess we all are.

"I don't want to marry the king," I say, feeling the need to confess something to ease the balance between us. "I don't want to be queen."

"And that's what has you wandering around in yesterday's clothes?" It's not condemnation in her gaze when she asks this time, more genuine curiosity.

"Something like that."

She nods but doesn't ask more.

"I don't want to marry him," I say again. "But if somehow I get stuck with him, I can make you the same promise Bailey did."

Cora snaps her head in my direction.

"I'll do whatever I can to help you stay here and keep your family away."

"You'd do that?"

"Of course. Why wouldn't I?"

She huffs. "I haven't exactly been nice to you."

"No," I admit. "But I think I understand your reasons a little more."

The sun has risen, the world fully wakening, and I can almost feel like sand in the hourglass running out before Fia comes to wake me with coffee. Except she won't find me.

I stand from the bench. "We should get back before our maids find us missing and panic."

"I'll keep it to myself," Cora says.

"Huh?" I glance down at her where she still sits on the bench.

"Whatever you were up to." She gestures around us. "I won't tell."

"Oh." I swallow, my mouth suddenly dry as memories of the night before rush back. "Thank you."

"Maybe..." She looks up at me, and when she smiles, I know it's the first genuine one I've seen from her. "Maybe we can do better with each other going forward."

I smile at her in return. "I'd like that."

My room is still dark once I slip inside and close the door behind me. There's no time to savor the feeling of relief before it all gets smashed to bits.

"I'm disappointed" comes a voice from the shadows.

I startle, whirling around with my back to door, palm gripping the handle in case I need to flee.

But running won't help. I've been caught. Again.

Fia stands from the stool at my dressing table, shaking her head like a mother who has caught her child sneaking in after a night of drinking and debauchery. Except Fia and I aren't that far apart in age and she doesn't have any kids to have practiced her disappointment on.

"Fia..." I start, unsure what to say.

"Sneaking out to spend time with the prince." She tsks.

"How— Why do you think that?" I lean farther back against the door, the solid mass at my back the only think holding me upright.

She sighs. "Tharin told me."

Tharin... I grit my teeth, the betrayal sharp and stinging. I know he's against us, but ratting me out like this?

"And who have you told?" I ask.

Fia frowns, her shoulders dropping. "You really think so poorly of me?" She crosses the space between us and hold out a hand to me. "I'm disappointed because it wasn't you who told me, not because you care for the prince."

I blink at her. "Wait, what?"

"You thought I wouldn't approve." She flexes her open hand, waiting for me to take it.

Finally, I do, and she leads me over to sit on the edge of the bed.

"Well, no," I say. "I know how much you want me to become queen. And being with anyone else while bound into The Choosing is treason. I'm the king's until he decides otherwise." Saying it out loud makes it all sound so much worse than it did a few moments ago.

"All true," she says. "But aren't we friends?"

"Yes?"

She sits next to me and takes my hand in hers. "I hope we are. There can only be one queen. Being the maid to the future princess sounds quite nice. Less pressure, all the fame. Besides, he's a better fit for you, I think. Much better."

"So you didn't tell anyone?"

"No."

I nearly sigh in relief, some of the tension slipping from my shoulders.

"Tharin was looking out for you, I think. He thought something like this might happen and didn't want me to find you missing in the night and panic, thinking something had happened to you, as I might have. I do get concerned for you." She tilts her head to the side, smiling that blinding grin of hers.

Something swells in my chest, and I make an effort to return her optimist. "I don't deserve you."

"But you do." She pats our joined hands before releasing me and rising. "Now that I know you are safe, rest. There is nothing planned this morning as of yet but..." She trails off, looking away. After yesterday, the king's sudden return. "It would be best to rest now, and I will wake you if an event arises."

Because no one knows what state the king is in now or how he'll want to proceed with The Choosing after all that's transpired the last few days.

"Thank you, Fia. For everything." I fill the words with all the gratitude I feel, and from the softening of her face and soft sparkle in her eyes, I think she feels it too.

"I am here for you," she promises. "Now sleep."

CHAPTER 39

WHEN I JOIN THE other women for an early lunch, there's an extra pep in my step that's been missing far longer than I'd like to admit. The sun shines a little brighter today, pouring into the room and lightening everything up. It's almost like fate has opened a window and maybe things won't be as bad as I'd feared.

"Saved you a seat!" Grace waves me over to the open space between her and Gabriella.

Cora, seated directly across from her, looks up as I approach and offers me a small smile—more than she ever has before. Sitting down with them for lunch feels relaxing, comfortable. Servers rush over with pitchers of drink and platters of food, all of which are divine. I don't know if it's something in the soil or maybe the magic flowing through the world itself, but everything here tastes a little better than similar foods would at home. Of course, with all the pesticides and stuff used back home, I guess it shouldn't be that surprising.

Zoe joins us a few minutes later, leaving just one spot open at the table. "No Katherine yet?"

Everyone shakes their head.

"And no word from His Majesty?" The slight bitter edge when she says his title is new. A few bird calls flit in from the large, open arched windows, but otherwise silence reigns.

"Nothing today," Adeline says after a weighty pause.

From the guarded looks and silence around the table, none of us are too excited about a follow-up to yesterday's horrific disaster.

Zoe has just settled into her plate of vegetables when the main door to the room opens without warning. Multiple women startle, glancing toward the door as guards file in, led by the Captain Avara, the king's right-hand man a step behind.

I brace, waiting for the king, uneasy anticipation of whatever he has planned for us churning up the food I've just eaten. After all, if he planned to apologize, why bring a host of warriors with him?

But the king doesn't appear.

Avara looks us over before settling on me. "Lady Mira, you're to come with us."

"Me?" I blink, taken aback.

"Right away," the king's personal guard orders.

Then Tharin is there, pushing through the other guards to step between me and the newcomers. "What's happening here?"

When his hand drops to the pommel of the sword at his side and stays there, my heart drops.

Wrong. Very wrong.

"King's orders," Avara says.

Dawning horror steals the warmth from my skin. He knows. Oh God, somehow he knows. I twist back toward the table, searching one face after another.

"Mira?" Grace grabs my hand.

Alex looks ready to leap out of her chair and fight the guards herself. Adeline is pale and drawn. Gabriella openly gapes in shock. Zoe has dropped her fork. I finally glance at Cora, expecting the sting of her triumphant gaze, but she looks as horrified as the rest. She gives the slightest shake of her head and mouths, *No*.

Not her. Not any of them.

Tharin is arguing with the guards closing in, but I barely hear him.

None of the women ratted me out. They wouldn't. And it wasn't Tharin—he's as shocked as the rest.

"Right now, miss." Avara waits, hand outstretched just a few feet away.

My heart is in my throat as I release Grace's hand, rise on shaking legs, and reach for the guard's outstretched hand.

But Tharin grabs my other arm first.

"I'm going with her," he snaps. He cuts his gaze to me, concern evident.

Thank you, I say silently. He must understand, because he gives a short nod before turning back toward the Captain of the Guard.

The moment I take Avara's hand, we shift. The air constricts, the world melts, and then we're in a dimmer room that swelters with warmth. My head is still spinning, my lunch tossing and turning, when the captain's strong arm lands on my shoulder and pushes me downward.

"Kneel," she says.

I drop, half falling, my palms slapping onto the stonework. Tharin is right there with me, down on one knee, his head bent in a show of deference. Flames flicker in my periphery, sending light and shadow dancing across the ground. Probably the source of the heat too, since it comes in waves from that direction. When the world stops spinning, I raise my head.

The king sits on a throne just ahead, head propped on his fist as he scowls at me. A few guards linger off to the side, but much of the room is empty and dark.

"This is the woman you saw this morning?" Vasilius asks someone.

"It is."

I twist my head toward the voice. Now I know why Katherine wasn't at lunch. She was here. And the bitch looks all too proud of herself, arms crossed, chin raised, and a sneer on her pointed face. Should have known it was too much to hope for us all to get along.

"What is it you thought you saw?" I demand, pushing back to my feet. I glance between her and the king, waiting for an answer.

"She"—the king points a finger at Katherine—"says she saw you out before dawn, and kissing my brother at that."

Fucking hell. I let the accusation roll over me, trying to show no reaction.

"And here you are, his guard at your side," the king adds.

Tharin, still kneeling, looks up. His form is rigid, hand still on the pommel of his sword. Holy hell, he wouldn't defend me before the king, would he?

"Tell me, Mira," Vasilius says. "How long as this little affair been going on?"

"Affair?" I gape. "We haven't..." I shake my head. "His mark is not on me. You know that."

Vasilius shoves to his feet. "What I know is that you are bound to *me*. Mine, until I decide otherwise." He stalks toward me, staring me down like I'm an inch high. "You were the one who gave such an impassioned plea about wanting to become my bride, my queen." A cruel smile pulls at the corner of his mouth. He stops an armlength in front of me. Warmth pours off his skin, causing sweat to dew on mine. "Ironic that my brother didn't want you to enter The Choosing then. Were all your words a lie, Mira? Had you chosen him even then?"

"No." The urge to step back is so strong, but Avara is there, blocking me in. "No. I'd never met him then. I promise."

"But you have now." He leans in. "And you prefer him?"

My back arches in my attempt to put some distance between him, but all I seem to do is make myself unsteady, like prey baring its neck for a predator to strike.

"Funny. I can't smell him on you, but I could smell your scent in his room, his bed no less."

My stomach plummets. This isn't an interrogation or questioning—it's a trial, and I'm already damned. And if he's been in Lysandir's rooms...

"Where is Lysandir?" I find a kernel of courage deep inside and cling to it, begging it to fortify me.

"See," Katherine snips. "She only cares about him, not you."

Vasilius turns his head toward her so slowly that it raises the fine hairs along my arms. "Leave."

"But my king—"

"Leave." He flicks a hand toward Avara, and then she's moving away from me over to the other young woman gaping at us.

"But I—"

"Have done more than enough," Vasilius says. "Return her to her room while I deal with this."

Katherine stammers again, looking affronted, but she barely gets the beginnings of another protest out before Avara grabs her arm and is gone.

Vasilius sighs and rubs his forehead. "Better. Now, where were we?"

"Where is Lysandir?" I ask again. I stand a little straighter. He dismissed his captain. The king doesn't see me as a threat, but if he's done something horrible to the man I love, I swear—

My brain trips over itself.

I love him. My mouth parts. My God, I really do.

"Come to some realization?" Mocking amusement shimmers in the king's gaze.

I snap my mouth shut and all but snarl at him.

The bastard just grins wider. "You do care for him, it seems. How interesting. And frustrating. Does he know? He must, right?"

Vasilius waves a hand toward the flames burning in a wide column on the other side of the room. All at once they die away, and I let out a strangled scream at the sight beyond. Lysandir is there, kneeling on the ground, cream-colored shirt sticking to his skin, hair plastered to his face and back.

He looks at me, eyes wide and pleading. "Mira."

I'm running toward him before I can think, but someone grabs my arm, jerking me back. I twist, slapping at the hand on my arm.

"Mira," Tharin says. "Don't."

"But he—" I gesture wildly.

But Tharin doesn't let go.

"So desperate." Vasilius tsks at me, shaking his head. "Is it love?"

"What have you done to him?" If not for Tharin holding me back, I'd likely punch him, king or no.

"He's fine," the king says. "Though even a prince of fire can have trouble taking the heat after a while, isn't that so, my brother?"

Lysandir remains on the ground, grimacing, and I only pray that's the extent of what's been done to him. If he's been tortured, suffered some other way too—

My throat starts to close up, and its everything I can do to pull in one breath after another.

"What to do? What to do?" Vasilius starts to pace back and forth. "Here I am, trying to find my bride, and my brother goes and seduces one of my women." He pauses and looks at Lysandir. "It's treason, you know."

Lysandir doesn't argue, just hangs his head, and it guts me, absolutely tears me up to see him like this to the point I can't take it anymore.

"It's my fault!" I step toward the king, demanding his attention. When he gives it, sliding his imperious gaze my way, my skin tingles from the pressure of his regard. Nothing in life has prepared me for this, but I summon everything I have anyway to make my stand.

"Mira!" Tharin hisses my name and hardens his grip.

I roll my shoulder, trying to shake him off.

"I kissed him this morning. I went to his room. I lay in his bed." Those were my choices.

The king stalks back my way. I brace, holding my spine straight. His gaze dips to Tharin's hand on my arm, and the king shoos him away. With a quick look of apology to me then Lysandir, Tharin goes.

Vasilius stops just in front of me, staring me down. "You are bound to me."

"Yes," I say. "And I wanted to love you. I did, with all of my heart. I wasn't lying when I said I'd dreamed for years about coming here and about becoming your bride. I really thought that I could be perfect for you." A strange calm settles over me as I share my truth. "You have many qualities that make you a great king, and many women would be happy to be your bride. But unfortunately, I am no longer one of them. I wanted to love you but..." I turn my head to look at Lysandir. It's hard to make out the look on his face with the distance between us, but just the sight of him, there, breathing, and suffering for caring for me, makes the words flow even more easily. "But I fell in love with Lysandir instead."

When I look back at the king, any illusion of humor has faded completely from his stony features. I wait, braced for his reply, when he turns on his heel and strides back to his chair. He drops into, propping one elbow on his need and leaning his head on his fist as he continues to look between the two of us in silence.

"What to do with you two," the king muses aloud to the quiet room. His attention lingers on me. "Perhaps I should just marry you."

I gasp.

"No!" Lysandir cries out, leaping to his feet.

Vasilius holds an open palm toward him, and Lysandir draws still and silent.

"It would be a fitting punishment for such a betrayal," the king drawls.

Darkness creeps in at the edge of my vision, and despite the warmth of the room, I'm suddenly cold.

This is it. This is how the vision comes true.

Somewhere behind me, a door groans open. I dare a glance behind me in time to see Elaine enter, making her way toward us on her cane—the spear.

"What's going on here?" she demands.

"I must deal with this treason," the king replies, unmoving save for his mouth.

"Treason?" she scoffs. Her gaze darts between myself, Lysandir, and the king. "Have they aligned themselves with the Unseelie then?"

"No," the king grumbles.

The end of her cane clacks against the stone as she continues to advance, all eyes in the room on her. She stops next to me. "What has this young woman done then?"

Vasilius lifts his head from his fist and sits straighter in his seat, staring down at me along the length of his nose. "She has broken the rules of The Choosing and been seen with another." There's a pause before he looks at his next victim. "My brother."

"Ah." She looks between us, seeming not the least bit surprised, which is shocking in and of itself. She stops on me. "You love my son?"

There's no judgment in her gaze. No condemnation, simply a mother asking what's probably one of the most important questions one can.

"I do," I say.

She nods and turns toward Lysandir. "And you love this young woman?"

But it's not his mother he looks at when he answers. Instead, he steps to the side, looking past her directly as me as he says, "I love her with my whole heart."

Oh, Lysandir. He may as well have reached into my chest and spread my ribs apart to speak directly to my soul.

"I see." Elaine folds her hands over one another on the ball of her cane and regards the king. "Well, I would say they have done you a favor by making your choice simpler."

"Simpler?" The king speaks the word echoing in my head. "Whatever shall I do with them?"

"It should be obvious," she replies. "The thing is done. You don't want to marry someone who is in love with someone else, do you? Someone who is favored by your brother and who would be a good match for him? Do you not think it would do my weary spirit well to see both my sons wed before I pass?"

I suck in a breath and hold it, barely able to comprehend what's happening. Hope balloons in my chest, and I try so desperately to hold it down, not to let it get out of hand. But my control slips when I look at Lysandir and see the same wonder and hope reflected in his face.

"Fine. Fine." Vasilius sighs and slips down in his chair. "I see that not even the rules of The Choosing can keep you apart, but some discretion would be appreciated. Perhaps you two should stay cloistered until the end of The Choosing. Wouldn't want the *entire* court to get the wrong impression of me."

My heart skips a beat. "Are you saying—"

But I never get the question out. Lysandir is there, having shifted directly in front of me. He pulls me into his arms holding me close.

"Mira. My Mira," he whispers against my hair. I cling to him, my legs barely holding me.

"This is real. We can be together?" My fingertips dig into his sweat-dampened shirt as I look up into his wide, glowing eyes. The bubbling feeling within me presses at my ribs, trying to burst free. A laugh bubbles up my throat, but nothing is funny.

Lysandir is mine. I am his.

The king coughs, drawing our attention. Lysandir releases me just enough for us to turn toward his brother, but his arm is still wrapped around my middle, holding me close to his side.

"While I am sure you two are excited, we have other important things to discuss. Firstly, I cannot remove your bond to me." The king points to his wrist. "It will remain until I have chosen my queen, but that shall not be you." He shares a look with Elaine, who has hobbled to his side, and then asks, "Are there any others who would choose someone else if given the choice?"

Oh... I swallow, unsure if he really wants the truth. My gaze darts away. Lysandir must sense my uncertainty because he adjusts his grip on my hip.

"There are." The king sighs, shoulders slumping. "Does anyone want to be my bride? Other than what's-her-name that tried to sneak in my bed this morning and then told me of you and my brother when I tried to make her leave." He waves his hand about, searching for the name.

She what? I nearly gape in shock. We weren't supposed to have such relations with the king until he chose a queen. I suppose I'm not one to talk, since I snuck into Lysandir's room, kissed him, and more, but at least we had a mutual understanding. From the way Vasilius just spoke about her, he and Katherine certainly did not.

"Katherine." He snaps his fingers.

"Oh, you cannot marry her," Elaine says.

He winces. "I'd rather not."

"Yes, Your Majesty," I say, trying to remain in his good graces. "There are human women here who would marry you." Cora for one, or rather, she wants the freedom such a marriage would grant. Possibly Zoe or Gabriella, but I can't be sure.

Damn, maybe there aren't any who want him for just him, but I've already spoken, and I'm not about to take it back.

"I don't suppose you'll tell me which ones are not interested?" he asks.

"I..." I pull in a deep breath. "That information is not mine to reveal, but maybe you could talk to each woman yourself? Assure them there are no ill repercussions if they have changed their mind? Each one I have spoken to would like to remain here in your court, even if becoming your bride is not their heart's desire."

"More humans here is good," the dowager reminds him. "No matter the reason."

"Do any of you know?" the king asks the others present.

They all shake their head, even Tharin. Funny, I would have thought nothing escaped his notice. Stranger still, there's a hint of a smile on his face, and it doesn't look sarcastic or forced at all. The oddness of it makes me want to rub at my chest.

Other than a quick response to his brother, Lysandir has remained quiet but attentive, almost like he worries one word out of his mouth might destroy this tentative hope we have or send our fates tumbling off course. But he's a solid, reassuring presence at my side.

And mine. My God, he's really mine.

"None of this is going as I'd hoped." Vasilius shifts forward in his chair. "I'd have you two keep out of sight until The Choosing is over. Be together if you wish, but stay in the royal quarters. Order the maids not to talk about this. I'd have it kept quiet."

A sensible suggestion. Finally.

"The other women may worry. We will need to tell them something," Elaine says.

"Fine." He waves his hand. "They can know." He stands, his voice rising as he does. "Do tell them that the rules of The Choosing are to be obeyed from here on out. If their heart lies elsewhere, fine, I shall soon discover that from them. But they are to keep such feelings to themselves until this is done. I won't have more of this." He gestures to us.

The others might be jealous, but they can get their happy endings too. Adeline and her guard. Alex and Grace. I hum with excitement at the thought of telling them, of encouraging them to be honest with the king when he asks. Things really are turning out better than I ever dreamed possible.

"You're certain of your choice," Vasilius asks his brother.

Lysandir grins down at me. "As certain as anything in my life."

"She is a lovely dancer," the king remarks. He tilts his head to the side, smirking, waiting to see how his blow lands.

But Lysandir, if he's bothered by the king's jab, doesn't show it.

"I'm sure she is," he replies evenly.

Vasilius frowns. "Not a great kisser though."

"Vasilius," Elaine hisses and lifts her cane, almost like she might whack him with it, but thinks better of it.

"I disagree." Lysandir cups my cheek, capturing my full attention. "I think she's a wonderful kisser." He pulls me close and leans in, and I think he means to prove it right there.

But Vasilius groans, and Lysandir halts, a hint of mischief in his eyes.

"Have the decency not to do it in front of me." He thumps back down into his seat. "It's a pity you know, you were one of my favorites after..." His eyes close as if he's in pain, and his hand balls into a fist on the armrest of the chair.

After Bailey. The weight of her loss makes the room a little dimmer, and I lean into Lysandir for comfort.

"Go, both of you. Take your happiness elsewhere," the king commands.

Lysandir doesn't wait before he shifts us out of the room.

CHAPTER 40

I EXPECT LYSANDIR TO shift us to his room—or near it, since the area is warded against shifting. However, a few heartbeats later, we appear somewhere completely new to me. Wooden walls made of thick beams support a high, thatched roof. A low, wide bed sits just off to our left, its forest green coverings neatly made. Fae lamps linger nearby but are out now. We don't need the light though. The wall opposite the bed provides plenty. Sheer curtains waft in the breeze where they are pulled back on either side of the large opening that walks out onto a wooden balcony and wide-open view beyond.

"Where are we?" I gape at the room around us.

The whole thing reminds me a bit of those over-water bungalows I've ogled in travel commercials, but instead of on the water, we appear to be high up in a mountain or something. A few trees with thick leaves and draping vines are visible at the periphery, but otherwise, all I can see is sky.

"A private getaway near Calida," he replies. His thumb rubs the back of my hand. "No one will bother us here."

The heated look in his eyes has my legs pressing together to stifle a sudden surge of desire.

"We're together," I say, still in disbelief that it's real.

"We are." He cups my cheek, tugging me close. "I still don't know how it's possible, but you're mine, Mira."

I bunch his sweaty shirt in my hands. "And you're mine, Lysandir."

I stretch up on my toes, closing the last of the distance between us, and kiss him with all the emotions racing through my blood.

He's mine. I'm his. Even the king has approved us. No one can come between us now.

We've defied fate. The passion in his kiss is all-consuming, a flame hotter than the one he was trapped in. He's a sweaty mess and I don't care. As long as we're together, I will take him however I can.

Lysandir's arms encircle me and slide low, and then he's lifting me. I wrap my legs around him, my dress riding up around my hips. He groans against my mouth as he moves us. Lysandir lays me on the edge of the bed, breaking our kiss and stepping back. My legs are still spread, my dress around my hips from the way he carried me. Instead of covering my underthings, I widen my legs. He scrubs a hand down his face.

"Little temptress."

"We've waited long enough, haven't we?"

His countenance grows serious. "Indeed we have."

And then his shirt is up over his head and gone. I'm tempted to lay back and watch as he removes the rest, but my clothing is suddenly too constricting. I need it gone. Now. Right now.

By the time I slip out of my underwear and kick it away, Lysandir is there, completely, gloriously naked. There's no time to appreciate the sight before he embraces me again. One hand cups the back of my head, dragging my mouth back to his. The other wraps around me, pressing our heated bodies together before he tumbles us back onto the bed.

His hard body is supported on one arm, keeping most of his weight off me, but enough lingers for me to feel him pressed against me head to toe. And I love it. I never want to be apart from him. My body already aches for him, crying out to have him inside of me. Another part still can hardly believe it. Only his body against mine, my arms around his neck, the press of his lips convince me its really happening. It's not some dream. Some wish.

Lysandir breaks our kiss and stares down at me. His hooded gaze dances over my face, like he's trying to memorize every line and convince himself that I'm real too. "I've waited so long to taste you."

"That's not our first kiss if you recall," I say between heavy breaths.

"Mmm." He rocks his hips, his hard length sliding against my skin and twisting up the knot of desire within me. "But I haven't tasted you elsewhere yet."

The words haven't fully sunken in before he's kissing his way down my neck, my collarbone, and then closes his lips over one nipple. I let out a little moan, arching my back as he flicks the peaked tip with his tongue. He lavishes the other, and then he's moving downward again, kissing my ribs, my belly button.

Lysandir slides off the foot of the bed and crouches on his knees. I whimper in anticipation as his gaze drops between my legs. A smirk quirks up at the corner of his lips before he grabs my legs and tugs my ass to the edge of the bed.

"I've dreamed of this." He licks his lips. "So many times." The prince on his knees dips his head between my spread legs, and then he's tasting me in a whole new way.

The feeling is electric—pure lightning through my veins. He devours me like a man starved, and I suppose he is. How long ago did he first see a vision of me? How many years has he dreamed of this? To have something you crave after so long without.

His lips close around my clit, and I nearly buck off the bed.

"Lysandir!" I tangle my hands in his damp hair.

"Mira," he growls my name against my core. "My beautiful mate."

A glow emanates from him, and it only makes me wilder with need. I writhe under his ministrations, taken to the edge but not quite tumbling over.

"Lysandir. Please." I tug gently at his hair. "I need—I want—"

He pauses to look up at me. Strong hands flex on my thighs. His face glistens with my wetness.

"Please," I whimper again, releasing him and letting my arms fall limp at my sides.

My prince stands and takes his cock in hand. A little bead of moisture glistens at the tip. "I'm going to mark you, make you mine."

"Yes." I slide back up the bed, beckoning for him to join me. "I want it. I want everything."

The mattress dips as he crawls onto the bed like a predator about to pounce and devour me whole. I watch, enraptured, as he closes the distance between us to cover me and position himself at my entrance. At the first touch, I gasp, my whole body tensing up with aching desire. The tip presses in, and I suck in a breath, marveling at the feel of him.

He releases himself to cup my cheek, brushing his thumb along my skin. "My mate. My Mira."

His glow flares brighter in a corona around us as he presses forward. I moan as he enters me, stretching almost to the point of pain but not quite. A sharp curse slips from Lysandir. He bares his teeth, and I know he's trying to take it slow, let me adjust.

"I can take it," I tell him. "Give me everything."

And so he does, bottoming out and holding himself still inside me. The feel of him is everything, like he was made for me and I for him. No one and nothing could ever be more perfect than this moment.

But then he moves, retreating and thrusting back in. And I was wrong. So wrong, because the pleasure is dizzying, so much more than I expected.

He fills me up in the best way, until there's no him or me, just us.

A few more thrusts and I'm hanging on the edge, the knot of desire within me twisted up so tight I can barely think. "Lysandir. I'm—I'm going to—"

He growls against the crook of my neck. His scent fills my nose. It's his warmth against mine. Everything is him. On his next thrust, I shatter, screaming my pleasure and bucking against him. His powerful form holds me to the sheets as he wrings out my desire, teasing it out with thrust after thrust until he flings his head back and roars his own pleasure.

We're both a panting, sweaty mess, clinging together through the last waves of pleasure tingling under my skin. It's then that I feel something cool slide under my skin near my hip. It circles once, twice, before settling.

"Mira. My Mira," Lysandir pants. Our foreheads are pressed together, our breaths mingling. The pure love and adoration shining in his eyes makes my chest swell.

I cup his cheek.

"Yours," I promise.

Lysandir slips from me with a groan and tumbles onto the bed at my side, still breathing heavily. His strong arm comes around me, pulling me half atop him. We lay that way for a minute, locked together, until his palm smooths down my side to settle on my hip. He rubs his thumb over the skin that had been cool just a moment ago.

"I feared I'd never see this," he says.

The mark is beautiful, swirls of flame chasing each other in a circle. I can't help but grin as I take it in. I'd always kind of wanted a tattoo but had never gotten one. A good thing, since none of them could ever compare to this. It's a mark of love. A symbol of our bond.

"I want to see yours." I scoot back on the coverings to get a good look at his hip. The mirror image of our mark is on him too. Just seeing it is like tossing fuel onto the smoldering fire of my desire, and I'd climb right back atop him in that moment if he were ready for it.

"What do you think?" he asks, almost hesitantly.

"I love them," I reply. "And I meant what I said in front of your brother. I love you."

He caresses my face, pushing hair back behind my ear. "I love you too, Mira. I will all my days if you'll let me."

"I wouldn't have it any other way."

We venture out of bed, not bothering with our clothes. I grab a blanket and wrap it around myself, but Lysandir doesn't seem to have the same modesty and thankfully doesn't mind me checking out all of his assets.

I wander toward the balcony, determined to finally learn a little more about this place he's taken us. "A private retreat, huh? And you just happened to have it ready for us? Just in case?"

A small huff of laughter slips from him as he follows after me. "No. I took a risk that it wasn't in use."

"If it was?"

He smirks. "Then whoever was using it would have had quite a story to tell."

A little laugh of my own bubbles up, but I nearly choke on it when I catch sight of the view beyond. We are high up on a mountain, clinging to its forested edge where it looms over a long valley.

"Is that Calida?" I point toward the large mass of buildings in the valley.

"It is. There are a number of other lodgings like this one around the mountainside, but it will be hard to see them among the trees." They seem to hug the building on either side of the balcony, almost like its nestled among their branches. It might be.

The valley stretches out for some distance, full of lush, green life basking in the afternoon sun. But out near the horizon, the green vanishes in an almost straight line, giving way to browns and grays.

"What is that?" I point toward it.

Lysandir's humor fades. "The Shadow Lands. Unseelie territory."

The pronouncement threatens to steal all my warmth. "So close."

It makes sense. It's why we came here after all, but I hadn't realized exactly how close it was.

Lysandir wraps his arms around me, pulling my back against his chest and placing his chin atop my head. "You mine, and I will keep you safe, no matter what comes."

"I know." I place my hand over his and lean back against him. Despite the grim reminder on the horizon, I could stay like this forever. Maybe the king will let us, at least until he chooses his queen and Lysandir and I can be more open with our relationship.

We're marked now. It's not just a visible symbol on our skin—any fae will feel it and know our connection.

Between the warmth of the male at my back and the languidness in my limbs from my release, I'm so relaxed that I let out an embarrassingly large yawn. Lysandir chuckles. He adjusts his stance, and I feel the press of his renewed erection at my lower back.

He leans in, his breath ghosting across my ear and raising goosebumps on my skin. "I hope you're not too tired, little mate, because I'm not done with you. Not nearly."

Any lingering sleepiness vanishes instantly. A few touches, some whispered words, and I'm a ball of aching need once more.

Lysandir frees me from the embrace of his arms and stalks around until he's the only majestic view in front of me. He grabs my blanket and gives it a solid tug. I let it fall.

He holds out a hand to me.

"Well?" He raises his brows in question, his grin devastating.

I take his hand and let him lead me back to bed.

CHAPTER 41

S OMETHING ROUSES ME FROM sleep. I blink, coming back to the world, conscious of the warm body I'm snuggled up against. Lysandir.

Memories flood back, bringing a smile to my face. I'm tucked up against his side under the sheets, and just the sight of him there—mine and with me—makes desire spark anew deep in my core. I push my hair back and sit up. He's still asleep, hair splayed over the pillow. Though his brow is pinched, his chest rising and falling like some nightmare has him in its thrall. How many horrors has he witnessed in all his years? Plenty recently, to be sure.

It's tempting to wake him and resume our earlier activities, but I know he needs his rest. It's doubtful he got much the night before or for several nights before that either, traipsing after his brother through Unseelie lands.

The world outside is still completely dark, showing no signs of dawn. I consider lying back down, snuggling up against his side, and finding rest once more. Goodness knows I need it too. But a sudden glimmer in the distance snares my attention.

I slip from bed as quietly as I can. Cool night air tickles my skin and raises gooseflesh along it. I grab a blanket from the bench at the foot of the bed and pull it around myself before moving to the railing and looking out at the valley in the distance. Dim light emanates from the Calida. There's a soft spot of glow here and there around it as well, likely more buildings or homes.

Far beyond the city, the sparkling comes again, stretching from some point near the horizon into the sky. It's strange and beautiful all at once. The glimmer sparkles again, but this time, it doesn't fade. Instead, it appears to widen, peeling back like the flaps of a tent. I squint at the distant light. What could it be? Lysandir hadn't mentioned anything that way, nothing but—

The sudden realization leaves me cold.

Nothing but Unseelie territory. The Shadow Lands.

Closer by, in the city, I'd swear more lights have illuminated, like the city is waking up, but still dawn shows no sign of being near.

The wrongness of it all has me shuffling back to the bed. Lysandir's head tosses to the side, and for a moment, I think he's awake. But his eyes are still pinched tight.

"Lysandir." I lay a hand on his shoulder, finding it warmer than I recall. "Lysandir." I give him a little shake.

He grips the sheets over his chest in a tight fist. His head thrashes again.

My worry spikes as I try to shake him awake.

Something is wrong. Very, very wrong.

His whole body jerks like he's fighting some enemy in his sleep. But whatever has him in its thrall won't let him free.

I drop my blanket and climb atop him in the bed. He twists, his body jerking in some fit, and I fear he's about to topple me to the floor. "Lysandir!"

His eyes fly open, wide and glowing with that strange fae reaction to strong emotions.

"Mira." He pants my name like a prayer, chest rising and falling as he pulls in one deep breath then another. Then his palms are on my hips, holding me close. His thumb rubs across his mark on my skin, and a shudder rolls through him as his eyes turn hooded and hungry. But then he flinches, and the look is gone, instead replaced by one of panic. "Something is wrong."

"I know. I tried to wake you." I slide off him and grab for my discarded blanket.

Modesty seems to be the last thing on Lysandir's mind as he slips from the bed and rushes to the balcony railing. I hurry after him. He grips the railing so hard it cracks.

A fae curse slips from his lips. "The wards are failing. I feel it."

"What?" I squeak. "How is that possible?

"I don't know." Lysandir whirls around. "We have to go. Quickly."

No sooner have the words left his mouth than a plume of fire soars into the sky from the center of Calida. I gasp, frozen at the sight of flames stretching into the sky.

Lysandir whips his head back toward the pillar of fiery light. "We're under attack."

Any lingering warmth in my body falls away. Horror threatens to root me to the ground, but I force myself to hurry inside and search for my clothes. Lysandir is already shoving his feet into his pants.

"The Unseelie?" I ask, tugging my dress over my head.

"Most likely."

Lysandir is there the moment I'm done, taking my hands in his, and I know we're about to shift. But he stops and says, "I need to go to the city, and it may not be safe for you to stay here."

"I'm coming with you." There's no way I'm getting left behind.

He doesn't argue, just gives a short nod. "I'll keep you safe, Mira." His hands flex on mine. "Don't be afraid."

"I'm not." Not with his hands in mine. I know he'll protect me. We've conquered fate and found a way to be together. No Unseelie is going to keep us apart. Not now.

"Good."

And then we're shifting, vanishing from our slice of paradise and into war.

CHAPTER 42

W E REAPPEAR INTO CHAOS. Sound fills the halls. Fae rush this way and that. Lysandir leads up off the intricate patterns on the floor of the central hall—a honing point, the fae call it. The designs channel magic which lets them shift to certain places more quickly and easily. It's the same place we arrived several days ago. Not too far from our quarters, if I recall correctly.

Lysandir grabs a passing guard and draws her to a halt.

Her eyes widen as she takes him in. "My prince."

"My mother and the human women?"

"Gathered in the queen's rooms for safety," she reports.

"The king?" Lysandir asks quickly.

"Gone to meet the enemy."

Lysandir curses and releases the guard.

"We are to—" she continues, but Lysandir has already turned away, hurrying toward a nearby hall and taking me with him. I have to jog to keep up his pace.

"I want you to stay with the others," he says as we rush through the halls. "It's the safest place for you."

"And you?" I ask.

But the sinking feel in my chest says I already know. He'll go to his brother, to face the enemy head-on a fight. An enemy that has somehow managed to rip down the wards. It shouldn't be possible, yet it's happened.

"I felt the wards tear and break." He clutches at his chest. "If they can do that, this is no unorganized and unprepared rabble. I will be needed at the front."

Tears burn at the corners of my eyes. I'm about to protest when we turn the corner and a familiar figure looms just ahead.

"Thank holy Aine," Tharin says as he catches sight of us. Gold-plated armor hugs his form. I might not have noticed him if he had been wearing the helm tucked under one arm. "I've been looking for you everywhere."

He and Lysandir meet, clasping shoulders in a friendly embrace.

"I need you to take Mira to the others," Lysandir says before he releases his friend. "Keep her safe for me and watch after her as you have these weeks."

Tharin opens his mouth like he might protest but then closes it and nod. "With my life, my prince."

Don't leave. Don't go. The words are right there on the tip of my tongue. But I know no matter what I say, he will. Begging will only make the inevitable harder.

So, when Lysandir turns from Tharin to me, I say, "Stay safe. I love you."

Lysandir cups my cheek and pulls me close. "I love you too."

He seals his words with a kiss. Tears leak from my eyes and slide down my cheeks. I taste their salt as he breaks the kiss.

"I'll come back to you, Mira." The same promise he made before, and he kept it then.

He drags his gaze up and down my body, in one scalding last look, before he turns and races down the hallway alone.

Tharin dons his helm and then wraps an arm around my shoulders. "Let's get you to the dowager."

When I arrive, all of the other women have already gathered. Elaine, or someone, must have filled them in on the state of affairs because I'm met with excitement and messages of congratulations. It's a bit embarrassing really, but their support warms me too. Having them near brings me comfort and strength, more than I anticipated, especially given the horror of war unfolding just outside the walls.

The only one who doesn't approach me is Katherine. She completely refuses to look at me, instead lingering near the corner with her back turned. It's fine. I'd rather not deal with her right now anyway.

"Ignore her," Cora whispers to me. "We're glad you're here and safe."

"We'll pray for your prince and all of the others," Gabriella assures me.

I guess that's what they expect us to do. Pray and remain safe like poor little damsels. Not that I know how to wield a sword. And I certainly don't have magic or anything else to fight with. I'd be a liability. This is the best place for me. But still, waiting, feeling helpless, is the worst. It'd be safer for us to leave, but we can't, not bonded to the king. It would hamper him too much if we were to be far away. The bonds would pull at him, being a terrible distraction and possibly impairing his ability to fight. The only place for us to be is here, in this extra-warded area where it's safest. But if the Unseelie can break through the wards protecting the territory, what's to stop them from shattering these as well?

Just the guards, the ones who haven't gone to join their king. Tharin has taken up residence inside the room, refusing to be anywhere else. Adeline's guardsman Erymis is here too, and they've shared enough longing looks to draw multiple questioning glances from the others. Though I suppose that shouldn't matter so much anymore if the king gives them leave to follow their hearts as he said.

Unable to sit still, I start to pace. It can't have been long. Minutes, not hours. But each one drags like a day, and it's already getting hard to block out the horrible possibilities that keep popping to mind.

I clutch Lysandir's ring in my palm, savoring its warmth. Alive. Well, if not safe.

Zoe suddenly cries out. I whip around toward her. The guards grab for their swords. Her arm is outstretched before her, and she stares at it like the world's biggest spider is crawling across her skin.

Something moves. But it's not a spider.

Thin tendrils of black smoke lift from the bond mark around her wrist.

My own suddenly feels cold, as if someone with hands of ice grabbed me. I glance down in time to see little whisps of smoke rising from mine as well, bits of the bond lifting off my skin and vanishing.

"What's happening!" Katherine has rushed toward the rest of us, her arm outstretched.

"Your Highness?" Cora says with a desperate glance at the dowager queen.

Elaine cries out, covering her mouth with her hand.

My stomach plummets. Breath comes short and quick.

It's then I know. The king is hurt. Dying.

When Bailey died, her bond to the king vanished. The same is happening now, just the other way around. The world seems to shift under my feet in a way it has only a few times in my life, the last when my father died. It was unexpected, the unthinkable, something so seismic as to shift the balance of my life for good.

Just like then, my chest is hollowed out, shock stealing my wits.

The king is dying. The Court of Fire is losing.

I grab Lysandir's ring so tightly the metal digs into my palm. It's warm, but how long will that last?

Ribbons of smoke continue unfurling from our wrists. They barely leave our skin before vanishing into nothingness.

Tharin takes charge, ordering the other guards in the room. "Get the women to the honing point! Take them to the capital at once!"

Because there's no reason for us to remain anymore. No bond to hinder the king. No king at all.

Tears slip down my cheeks.

"Time to go." Tharin latches onto my upper arm and tries to haul me toward the door.

But I dig in my heels and jerk out of his grip.

"No! I won't leave him." I can't bear to leave him to fight and die, to hide away when at any moment the ring he gave me might cool.

"I have to take you to safety."

Already the guards are ushering the other women up and toward the door.

"There has to be something we can do to help," I all but shout at him.

"Mira," Tharin grates, a hard edge to his voice. "I have to—"

A sound like shattered glass rings through the room. We freeze and look toward its source.

Queen Elaine stands with the spear in her hands. Its shaft has been extended. The shattered remnants of its top lie in pieces on the stonework as she rights it and holds it out toward me.

"Take the spear." It's the order of a queen. A command. "Help my son."

Something fierce and hot burns in the center of my chest, racing like tingling likes of flame through my veins.

Tharin sucks in a breath, and I know he wants to demand I do otherwise. But even he won't go against her wishes.

Her unblinking, powerful gaze calls me, tugging me forward like a rope I'd be helpless to wiggle away from even if I wanted to.

I cross the room to her and take the spear. It's warm under my palm. Just the feel of it gives me strength—and something else. At the edge of my senses, I hear a song, a whisper urging me to go, to protect.

I straighten my shoulders and meet her resolute stare with one of my own. "I will."

She gives me one solid nod. "Good."

"Mira..." Adeline stares at me wide-eyed as I turn back toward the others.

"You can use it?" Cora asks.

I flex my fingers on the staff. "Yes."

And I know it without a doubt. The magic already calls to me, begging to be unleashed. Elaine is too old and frail for the battlefield, but I'm not. I can do this.

I glance at Erymis, for I know he'll do exactly what I'm about to ask. "Get them to safety. Now."

"Right away," he responses, grabbing Adeline and moving her toward the door. The other women follow, guards ushering them away. A pair help the dowager to her feet, and for once, she doesn't rebuke their assistance.

"Tharin." I pull the ring from around my neck and hold it up. "Take me to Lysandir."

He gathers the ring into my palm and clasps it between our hands. "You're sure?"

"Absolutely." I can help. I can do something more than hide. And I will not lose him now.

CHAPTER 43

T HERE'S NO TIME TO worry or second-guess before we're shifting. My feet land on lush ground. A forest cloaked in night appears around us, bits of flame burning on grass and shrubbery. A few dark masses lie unmoving. Cries ring out in the distance. I blink, trying to adjust my sight to the dimness when a groan of pure agony emanates from a few feet away.

A figure in golden armor kneels on the ground, body hunched over in the grass, hands grasping their head as they rock and writhe in pain.

My heart skips a beat then stops altogether before jolting into a gallop.

"Lysandir!" I lunge toward him and drop to my knees at his side, letting the spear fall between us. Then my hands are on him, trying in vain to discover where he's injured as he rocks and holds his head like it might split in two.

"Where are you hurt? What's happened?" I ask, but he doesn't respond.

"It's the magic settling on him," Tharin says, coming to crouch beside us.

"The magic?"

"The king's magic." Tharin places his hand on Lysandir's back. "Lysandir is the King of Fire now."

Lysandir is... A tear wells up from nowhere and slides down my cheek. The king is truly dead then.

"Mira." Lysandir reaches out and grabs a fistful of my dress.

"I'm here." I caress his armor, not that he can likely feel it.

"No," he groans. "You must go." Lysandir plants his hands on the ground but struggles to push himself up, almost like the weight of a beast sits upon his back.

"I'm not leaving you here." I grab his arm and try to help him sit.

He stiffens under my grip. "The spear." He twists his head to stare at me in horror. "My mother?"

"Is fine."

His whole body sags in relief.

"She sent me here to help you." I grab the spear, and with Tharin's help, we get Lysandir to his feet.

"The battle nears," Tharin says urgently. "I can shift you both away."

"That would—" Lysandir's attention shifts past his friend toward the something in the distance. Before I can glimpse it, he shoves me behind him and pulls his sword free. Tharin whirls and does the same.

"We must go." Tharin snaps. "Now!"

"No." Lysandir growls. Waves of magic pour from him, creating a corona of fiery light.

I lean around Lysandir and stare at the wavering shadows beneath a thick grove of trees. A gasp lodges in my throat as I spy figures stalking our way. Several stop, but one advances, stepping out into the small clearing we occupy.

The light from a smoldering bush shines on the figure's black armor. Spikes protrude from the shoulders and upper arms. Long, pale hair shimmers like a banner from under their dark, fearsome helm and falls in a cascade down their back. They carry two objects, one a long sword dripping red with blood, the other, a golden helm decorated with a crown of flame.

The sight strips the heat from my body. I clutch the spear tight to my chest.

I know who stands before us.

I feel it in my bones. Hear it in the discordant whispers of the ancient spear in my hands.

The Unseelie King tosses the helm toward us. It bounces once and rolls to a few feet away. I try not to look too closely at the blood smearing the metal or to speculate at its source. Though somewhere inside me, I know.

A cry of alarm rings out behind us. I twist to see figures in gold and red advancing. Our allies. But I feel no relief at the sight of backup.

"Your king is dead." The resonate voice of the Unseelie King snares my full attention. "Killed for the atrocities against my people. Cede this city to us to compensate for the loss of our innocent, and I shall let you take your people and leave, new Fire King."

I clutch the spear a little tighter, my fingertips digging into the shaft.

"You killed my brother!" Lysandir snarls. "You think I'll walk away?"

Lysandir... I bite my wobbling lip as I stare up at him. I ache to reach for him, to hold him close, but I won't compromise him in this moment.

"If you know what's good for you," the Unseelie King replies, his deep voice even and calm. "Your brother started this by attacking my people. You can stop it or continue the bloodshed."

A humorless laugh spills from Lysandir. "You starting this by killing a human in our territory. One of my brother's potential brides, no less! You think he wouldn't retaliate?"

The Unseelie King shifts his stance and takes a half step back. "Killing a human?" he echoes. "My people know I forbid violence against humans."

"Then you don't have the control of them that you think," Lysandir snaps. "Only days ago, your people entered our land, killed a human woman, and injured one of our court's chief advisors. Do you deny it?"

"I do deny it. Why would we harm a human?" He gestures to those behind him looming among the trees.

Human. Human. Human. Each use of it grates against me, boiling the emotions I've tried so hard to hold in check, until I can't stay silent.

"Bailey!" I shout, stepping to Lysandir's side. "Her name was Bailey. And she was innocent and kind. She deserved better!"

"Mira." Lysandir throws an arm out in front of me, trying to block me from view, to no avail.

The full weight of the Unseelie King's regard falls on me, and it takes everything I have not to shrink back in fear. The world seems to hold his breath as the Unseelie King looks from me to Lysandir.

"Last chance, Fire King. Cede and flee or stay and atone for your crimes," he says. I catch the barest hint of a smirk as he glances back at me. "I'll even see that your human remains unharmed in my court."

Lysandir erupts, sending a blast of flames straight at the Unseelie King. His roar of fury follows with it. The blast of heat blows my hair back and rolls across my skin. I wince, pinching my eyes shut until it passes. When I open them again, Lysandir has rushed forward and meets the Unseelie King in a clash of swords that rings out like a gong. And suddenly both sides are racing toward each other, the Court of Fire coming up from behind us and the Unseelie slipping out of the forest. Tharin steps into the spot Lysandir vacated, his sword up to protect me, but it doesn't change the fact that we're in the middle of a battlefield.

Sweat breaks out on the back of my neck as I glance around. Panic has my breaths coming short and quick. Lysandir leaps back, then clashes with the Unseelie King once more. He moves with swiftness and grace that would be the envy of the best human swordsman, but even I can see he's unmatched against the power of the Unseelie King.

From out of nowhere, a sudden quiet surrounds me, and then I hear the whispers I missed amid the chaos. The words are strange, a language I do not know and could not begin to recite, but I know what they ask of me all the same.

Use the spear. Protect your people.

With a hard shove, I plant the butt of the spear on the ground and call to the voice with all of my soul, *Shield them. Protect them.*

The moment I think it, a burst of magic rolls out from me in a shimmering wave. It flows over the members of the Court of Fire, enclosing them in a dome of pale, glittering light. The nearby Unseelie are shoved back, even the Unseelie King.

Lysandir shifts back to stand just in front of me and glances over one shoulder. I swear there's pride in his gaze, clouding out his worry.

"I'm with you," I promise.

Beyond the shimmering wall, the Unseelie King has let his sword dip and lays an open palm against my shield. I *feel* as he pushes against it. Not pain but a soft pressure, an awareness, reaches me through the shaft of the spear.

And that's not all the spear tells me. It lets me know something else too, an advantage I don't think the Unseelie have grasped.

"Light them up, Lysandir," I say.

His eyes widen ever so slightly before a vicious grin spreads across his face. He turns back toward the Unseelie King. "With pleasure."

Lysandir unleashes a fireball that soars through the air straight at the Unseelie King. It slips through the barrier without incident. The king barely raises his sword in time, holding it blade out in front of himself. The ball of fire strikes it and splits into a rain of sparks that the Unseelie King ignores.

Damn magical sword. It's true then. He did find the sword that was thought to be lost.

The other warriors of our court catch on. Fire races by me toward the Unseelie, who scramble to defend. When the heat buffets me, I no longer fear it. I embrace it instead, savoring the sting, the sweat that runs down my skin. Hope swells within me as the Unseelie begin to retreat. Some of our troops rush past the barrier to chase those escaping, and I push out my awareness, making the barrier larger.

Pressure comes again as the Unseelie King plants his feet and pushes back against the magic. It retreats as he does, stepping back as Lysandir stalks his way, shooting bursts of flame with one hand, sword at the ready in the other.

The Unseelie King raises his sword. My brows pinch in confusion at his aim until he slams the blade against the barrier.

I cry out at the sudden impact as tremors race up my arms and through my chest.

"Mira!" Lysandir shouts back at me.

I brace my feet and the spear, readying for another blow. "I'm fine. Get him!"

With another roar, Lysandir engages the Unseelie King again, blending fire and blade, staying just inside the safety of the barrier.

The sword strikes against my shield again, and though I'm ready for it, the blow has me wobbling on my feet. My muscles cry out in protest.

The barrier flickers.

Please. I close my eyes and will the protective bubble I've created to strengthen and grow once more. Another blast of flame races by me, nearly singeing my skin.

Lysandir cries out.

My eyes fly wide. My stomach drops. A new smear of red mars the Unseelie King's blade, but Lysandir is still on his feet, still fighting. His next blow has the other king lurching backward and growling in pain.

"Stop her!" the Unseelie King yells.

It could mean anyone, but the pit in my chest says he means me. I glance around for danger, as does Tharin, who has sent a few blasts of fire toward the enemy but hasn't left my side. Finally, I spot a flash of pink—a most unusual color for a battlefield. A lithe warrior in lightweight, black armor darts through my barrier, and I *know* they're not friendly.

The way they—she—moves is like dance, springing this way and that until she's nearly upon Tharin, her twin short swords unsheathed and gleaming in the light from the burning shrubbery. But he's seen her too and is more than ready.

"Focus on the shield!" he calls to me.

And though I try, I can't help looking between him and Lysandir. Tharin moves to intercept the newcomer. She must be the null we've heard about. No one else could so easily slip past without causing so much as a twitch against my barrier. Was she the one who killed Bailey? The thought has my shield flickering, doubt nagging at me. An enemy, to be sure, but somehow I don't think she did it. This warrior answers to the king. If he denied it, it would not have been her to carry it out.

Tharin is quick, even more than I would have given him credit for. The Unseelie woman may have two blades, similar to the two cat ears on her head, but its not enough to unbalance or unsteady the skilled warrior. He's the prince's—no, the king's—guard for a reason.

Another hit crashes into my barrier, and I'm taken unaware. I fall. My knee slams into the ground, and I yip in pain but cling to the spear. The shimmering shield flickers like a bad screen, so I stay there, clinging to the spear and doing all I can to shove my will, my desire for protection, into the magical object.

But my shield has shrunk, and I can't seem to make it bigger anymore. Sweat rolls down my body, and it's not just from the flames.

That sword the king wields is harming the power of the spear.

I search the area nearby and finally find Lysandir again. He's locked in a sword fight with the Unseelie King once more, but this time, he's outside my barrier.

Get back. Come back to me, I yearn to cry but hold my tongue.

A sharp hiss fills the air near me. Tharin and the Unseelie woman have closed in, just a few short feet away. She reels back. Blood drips from a wound on her arm.

Tharin twirls his sword in a taunt. She snarls but refuses to flee. Tharin presses his advantage and rushes her. The clash of metal rings out as she blocks once. Twice. But on the third time, Tharin hits her arm again, and she cries out.

"Katiya!" The Unseelie King roars.

Like I thought, she's not just another warrior in his horde. She's someone to him.

And Tharin knows it too. He knocks the blade from her injured arm with a quick swipe of his sword. Katiya darts away, but Tharin is faster, shifting in front of her. He swings. She dodges. But not quite fast enough. His blade slices along the thin armor on her side, and she cries out in agony. Katiya hits the ground hard, clutching at the bleeding wound.

The next bellow from the king shakes the very ground. He rears back with his sword and then leaps into the air over Lysandir's head. The move is so fast a scream barely has time to form on my tongue. Lysandir ducks and whirls, ready to meet a strike from behind, but it doesn't come. Instead, the Unseelie King aims the tip of his blade at my shield and lands against it with the full force of his jump.

The blow to my shield strikes like a punch to my chest. One moment, I'm upright; the next, the wind has been knocked from my lungs, and I crash to the ground, pain radiating along my head and back from the impact. Stars dance before my vision.

Lysandir cries my name. Someone else screams. Tharin lets out a bellow.

Then hands are on me, feeling for injuries. Lysandir says something, though I can't quite make it out, but I feel his nearness, savor it. I blink, my vision returning. As it does, I see glimpses from where my cheek lays against the cool ground.

The Unseelie King deflects a blow from Tharin. Half the length of his sword is blackened. It makes an odd sound when struck. Katiya throws something at Tharin, and he backs away, coughing. The Unseelie King scoops Katiya into his arms and speeds away.

"Mira!" Lysandir cups my cheek in his palm and turns my head toward him. "Where are you hurt?"

Everywhere. Each breath is a harsh rasp, but they come. I can wiggle my fingers and toes. I'm going to be bruised like crazy, but I don't think anything is broken, at least nothing major.

"I'm fine," I manage to say. "He's getting away."

Lysandir looks back over his shoulder. Warriors from the Court of Fire have closed in around us, offering protection.

"Maybe for the best," he mumbles.

He meets my gaze, and I read the things he doesn't say. Because he might not have won. Even with my shields, the Unseelie King was a formidable opponent, one he was not prepared for.

Lysandir looks to the surrounding fae and shouts, "Medic!"

"I'm fine," I protest again and attempt to sit. My breath comes easier now. "But you're not." Blood leaks down his arm.

A fae I don't know drops to their knees beside us. They lay a hand on each of us before I can ask what's happening. Magic shivers under my skin, and suddenly my aches and pains fade away. They drop their hand from me, but healing Lysandir takes longer.

I grab the spear where it fell on the ground beside me. It looks none the worse for wear, but the whispers of power I heard and felt from it before are quiet.

"Almost had her." Tharin wipes at his face as he joins us. Whatever the Unseelie woman used worked to distract him but doesn't seem to have had any lasting effect, thank goodness. "Should we pursue?"

"To the borders only. No farther," Lysandir commands.

Immediately, Tharin begins barking orders at the others.

The sun has begun to rise, brightening the sky and casting a muted light over everything. Smoke rises from the fires caused by magic. Some of the fae rush to put them out, seeming to suck the flames away and extinguish the smoldering embers.

"You're safe. You're okay." Lysandir says, maybe more to himself than to me.

"I am." I lift the spear just a bit and try to push my awareness into it. It flares weakly but then sputters out. "But it's quiet now. I... I didn't break it, did I?" Oh gosh, if I destroyed the spear, what does that say about me?

"It's fine." Lysandir curls his hand around mine over the spear. "All magic must recharge. Mine. The spear. It likely just needs time."

I breathe a sigh of relief. "Thank goodness."

We're an island of stillness in a sea of activity. I glance around but quickly avert my gaze as I spy a few unmoving figures in the distance. Instead, I focus on Lysandir. His bleed has stopped, and though he still breaths heavily, I know he's okay.

"What happens now?" I ask.

"Let's hope the Unseelie have fled for now." His expression turns somber. "This night has seen too much death and bloodshed."

My heart aches for him. I lunge forward, throwing my arms around his neck and hugging his armored form. "I'm so sorry."

He trails his fingers through my hair and holds me close. I hear his breath catch, and I nestle a littler closer, offering whatever support I can. When my father passed, there weren't any words that made it better. People feel the need to say them, I think, to offer support however they can. After all, didn't I just do the same? But the thing that actually helped was closeness. Mom was too distraught, as were my brothers, but Selena held me close, an arm wrapped around me as I cried on her shoulder. She didn't say anything. She didn't need to. Just being there was everything. I can be that for Lysandir now. Someone to lean on when all the world feels like its crumbling and shifting.

We cling together like that for a while until Tharin comes back and drops to one knee beside us. He places a hand on Lysandir's shoulder. "The Unseelie King and his host have fled past our borders. We're sweeping the area now for any others."

Lysandir's cheeks are dry when he raises his head to look at his friend, but there's a weariness in his eyes I've never seen before. Already, the crown sits heavily.

"Good. See it done." He rises to his feet and pulls me with him. "I will take Mira to the capital. You're in charge until I return."

The thought of him coming back, of leaving me somewhere else, makes me ill, but I swallow down my discomfort and stay silent. He's a king now. His responsibilities are bigger than me, and I won't make them even harder by adding my fear to his burden.

CHAPTER 44

S HIFTING TO THE CAPITAL takes time and a toll. Lysandir doesn't stand quite as straight and strong as we enter the dowager's room, where she waits with the other women, and I know its not just emotions weighing him down. He hasn't had a full night's sleep in days, and he poured everything into his fight with the Unseelie King. Between that and shifting, he must be on fumes.

"Mira!" The chorus of my name as we enter should be a relief. They are safe. The battle is done for today. But the war, I'm afraid, is just beginning.

"My son." Elaine's whisper cuts through the commotion.

Lysandir makes a beeline to her and falls to one knee beside her chair. He pulls his helm free and bows his head. "I never made it to him. I wasn't there when he needed me."

It should be a blessing that he was spared seeing what happened, but the wondering, the doubts about whether he could have done something, may be just as tough to live with.

"You were where you needed to be." Elaine cups her son's cheek. "He would not have had you there. No matter your differences, he would have had you safe."

"But maybe I could have—"

"No. His haste and anger led to this. Not you. You tried to show him a wiser path. It's not your fault he did not listen."

The other women silently look to me with mixed expressions of curiosity and discomfort. I shift on my feet, the spear clutched in one hand, unsure of what to do with myself. I feel like a voyeur listening in, but there's no way I'm just going to turn and leave right now either.

After a moment, Lysandir rises and turns toward us. We all look to him, waiting.

"As you likely know, my brother is dead. The Choosing is ended." He looks at each of them in turn before settling on me. "Mira is my choice. I will have none but her."

Love swells within me, but strangely, all I want to do is cry. It's so much—so many emotions in too little time.

Lysandir holds out a hand to me. The women part as I walk past them to take it.

His hand closes around mine, and he stares into my eyes. "I would make you my queen, if you'll have me."

It should be a big thing. Momentous. But his words are quiet, just for me. Our audience is small. It's intimate. It's perfect. I should probably think about my response, but deep in my soul, I already know. "I will."

"Long live the queen." Cora smiles at me and dips her head.

"Long live the queen," the other women echo.

The spear feels heavy in my hands. I turn and present it to Elaine, but she shakes her head.

"It is yours now. Wield it with pride for our people." The sad smile she offers warm the deepest parts of me while making me want to cry anew.

"I will."

To her son, she says, "We will hold a public ceremony to anoint you both as soon as you are ready. The court should see your unity and take strength from it in this time."

The whole court, take strength from me... It feels surreal. A dream. A fantasy. The weight of it hasn't landed, but I know it will at some point, once the shock has faded.

Lysandir turns to the others. "You're free to return to your homes at your earliest convenience. With all that's happened, I cannot guarantee your safety here, much as I would wish to."

It should be good news, relief, but the looks on most of their faces are anything but. Alex and Grace clasp hands and stare at one another. Adeline looks away—her guard isn't here, but hopefully he's safe. He should be if he brought them here. Cora, however, stares right at me, and I know exactly what she's begging for in silence.

"We should let them stay if they choose. Even if it's not safe, it should be their choice," I say to Lysandir.

He takes my hand in his and squeezes. "If you think it best."

"I do. And there's what Vasilius said yesterday." I swallow the knot that forms in my throat at the mention of him. I squeeze his hand a little tighter and look at the women. "I'm not sure if he had the chance to tell you all, but he was going to encourage you to follow your hearts. If you didn't want him, if your heart was elsewhere, he wanted you to be able to be with that person, regardless of The Choosing."

"You mean that?" Adeline says, wide-eyed.

"Yes. And you are all free to stay here however long you like. Forever, if that's your choice. With any power I have, I will make sure that your families cannot demand you returned nor will you be forced to wed a fae noble. Your choices in all things will be your own."

"Oh, Mira!" Adeline runs forward and wraps me a hug, nearly ripping me away from Lysandir and knocking the breath from my lungs with her fierce embrace. Beyond her, Grace nearly jumps into Alex's arms as the two meet in a kiss. Some of the others look a little surprised, to say the least.

But Cora just crosses her arms, grins, and mouths, *All hail the queen.*

Adeline finally releases me and returns to the other women, who muse over the revelations I just presented.

"I hope I didn't misstep," I whisper to Lysandir. "I don't really know if I have any authority..." Something I probably should have considered before, especially since I'm not actually queen. Yet.

But he just wraps an arm around me and pulls me close. "You will have all the authority you want, and I believe you will use it well, as you just have."

"I don't know. Some of the gifted families may be upset by this." I pull my bottom lip between my teeth, already contemplating the nasty messages we're sure to receive.

Lysandir shrugs. "Let them be upset, then. But I think they'll come around. From what I've heard, it sounds like they've become almost as dependent on us as we have on them."

"You have no idea," I grumble.

It's a happy moment in a horrible morning. Hopefully, it's the promise of change, of good things coming with the dawn.

CHAPTER 45

NOT LONG AFTER OUR reunion in the capital, Lysandir sets off to return to the border and rebuild the wards that the Unseelie King was able to destroy. Elaine ordered letters written up to be sent to the human world informing them of all that transpired in the night. I don't envy anyone on the receiving end of those letters. I can't imagine any of them will be happy, except maybe my uncle. Assuming they include mention of me, which I'm not entirely sure they will. The dowager suggested I write to my family myself, but no matter how long I sit here and stare at the blank page in front of me, the words aren't coming.

Hi Mom. You were right, I guess. I was destined to become queen after all. Sorry it's your worst nightmare come true.

I wince and throw the pen down in frustration. Maybe if they were the ones Lysandir had gotten me they'd help me find the right thing to say, but they're not. Retrieving our things is low priority, as it should be. And though I sit in Lysandir's quarters, at his desk, his pens are all boring ones with black ink. Suppose we'll have to change that.

But maybe the reason I can't find the words is because I haven't been able to sort it all out myself. Just over a day ago I was being dragged before the king, my sins laid bare. Now? That king is dead, and the man I love has vowed to place me on the throne beside him. Just thinking about it makes me want to laugh and cry in equal measure, and none of it feels real. Especially since Lysandir has not returned.

The sun has fallen, and logically, I know I should sleep. A full night's rest might be just what I need to sort out my thoughts and emotions. However, it feels impossible to rest when Lysandir is not here and I don't know what's happening to him. The ring around my neck is warm—a good sign, but last night showed just how quickly things can change.

I grab the pen again, determined to write *something*, when magic shivers across my skin. The moment it does, I drop the pen and leap from the chair, whirling toward the source of the feeling.

The sight of Lysandir leaning heavily on Tharin, both sagging in their armor, makes my heart stutter-step.

"What happened?" I race across the room toward them.

"Mira," Lysandir whispers my name.

"No need to panic," Tharin says at the same time. "He's just exhausted."

Lysandir's head lolls as Tharin lays him on the sofa. Worry races through me despite Tharin's assurances. Lysandir may be healthy, but he sure doesn't look it.

"Help me remove his armor," Tharin says. "I'd call for someone else to assist, but Lysandir generally prefers his privacy."

"It's fine," I say and set to helping him remove it piece by piece.

Tharin tsks as he works. "Burned straight through his magic in his determination to get the wards repaired. It's always a hard job, and this was...different."

"How so?" I ask.

His lips thin as if he thinks better of it, but then he continues, "The Unseelie King cut our wards to pieces at the spot they broke through. It was quick. Brutal and efficient. So much different than the first time the king cut through our wards to create a breach."

Shit. That's even worse than I thought. "What's to stop him from breaking through somewhere else."

The grim look he gives me says more than enough. I swallow, my throat suddenly dry.

"And that's why we need our king to rest and get back on his feet as soon as possible. Good thing he has you to help with that." He gets his king down to just his underwear and then hoists Lysandir's unconscious form into his arms and carries him to the bed.

"How do I do that?" I ask. "Force him to stay in bed?"

Tharin groans as he finally gets Lysandir somewhere he can rest.

"Surely you know?" He raises a brow at me.

"Humans give fae power, yes. A mark even more so."

"Uh huh. And the more you work on that mark and build the bond between you, the more powerful he'll get. Just being near you will aid him. So, it'd be best if you get in the bed, preferably naked so your skin touches his. And when he wakes up, you can show him just how much you've missed him." He winks.

I want nothing more than to vanish through the floor. "We are not having this discussion right now."

He smirks. "Oh, but we are. You're the best thing for him. How do you think he held his own in the fight after so little rest and still had enough strength to re-raise the wards that the Unseelie King ripped apart?"

"Fine." I want nothing more than to help Lysandir and strength-en him. Discussing it with Tharin? No thanks. "But I'm not about to strip with you here."

"Then I'll see to my own rest. But first." He drops to one knee before me. "I'm sorry."

I lean back in confusion. "For what?"

"For my wariness of you being near Lysandir. For doubting. I promised you would have my apology if your bore his mark." He glances to Lysandir and back to me. "So, you have it, along with my trust and protection from this day until my last."

I sober, the reality of what he's pledging sinking in. It's so much more than an apology. "Thank you," I whisper, barely able to form the words over the weight of his proclamation settling over me.

He rises to his feet before giving a sweeping bow that manages to be both respectful and amused in equal measure. "Good night, future queen."

Lysandir woke a few hours after Tharin returned him and we did work on rebuilding our mark. And the next morning too. The sting of loss hit him hard then, and I held him close until he fell back asleep and I laid down beside him. When I wake again, the room is bright, but the comforting weight and warmth at my back says Lysandir is still close by. I sit up carefully so as not to wake him, but when I look over, I find him watching me, wide awake.

"Good afternoon?" I tug a sheet up to cover my chest, though he's seen all of me multiple times now.

"Afternoon indeed." He reaches up and brushes a piece of hair back behind my ear. The simple act stirs up an ache between my legs. But even though he smiles up at me, the look on his face is a somber one.

He beckons me, close and I curl up at his side again, my head on his shoulder, one arm draped over his chest.

"I've been thinking," he begins.

"About?"

Lysandir sucks in a deep breath and then lets it out again. "What the Unseelie King said before the battle."

"About Bailey?"

He nods. "He seemed genuinely confused, and even Unseelie cannot lie. The more I think about what happened, the stranger it seems for it to have been Unseelie. They need humans. They've tried to capture them, sure, but harm them? They didn't even really hurt Wren when they held her captive, but they could have to force the King of Air into action."

"It does seem strange."

"I thought so earlier, but with everything that happened, there was little time to focus on it. But why kill her? Why not even try to take her away? Plus, how could they know where she would be and the impact it would have upon my brother?"

A sinking feel takes root within me, and I snuggle closer to Lysandir. "Unless it wasn't the Unseelie but someone who knew the king's preferences and where we would be."

"Exactly."

"But who all knew how much he cared for her? That she was his top pick? We women discussed it later, but I don't think any of us were really sure."

"The council," he says calmly. "Maybe some of the guards."

I half sit up in urgency and stare down at him. "You think someone in the court did this. That there's a traitor among us."

Lysandir pulls me back down. "I want to know what you think. Talk out your thoughts with me."

"If it wasn't the Unseelie, whoever did it wanted us to believe it was."

He nods again.

"And they likely knew that the king would not be one to sit idly by and not react to such a tragedy."

Another nod.

"So, who would benefit from such a thing? From inspiring war?"

When I don't continue, he says, "Someone who wanted one?"

"Memnon?" It's the first name that pops to mind. He was so adamant at the council sessions about the need to go on the offensive to defend the court before the Unseelie could gain more power. "But he was injured in the attack. Gravely so. He didn't appear to have done it to himself, did he?"

"No. But what better way to avoid blame than to be a victim yourself?"

I roll onto my back, blinking. "If it was him, he had help." Multiple traitors. Members of the court moving to force things to go the way they wanted them. I turn my head back to Lysandir. "How do we find out if you're right?"

He takes my hand in his and squeezes it. "I have an idea."

CHAPTER 46

W ITH A LAST SWEEP of the brush across my cheeks, Fia steps back and smiles at her work. "There." She smiles at me in the mirror. "What do you think?"

"Perfect, as always."

Fia arrived just after dawn this morning to help me get ready for the day. I once read that makeup was a woman's body armor, and I believe it in this moment. Between her cosmetics, the way she's styled my hair, and the beautiful gown I'm about to step in to, I feel stronger—more confident.

She steps behind me and places one hand on either shoulder. "You will make a wonderful queen."

I suck in a deep breath. "I hope so."

"I know it. I've believed it since the beginning." She leans in, giving me a sort of hug. "And I'm honored to be here, to help you in whatever little way I can."

"You're a huge help. More than you know." Tears burn at the corners of my eyes as I stare at our reflection in the mirror.

In minutes, I'll come before the dowager queen to be anointed as the next via the ceremonial passing of the spear. Hundreds of fae will be in attendance. Some humans too. According to what Fia told me earlier, Selena will be there with my aunt and uncle too. If only Mom could come, but she's a literal world away from all of this.

"None of that." Fia releases me and pats my shoulders. "Wouldn't want to ruin all my work." She winks.

Another deep breath fills my lungs. "Of course not."

"Let's get you dressed and on your way."

Minutes later, I stand just outside the massive throne room as the doors are pulled wide. This is where it all started weeks ago, where I entered The Choosing and was bound to the king as a potential bride. It was always going to end this way for someone. I yearned for it to be me. Oh, how things have changed since then. What a strange and curving path I've walked to end up at this moment.

The room is packed to the gills, but an empty pathway runs from the doors to the dais at the far end where Elaine waits, the spear lying in her lap. Lysandir will be off to the side somewhere, waiting and watching. This moment isn't a time for kings but queens alone.

Silence falls as those assembled wait for me.

Like a bride, I start my march down the aisle, but no one escorts me. This walk is one I make alone, my head held high, all my focus on the destination. It's a long walk, but it passes quickly. I pull up hem of my dress and ascend the stairs before dropping to the ground in front of the queen. I kneel there, head bowed.

Elaine rises from her seat, the spear extended to its full length clutched in her hand. "Mira Rivera, Chosen of the King of Fire, I anoint you the future queen of our court. May you bring prosperity to our people."

She touches the spear to my shoulder, like a monarch naming a knight.

On a pedestal by her chair looms a golden band spotted with rubies. She lifts it and places it upon my head. My whole body nearly vibrates with emotion as it settles on my head. The crown is dainty, light, yet the weight of it isn't lost on me.

"Rise and take the spear," Elaine orders.

I do. She bows her head to me and then retreats to her seat. I turn toward the deathly quiet assembly, searching for Lysandir as I do. I find him almost immediately, standing near the front and just off to the side. He beams with pride, Tharin at his side.

Breath catches in my throat as I notice those near him—Selena, my aunt and uncle just behind her. And they actually look happy—joyful. Several of the other women from The Choosing are around them. Grace, Alex, Adeline, and Cora. Zoe and Gabriella returned to Earth with promises to visit again soon. Katherine... Well, she said nothing about returning, and I wouldn't be surprised if I never see her again. Tears threaten at the sight of so many people there for me, but Selena gives me two thumbs up, and a little laugh slips out instead. It's lost amid the cheers that rise from those assembled. The wave of their support is the highest high, a swell of encouragement that could lift the most dejected soul.

When the cheers slow, Lysandir ascends the dais, takes my hand in his, and kisses the back of it. That sends another round of whoops and applause ringing out. With all the joy filling this room, one might never know their king had just died, that the ceremonial burning of his body and sending on of his soul is still to take place later today.

But maybe people need something to cheer for in the hard times.

Lysandir speaks to the crowd, recounting his brother's loss, his ascension as king, and choosing of me as his queen. He pledges to defend the court and its people, to lead with honor and dignity.

"For our court to be strong and prosper, we must be united toward its security and the well-being of its people. To that end, I ask my brother's counselors to continue their great service to us and to acknowledge their pledge to that end before the members of the court assembled here today." He waves a hand toward his brother's closest advisors where they stand in a line at the front of the crowd. The fae cannot lie. And they will either confirm their innocence and loyalty or condemn themselves for all to see.

This is the plan, the trap. They all assembled for my anointment, but no one save Tharin, Elaine, and I knew about this part. If anyone were to leave now, it would be an admission of guilt in itself.

Lysandir gives them words to recite, and they do, one after another. Most are eager to do so.

Captain Avara advances next and drops to one knee at the foot of the dais. "I pledge that I have never sought to harm the Court of Fire, the royal family, or any of our treasured human friends and never shall. I will serve to the best of my ability and work for the safety and prosperity of the Court of Fire."

Eventually, only Memnon is left.

I've watched him squirm, gaze darting, shifting his stance, pulling at the collar of his tunic. It's as much an admission as anything, and maybe I'm a horrible person, but I savor watching the noose slowly draw tight around his neck.

He drops to one knee before the king. "I pledge that I have always worked for what I believe to be the best for the Court of Fire and I will continue to do so."

Lysandir crosses his arms and stares down at him. "Those are not the words I asked for."

"My King." He bows lower, nearly placating himself upon the ground. "I have always advised and sought what I thought was best for the Court of Fire, and I pledge to do the same for you."

"Still not what I asked of you. Let's try something else." His voice has lost some of its calm.

The trap is sprung, and the culprit on the edge of admitting their guilt.

"Can you swear that you had no involvement in the plotting or act of killing one of my brother's potential brides?" Lysandir asks.

A collective gasp echoes through the crowd. Cries of disbelief ring out, even a sob, and I can't help but wonder if someone from Bailey's family is here.

I hold my breath, pulse pounding.

"I—" Memnon start. "My king, I—"

"Can you not deny it? If you can, this is your last chance."

Guards move in from the edges of the dais. There's no escape. Memnon could shift, I suppose, but he'd be the most wanted person in the entire court. Even the Unseelie lands would hold no sanctuary for a traitor who killed an innocent human—an act abhorred by all fae.

"Action was necessary. The Unseelie were growing in power and needed to be stopped!" Memnon's voice rises in a fervor. "The king failed to act to stop them. He let them continue to amass, and see what happened?" He gestures wildly. "The Unseelie King was able to break down our wards and attack our court in the middle of the night. They took us unawares and killed many, including our king!"

Murmurs rise throughout the crowd. Lysandir steps to the edge of the dais and frowns down at the advisor below him.

"They attacked because we moved against them first—killed their innocent in retaliation for what we believed was their killing of the king's favored. I was there." He looks up at the crowd, speaking to them. "I saw the acts we committed, ones that I would have avenged just as their king sought to do. *We* were wrong. The Unseelie did not commit the atrocity against us. They have attacked us in the past, yes, but with purpose, not the indiscriminate violent wrath that we inflicted on them. And the cause? The spark that ignited such fury?" He points an accusing finger at Memnon. "Treason from within. The murder of a human, one who the king favored, who would have been his bride, his queen. And you knew it."

Memnon shoves to his feet and snarls toward Lysandir. "Ruling requires action. Sacrifice! I did what was necessary!"

"You murdered an innocent and brought war to us."

Avara pulls her sword and advances. The guards close in. But Lysandir waves them to a halt.

"You're right about one thing," Lysandir says. "Ruling sometimes does require action and sacrifice. Let it be seen and known that I will abide no harm against innocents in my court."

Lysandir's gaze hardens as he lifts an open palm toward the former advisor.

Memnon's eyes fly wide.

"Wait!" He steps back, but it's too late.

A pillar of fire erupts where he stands. The heat of it makes me wince, but I refuse to move, to cower. In seconds, the fire is gone, and only a small pile of ash remains where Memnon once stood.

Lysandir is almost frozen in place, hand still extended. His throat bobs. I lay my hand on his arm, and he finally relaxes, blinking at the spot where he carried out the sentence. The hardness in his expression breaks, flickering to sorrow before he shuts that down and puts on a front for his people. But I saw. I know how hard it was for him. I twine my fingers through his and move closer to his side.

Tharin steps up and starts into a speech about how members of the court can pledge their support to their new king and the ceremony to be held for Vasilius's passing later in the day. Lysandir and I retreat further into the dais.

"I got caught up and forgot to demand his accomplices," Lysandir whispers to me.

"It's okay," I say. "We'll figure it out. We'll figure all of this out in time."

He stares down at me and gives my hand a squeeze. "I'm honored to have you by my side. I don't... I'm not sure I could do this without you."

"Same." I lean into him. "If you were anyone else, I would have definitely run away by now."

Lysandir chuckles. "If you do, take me with you."

"It's a promise." I beam up at him.

"We can't run away yet, but perhaps you'd step away with me for a little while?" He arches one brow.

"Of course."

We shift, the throne room and the crowd falling away and trees rising up in their place. Their trunks glow with inner light like flames, their colorful foliage brilliant in the morning light slanting through the boughs. The ground we stand upon bears a number of swirls and glyphs. It's familiar, but I don't fully place it before Lysandir snares my full attention.

"I've thought a lot about what I meditated on before I had the vision of you being anointed as the next queen by my mother."

"Oh?"

He nods, solemn. "Did I ask who my brother would pick in The Choosing? Did I ask who the next queen would be? Probably both. I asked many things in many ways in search of answers. So which question was the vision an answer to? I can't be sure anymore. I thought then that I was being shown who my brother would choose. I never imagined that, when I had a vision of you being anointed by my mother, when I caught a glimpse of what just played out in the throne room this morning, that you would be *my* queen."

Lysandir pulls me close, leaning in until his forehead is pressed against mine.

"I never imagined this either," I say. "So many times I thought all was lost. But we're here. Together." But others aren't. It's a heavy truth, a weight holding down my joy. "Do you think it's wrong to be happy when they..." *When they're dead. When they lost everything.*

"It's not wrong. Neither of us wished for others to die, nor can we reverse time to save them. All we can do is make the best of what they sacrificed. Who is to say if this was always our fate or if we did manage to change something? But either way, even knowing all that has happened and the way it hurts, I cannot regret it. Because it brought me to you." He holds my face gently between his palms. "My mate. My destined one. Finally mine."

He seals it with a kiss, full of longing and promise.

After a moment, he breaks our kiss but lingers close, sharing the same breath. "I worry I'm bringing you with me into danger, into war. It's safer for you back in your world."

I scoff. "Don't you dare try to send me away."

"I won't. Your choices are yours. But if you ever want to leave..."

I tap him with the spear I still hold clutched in my hand. "I have a responsibility here now too. This war, whatever is ahead, it's not all on you. We'll do it together."

"Together then," he says. "Though..." He steps back and looks out over the clearing where we stand. "I thought we could step into your world together for a short time."

The doorway. I take in the area with new understanding. This is where I entered Faery all those weeks ago. No wonder it looked familiar.

"Your uncle mentioned that he brought someone with him this morning. Someone I think you'll want to see."

My mouth drops open as my heart gives a leap. "My mother?"

Lysandir smiles. "You've met mine. I thought I should meet yours."

"She's not gifted," I say.

"I know. She will not be able to see me, but I could see her, meet her in a way, if that's acceptable to you."

"You'd risk that? Stepping into my world?" Not that there should be anything dangerous at the coven house, but most fae won't dare it. It's too much of a risk getting trapped on Earth and dying from the lack of magic.

"Of course. You have risked far more for me." He holds out his hand. "Well? We should have a few hours until we're due back."

I take it, my heart full of love for my fated mate, my destined king. "Let's do it."

Thank you for reading *Destined for the Fae King*!

Stay in the loop on this series and other by signing up for my newsletter. You'll also receive a free prequel novella: https://www.authormeganvandyke.com/newsletter/

Reviews are so important for authors, so I hope you'll take a moment to share your thoughts on this book via your favorite online retailer or book review site.

ALSO BY MEGAN VAN DYKE

The Castamar Duology

The Musician and the Monster (Beauty and the Beast)
The Artist and the Dragon (Sleeping Beauty)

Reimagined Fairy Tales Collection

Second Star to the Left (Peter Pan)
The Ugly Stepsister (Cinderella & Snow White)
The Alice Curse (Alice in Wonderland)

The Courts of Faery

A Gift for a Fae Warrior (Optional Prequel)
A Bargain with the Fae King (Book 1)
Bound to the Fae King (Book 2)
Forgiving a Fae Warrior (Book 2.5 - Optional Novella)
Destined for the Fae King (Book 3)
Marked by the Fae King (Book 4)

Stolen Empire

Captive of the Stolen Empire (Book 1)

ABOUT THE AUTHOR

Megan Van Dyke is a fantasy romance author with a love for all things that include magic and romance, especially fairy tales and anything with a happily ever after. Many of her stories include themes of family (whether born into or found) and a sense of home and belonging, which are important aspects of her life as well. When not writing, Megan loves to cook, play video games, explore the great outdoors, and spend time with her family. A southerner by birth and at heart, Megan currently lives with her family in Florida.

Connect with Megan

www.authormeganvandyke.com
www.authormeganvandyke.com/newsletter/
facebook.com/AuthorMeganVanDyke
instagram.com/authormeganvandyke
tiktok.com/@authormeganvandyke
bookbub.com/authors/megan-van-dyke

www.ingramcontent.com/pod-product-compliance
Lightning Source LLC
Chambersburg PA
CBHW021233190726

48289CB00005B/1311